Not Exactly Chaucer

Not Exactly Chaucer

Published by The Conrad Press in the United Kingdom 2020

Tel: +44(0)1227 472 874
www.theconradpress.com
info@theconradpress.com

ISBN 978-1-911546-91-7

Copyright © Wendy Mason, 2020

The moral right of Wendy Mason to be identified as author of this work has been asserted in accordance with the Copyright, Designs and Patents Act 1988.

All rights reserved.

Typesetting and Cover Design by: Charlotte Mouncey, www.bookstyle.co.uk

The Conrad Press logo was designed by Maria Priestley.

Printed and bound in Great Britain by Clays Ltd, Elcograf S.p.A.

Not Exactly Chaucer

Wendy Mason

By the same author
St Francis – An Instrument of Peace (Novum: 2018).

For my wonderful husband, Harold, whose endless support has made this book possible.

The Characters in
Not Exactly Chaucer

Kate Bailey is the tour guide. She is forty years old, divorced and misses her son, Duncan, who now lives in Scotland. She loves her job and is totally dedicated to providing the best possible care to her clients – no matter how difficult they may be.

Barbara Bath is a seventy-year-old, flamboyant retired agony aunt. She is currently a widow, having been married five times, but is frequently on the lookout for a replacement. She dresses in silk suits, wears hats and several valuable diamond rings.

Cynthia Clerk, a sixty-five-year-old spinster and recently retired Hospital Administrator. She tends to be rather shy in social settings.

Angie Cook is a retired sixty-eight-year-old widow, with a tendency to drink too much. She always wears brightly coloured kaftans and turbans.

Brigadier Andrew Friar is a fifty-year-old retired military man and fundraiser for Help the Hero's. He is single, with pleasant manners, and well spoken.

Dr James Hunt is a sixty-five-year-old wine importer, travelling with his long suffering, fifty-six-year-old wife, March. He always has a lot to say about everything, especially wine, and very loudly. She has an interior design company and hopes that the holiday will patch up their marriage.

Tony Knight is a thirty-eight-year-old former soldier. Always polite and charming, he is single, tall and good looking – in a roguish kind of way.

Frank Lynne is a sixty-year-old farmer travelling with Paul Pardoner, a twenty-eight-year-old social worker.

Maddy Mancipal is an attractive, single, thirty-two-year-old, who works for the police. She is on sabbatical from her job for a year.

John Miller is an ostentatious stockbroker is in his mid-forties. His humour sails close to the wind at times, and he scoffs at the very idea of commitment.

Nigel Monk and his wife, Pryor, are an 'adorable' sixty-five-year-old couple. Pryor wears a pendant inscribed 'love conquers all' and has two very spoilt dogs, who she keeps in touch with through Skype.

The Nunnes, both sixty-eight-years-old, are very challenging guests that like nothing more than to find something to moan and complain about.

David Parsons, the retired Dean, is a calm, gentle, sixty-eight-year-old widower, who always wears his clerical garb.

Professor Harold Reeve is a retired seventy-year-old Black African American from Arkansas. He is devoted to his English wife, Cher, aged sixty-one, to whom he has been married for sixteen years. She is a published author.

Fyrne Schipmanno is a dark haired, attractive, forty-year-old physiotherapist. She is single, of Sicilian heritage and a feminist.

Jujh Singh, a Sikh is in his late thirties and joined the tour from India. His father is a hotelier and a Maharajah.

Sumoner White is a photographer in his late forties. His interests lie with younger women because he believes they become 'clucky' as soon as they reach thirty. He is not interested in marriage or becoming a parent.

PART ONE

1. Day One – Perth

Bailey sat at the hospitality desk, positioned to give her a panoramic view across the hotel's lounge. She checked the guest list and fiddled with her badge. The logo: *Australia Unleashed*, underscored her name: *Kate Bailey*. Not that anyone called her Kate, nor did she encourage it.

She glanced at her watch: eight-fifteen. Some of the early risers should be finishing breakfast anytime now. She breathed in the irresistible smell of bacon. Her stomach twisted into a knot. Hunger, or the apprehension she always experienced on the first day of a tour?

The door to the dining room whooshed open. Her heart quickened. Her first guest?

A familiar waitress emerged balancing a tray on one hand.

'Coffee?'

'That's so kind of you, Cheryl.'

'You looked in need. How's that handsome son of yours? Duncan, isn't? He must have finished university by now, is he home?'

'I wish.'

'Oh, dear. Is he all right?'

'He's met a girl. His "soul-mate." She wants to stay in Scotland to be near her parents, and he's been offered a really good job with a top accountancy firm in Edinburgh.'

The idea of Duncan being away for three years had been bad enough, but the thought of it becoming a permanent arrangement had never crossed her mind. Karma. Now she knew how her parents must have felt when she'd married at seventeen and abandoned Scotland in favour of Australia.

'I'll see him at Christmas, but only for a couple of weeks.'

'You know what they say: "a son's only a son until he finds him a wife." What you need – apart from coffee – is a touch of romance in your life.'

Bailey flinched. Why did everyone presume she needed a man, just because she was forty and single?

'I tried that once,' she shook her head slowly. 'Never again.'

Cheryl placed the tray on the table.

'Thanks for the coffee,' Bailey said. She sipped her drink. Hot, black and strong, exactly how she liked it.

A flurry of rain, sprinkled with tiny hailstones, splattered against the ceiling-to-floor window beside her. Her guests would be disappointed to wake to this unseasonal weather, especially after the sweltering heat of their various stop-over breaks in Hong-Kong, Dubai, or Singapore. Not an impressive start.

Of course, it would improve. For the next three weeks her guests would enjoy a stunning array of colours, scents, and sounds: the cool greens, fragrant lilies and laughing kookaburra of the Margaret River region; the hot reds, eucalyptus and didgeridoos of Uluru; and the turquoise blues, ozone and crashing surf of the Barrier Reef. In stark contrast, Australia's vibrant cities awaited, including their current location, Perth, together with Melbourne and Sydney. For some guests, this would be their holiday of a lifetime. Expectations would run high and as Tour Manager she needed to ensure they were met.

The door to the dining room whooshed again. Five guests strolled purposefully towards her. She felt the familiar thrill as the adrenalin surged, part nerves, part excitement. It always happened when she met her guests for the first time.

The first man looked like the amicable villain in her favourite TV soap – six-foot-tall, muscular, late thirties, with his hair shaved short. His jeans and black T-shirt were smartly pressed, and he carried a leather jacket draped over his arm.

Two older couples followed.

The first, a silver-haired pair, dressed identically in Burberry check trousers and white tennis shirts, reminded her of Tweedledum and Tweedledee; with mutually unfriendly expressions, furrowed brows and pursed lips. The man carried their matching red anoraks as his partner foraged in her large purple tote bag. Her hand emerged clutching a bottle of antibacterial gel. As they approached, she proceeded to spray first her own, then her partner's, upturned palms. He rubbed his podgy hands together and glanced at his watch.

The second couple chatted together quietly as they approached, heads touching, arms entwined. His navy polo shirt with burgundy stripe complemented the pale blue of hers.

Bailey stood to greet them. 'Welcome to Perth.'

Her first guest reached across the desk and firmly shook her hand. His brown eyes twinkled as his face broke into a broad grin.

'Good morning. You must be Kate? I'm Tony Knight.'

'Please. Call me Bailey. Everybody does. Did you enjoy your stop-over, Tony?'

'Brilliant. Great hotel in Singapore – very central.'

'And your connection flight?'

'I got in about six last night, which gave me plenty of time to explore.'

Bailey turned towards the silver haired couple beside him. The man glared at her; the woman sniffed.

'Mr and Mrs Nunne,' he said, ignoring her outstretched hand.

Bailey's hand trembled slightly as she ticked their names off her list. 'Welcome. What time did you arrive in Perth?'

'Two o'clock this morning, after a five-hour delay in Dubai. Ridiculous.'

'I'm very sorry. I did hear that a flight got delayed for technical reasons.'

'And now we hear that our schedule has changed – Melbourne after Uluru and then back up to Cairns? Extra travel. Huge temperature changes. I'll be surprised if we don't all go down with pneumonia.'

Bailey's heart sank. Why was there always one?

'I'm so sorry. The alterations to our planned schedule are due to internal flight issues. You'll find a complimentary bottle of wine in your room as an apology for any inconvenience.'

Mr Nunne grunted. 'Poor planning, more like. We'll be writing to complain.'

Bailey fixed her smile firmly in place and turned to the next couple.

'Nigel Monk and this is my wife, Pryor. We're pleased to meet you, Bailey. What have you done with the weather? This temperature's a bit of a shock after Hong Kong.' His voice, gentle and teasing, delivered with a friendly smile.

'I'm assured this weather front will clear later today.' She handed each of them an envelope. 'I've prepared these. They contain a map of the city, details on the free tram service, a few ideas on places to visit, and complimentary tickets for the famous Swan Bells Tower. There's also a card with my cell phone number. If you have any queries give me a call. Tonight, we meet at six in the Compass Lounge, down that staircase over there.' She pointed towards the highly polished brass hand rail and marble steps. 'It's an opportunity to get to know each other, enjoy a complimentary cocktail, some entertainment, and then we'll walk down to the boat for our river cruise and evening meal.'

'As a retired soldier,' Tony said, 'I couldn't resist checking out the Barrack Street Jetty last night. It's only a short walk away.'

'That's as may be.' Mrs Nunne folded her arms over her ample bosom and glared at Bailey. 'But what if it's still raining? My evening shoes are black satin.'

'I'm happy to arrange a taxi for you.'

'And how much is that going to cost?'

'Nothing at all. My pleasure.' Bailey glanced at Tony, who winked.

The five travellers dispersed, Mr Nunne still moaning about the changed itinerary.

Bailey thought about her new plans for evening entertainment. While they enjoyed their cocktails, she would invite one guest, each evening, to tell a story. Of course, not everyone would want to take part, but she knew from previous feedback that some travellers found the socialising before dinner difficult, particularly those travelling alone. She hoped the stories would act as an ice-breaker. She wondered who to enlist as the first narrator. Tony Knight could be a good choice. Not the sort to refuse a damsel in distress. She'd leave a note for him at the reception desk.

Bailey's cell phone rang. She glanced at the screen before answering. 'Hi Suzy, how are things at Head Office? Don't tell me the Nunnes have phoned to complain already?'

'The Nunnes? Why is there a problem?'

'You know how it is sometimes.'

'Well, you'd best charm them out of it. It's all going crazy back here in Sydney. Australia Unleashed has a new owner.'

'What! Who?'

'Your guess is as good as mine. Rumour has it they have spies in every camp.'

'Why?'

'Looking for savings?'

'Anything else?'

'Smithy's gone. We don't know the new MD's name but, apparently, he, or she, is really hot on customer service. Jim told us at this morning's briefing that any member of staff who elicits a complaint will get their marching orders.'

'I bet Jim enjoyed that. Any excuse to bully.'

'Be careful. I'll let you know if I find out any more. Oops, got to go.' Suzy hung up.

'Dammit,' Bailey muttered.

'Trouble?'

A smartly dressed man in his mid-forties, her own height, stood before her, his gold Rolex partially obscured by the cream raincoat draped over his arm. She noticed the coat's label: *Aquascutum*. Obviously not afraid of wearing his wealth. His hair was the most amazing shade of red – as in carrots – his face sprinkled with freckles. She hoped he'd brought lots of high factor sun cream.

'I'm sorry,' Bailey jumped to her feet and held out her hand.

'Bailey. Welcome to Perth Mr…?'

'Miller. Call me Miller.'

His handshake oozed self-confidence.

'Welcome, Miller. I trust you enjoyed your stop-over and arrived without incident?'

'All good until now, but here's the test… how are you at performing miracles?'

'I'll try my best.'

'I want to see the gold pouring at the Perth Mint. Making money, well, that's something I'm used to, but making gold ingots would be a first. I rang this morning but they say they're fully booked. Can you fix it?'

Bailey smiled with relief. She knew most of the receptionists at the Mint. This was one challenge she could easily pull off. 'Have you had breakfast, Miller?'

'Is that an invitation?'

She laughed, 'I wish. No. But if you go through for breakfast, I'll make a couple of calls and see what magic I can conjure up.'

Fourteen guests later, Bailey jumped as a folded pink newspaper slapped onto her desk.

'Sorry, Miller, miles away.'

'Well?'

'Very well. Thank you for asking.'

'I mean, were you able to get me in?'

She handed him her business card. 'Give this to the receptionist at the Mint. I've written her name on the back. She's expecting you for the eleven o'clock tour.'

'Abracadabra, eh?'

'I'll look forward to hearing how it goes. We're all meeting at six, in the Compass Lounge downstairs.'

Bailey returned to her list. Only one name remained un-ticked: a Mrs Angie Cook. So far, they seemed a nice bunch, except perhaps the Nunnes. Maybe they'd warm up, along with the weather?

2. Evening – Perth

Sidecar Cocktail

- *40ml Cognac*
- *20ml Cointreau*
- *20ml fresh lemon juice*

Decorate cocktail glass by dipping 0.5cm of rim in egg white, followed by fine sugar. Place in freezer to chill. Shake all ingredients together with ice cubes, strain and serve in the chilled glass.

Bailey glanced around the Compass Lounge; named after the parquetry compass inlaid into the marble floor. At least three metres in diameter and so precisely cut. Not one gap existed between the tiles. How many of her guests would appreciate the workmanship as they strolled across its surface in an easterly direction towards the corner bar?

Giles Sumner and Barbara Bath were the first to arrive. Sumner, at almost six foot, towered above her. He leaned down to hear something she said and his paparazzi style camera knocked against her arm. Barbara didn't seem to mind; she clearly enjoyed the attention of a younger man. She smiled at him and fluttered her obviously false eyelashes.

Bailey knew, from their conversation that morning, that Sumner disliked his first name and preferred to be called

Sumner. She could understand that. She enjoyed the *distance* the use of her own surname gave her. He'd explained that as a professional photographer, he'd booked the tour after being commissioned to produce scenic and wildlife photographs for an Australian calendar.

Barbara Bath, a seventy-year-old retired agony aunt, dressed in a pink silk suit with matching pillbox hat, looked as though she'd just arrived from a 1960's wedding. As the couple approached, Bailey could see that Barbara wore several rings, set with large diamonds that flashed as they reflected the lights. Bailey hoped they were well insured.

'Good evening, Barbara, Sumner. Please, help yourselves to a cocktail.'

Two younger women entered the room. At thirty-one, Maddy Mancipal was the youngest female of the group. She wore her hair down and the honey-blonde tresses rippled around her shoulders. A long slinky black dress showed off her slim figure.

The second woman, Fyrne Schipmanno, was forty, but looked a good five years younger. Her tanned complexion and long black hair paid tribute to her Sicilian heritage. Fyrne also wore black, but had chosen a short woollen sheath dress to show off her curves.

'Good evening. Have you enjoyed your first day in Perth?' Bailey asked.

'We bumped into Miller leaving the Mint,' Fyrne said. 'He claimed he'd got a taste for making money and dragged us off to the casino to play roulette.'

'Did he win?'

'At first. He built skyscrapers with his winning chips, and

then casually threw them back. Always on red – apparently his lucky colour – it matches his hair. And such random numbers! First my birthday, then Maddy's, the year of the champagne he ordered – vintage of course – and then his room number.'

Maddy laughed. 'We decided to leave at that stage, before he asked for ours.'

'Well, cocktails may seem tame after vintage champagne but, please take one.'

Next to arrive were Nigel and Pryor Monk, together with Tony Knight. Pryor had her arm hooked through Nigel's. He smiled at her affectionately as she chatted to Tony. As they drew level, Tony looked up from his conversation and gave Bailey a salute.

'Reporting for duty.'

'Thanks, Tony. We'll be ready for your tale as soon as everyone arrives. Cocktails, at the bar.' She pointed.

Mr and Mrs Nunne came next. Mrs Nunn tottered across the floor clutching her husband's arm. Unlike the Monks, her grasp did not appear to be one of affection, rather a desperate attempt to maintain her balance. Her shoes were not only satin, as promised, but also had extremely high heels. His black lounge suit contrasted with his red silk waistcoat and dickey bow, which perfectly matched his wife's ankle-length evening dress. He ignored Bailey and steered his wife towards the bar.

A buzz of conversation from the stairs alerted Bailey to the arrival of a larger group of her travellers. She directed them to the bar, counting them as they walked past. Twenty guests – one missing. She scanned the group. Angie Cook. Again.

'Coo wee.'

Bailey glanced back at the staircase, just in time to see Angie reach the bottom step, wobble, and grab the handrail. Bailey rushed forward and offered her hand.

'Oh, thank you, darling. The last one is a bit steep, don't you know?'

The aroma of Chanel No 5, tinted with alcohol, wafted over Bailey.

'Let me help you to a chair, Angie. Then I'll fetch you a cocktail. Or would you prefer sparkling water?'

'I never drink water, darling. But a cocktail would be lovely.'

Bailey linked arms with Angie and steered her towards the chairs she'd arranged into a horseshoe earlier. Angie sank rather heavily onto one, smoothed her long blue and green silky kaftan around herself, and straightened her matching turban. Her feet, encased in silver ballet shoes, peeped out from under her gown.

Bailey rushed over to the bar. 'Ladies and Gentlemen, as soon as you have your drinks would you please make your way to the seating area.'

She handed Angie her drink and then waited for the others to settle.

'I hope you're enjoying your cocktail. Tonight, we have the legendary Sidecar, created by the Ritz Hotel in Paris – or so they claim. As you will have seen in the newsletter, Australia Unleashed will provide you with a complimentary cocktail each evening. The recipes, should you like to replicate them back home, are included in your newsletter.' Bailey indicated their whereabouts. 'As you will also see, one of you each evening will be invited to tell a story.'

Mrs Nunne turned to her husband. 'Do-it-yourself entertainment. How cheap.'

Fyrne raised her hand. 'I'd be hopeless. Must we?'

'Obviously, this is completely optional, but I hope you will embrace the challenge. It can be a true – something biographical – complete fiction, or even a poem. If anyone gets stuck, I have a bank of stories for you to draw on. Our storyteller this evening is our volunteer, Tony Knight, who I enlisted earlier today.'

Tony marched to the front. He stood with his feet slightly apart, back straight. Bailey wondered how he managed to get perfect creases in his grey trousers, and yet none at all in his open-necked white shirt or navy blazer. He ran his hand through his short-cropped hair and gave Bailey a cheeky smile.

'Whenever you're ready,' she prompted.

'Thanks, Bailey. And may I say, I think this story malarkey is a great idea. Mine is autobiographical. I joined the army at sixteen, but I'd always promised my father I'd retire my commission after twenty years and take over the family business. My story begins two years ago, on my last tour of duty in Afghanistan.

'Retired,' gasped Barbara. 'My dear, you don't look old enough to enlist, let alone retire.'

'Thanks, Barbara." Tony grinned at her. 'Anyway, here goes:'

Tony Knight's Tale

The sun seared my skin. The sunlight blinded me. I lay still, not daring to blink, barely breathing. The slightest movement could alert the Taliban snipers to the fact that I was still alive.

Beside me, I could sense Archie, also unmoving. Weird how peaceful it was now that the rat-a-tat of the gunfire had stopped. Unless the grenade had deafened me? But no, I could hear a bird singing in the undergrowth.

'Archie,' I whispered.

No response.

'Archie, are you OK?'

Still nothing. Turning my head, I realised why. Archie had taken the full blast.

'Archie, wake up.'

I sat up, forgetting that the Taliban might still be watching, guns aimed ready to shoot. I leaned over my buddy and my stomach lurched. His face was covered with small shrapnel wounds and a wound in his neck oozed blood that soaked into the sand. A slow pulse throbbed near his collarbone; alive – but only just.

The hill from where the attack had come looked deserted. I stood. The hairs on the back of my neck bristled with anticipation of the bullet that could come at any moment. I grabbed Archie's waist and shoulder, and pulled him into the recovery position.

'Come on, mate, stay with me.'

I didn't have any idea if he could hear me but, somehow, it made me feel better to have a conversation with my best friend, even if one-sided. 'Archie,' I told him. 'I have to stop this bleeding.'

I packed my scarf onto his injury and applied pressure. The flow of blood slowed. He turned his head towards me and groaned. I tried to sound reassuring.

'*You're OK. I'll get you out, I promise. You have a proposal to make, remember?*'

Archie and I met Emily when she first arrived in Afghanistan for her tour of duty. I think we'd both fell in love with her at first sight, but while I tried to pluck up the courage, Archie was quicker off the mark and asked her out. Moments before the snipers threw the grenade, he'd pledged that if we escaped this ambush alive, he would ask Emily to marry him. I would not forget that promise. How could I? His declaration of intent had destroyed my long-term hope that eventually they would tire of each other and part, leaving me to pick up the pieces.

Scooping him into my arms, I staggered towards the jeep. Our progress met with silence. I laid him in the back, jumped into the driver's seat and reached for the radio.

'*Man down! Badly injured!*' *I screamed into the handset.* '*Request big-bird!*'

They told me they were tracking us on the drone, and that I should drive due south for two miles. The helicopter would be with us in ten minutes.

I drove far too fast and hit a pothole. Archie let out a chilling groan. I realised that any jolts could escalate the bleeding and immediately slowed to a more sedate pace. After the longest ten minutes of my life, we arrived at the rendezvous point. I could see why they had chosen this place to land. High and flat, with a good view of the surrounding countryside and no cover for snipers.

I killed the engine, jumped out and opened the back door of the jeep.

By now I could hear the chopper. It hovered above us and then descended slowly. Dust pluthered around, partially obscuring my view of the co-pilot as he jumped down and raced towards us. He took Archie's arm and wrapped it around his shoulder. Between us, we half-carried, half-dragged Archie to the side door. The co-pilot jumped in first and pulled Archie while I pushed. As my friend's feet crossed the threshold, I threw myself in beside him. The Chinook took to the air before I had the chance to breathe.

'We'll be at Camp Bastion in no time,' the co-pilot assured me.

The consultant surgeon walked into the room; his eyes full of compassion. I searched his face for any sign of the news I dreaded. Had Archie survived? Would he make it?

The surgeon's calm words answered my first question, but not the second.

'You do know he's critical, don't you?'

'I guessed.'

'Does he have a wife, parents, anyone we should contact?'

'Emily. His girlfriend. Just before the grenade went off, he told me that if we got out alive he would propose.'

'Well he won't be going down on one knee, I'm afraid.'

My head spun. 'I thought the blast injured the artery in his neck.'

The consultant explained, slowly and plainly, that shrapnel had destroyed Archie's right eye – which they had to remove, sliced through the optic nerve of his left eye and severed his spinal cord. Nothing they could do. Archie would spend the rest of his life – if he had one – in a wheelchair. A blind paraplegic.

I slumped onto a chair, my head in my hands. 'Oh my God,' I gasped. 'He'll never cope. He's such a sports fanatic.' I struggled to take it all in. I'd got him out alive, but what sort of life had I condemned him to? And Emily? How would I explain this to her?

The consultant paused, giving me time to gain some composure. I began to think about the practicalities and asked when Archie could go back to the UK.

'We don't want to move him for a couple of days. He needs to stabilise, but then he'll be transferred to the Queen Elizabeth Hospital in Birmingham.'

'I'll let his girlfriend and parents know,' I said, my heart heavy with the responsibility.

Remembering that we owed this man for saving Archie's life, I thanked the consultant for everything he'd done. We shook hands.

I rang Emily. The hardest phone call I have ever made. She was on leave in the UK for a friend's wedding. I stumbled to find the words to describe Archie's injuries, trying to be gentle and optimistic but at the same time as truthful as possible.

Over the next two days, I supervised the arrangements for our journey. My tour of duty, my last before I retired, came to an end that week. The Major gave permission for me to finish a few days early and travel back with Archie.

The flight to Birmingham went well. Archie cocooned in an induced coma.

I left him to drop my suitcases at my room in the hotel, grabbed a quick shower, rang Emily and then dashed back to the hospital. Emily stood waiting for me at the reception desk. She threw herself into my arms. I tried to find the right words to give her some comfort. An impossible task.

'I'll always be here for you both,' I told her. 'You know I love you guys?'

'I know,' she sniffed. I reached for my handkerchief. She took it and blew her nose. 'Come on, let's get this over with.'

He lay flat on his back, his head swathed in bandages, a patch of gauze over his right eye – or at least where his eye had been. He looked as white as the sheet that covered him. Cables and tubes ran in every direction. An overpowering smell of disinfectant threatened to choke me.

'Can he hear us?' Emily whispered.

'I'm not sure. The nurses talk to him, but they say it varies. Some people come out of the coma and know everything that has happened, every word that's spoken. Others know nothing until they come around.'

She leaned over, kissed his cheek and stroked his fingers, taking care to avoid the PICC line delivering his cocktail of drugs.

'I'm here sweetheart. Tony and I are both here. We love you. You're home with us now. Don't worry, I've followed your instructions. We haven't contacted your parents yet. Not until you're ready.'

We sat for a while, reminding Archie of silly stories about our times together, but eventually, they wore a bit thin. We fell into an uncomfortable silence, punctuated only by the hiss of the breathing apparatus and the beep of the monitors. We said our goodbyes and left.

As we reached the car park, Emily asked me where I planned to stay. She offered to drop me at the hotel. 'Or…' she said, 'you could come back for coffee and tell me more about what happened. I could do with the company.'

We sat listening to music and drank our way through two bottles of red wine. Neither of us felt like eating.

I glanced at my watch. 'It's way past midnight. I should phone for a taxi.'

'Please don't leave. I can't bear to be on my own.'

I agreed, but don't get me wrong folks. I spent the first of many uncomfortable and virtually sleepless nights on the sofa. There's no way either of us would have been unfaithful to Archie.

Returning to the hospital the next morning, we found that Archie had come out of the coma. Awake, although extremely groggy.

Emily leaned over and kissed his forehead. 'How are you feeling sweetheart?'

'How do you think?' He croaked harshly. Obviously, he'd been told about the extent of his injuries.

She tried to reassure him. 'I'm here for you. I'll always be here for you.'

Her words were an agonising blow to me. I knew she meant them.

'Until someone else comes along.'

'I'd never leave you, Archie.'

'I want you to leave me. Now!'

'You can't mean that.' Tears poured down her cheeks. She wiped them away with her sleeve and grabbed his hand. 'I'll always love you. Whatever we have to face, we'll do it together.'

'Get out!' he snarled.

Emily ran from the room.

I put my hand on his shoulder and gave it a squeeze. 'Come on, Archie. Don't take it out on Emily. She loves you to bits.'

'How appropriate. That's all that's left of me.'

'Archie!'

I could hardly believe his response. It's difficult to know how I, or anyone else for that matter, would react to the distressing prognosis, but Emily didn't deserve all this bitterness.

'I'll come back this evening. I'd better go and find her, make sure she's all right.'

'She'll be all right. She's got the rest of her life in front of her.

Unlike me.'

'Mate…' I patted his shoulder again. 'I know this is awful, and I can't imagine how you must feel, but—'

'But what? Try and lighten up? Make an effort? Be grateful that you got me out instead of leaving me to die? That would have been kinder. Then you'd be free to be with Emily. I've always known how you feel about her.'

I couldn't reason with him or deny how I felt about Emily.

'I'll come back this evening,' I told him.

'Tell Emily I won't see her. Hah. See her? That's a laugh.'

I went in search of Emily. She stood near the coffee machine, watching as the espresso frothed over the top of the beaker and filled the slops tray. She picked up the misshapen beaker, took a sip, grimaced and placed it on top of the machine alongside several others. She looked up as I approached; her eyes bright with tears.

It seemed natural to float back to Emily's. We ordered pizza and talked, and talked, and cried, and hugged. I went back to see Archie that evening, and the next, and the next, but each time he refused to allow Emily to visit.

She took compassionate leave to extend her stay in the UK, but eventually she had to return to Afghanistan. She worked for the Army as a clinic nurse, taking essential supplies and drugs out to the remote villages, treating the children's minor illnesses and injuries, offering dietary and health advice to the mothers.

On our last evening together, she cooked me a meal of fillet steak and salad, and I bought a couple of bottles of Châteaux Neuf de Pape. We danced to a romantic Enya CD and, as I held her, I wondered why it couldn't have been different. What if I had asked her out first? What if I had been the one injured? Would

Archie be here dancing with his fiancé now? Why were three people so unhappy?

I looked down into her startling blue eyes. She looked so lonely and so in need of affection that I nearly told her then how much I loved her. But I realised, in that moment, that she already knew. Perhaps she always had. I also knew that if we betrayed Archie, neither of us would be able to live with ourselves

Neither of us could sleep that night. We danced for hours. Eventually, exhausted, we collapsed on the sofa. I held her in my arms until the morning came and she had to leave.

I stayed on at her flat and visited Archie every day. He didn't want his parents to know anything about his injuries. Not until he was ready to go home. We set up an elaborate postal diversion: he dictated the letters; I posted them to a colleague in Afghanistan; who then re-addressed them to Archie's parents in the UK.

Archie's wealthy parents had retired several years before to a large house in the country. As I read him their sparse re-routed letters, I came to understand his reluctance for them to know about his condition, or any details about his slow battle for some semblance of recovery. They described a social whirl of charity functions, dinners and cocktail parties. A butterfly life, as my mother would call it.

Emily also wrote every week. In contrast, her letters were full of love and tenderness. As I read Archie the letters, I constantly tortured myself, wishing they were intended for me.

I rang her every week to keep her updated on progress, but Archie refused to speak with her, or reply to her letters.

After three months, Archie's doctor decided that he could return home, as long as he had nursing care and specially adapted accommodation.

'Come on,' I told him. 'It's time to tell your parents.'

He refused to discuss it.

When I arrived the next day, I found him sat in the chair beside his bed. He seemed a bit brighter. Again I offered to contact his parents.

'No, I realise you're right, but I need to do this for myself. You've read their letters. You know what they're like.'

I did. Only too well.

'Could you stay with me while I ring them?'

I took out my mobile, switched it to loudspeaker so that he could use it from the bedside locker beside him, and tapped in the number he gave me.

It rang.

'Hello, this is 564580, Tina speaking.'

'Mother, it's me.'

'Darling, how are you? Where are you?'

'I'm in the UK. I came back with a friend of mine who got injured in Afghanistan.'

'That's nice, dear. When are you coming to see us? I must know. Only we have several important engagements coming up.'

I could hear her turning pages, presumably a diary, searching for the dates where Archie could be an inconvenience.

'I'm thinking of coming over in a couple of weeks, if that's OK?'

'Yes, I'm sure it will be. Let me know the dates as soon as you can and I'll check the diary.'

'I'd like to bring my friend, the one I told you about who got injured.'

'Is that really necessary dear? You know how your father hates illness.'

'He's not ill, Mother. Just injured. Quite badly in fact. Blown

up by a grenade. Lost his sight. Confined to a wheelchair.'

'Well, how will we manage dear? You know we don't have a lift to get him upstairs?'

'I thought he could use the smoking room as a bedroom. It's next door to the downstairs bathroom. It would only take a few alterations.'

'You can't possibly be serious. You know we use both of those rooms whenever we host a dinner party. We could probably work around him for a few days, but alterations... I don't think so.'

Archie shrank in his chair. 'I...'

'Speak up dear. I can't hear you.'

'I'm thinking of coming home to live. Permanently. Bringing him with me?'

'Have you gone mad? Darling, you can't really believe that I'm going to make our home available to someone you've adopted as a charity case.'

I could barely look at Archie as his mother went on and on about their important social engagements and asked how Archie could even suggest that they could put their lives on hold for some blind cripple.

'Oh, that's the doorbell, I'll have to go. Kiss, kiss, love you, bye.' She put the phone down.

Archie bowed his head. His shoulders shook.

I placed my hand on his arm. 'She'll get used to the idea. Let me go and talk to her and explain.'

'She meant every word. It would make no difference. She would always think of me as a blind cripple, some creature to be tidied away and pitied. I'd become an embarrassment. I wish I were dead.'

I tried to talk some sense into him but he said he wanted to be alone. As I left, he asked me to get his bottle of cola and a straw from his locker. That way he could take a drink without bothering the nurses.

If only I'd known.

The next morning, I received a phone call from the hospital. Archie had died in the night. Over several days he'd tricked the nurses as they'd dispensed his pain killing tablets. He'd pretended to swallow them, but had in fact spit them back into his cola bottle where they'd dissolved. The previous night, he'd drunk the lot.

I told them I'd inform his parents and Emily. I thought it would be better coming from me.

I telephoned his parents first. 'Hello, this is Tony Knight. I'm a friend of Archie. I'm afraid I have some bad news for you. You remember he told you about his friend, the one badly injured in Afghanistan?'

'Yes, I hope he's not still harbouring these silly ideas of dumping him on us, disrupting our lives.'

'No, he won't be doing that. Unfortunately, he died last night. He took his own life.'

'Perhaps that's the best for everyone. But why is it you're ringing to tell me Archie's friend died?'

'I'm ringing you to explain that Archie described his own injuries. I'm sorry, but your son committed suicide last night.'

I could hear her gasp, followed by a long pause. She eventually recovered her sharp, staccato voice. 'Thank you for calling. Goodbye.' The phone went dead.

I suppose I could have been a little more understanding, a bit more subtle, but the uncaring way she'd spoken to Archie left me somewhat short on sympathy.

Then I had to make the second most difficult phone call I have ever made. I rang Emily. Her phone went directly to voicemail.

'Emily here. Can't get to the phone, so leave me a message after the tone. B-e-e-e-p.'

'Hi, it's Tony. Give me a ring. Love you.'

Not a call I looked forward to receiving. However, it would have been so much better than the one I got. Her supervisor rang to explain that Emily had been driving to deliver medicine to one of the villages. She's normally a very careful driver, but on this occasion, she'd failed to notice the freshly dug earth by the side of the road and driven over an IED. The blast had killed her instantly. My two best friends. Dead within twenty-four hours. The woman I loved... taken from me.

Barbara Bath spoke first. 'Oh Mr Knight, that's the saddest love story I have ever heard. You poor, poor dear,' her eyes filled with tears. 'How brave of you to share it with us.'

'I'm not usually one for wearing my heart on my sleeve, Barbara, but my doctor said the more I talk about it, the sooner I'll be ready to move on.'

'Exactly what I would tell my clientele. Well done you.' Barbara reached over and patted his arm.

Bailey glanced at her guests. Most appeared stunned. An interesting tale, but *so* sad. This is a holiday, for goodness sake. She sprang to her feet. 'Ladies and Gentlemen, please put your hands together for Tony, our first storyteller. What an amazing start.'

Everyone clapped.

'I can't believe how Archie's mother behaved so harshly,' one woman said quietly. Bailey remembered meeting her earlier – March Hunt. She'd explained her unusual name. Her parents planned to name her April, but she arrived two weeks early.

'Prejudice and selfishness,' Barbara said. 'I used to get numerous letters from disabled clients. They frequently complained they were treated as if they had cognitive issues as well as physical, just because they used a wheelchair.'

'Good story, Tony.' Sumner clapped his hand on Tony's back.

Bailey agreed. Just a bit dark. She'd need to give careful consideration to her choice of tomorrow's storyteller. But for now, it was time to move them on.

'OK, everyone if you would follow me, we'll make our way down to the pier for our dinner cruise. Mr and Mrs Nunne, your taxi driver is at reception. He knows where to drop you. We'll see you down there.'

Bailey led the way out through the hotel's rear entrance and waited for the group to gather around her. At least the rain had stopped and the clouds were gone. The evening river cruise had always been a success. Things could only get better.

3. Day Two – Trip to Freemantle

Bailey sat at the hospitality desk and checked her e-mails. Nothing from Suzy. One from the hotel manager confirming they could use the main lounge for tonight's entertainment. Great. She liked the Compass Lounge, but this one was far more comfortable, and she loved the décor. The thickly piled navy carpet complimented the comfy dark blue armchairs and two-seater sofas with scatter cushions, some pale blue and others pale yellow. On the far side of the room, the marble pathway meandered past the elevators and into the reception area. The walls – also marble – were adorned with large gilded mirrors. Floor-to-ceiling windows ran from beside her desk to the main entrance doors in reception. Bailey always wondered how they cleaned the six large chandeliers suspended from the high ceiling. They obviously did, because today with the first hint of sunlight, the crystals sparkled like diamonds.

Bailey stifled a yawn. She'd hardly slept last night for worrying about what this takeover could mean. Did she have time to call Suzy again? She checked her watch: eight-thirty. A bit early. In any case, her guests would finish their breakfasts and join her any time now. She'd try later.

First to leave the restaurant were her favourite couple, Nigel and Pryor Monk. They both smiled at Bailey as they approached her desk.

She stood to greet them. 'Morning, Nigel, Pryor. You're nice and early.'

'I need the internet password, Bailey,' Pryor said. 'I promised I'd check in with my boys.'

Boys? Hadn't Nigel told her they had no children?

'I promised them I'd Skype before they go to bed. I'm worried they won't eat their food unless I say goodnight.'

'Honestly, Pryor, you don't need to worry about those dogs. You know they adore Christine.' Nigel turned to face Bailey. 'Our dog walker moves in with the dogs whenever we're away.'

'I know you think I'm fussing, Nigel, but they expect to see me. Anyway, it will put my mind at ease.'

'Whatever you say, my dear.'

Bailey handed Pryor a slip of paper. 'This code only works here and in the reception area. Let me know if you need help.'

'Thank you, but I'm sure I'll be fine.'

Nigel placed his hand on Pryor's shoulder and steered her towards the nearest sofa.

Pryor fluffed up a couple of scatter cushions, opened her tablet and proceeded to tap away. Nigel snuggled down beside her and opened his morning paper.

Well, two happy customers. What next?

She didn't have long to wait. The guests began to arrive in ones, twos and small groups. She noticed Frank Lynne arrive, he chatted to Barbara Bath. No sign of his partner, Paul. She'd noticed they'd sat apart last night and hoped they hadn't fallen out.

At eight forty-five, Bailey carried out a quick head count. Nineteen. Two missing. She knew the Dean, David Parsons had other arrangements. The second absentee was, of course, Angie Cook. Bailey decided to go ahead and explain the excursion details. She'd worry about Angie later.

'Good morning, Ladies and Gentlemen. I know from you're feedback that you enjoyed last night's dinner cruise. Today we're back on the Swan River as we cruise down to Freemantle. Ah…'

Angie bustled across the room to join them. 'So sorry, Bailey. Sorry everyone. My alarm clock failed to wake me.' She sank into an armchair and adjusted her turban. 'Please continue.'

Bailey quashed her feelings of irritation and glanced at her notes. 'Once we arrive – it takes about an hour and a half – we'll take the tram tour of the town before we visit the Mariner Restaurant for our fish and chip lunch. You'll then be free to explore Freemantle until our boat leaves at 4:30. Please be prompt. It's a long and expensive taxi ride back if you miss the boat. Any questions?'

'I haven't seen David Parsons this morning,' Cynthia said.

Ms Clerk had hardly said a word to anyone since her arrival, and yet here she was, the recently retired hospital administrator and spinster, taking an interest in the whereabouts of David, the retired Dean and widower. Did she have a potential romance on her hands?

'He won't be joining us today. He's meeting the Bishop of Perth for lunch. I understand they studied Theology together at university.'

Sumner raised his hand. 'I'd like to visit Rottnest Island to photograph the Quokkas?'

'No problem, Sumner. The ferries are frequent. I'll point out the ticket office when we arrive in Freemantle.'

'I thought you were collecting pictures of scenery and wildlife,' Barbara said. 'Why do you want pictures of Quakers?'

Sumner laughed. 'Not Quakers, Barbara. Quokkas. They're little furry animals.'

James Hunt leaned towards his wife, March, and whispered in a voice loud enough for Bailey to hear, 'Daft bat.'

Bailey flinched and glanced at Barbara who appeared unperturbed as she continued to chat to Sumner.

'Shush, James,' hissed March. 'She'll hear you.'

He grinned. 'So?'

'How can you be so rude?'

'Moi?'

'And pretentious.' March pushed past her husband and sank into an armchair.

Bailey turned away, pretending she hadn't noticed the exchange.

'Ladies and Gentlemen, could you follow me? We'll retrace our steps from last night, and head back to the Barrack Jetty. Mrs Nunne, will you be OK, or shall I get you a taxi?'

'I can manage,' she sniffed.

'Great. Let's go.'

The Pilot eased the boat away from the dock and into the central channel of the river. Most of the guests had climbed to the top deck, but Barbara remained on the one below. She had yet to find her sea legs, couldn't face the stairs and preferred to be out of the direct sun. She'd discovered the perfect shady spot; a table, surrounded by four comfortable chairs, sheltered by a large cream parasol. From her vantage point at the stern of the boat, Barbara had a perfect view of the receding Perth skyline as it slipped away.

She could see the others milling around on the top deck, including James. What a horrible man. He stood talking to Sumner and the farmer, Frank Lynne. Perhaps she should confront him. She might be a daft bat, but she wasn't a deaf one. Then again, what's the point? She felt sorry for his wife, March, who seemed to be a thoroughly decent person. She deserved better.

Barbara glanced up as a shadow fell across her. Maddy Mancipal stood before her. Her fitted shirt, jeans and pumps were sensible and casual, but still elegant. She wore her long blonde hair tied back in a ponytail.

'Hello Maddy. Enjoying the cruise?'

'I'm just going to fetch Angie some tonic water, and grab a coffee for me. Can I get you anything?'

'That's very sweet of you, but I have my water... on second thoughts, a plastic cup would be good. That way I won't get lipstick all over my water bottle.'

Maddy returned a few minutes later. She placed the tray on the table.

Barbara patted the chair beside her. 'Here, sit with me while you drink your coffee. Tell me, what did you think of Tony's story last night?'

'So sad. I wanted to give him a big hug.'

'Perhaps you should?'

Maddy laughed. 'In my dreams.'

Barbara reached for one of the plastic beakers and poured water over the ice. 'Thirty years as an agony aunt has convinced me that dreams do, indeed, come true.'

'Well, I of all people should know that,' said Maddy.

'Oh?'

'I'm only here today because I had a win on the lottery.'

'Oh, my dear, how wonderful. I've never played.'

'Me neither, but I'd had a really bad day at work and couldn't be bothered to cook, so I called in at the supermarket to get one of those ping meals.'

'Ping?'

'You know those plastic trays of processed food you heat in the microwave until it goes *ping*. I don't know why, but I found myself asking for a lucky dip ticket. To my amazement it turned out to be a winner. Enough to pay off my mortgage, take a year's sabbatical, and book this trip to Australia.'

'There you go. Dreams.'

Maddy finished her coffee. 'I'd better get back to Angie.'

As she watched Maddy walk away, Barbara's mood lifted. She welcomed the challenge of a worthwhile project to keep her occupied.

Maddy climbed the steps in search of Angie. She found her leaning on the railings, her pink and orange kaftan flapping in the breeze.

'Thank you, darling, so kind.' Angie smiled at Maddy as she took the plastic beaker and bottle of tonic water. 'What do I owe you?'

'My treat. Sorry, the ice has melted a bit. I stopped to chat with Barbara. She's found a nice shady seat on the deck below.'

'I wondered where she'd got to.'

Angie suspended the beaker over the railings, and with one finger holding back the ice, she tipped it, allowing the water to run off. She unscrewed the bottle and poured half the tonic water over the remaining ice. 'I'll save this for later,' she said, screwing the top back on and stuffing the bottle into her shoulder bag. 'I think I may go and join Barbara. I could do with getting out of this sun. Where did you say she is?'

'Down that staircase, then straight on. You can't miss her.'

Maddy watched as Angie swayed towards the flight of stairs, paused, pulled a silver hip flask from her shoulder bag and topped up her beaker. Maddy sighed.

'She'll be OK.'

Paul stood at her side. His long blonde hair, tied back in a ponytail much like her own. On the dinner cruise the previous night, she'd briefly chatted to him. She'd thought at the time that they were about the same age, but in daylight he looked about three or four years younger.

'I feel somewhat responsible. I provided the tonic water.'

'Strikes me she's one of these people that keep themselves constantly topped up to the happy stage. I don't think she'll do herself any harm. I work with several alcoholics – clients, not colleagues.'

Maddy laughed. 'Fyrne told me you were a Social Worker.'

'Where is your friend?'

'We not travelling together. We only met yesterday when the waiter asked if we would share a table for breakfast. Last time I saw her she was in the bar downstairs, drinking coffee.'

'Coffee sounds like a good idea. Coming?'

'I've just had one.'

'OK, see you later.'

Maddy looked across the river. A small boat, with a huge outboard motor, tore through the water pulling a man on skis. The skier swung from side to side, riding the wake. It looked such fun. She felt a surge of anger at Peter, which quickly translated into annoyance at herself. All those wasted years of waiting in for him to call. She could have been out with friends, having fun. She must have been crazy.

Below her, in the water, a streak of pale grey caught her eye. Then another.

'Dolphins!' she shouted.

'Where, where?'

Maddy glanced up as Cher Reeves joined her at the rails.

Cher clapped her hands. 'Oh look, aren't they gorgeous? I love dolphins. Harold, quickly, can you see them?'

Professor Reeves reached his wife's side, placed his arm loosely over her shoulder and followed her gaze into the dark blue water.

Sumner rushed over to join them. His camera whirred as he took shot after shot.

One dolphin's fin broke the surface of the water leaving swirls of glistening ripples. Another swam on its side close to the boat. It seemed to be smiling at them, enjoying the attention. Maddy spotted Angie's turban and Barbara's sun hat, as the two women stood on the deck below and watched the performance.

And then, as quickly as they had arrived, the dolphins were gone.

Sumner replaced his lens cover. 'Thanks for the tip-off, Maddy. Got some good shots.'

'I may need you to send me a few,' Maddy said. 'In the excitement I forgot to get my camera out.'

'And me,' Cher said. 'Such a beautiful moment, but it ended so quickly.'

'My pleasure. I'll get your e-mail addresses later. I'm off now, hopefully, to capture black swans. Digitally, that is.'

'It looks as though your friend missed the excitement,' Cher said. 'Where is she?'

'Downstairs in the bar,' said Maddy. 'But we're not travelling together. We only met yesterday, over breakfast.'

'Oh, sorry. I'm terrible at jumping to conclusions. Doesn't that just prove that we shouldn't make assumptions? Harold's always telling me that, aren't you, dear?'

Professor Reeves nodded.

'Coffee sounds like a good idea, don't you think, Harold?'

'Yes, dear.'

'Would you like to join us, Maddy?'

'I've just had one.'

'Come on, Harold. We told Tony we'd meet him down there for coffee.'

Maddy looked around the deck for somewhere to sit. Both sides of the top deck were lined with containers, which the labels identified as storage for life jackets. Covered with two-inch thick cushions, they doubled as seating.

On the first bench Maddy recognised the farmer, Frank, talking to James, the unlikely husband of the lovely March, and that pompous oaf who insisted on being called by his rank – Brigadier. He'd bragged the previous evening about working as a volunteer fundraiser for *Help the Heroes*, raising thousands of pounds every month.

On the second container sat Mr Singh, watching the riverbank through a pair of binoculars. Maddy hesitated, but then he looked up and waved.

She crossed the deck.

Mr Singh sprang to his feet and bowed. 'I would be greatly honoured if you would join me.' He remained standing until she'd settled on the cushion.

'Are you enjoying the trip so far, Mr Singh?'

'Please, call me Jujh.'

'You're a judge?'

'J-u-j-h, it's short for Jhujhaar. And yes, I am very much enjoying the tour.' He looked over her shoulder. 'Where is your friend?'

'She's not a friend, we only met yesterday.'

'Are you then perhaps travelling with your parents?'

'Unfortunately, my parents were both killed in a car accident the week before my eighteenth birthday. I'm travelling alone.'

Alone described her very well she thought; no parents, no sibling, no partner, and no friends.

'This is very regrettable. I remember my eighteenth birthday – a joyful time. My dreams had begun to come true – I played cricket for my country. And then even more happiness. Delhi University accepted me, to study Law.'

'Me too. Not Delhi, you understand, I read Law at Birmingham University.'

'Do you, like I do, aspire to be a politician?'

'No way. I'm interested in enforcing laws, not making new ones. I'm a detective sergeant in Birmingham CID.'

'A detective?'

'Yes, I know. Everyone seems surprised when I tell them. What about you?'

'My father and I run a hotel.'

He reached into his pocket, pulled a photograph from his wallet and handed it to her.

She looked at the rambling palace of pink sandstone, surrounded by formal gardens.

'We have thirty suites, and the occupancy is over ninety percent.'

'It looks wonderful. I can understand why it's so popular.'

'It used to be our family home, but it became impracticable. My father had a modern wing built for the family to live in and had the old building refurbished into hotel suites. My father always says that success is all about spotting an opportunity and then being brave enough to take it. The hotel is a triumph, but I do miss our old home.'

He took the photograph and stroked it gently before putting it back in his wallet.

'I know how you feel. When my parents died, the bank manager tried to persuade me to sell our home, buy a small flat, and become mortgage free. I loved the house. All my memories lived within it. I totally ignored his advice and increased the mortgage to cover my university expenses. I had to work every weekend and through the holidays to cover the repayments. But I'm glad I did.'

'You are a very resilient and determined young lady. I am full of admiration. When we value something, we shouldn't let it slip from our hands.' His brow furrowed.

'I hadn't thought about it like that. Now, if you'll forgive me, I think I'll go and get myself a coffee before we arrive.'

Bailey walked past Freemantle's historic Round House, the oldest building in Western Australia. She'd booked it for Duncan's tenth birthday party. The boys ('soppy girls' hadn't been invited) had enjoyed the experience, especially taking part in firing the one o'clock cannon. She wondered if Duncan ever watched the firing of the one o'clock canon at Edinburgh Castle. Did it remind him of that birthday?

She checked her watch. Ten past four. Time for the final round up. By now, most of her guests should be close to the harbour. As she walked up High Street and into Cliff Road, she kept a constant look out for stragglers. A flash of orange and pink caught her eye. She sighed and crossed the road.

'Good afternoon, Angie. You do realise you're going in the wrong direction?'

'Hello there, Bailey. I'm looking for an off-licence. I need some brandy. Purely medicinal you understand.'

Bailey's heart sank. Only the second day in Australia and already Angie needed to top up her supplies.

'We'll be cutting it a bit fine if we don't start back now.'

'There must be one here somewhere?'

The best option, Bailey decided, would be to satisfy Angie's needs. And quickly.

'You need a liquor store. There's a Woolworth's just up the street. It's on the way back to the boat. I'll show you.'

'I never knew Woolworths sold alcohol. I must have walked past it three times.'

Bailey escorted Angie to the shop door. 'I'll wait here for you. I need to call the office.'

Angie emerged from the shop a few minutes later with a plastic bag that clinked as she approached. 'Did you make your phone call?'

'I tried to reach my colleague, but she's not in today. Got what you need?'

Angie held up her bag and the bottles rattled in answer.

'We need to step on it now, or it will be the tour guide who's missing the boat, and that would be an embarrassing first.'

Jim would have fun at her expense if that happened. She'd never live it down.

4. Final Evening – Perth

Cosmopolitan Cocktail

- *40ml Vodka*
- *20ml Cointreau*
- *15ml fresh lime juice*
- *15ml cranberry juice*

Shake the ingredients together with ice cubes, strain and serve in a chilled cocktail glass with a twist of orange zest.

Bailey admired Brigadier Friar's military bearing as he collected his cocktail and strode over to join her and Sumner. He stood with his free arm tucked into the small of his back, every inch a services man. She enjoyed his company; not only his conversation, but also his charisma and charm.

'G'day, Bailey. Great camera, Sumner. Puts my happy snappy to shame.'

Sumner looked up from his camera. 'It's a new lens. I invested the advance from my calendar commission.'

'Any potential shots today?'

'Lots of Quokkas. Rottnest Island is the only place that they still live wild. Look.' He held his camera towards them both. The screen showed an animal resembling a small kangaroo. It sat on its haunches, as though posing for the photograph.

Bailey laughed. 'They're such cute little critters, and so tame.'

Sumner switched off his camera. 'What about you, Brigadier?'

'Freemantle tram tour, fish and chips and a leisurely shop browse.'

The other members of the group had gradually drifted into the corner of the main lounge. She picked up her papers from the hospitality desk and turned to face them.

'Ladies and Gentlemen, I hope you all had a wonderful day. Isn't the colonial architecture in Freemantle amazing?'

She paused as her guests nodded and murmured agreement.

'You'll have received my newsletter with details of the story rota and tomorrow's departure to the Margaret River region – nine o'clock sharp from the front car park. Today's cocktail is a Cosmopolitan.' She indicated the array of colourful glasses. 'Please help yourself, then settle back and enjoy tonight's tale. Miller has kindly agreed to entertain us this evening. Miller, whenever you're ready.'

Bailey sat back in her chair. She hoped Miller's story would be entertaining. He gave the impression of having quite a mischievous sense of humour. Hopefully his offering would reflect that, and banish any lingering blues from Tony's offering.

Miller strolled forward to the front of the group, perched on the arm of a sofa, and waited while everyone settled down with their drinks. He cleared his throat.

'When it comes to evaluating women, most of the men I know start at the top and work down. Not me.'

Miller's Tale

I watched her high heels as she walked slowly towards me. My God, they were high. Black, patent leather, with mirrored stilettos. I perched on a bar stool sipping my Jacks and Coke and continued my leisurely appraisal: Nice ankles; slim bare legs; knees perfectly structured. So far so good. She had a body like Jessica Rabbit: cupid mouth; cute nose; huge blue eyes and then, horrors – I noticed the green hair.

Green! I ask you. Who wants green hair? Now, red I can understand. A lot of women would give their hind teeth for hair like mine. But green? Still, she had a knock dead figure and I decided I wouldn't notice the hair with the lights off.

Fyrne groaned.

Bailey's stomach flipped. Oh no.

'Evening beautiful,' I quipped. 'Where have you been all my life?'

She gave me a withering look.

'Well she would, wouldn't she?' Fyrne called out.

'It wasn't the most original chat-up line,' Miller agreed, 'but it usually gets a smile.'

'Brandy, please,' the green goddess said to the bartender. 'Neat. Make it a double.'

She sat on the barstool next to mine and took a large gulp. Small beads of sweat appeared on her top lip and forehead. Could she be on drugs? I don't do drugs.

She gasped and gripped her side.

'Are you OK?' I asked. 'Is there anything I can do?'

'I need…' She gripped the bar with both hands and grimaced. 'I need to get to the hospital.'

'My car's just outside the back door. I can take you.'

She stared at me, obviously torn between her personal safety and the pain.

The bartender leaned over. 'Miller's OK, darling. I can vouch for him. He's one of my regulars.'

'Trust me,' I added. 'I'm a Doctor. Or at least my brother is, and I can get you to one quickly.'

I steered her out of the back door and towards my pride and joy, my black BMW Z4 Roadster Convertible. I expected her to gasp at its beauty – girls usually do – but she just groaned.

'What's up, exactly?'

'The pain… it's unbearable.'

'Do you feel sick?'

'Don't worry.' She threw me a look of disapproval. 'I won't mess up your car.'

I opened the passenger door, did my good cop, bad cop thing. You know, making sure she didn't bang her head and then watching her dress ride up high enough to reveal a well-toned thigh.

It took ten minutes to reach A and E, two to locate a wheelchair, and a few more seconds to arrive at reception. I'll give them this, they didn't hang about. They had her on a trolley and into a cubicle before you could say triage.

A young man arrived. He looked sixteen, but introduced himself as Dr Young and started to ask questions. She gave her name as Hazel Harvey. The pain had niggled for a couple of days but had got worse as she walked home. It became acute as she got to the bar. No, she hadn't eaten all day. Yes, it did hurt more when he pressed.

'Nurse, ring the surgical team. Tell them we have a case of appendicitis on its way.'

One nurse left to make the call; the other pulled up the trolley sides and deactivated the brake. A porter joined him and helped manoeuvre the bed into the corridor. Without thinking, I followed. The nurse told me I could stay in the relative room and wait for my partner.

My partner, I ask you. Do I look like someone capable of making a commitment?

Laughter rippled through the group, although Bailey noticed that Fyrne didn't join in.

He assured me that Hazel wouldn't be long. Apparently, it's a very simple operation, nothing to worry about.

It seemed a bit churlish to desert Hazel in her hour of need. I could still hear those groans. I certainly wouldn't mind hearing them again under different circumstances. Perhaps I could persuade her to lose the green hair.

I settled down, picked up a magazine, and prepared myself for a long wait.

A young nurse stuck her head around the door of the waiting room. 'Hazel Harvey's partner?'

I nodded.

'Hazel's doing well, but she's sleepy right now. I suggest you come to see her at visiting time tomorrow afternoon, between two and six. She'll be on the Nightingale surgical ward. And remember, no flowers. They're an infection risk.'

I arrived the next day, two o'clock on the nose, grapes in hand. I spotted her as soon as I entered the ward. She looked stunning, even in the hospital gown, very pale but still gorgeous. I even decided I liked the green hair.

'Hi, Hazel. I'm Miller. Remember me?'

'How could I forget my knight in shining armour?' She smiled and I melted.

'Grapes,' I said, thrusting them into her hand. 'Apparently they don't allow flowers.'

'Thanks.' She waved seductively towards the chair beside her. 'Take a seat.'

A tall man, mid-fifties, wearing an expensive suit appeared. His presence clearly made the statement: I am your consultant surgeon. His name tag identified him: Mr Absolon. A gaggle of youths in white coats followed him.

'And how are we feeling this morning, Hazel?' he asked.

'Much better, thank you.'

'And how's your sense of humour?'

A slight frown creased Hazel's brow and one perfectly groomed eyebrow arched.

Mr Absolon smiled and leaned across me to whisper into Hazel's ear.

'You will find that we had a little joke at your expense. We had to shave you for the operation you understand?'

Hazel smiled demurely. 'Of course.'

'I don't think we have ever had to remove green pubic hair before. We found the tattoo on your right thigh: "Keep off the grass." You will find a sticking plaster on your left side: "Sorry we had to mow the lawn".'

James burst into laughter. 'Good one, Miller. I don't think mowing the lawn will ever be the same again.'

Miller smiled.

Fyrne put her head in her hands.

Bailey cringed.

Hazel giggled. What a girl. She wagged her finger at the doctor and smiled at him provocatively. 'You're a very naughty man, Mr Absolon.'

I bristled. I was the gallant knight, here. I didn't need competition.

He returned her smile. 'I'll be back to see you later tonight. We'll talk then about you going home. Probably tomorrow.'

A dark sultry female swept into the ward and strode towards us.

'Hazel darling. How are you?'

'They say I'll have a tiny scar. But otherwise, I'm as good as new.'

'I can't wait to get you home. Lots of cosseting, that's what you need.'

Hazel kissed her visitor. Not a peck on the cheek, but a long lingering smooch. They eventually pulled apart.

'Let me introduce you,' Hazel said. 'This is Miller, my knight in shining armour. Miller,' she turned towards her visitor, grabbed her hand and smiled into her eyes. 'This is Nicola, my wife, the love of my life.'

Miller glanced around the audience and laughed.

'Would you believe it? They were both... well, queer.'

Fyrne laughed. 'Did they threaten your masculinity, Miller?'

'Not likely, but they were clearly off limits, all the same.'

'If you used language like "queer" in the Health Service, you'd be sent on an Equal Opportunities course,' Cynthia said.

'We were told you can't say black coffee; you have to say coffee without milk.'

'And you mustn't say nitty-gritty,' Maddy said. 'I had a boss who said it in a press conference. He got disciplined.'

'How is that offensive?' asked March. 'I hear it all the time.'

'The nitty-gritty is the effluent left in the bilges when the slaves disembarked,' Maddy explained.

'Rubbish,' laughed Miller. 'No offence, Maddy, but I think you will find it has a sexual connotation in blues music. Let's get down to the nitty-gritty.' Miller winked and nudged Maddy's elbow.

Bailey gave Miller what she hoped was a stern look.

'Take no notice, Miller,' James said. 'There's far too much of this "political correctness" as far as I'm concerned. What else should we call two lesbians? Other than misguided, of course?' he laughed.

Bailey caught a glimpse of his wife, March. She appeared to be shrinking into her chair, her flushed cheeks co-ordinating with her pink tie-dye top and crochet jacket. Poor woman.

Miller laughed. 'Come on, Bailey. It's just a story.'

'OK, Miller, we'll take that as an apology.' Bailey clapped her hands. 'Shall we go through for dinner now? I think they're ready for us.'

She watched her guests file through to the dining room. At least the banter towards Miller had been fairly amicably. Still, she hoped no one would complain to Head Office.

5. Day Three – The Margaret River Region

Manhattan Cocktail

- *40ml Bourbon*
- *20ml Martini Rosso*
- *Two dashes of bitters*

   Stir the ingredients together with ice, strain and serve in a chilled cocktail glass with a cherry.

Maddy entered the bar and quickly became cocooned in a sense of warmth and cosiness. This new hotel, in the heart of the Margaret River region, reminded her of the child-friendly pub she used to visit with her parents. Similar décor. The walls and ceilings were constructed with dark oak beams that contrasted sharply with the rough white plaster. Brass horseshoes adorned the beams and glinted in the flickering light from the log fire. A deep pile burgundy carpet covered the floor except for the area that surrounded the bar, where wooden flooring allowed for the occasional spillage by a careless customer. The sofas and chairs were covered in black crushed velvet and burgundy scatter cushions. Dark oak coffee tables complemented the décor.

Maddy collected her Manhattan from the bar and glanced

around the room. Her eyes focused on Tony, who stood by the fireplace, deep in conversation with Sumner and Miller. He looked up and smiled warmly as she walked over to join them.

'Cheers Maddy, we were just talking about you,' Tony raised his glass in a salute.

'Oh dear, that sounds ominous.'

'Not at all,' Sumner said. 'We had a wager on what you do for a living. I said you're a teacher. Tony here says that can't be, because it's term time and suggests you might be a lawyer. Miller thinks you're in Public Relations.'

'All wrong. I'm a Police Officer.'

'Hello, hello, hear that, Tony?' Miller winked at her. 'We'd best behave ourselves. On leave?' He nudged her arm and winked again. 'Or undercover?'

'On sabbatical. For a year.'

'We were worried you weren't coming down tonight. You're the last to arrive.' Tony waved his glass towards where the other tour guests stood in small clusters or sat around in the overstuffed armchairs. 'Even Angie's here.'

'Delayed by a visitor.'

'Anyone we know?' Miller quizzed. 'Should we be jealous?'

'A very tame parrot. Beautiful, with emerald green plumage, a yellow collar and black tail feathers. Not your kind of bird, Miller. Although he was green.'

Miller grinned.

'Known as twenty-eights for some reason,' Sumner said. 'Ah, here comes Bailey.'

Bailey paused as she reached them. 'Has anyone seen Professor Reeve?'

Sumner pointed into the far corner. 'His wife is on the sofa, over there.' He looked over Bailey's shoulder. 'And here comes her husband.'

'Professor Reeve,' Bailey greeted him, 'I wonder if you are ready to tell us your tale tonight?'

'I am indeed. But please, call me Harold. Let me just tell Cher we're ready. She's got her nose stuck in a book. I do believe we could suffer an earthquake and she wouldn't notice.'

Maddy could tell from the way Harold gently touched his wife's shoulder, smiled at her and offered his arm, that he absolutely adored her. Cher's returned smile convinced Maddy that their relationship was one to be envied.

As in Perth, Bailey had clustered sufficient sofas and chairs together in one corner of the lounge to create a cosy space for their story.

Harold and Cher joined the group to a chorus of 'good evening.' Cher sat in an armchair while he stood next to her and turned to face his audience.

'My tale is based on a true incident and takes place in Arkansas, in the Deep South of America.'

'Home of the Blues. My favourite music.'

All eyes focused on the retired Dean, decked out in his usual attire of black trousers and grey shirt with glistening white clerical collar. His eyes widened. His bushy eyebrows twitched. 'What's the matter?'

Sumner recovered first. 'You're a dark horse, David. I had you down as a Bach kind of a guy.'

'You know what they say: "Still waters run deep".' David smiled. 'I'm so sorry, Harold, I interrupted. Please continue.'

'No problem. It's good to know we share a passion for good music.'

Maddy settled back in her chair, mesmerised by the melodic tones of Harold's voice.

'At the time of my story in the late 1940's, slavery is abolished, but segregation is absolute. Separate schools, hospitals, public transport. To put this into context, this is ten years before the famous case of Rosa Parks. You may remember, they arrested her in Montgomery, Alabama, after she refused to give up her seat on the bus to a white passenger. Black folk had the right to vote, but the majority of the Southern States introduced an entry exam and poll tax which prevented most from doing so.

Harold perched on the arm of his wife's chair. She smiled up at him, reached for his hand and gave it a squeeze.

'Porter was the headteacher of Coffee Creek, the local elementary school for black children, but the pay wasn't good and he supplemented his meagre salary by farming his forty-acre cotton farm, where my story begins:'

Professor Harold Reeve's Tale

Porter heard the horses coming long before they arrived. He stood on his porch and scanned the winding track that led from the main road and ended at the dusty driveway of his home.

Please God, don't let it be them. His pulse raced as the three horses galloped towards him. Their riders wore white robes with hoods.

Porter glanced through the open door at his wife, Lydia, who sat at the table, her arms around the shoulders of their two youngest children: Harold, five years old, and Barbara, their youngest, at three. After three boys, they'd given up all hope of ever having a girl, but she'd finally arrived – as sweet as pecan pie. At least his two older boys, Harvey and John, were down by the river fishing, out of harm's way.

'What is it, Papa?' Harold asked.

'Is it them?' his wife asked.

He nodded and turned back to check the riders' progress. They had reached the driveway. No chance to get the children out and anyway, where could they possibly hide?

'Get those children under the table,' he said.

'But what–'

'Do it now!' he snapped.

He shared her fear, but guilt intensified his.

As the horses raced past the pig sheds, Porter slammed the door shut, ran to the window and closed the shutters.

He turned to his wife. 'I'm sorry,' he said.

'You did the right thing,' she answered softly. 'The Lord will surely protect us. Hush children.' She pushed her son and daughter under the table and pulled down the tablecloth to hide them from

view. 'Stay very quiet,' she begged. 'It'll be all right.'

Her words seemed to echo what JD had said as they stood beside the rickety wooden church a month before: "It'll be all right," he'd said.'

The service had been over for a good twenty minutes, and all the congregation had drifted away, except for Rosie Wellington, who seemed to be struggling with her bootlace.

'Let me,' JD had offered, and he'd bent down and tied the lace so tight it wouldn't be coming loose again anytime soon.

'Thanks,' Rosie had said, but it hadn't sounded much like she meant it.

As she turned to go, Porter winced at the purple patches on her dark skin: bruising that had no place on a woman's neck. JD put a hand on Porter's shoulder and they both watched Rosie walk away.

JD was Porter's uncle, and one of the wealthiest men in the neighbourhood. No one knew how JD had managed to amass such a fortune, but he owned the biggest plantation for miles around, getting on for 850 acres. He employed more hands than most of the white folk in the area. Ten men and a cook worked on the farm full time. During the weeks of cotton chopping and picking, JD employed additional casual labour. He had a reputation for providing good living conditions for his workers and their families, paying a fair wage, and for being something of a political activist.

He patted Porter's shoulder. 'Come on, Porter, the Fifteenth Amendment gave our folk the vote, and we ain't gonna let these politicians steal our rights. We were equal enough when they needed us to fight the Germans.'

JD locked the church door and turned back to face Porter.

'We didn't need some fancy certificate to say we could read and write before they packed us off to war. How come we need one now

to prove we're fit to vote?'

'I know it's unjust, but what can we do?'

'I'm not gonna let them get away with it. I'll find the funds to pay the poll tax if you teach them to pass the literacy test.'

'But, JD, what happens when the Klan find out?'

'They won't. We'll use the church on Sunday's, after the mid-day service. We'll call it extra bible study. It'll be all right.'

It had seemed easy enough. Porter taught them well. Within three weeks, thirty-two men and women had travelled to the town of Marvell, where they'd taken the exam, got their certificates, and become eligible – with their fees paid by JD – to vote in the next election. There were plenty more folks keen to take up the offer. How could the Klan possibly find out when only negroes attended their church?

But clearly, they had.

Porter peered out through a gap in the shutters.

The riders screamed and yelled as they galloped their horses into the yard and pulled up. The horses flared their nostrils, reared and pranced. One rider drove a four-foot stake, shaped like a cross and covered with dry grass, into the dusty ground. A second rode up beside him, tipped a container of petrol over it and used his tinderbox to set it alight; the distinctive and terrifying fiery cross.

Porter wondered if the neighbours would see the blaze, but then realised that even if they did, they wouldn't dare interfere.

'Lydia, my gun. Get me my gun.'

'No, Porter.' Lydia cried. 'If you kill them, they'll see you hang.'

'What am I supposed to do, stand here while they burn our home around us?'

'If that's what it takes.'

The riders circled the wooden house, firing their rifles into the air. One rode his horse onto the veranda. The hooves thundered across the planked decking until he reached the window where Porter crouched. The rider swung the butt of his gun and shards of glass fell through the slats and crashed around Porters' feet.

Barbara screamed and began to sob.

'Hush little one,' Lydia crooned in their daughter's ear. 'Don't be afraid. That's exactly what they want.'

Porter peered through the shutters and broken glass. The sun sank behind the smoke shack painting the evening sky mauve. Usually, at this time of the evening, he'd be sat on the veranda, his daughter in his lap, watching the chickens scratch for food and his sons horsing around in the yard.

The terrifying trio continued to circle the house uttering blood-curdling yelps. The chickens squawked and flapped as they tried desperately to avoid the murderous hooves.

Porter heard Lydia gasp.

He swung around, fearing the worst. Lydia's eyes were wide as she stared at their son, who stood right next to Porter, so close he'd almost knocked him over.

'Harold,' Lydia's voice trembled. 'Whatever are you doing? Get back under the table.'

'Take this father.' Harold held up his slingshot. 'It works real good on the snakes.'

Porter remembered teaching Harold how to take aim and shoot at them with his slingshot. He'd watched him since on many occasions. The boy never missed. The snakes – rattlers, green garters, and the aptly named cottonmouth moccasins – were always his biggest worry when it came to the children's safety.

Until tonight.

Porter took the slingshot. 'Ammunition?'

Harold searched his back pocket, brought out a selection of dried peas and handed them to his father.

'Well done, son. You get back now, and look after your mother.'

Porter crouched at the window, parted the shutters a few inches, armed the cup of the slingshot with the peas, waited until the next horse mounted the veranda steps and charged across in front of him.

He unleashed his son's weapon.

An explosion of noise erupted as the peas hit the horse's withers. The horse snorted in shock, whinnied, and reared, front legs pawing the air. The rider's head struck the roof timbers. He let out an excruciating howl of protest. The horse snorted, and bucked, and the white-robed rider tipped to one side and crashed to the floor in a crumpled heap. The crazed horse raced off the veranda, across the yard, and disappeared into the trees.

One of the other riders dismounted, clambered onto the porch and gathered up his half-conscious colleague. He wrestled him off the porch and, with the third man's help, threw him over the neck of his horse and jumped back into the saddle. Together, they galloped off towards the town, leaving a cloud of dust in their wake.

Lydia ran over to Porter, threw her arms around his neck and kissed him. 'Thank the Lord. Saved by a few dried peas.'

Porter proudly placed his arm around his son's shoulder. 'Saved by Harold's quick thinking,' he said.

Half an hour later, Porter sat on the veranda in his rocking chair, gun laid across his knees as he sipped a cold beer. He didn't expect any further trouble that night, but the gun helped him feel better prepared. The moon had risen and the stars peppered the night sky. Bats flew over the charred remains of the cross. The smoky smell mingled with the heavy scent of honeysuckle, roses and lavender.

Their scent soothed him as he reflected on the events of the evening and tried not to fret that his oldest two were not yet home. It wasn't unusual for them to be out this late, not at all, but after tonight's events he couldn't help but worry.

Just as the moon disappeared behind a cloud, he heard a crunching sound coming from the woods. He sat bolt upright, gun at the ready, and peered into the darkness. Something glinted near the shed. He leapt to his feet and flicked off the porch light, heart pounding, eyes straining.

The distinctive shape of Harvey, returning from his fishing trip came into view. He carried a line of six Grinner fish threaded together through their gills; their scales glittered as the moon reappeared. Porter's hand shook as he lowered himself back into his chair.

As Harvey grew closer, he started to run. 'What's with the cross, Father? It's not—'

'We had visitors,' Porter said, peering desperately behind Harvey for sight of his eldest son.

Relief surged through him as he made out John's figure in the shadows, but what was that behind him?

Harvey pointed. 'Look what we found.'

John emerged, leading a Palomino horse.

Porter came down from the porch and took a closer look. It was him all right, the horse he'd startled with Harold's slingshot.

'Put the beast in the shed, John,' he instructed. 'And, Harvey, put those fish in the cool-box and grab you both a root beer. We need to talk.'

Harvey and John did as they were told, then joined their father on the veranda. He brought them up to date on what had happened.

'What if they come back?'

'They won't come back tonight. I think one of them has a mighty big headache, and the others will be considerably shook up. They're not used to any form of resistance. But you're right. We need to make plans. I'll go and see Uncle J.D. tomorrow – see what he suggests. Problem is, we don't know who we're dealing with.'

John grinned at him. 'It'll be easy enough to find the owner.'

Porter frowned. 'Nobody in the Klan is going to admit it. Not given the way we came by him.'

'They don't have to. All we gotta do is release the horse and follow him.'

'Yes, that could work.' Porter sipped his beer and tried to think. 'But then again, what's the use? The sheriff won't take action against the Klan. Half his deputies are probably Klan members.'

John shrugged. 'We won't know what we can do until we find out who we're up against.'

'True,' Porter conceded.

The next morning Porter saddled up his mare, released the raider's horse and followed as it trotted out of the yard, cantered up the drive and onto the gravel track. The horse reached the main road and turned towards the small town of Postelle. The railway crossing lay in front of them and, beyond that, the general store, but before they reached the train track, the horse turned into a yard and passed under a sign that read: Frank Wright's Ginning Mill.

The cotton-picking season had begun and the first customer already had his trailer lined up underneath the suction pipe.

'Morning, Tommy,' Porter said. 'Let me give you a hand here.'

Porter tied his horse to a post and clambered into Tommy's trailer, positioning himself so that he could keep an eye on the Palomino.

'Mighty good of you, Porter. How's the family?'

'Growing up fast. Barbara's three now, and Harold starts school this fall.'

'Shucks, it don't seem five minutes since Lydia birthed him.'

Porter grabbed an armful of cotton bolls and pushed them towards Tommy, keeping an eye the whole time on the Palomino. The small puffs of raw cotton were sucked into the sixteen-inch diameter pipe and up into the gin. From here they would be loaded through a hopper onto a large tray containing rollers of evil looking metal teeth that separated the seed from the cotton threads. Metal hooks would pull the thread through holes in the tray and deposit it onto a conveyor belt, which transported it into a wooden box lined with fine muslin. The cotton would then be compressed into bales.

The seeds – too big to fall through the tray – continued down a second conveyor belt into a trailer. Once full, this would be taken to Memphis and either processed into oil, or cleaned, dried and treated to prevent mildew, before being packed as seeds for the following year.

Porter loved to watch the process, especially for his own crop. It made all those hours of backbreaking work worthwhile. Not that you thought it as you chopped the soil between the cotton plants to keep them weed free, and picked the bolls under the relentless hot sun, an endless task it seemed, until eventually there was sufficient to fill a trailer. Only on that trip to the ginning mill did it begin to feel worthwhile. Even more so when you watched your cotton bale released from the wooden press, veiled in its thin cotton cover. How much did it weigh, did it constitute a good crop, would it be sufficient to supplement his teaching salary and put food on the table for the next twelve months?

Porter continued to swing armfuls of bolls over towards Tommy, but not too quickly. He didn't want to finish the job and lose his excuse to hang about unnoticed, before someone claimed the Palomino.

'How's your crop coming on, Porter?' Tommy asked.

'Can't complain. What are you doin' this year, taking your bale or selling it through the factory?'

'I've sold it to Wright. He offered me thirty-five cents per pound.'

'You'd get thirty-eight in Memphis.'

'But then I'd have to get it there, and pay Wright's ginning fee. None of us like paying over the odds for cleaning up and baling, but Wright's the only service for miles around. As I see it, taint worth the hassle going elsewhere.

Finally, somebody emerged from the factory and walked into the yard. Porter ducked low as the man caught sight of the Palomino and pulled up short.

'Hey up, Frank!' he yelled. 'Your horse is back.'

Frank Wright came rushing out from the packing area, sporting a limp and a bandaged elbow. 'Ginny, thank God. I thought I'd lost you. Come here, come to Daddy.'

The horse whinnied when she spotted her owner and recognised his voice. He returned the affection by patting the horse's neck and stroking its velvety nose, murmuring soft, comforting words as he led her towards the stables.

So, Frank Wright, was the leader of the local Klan.

Porter pushed the last armful of cotton towards Tommy.

'Thanks, Porter. Hope I can return the favour soon.'

'You take care now,' Porter said. He backed off the trailer, trying to stay out of sight, as he headed over to JD's place.

The next morning, the same man who'd come out and found the Palomino, ushered Porter and JD into Frank Wright's office, where

Frank had grudgingly agreed to see them. Dressed in a long-sleeved shirt that almost hid his injured elbow, he sat behind his large desk, and made a point of leaving them standing.

'You can have five minutes, JD. I'm very busy.'

'That's all I need Frank,' JD said. 'I've come to tell you I'm calling in your loan on the mill.'

'You can't do that!' Frank jumped to his feet, yelped with pain, and sank carefully back into his chair.

'I can and I will,' JD said.

'But where am I going to find somebody to cover the loan?'

'Everyone knows about your gambling habit. You won't.'

Frank made a visible effort to rally. 'Look, this is stupid. If you want your stinking money back, then fine. I'll pay you after the harvest.'

JD sat down opposite Frank and made a show of brushing off his hat. 'How? I'm organising a boycott.'

Porter had to bite back a grin.

'Boycott,' Frank spat. 'Where? How?'

'I shall make my trucks available for everyone to take their cotton to the ginning mill in Marvell.'

'But that's miles away,' Frank laughed. 'No one will take you up on that ridiculous offer.'

'They will when they find out that you're the leader of the local Ku Klux Klan,' JD said, quietly.

'Prove it.'

'You left your horse behind, Frank. Very foolish. She led us right back to you.'

A terrible silence filled the room as JD's words sank in. Frank put his head into his hands.

'I'll release you from your loan and pay you $2,000 for the

factory on condition that you walk away today, take your cronies with you and leave the town by the end of the month.'

Frank swore.

'Come on, Frank. You gambled and lost. You've no wife or family, no future, no choice. Time for you to sell up and move on.'

Frank looked around the room like he sought some form of escape. His gaze came to rest on Porter. 'You can stand there now, Porter, all big and brave, but you've got to admit we scared the crap out of you.' He laughed. 'That'll make you think twice about helping more of your kind to get the vote. How dare you teach those niggers literacy and pay their poll tax? They should be taught to know their place.'

'Like you taught, Rosie, you mean?' JD said.

'That bitch knows her place all right. I taught her well enough.'

JD stiffened. 'Forget what I said about the end of the month. I want you out of here today.'

'Don't bother getting all gallant defending, Rosie. Who do you think told me about the lessons?'

Porter stared at Frank. Of course. Rosie. Frank Wright's lover. That's why she'd been hanging around, spying on them after church, sniffing out information she could pass on. Frank's boast, that he taught her well enough, explained the bruises. He looked at JD to see how he had taken the news.

JD just sat there grinning. 'You've got until midnight,' he said. 'Oh, and by the way, I'm keeping the horse.'

They walked towards JD's farm, the Palomino trailing behind them.

Porter turned towards his uncle. 'You set me up, JD. You made damn sure that Rosie told Frank Wright all about those lessons, didn't you? Just so you could smoke him out.'

'I did,' JD admitted. 'I knew Frank led the Klan, but I couldn't prove it. I've been picking up his gambling bills for a couple of years now. I just needed something to push him into a quick sale.'

Porter couldn't believe it. Uncle JD didn't have family of his own and had always treated Porter like a son, his kids like grandchildren. But he'd put them all in danger.

JD stepped in front of Porter and forced him to halt.

'Look at me, Porter. I would never risk the well-being of you, or your family. Never. I heard about the raid well in advance. Frank used his fists one time too many. Rosie came and told me what he planned to do. I had my two best sharpshooters hidden in your shed, ready to take over if things got messy. I swear.'

Porter glared at him. 'But you couldn't have known that we'd follow the horse home.'

JD laughed. 'You didn't need to. I had other men on the road. They followed them home. I already had my confirmation, but you finding the horse put the final nail in his coffin.'

Porter stared at JD, and then grinned. 'So, you had my back covered all along?'

'I did, but I'm proud of how you handled things. When it came down to it, you didn't need my help.'

'Thanks to Harold,' Porter said. 'I owe that boy some peas.'

'Forget the peas,' JD said. 'Who do you think the horse is for?'

The two men turned and looked at the Palomino, burst out laughing and then set off down the road together.

'And that's how I got my first horse.'

An explosion of applause erupted as Harold finished his story.

'What a cracking tale, justice for the black community,' Sumner said as he raised his camera and took a photo of Harold.

'My dear man,' gasped Barbara, eyes blinking as she addressed Harold. 'Are we allowed to say black?'

'Black is fine, Maam. That's what we are.'

'It sounds so... so harsh somehow.' She grasped her hands in front of her, the dark pink nail polish – a perfect match to her badly applied lipstick – setting off the brilliance of her diamond rings. 'Isn't it kinder to say *coloured*?'

'I have heard some women refer to themselves as *women of colour*. But most of us are happy with *African American* or *Black*. Both are OK.'

'It least there's more tolerance in America these days,' Sumner said. 'After all, you voted in President Obama.'

'Believe me; the British are far more open-minded than folk in the US. Chicago, where I lived when I met Cher, is still one of the most racially divided cities.' Harold reached over to his wife and took her hand gently in his. She smiled encouragingly as he continued. 'My wife and I married in 1999, but it wasn't until a year later, in November 2000, that Alabama overturned the law banning interracial marriage. Ironic, not only the last state to do so, but also the one-time home of Martin Luther King.'

'I'm shocked.' Bailey said. 'I thought we Australian's were the poor relations at conquering our prejudices, but it appears we all have a lot to learn. Thank you for sharing your story with us, Harold. Now, would you all like to make your way through to the dining room?'

Bailey breathed a sigh of relief. At last, a story they all enjoyed. Not too sad, not too rude, but just right. Even the discussion that followed went OK and not one complaint today from the Nunnes. Things were definitely looking up.

6. Day Four – Trip to the Leeuwin National Park

Paul felt a twinge of guilt as he turned the corner and saw Frank pacing up and down, checking his watch and glancing first in one direction and then the other.

'Paul, thank goodness you're here. At last,' Frank said as he caught sight of him.

'I'm bang on time.' Paul tapped the face of his watch.

Frank climbed the steps, walked along the aisle to the first vacant places and shuffled into the window seat. Paul followed and threw himself down beside him.

'Paul, I–'

'I'm not listening. I need a nap. Couldn't sleep for your snoring last night.' Paul closed his eyes and feigned sleep. He knew his behaviour was childish, but Frank had really annoyed him at breakfast. He'd claimed there wasn't time for Paul to go back to their room – fifteen minutes before they were set to leave. For goodness sake.

Bailey tapped the microphone. 'Good morning Ladies and Gentlemen. We have an interesting excursion for you today, but first we have quite a long drive, so if any of you need a snooze, please feel free.'

Paul woke up as he heard the bus driver speaking.

'Couple of minutes to the lay-by, Bailey.'

'Thanks, Stan.' Bailey got to her feet. 'OK, Ladies and Gentlemen, this is the centre of our Boranup Forest, part of the Leeuwin National Park.'

'Could you spell that for me please?' Cher asked, with her pencil poised over a note book.

'L-E-E-U-W-I-N and the forest is, B-O-R-A-N-U-P, an Aboriginal word that means "place of the male dingo." Unfortunately, you won't be seeing any today. You may come across them later in the tour, but the wild dogs hereabouts gained a reputation as sheep killers and were hunted to extinction.'

The driver pulled into the lay-by and the bus came to a standstill.

'We'll be here for about twenty minutes to give you a photo opportunity with these amazing karri trees. They belong to the eucalyptus family and rank among the tallest trees in the world. Some of them reach heights of eighty metres or more.'

Paul jumped as Frank clutched his arm.

'Don't stray too far from the bus, Paul. Please.'

'Oh, for goodness sake.' Paul shrugged Frank's hand away. 'She said twenty minutes. I'll be back. Not a minute before, nor a minute after.'

Paul checked his watch and walked to the front. The door sighed and hissed open. He jumped down the steps, ran across the road and down a wood-bark path leading into the forest. He continued to jog until, when he turned to check over his shoulder, he could no longer see the bus or any sign of the others. He stepped off the trail, pushed his way through the ferns and sank onto a network of moss-covered roots. All around him the tall pale-barked trees reached for the skies, their trunks of ghostly grey, occasionally blotched with pale terracotta smudges. He looked up through the sparse canopy of branches and leaves growing in tufted clumps, to the bright blue sky above.

He breathed deeply and the refreshing, earthy smell calmed him – a quiet and fragrant place for him to stop and think about his overwhelming problem. He'd been carrying this feeling of entrapment for six months, since the day he visited his mother in the hospice where she lay dying.

'I'm so worried about you. Where will you live?' she'd asked. 'Perhaps the council will let you keep the house?'

'It's a large family home. They'll need it. But even if they agreed, I couldn't afford to stay. Not on my salary.'

'Take Frank's offer and move in with him…please. He'll look after you.'

'But Mother, (a) I hardly know him, and (b) I don't need looking after.'

'But he's offered you a home. A nice home. And it's not far from where you work. Please, I beg you… please promise me?' Tears rolled down her pale cheeks. 'I *need* to know you're settled before I go.'

His heart had ached; he could hardly swallow for the lump in his throat. He'd foraged in his pocket for a clean handkerchief, passed it to her and patted her hand. How like her, putting her concerns for him above her dislike of Frank.

'Shush, Mother, don't fret. Please don't cry. Of course, I promise.'

She'd died three days later. Now here he was, six months on, trapped by his promise.

He heard the cry of a kookaburra and looked around, but it remained hidden in the undergrowth.

Pondering his predicament brought back the panic. His chest knotted; his heart raced. How the hell could he survive the next three weeks, let alone the months or years ahead? He liked Australia, although he'd prefer to be backpacking, but the way Frank insisted that they always did everything together suffocated him. He needed some space. His best option on their return would be to look for a small flat, before breaking the news to Frank. Of course, he'd still visit; stay over from time to time. He'd become very fond of him. But he found this living together extremely oppressive.

He knew he'd reacted to Frank's demands by behaving like a petulant child. Knowing how fastidious Frank was, he'd been deliberately untidy, leaving his clothes all over the place and his toiletries scattered around the bathroom. He'd left it to the very last minute to be ready for meals, Bailey's meetings or even, like this morning, getting to the bus.

He should know better with his training. If you act like a child, you will be treated like one. Time he started behaving like a mature twenty-eight-year-old. He glanced at his watch. He'd better make a start by getting back to the bus before Frank suffered apoplexy.

7. Second Evening – Margaret River Region

Aviation Cocktail

- *40ml Gin*
- *20ml fresh lemon juice*
- *4ml Maraschino Liqueur*
- *4ml Creme de Violette*

   Shake all the ingredients together, strain into a chilled cocktail glass

Bailey sipped her cocktail and smiled. It tasted great. She still hadn't received a reply from Suzy, but on the whole, today had been good. The restaurant had managed to rustle up brown bread for breakfast – not that the Nunnes noticed. The excursion had gone to plan. And, wonder of wonders, Angie had arrived on time to tell her tale. Yep, a good day.

'Good evening, Ladies and Gentlemen, I hope you enjoyed the Cape Leeuwin Lighthouse. I'm always amazed at the abundance of wildflowers that grow in such an exposed location. It is, after all, the most south-westerly point in Australia. Someone asked me the cause of those spectacular wave plumes we witnessed. They're the result of the Cape being the meeting point of the Southern and Indian Oceans. And wasn't the wine tasting and lunch simply wonderful?'

A general buzz of agreement circled the room, fueling Bailey's up-beat mood.

'Make sure you have your glass of Aviation. Tonight, I'm delighted to introduce Angie Cook, our storyteller for the evening. Angie, over to you.'

'Thank you, everybody.' Angie remained seated in her armchair.

'My story is about PR. One of these... what do you call them, a thinger-me-bob... erm... modern apprentice, that's it. He worked in my local pub. Nice boy, he would slip me a gin when no one was watching, don't you know?' She raised her glass and took a large gulp before she continued.

'PR liked a drink.' Angie drained hers and turned to the waiter collecting empties. 'Such a pretty shade of blue.' She twirled the stem of her empty glass between her fingers as she held it out to him. 'Could you possibly get me another, darling?'

'Of course, Madam.'

'Now, where was I? Oh yes, PR, or JR? No, silly me, that's the one married to Sue Ellen who got shot.'

Bailey sighed.

'PR used to get quite tipsy by the end of the night. Couldn't hold his drink.'

'Unlike you, eh, Angie?' Miller nudged Bailey's arm.

Bailey shot him a look.

Angie thanked the waiter as he handed her another glass of Aviation. She took a large gulp, and licked her lips. 'Lovely. Now... for his party piece he would do this dance... what do you call it? He would roll about on the floor with his feet in the air and spin like a top.'

'Break dancing?'

'That's it, Miller, break dancing. I told him, "you'll break your neck one day," but he took no notice. Then one night he spun around so much that when he stood up, he lost his balance and fell across one of the tables. You should have seen it. Drinks everywhere. The prop... pop–'

'Proprietor?' offered Miller.

'Yes, the prop... pop... the owner, he came over and sacked him on the spot. The boy was dev... deva... really upset. He had nowhere to go, you see. He lived above the pub. Then this woman customer – rather racy – you know the sort, Miller, she ran an escort agency. Well, she offered to put him up.'

'As the actress said to the bishop.'

'Miller!' Fyrne wagged her finger at him.

'Sorry.'

Bailey had never seen anyone look less sorry. 'Angie, please continue... Mrs Cook. Oh, my goodness, she's nodded off.'

'Not surprising really,' Miller laughed. 'Those Aviations pack quite a punch.'

'Especially on top of all that wine she consumed at lunchtime,' Maddy added.

'Miller–'

'I'm saying nothing. Promise.'

'I was about to say, would you mind helping me get Angie back to her room?' Bailey leaned towards him and whispered. 'At least that way I can make sure you don't say anything outrageous while I'm gone.'

He grinned and stepped forward to help.

Angie's bedside table contained an array of bottles; gin, brandy, vodka. All half full – or half empty, depending on your point of view. Bailey felt a surge of annoyance.

'Help me to lay her on the bed, Miller, and then we can role her over into the recovery position. She'll be safer that way if she's sick.'

'Poor thing,' Miller said. 'I wonder what's wrong with her.'

'She's drunk.'

'I know that. What I mean is I wonder what's causing her to drink. She must be very unhappy.'

A flush of shame rose up Bailey's neck and into her cheeks. For goodness sake, it was her job to care for her guests and yet Miller, the most uncouth member of the group, displayed more empathy for Angie than she ever had.

She slipped Angie's sandals from her feet and placed them beside the bed.

'I think she'll be OK to leave now.' Bailey smiled at Miller. 'I'll drop by later and check on her. We'd best get back to the others.'

'Before they start gossiping about us?'

The blood rushed back into Bailey's cheeks. It hadn't taken Miller long to revert to character. She followed him out of the room and closed the door carefully behind them. She wondered what she could do to rescue the evening's entertainment now that Angie had ruled herself out. With a bit of luck – and, my goodness, she needed some – Mr Singh might have his story ready. Worth asking.

8. The Evening Continues

Bailey and Miller walked back into the lounge.

'Is she all right?' Barbara asked.

'She will be when she's slept it off. I'll take a sandwich up to her later. Mr Singh, I wonder if we could perhaps trouble you for your tale.'

'Why, yes, of course. I will be honoured.'

Mr Singh sprang to his feet, clasped his hands together and looked around the room.

'For those of you who do not know me, my name is Jhujhaar Singh, but my friends,' he paused and swept his arm before him in a gesture that embraced them all, 'and I count you all as friends, call me Jujh. I work for my father, a famous hotelier. We run a truly splendid hotel.'

He took a sip from his water.

'In my late teens and twenties, I played cricket for the national team. He pulled back his shoulders, straining the buttons on his yellow silk paisley shirt. 'I hope one day I will again represent my country, but next time as a politician.'

Miller leaned over to Bailey and whispered behind his hand. 'Is he ever going to get around to telling this story?'

Bailey glared at him.

'I love it when you pretend to be angry,' Miller grinned.

Bailey gasped. She could not believe the audacity of the man. Just when she thought she'd glimpsed a thoughtful side to him.

Jujh cleared his throat. 'And now for my story. It is a true story. In my early years, I am ashamed to say, I was very spoilt and selfish. My Father decided the time had come for me to see, how do you say it, "how the other half live." Just after my thirteenth birthday, he took me on a trip into the jungle to visit a tribe of folk who still lived in very primitive conditions.

Father had visited the village several times as a teenager. My grandfather always took him along whenever he went on one of his trips to pay respects to the chief, Sabak. The inhabitants always celebrated a visit from their Maharajah.'

'Oh, my goodness, you mean to say that your grandfather's a Maharajah?' Barbara gasped.

'He was. The honour passed to my father when Grandfather died.'

'And you're the oldest son?'

'His only son.'

'Oh, my.' Barbara settled back in her chair, her gaze focussed on Jujh with renewed intensity.

Jujh clasped his hands behind his back, puffed out his chest and began his story in his soft, lilting voice:

Jhujhaar Singh's Tale

The village nestled deep within the forest, accessed by a long, narrow and very bumpy dirt track. Our driver swore under his breath as he inched the Land Rover along. The vehicle sank into one pothole after another, causing us to sway and lurch. I began to feel quite nauseous.

'Are we nearly there?' I asked my father.

'You need to learn patience, my boy. Where's your sense of adventure?'

Feeling somewhat hurt by his chastisement, I turned away and concentrated on tracking the progress of a troupe of brown monkeys that swung through the undergrowth beside us. Their name: Macaca Mulatta, brought back memories of my Amah, Jarita, as she read me Kipling stories.

A young female monkey paused to readjust her tiny baby, which clung to the soft grey fur of her chest. She stroked its head in a comforting gesture that reminded me of how my mother had ruffled my hair and kissed my forehead as we had left home earlier.

I also remembered her parting words: 'Remember to do as your father tells you. This visit means a lot to him. He wants to introduce you to Chief Sabak. He is proud that you are now a young man – no longer a child.'

So why did I behave like one?

At last, we arrived at the village, which consisted of about twenty shacks constructed from wood and tarpaulin, and positioned around the edges of a clearing. Two large cooking pots and a griddle hung from a metal frame over a blazing campfire.

A small, muscular man awaited our arrival. Behind him,

stood a large group of his family and neighbours – around fifty in number.

Excited shouts and the sound of laughter heralded the arrival of four children and three dogs. Scampering towards us, they disturbed some chickens, which squawked, and fluttered away in protest. One child tripped in his hurry to reach us, upsetting a pile of round patties baking in the sunshine. They were made from cow dung and would be used as fuel when completely dry. I could see the palm prints, made by the women as they moulded the dung into shape. I could only hope and pray that whoever had made them had remembered to wash their hands before preparing our meal.

I could not believe how appalling the living conditions were, and could only guess at what they used as their bathroom facilities; no toilet blocks were apparent. I dare not ask and reveal my ignorance.

Father jumped from our vehicle and I clambered out behind him. He ran towards Sabak and greeted him with a huge bear hug. My father lifted him easily and spun him around. They slapped each other on the back and laughed.

'My dear friend,' Father said. 'I bring you my son, Jhujhaar.'

I stepped forward, and we shook hands. Sabak bowed his head and welcomed me to his humble home. He told me how I resembled my father, who had been my age at the time they first met. To be compared with my father filled me with pride.

He told us, with tears in his eyes, how sorry he had been to hear that Grandfather had passed, two years earlier.

Sabak pulled a young man from the group. 'This is my son, Sonu. My wife and I were blessed with our only child late in life, so we called him Sonu, which means God's gift.'

Sonu knelt before my father and kissed his hand. He spoke in a dialect I did not understand.

'My son wishes to welcome you.' Sabak interpreted his son's words. *'He also wishes to express the thanks of the entire village for my safe return from the Kashmir campaign. You will no doubt be aware, Jhujhaar, I owe my life to your grandfather.'*

'I know very little about my grandfather's fighting days. He would never speak of them. Do tell me, Sabak,' I begged.

'I will. But first, please, take a seat and be comfortable.'

Sabak guided us to the tree trunks and we settled around the camp fire while the women busied themselves putting the finishing touches to our meal. Sabak stood before us as he told his story.

'The Maharaja of Kashmir requested help from the Indian government to repel the Pakistani army who wanted to annex Kashmir for themselves. Your grandfather, a personal friend of the Maharaja, volunteered to help. With me at his side he played a major role in preventing the fall of Srinagar.'

'You also played a major part in the success, Sabak,' my father said.

'Perhaps,' Sabak smiled. *'However, on our return across the border, we were ambushed. I was badly wounded but your grandfather ignored the hail of bullets, and carried me down the mountainside to safety.'*

'A hero, but a very humble man,' my father said, softly. *'We should all take a lesson from his modesty.'*

'A wonderful man. I'm very lucky to have had the opportunity to serve him.'

It made me feel proud to hear my grandfather spoken of with such respect.

We sat around the fire while Sabak's wife and daughter-in-law placed chapattis on the griddle to cook and ladled rice and curry from the cooking pots into small bowls. The meal smelt and *tasted delicious.*

As we enjoyed our meal, Father began to chuckle. 'Do you remember the day of my thirteenth birthday, when you took us all to the tiger sanctuary?'

Sabak smiled, and his eyes twinkled with pride. 'Dilip, tell me, you have shared the story of our adventure with Jhujhaar?'

'Do you know, Sabak, I'm not sure I ever did. Perhaps now would be a good time?' My father patted the log beside him. 'Sit here my son, and I will tell you the story of my thirteenth birthday treat. As part of the celebration, your grandfather and Sabak organised a tour of a tiger sanctuary with one of the rangers. We drove in a Land-Rover, through acres of dusty terrain, until we reached an enormous lake and parked beside it. The guide assured us tigers frequently visited here. They would come to bathe and kill the small crocodiles whose meat they found particularly tasty. We waited in silence for over an hour. Lots of colourful birds waded in the shallows and a few deer came for a drink. We even spotted a couple of the small crocodiles. But no tigers.

'By this time, boredom had set in, as it would with any young boy after all that sitting around. You see, Jhujhaar, I do remember what it's like to be thirteen. 'We should have brought food as bait,' I suggested. 'That way we would be sure of seeing a tiger.'

'This is a reservation, not a zoo,' said the ranger. 'We never feed the animals. The park's natural eco-balance provides an ample food supply. We maintain a policy of minimal intervention to ensure the animals remain wild.'

Occasionally, we would hear a tiger roar or see a group of deer break cover and run across the track in front of us, but nothing followed. Not a tiger to be seen. Eventually, disillusioned, we headed back to the hotel.

As we drove down the hotel drive, we were met by guests and staff, running towards us, screaming.

'Go back!'

'Save yourselves!'

'Stop!'

'What is it?' your grandfather demanded. 'Is it a fire?'

'A tiger!' a woman screamed.

'Oh please,' I begged. 'Let's get closer. I must see a tiger. It is my birthday.'

Your grandfather looked at the ranger, who nodded. 'Most of them are very placid when it comes to humans, unless they're either provoked or protecting their young.'

We drove on, reached the end of the drive, and saw the huge beast. He stood on the ramp which led down into the shallow end of the swimming pool, gently lapping the water. As we watched, he turned around and slowly backed into the water until his body was completely submerged. He looked up, and we could see the magnificent markings on his face.

'I now know why they say a tiger smiles,' I laughed.

'He may be smiling now, but I think we should leave, and quickly.' The ranger turned the ignition and the engine whirred.

'Why the hurry?' I asked.

'Every tiger has different markings. They are like a fingerprint. This tiger is none other than Tekhurho. He's a maneater. Once they get the taste for human meat, they will continue to kill.'

The engine whirred again but did not start. Sabak jumped out and lifted the bonnet.

The tiger emerged from the water, shook himself, and calmly padded toward us. I froze with fear, but fortunately your grandfather took control and shouted to Sabak.

'Watch out! Get back in the truck!'

Sabak continued to fiddle under the bonnet while your grandfather shouldered his rifle and aimed at the ferocious looking creature.

'Be careful,' the ranger said. 'It's difficult to hit an enraged tiger as it attacks, and if you miss—'

'I get the picture. Hurry up, Sabak.'

'Never fear, Master. I will soon have it fixed.'

'Sabak, I'm ordering you, get back in the truck. I may have saved your life once before, you skinny runt, but we may not be so lucky a second time.'

The engine burst into life, Sabak leapt into the Land Rover and the ranger reversed. Stones and dust spat up from the drive as the wheels spun and we put some distance between ourselves and the tiger. He stood, watching us, motionless except for the twitching of his tail. Then he turned and padded back up the hotel drive and off in the direction of the reserve.

My father and Sabak chuckled at the memory as we finished our lunch. By now I was getting bored. I kicked a pile of leaves. A loud hiss alerted us all to the fact that I had inadvertently disturbed a snake. Paralysed with terror, I watched as it lunged towards me and sank its fangs into my leg. Sabak's son, Sonu, immediately sprang to my side and chopped off the snake's head with his knife. Sabak told me not to worry, the snake wasn't especially dangerous but, he explained, the venom should be removed as quickly as possible. Sonu knelt at my feet, sucked the two puncture marks and spat out the blood. After repeating this process several times, he tied his scarf around my leg, inserted a twig and twisted it round to form a tourniquet.

My father sat beside me and stroked my hand. He told me to be brave, and not to worry.

One of the women rushed to his side with a hot poultice made from a fine muslin cloth filled with a variety of herbs and some rice from the pot. Sabak explained it would continue to draw the poison from the wound and that I should keep it held over the puncture marks. By this time, the bite and the surrounding skin were bright red and my leg had swelled alarmingly.

I became drowsy at this stage and remember very little about the dash to the hospital. I can't imagine how the rear axle survived as we drove at speed down that dirt track but we made it to the main road, into the nearest town and arrived at the hospital.

You can imagine the scare we had when we found out that the snake had been a deadly cobra. Sabak had played down the danger of the poison, so that I didn't panic, create adrenalin, and increase the rate of absorption. The quick actions of Sonu had undoubtedly saved my life.

I am ashamed to say that as I progressed through my teenage years, I continued to be somewhat selfish and arrogant, but I always remembered the small community in the forest. Seven years later, during a game of cricket, I realised we were close to the village. I thought it would be interesting to pay a return visit. I wanted to meet again with Sabak and with his son, Sonu, the man who had saved my life. I sought to express my thanks. A bit belated, I accept, but better late than never.

Imagine my distress when I discovered that Sonu had died the day after our visit. The snake poison had entered his blood stream through an infected tooth. He had sacrificed his life to save mine. His death had deprived three very small children of their father. Sabak also died a year later. They said from a broken heart – grief at the loss of his only son.

'Oh, my dear boy, how absolutely dreadful,' Barbara said. 'You must have been devastated.'

Jujh nodded.

'Exactly Madam. I felt very guilty and responsible for his death. My father took me to the village to learn some humility and I had persisted with my selfish and arrogant lifestyle.' He cleared his throat. 'With my Father's agreement and support, I established a Trust Fund that covered the educational costs for Sabak's grandchildren. All three children now hold a degree, but the Trust Fund remains in place to fund the education of other children from the village.

'How wonderful,' Barbara clapped loudly. 'Isn't he simply brilliant?'

Bailey joined in with the applause. What a relief. Tony's first story had been superb, but so sad. She counted herself lucky to have escaped from Miller's offering without someone making a formal complaint. Harold's tale had been entertaining. This evening had started badly with Angie, but this contribution from Jujh, although sad, had been both different and enjoyable. Perhaps her experiment would work out well after all. Thank goodness.

'Ladies and Gentlemen, after all that excitement, are we ready for dinner?'

Bailey followed her guests into the restaurant. Several were congratulating Jujh on his story and she realised that she had failed to give him sufficient time to bathe in their compliments. But the restaurant staff had been waving franticly at her to get the guests in for dinner, pronto. She couldn't do right for wrong. She fought back unexpected tears. Goodness, she needed a good sleep tonight.

9. Day Five – The Drive to Perth and Flight to Alice Springs

Maddy had dressed carefully that morning – dark blue vest, pale blue fitted cotton shirt and her new, and very expensive, blue jeans. Her make-up took an age to apply but she liked the result, especially the way it emphasised her eyes while remaining minimalistic.

As she'd waited to board the coach, she'd experienced a surge of excitement to see Tony walk over to join her.

'How's your parrot this morning?' he asked.

'I'll miss him. Such a colourful character.'

'And here's another. Good morning, Angie.' Tony jumped onto the coach and held out his hand. 'Let me help you up these steps.'

'Oh, thank you, darling. Knight by name and knight by nature. So gallant.'

'My pleasure.' He returned his attention to Maddy. 'Your hand, fair lady.'

'Sir.' Playing along with his pantomime she held out her hand. He took it firmly and pulled her towards him. His eyes twinkled. The excitement fluttered in her stomach. Now she understood what people meant when they said they had butterflies.

'Where would mademoiselle like to sit?' he asked.

'That one will be fine.' She indicated two vacant seats half way down the bus. She paused as she reached Barbara, who looked cool and comfortable in a pale pink trouser suit and a white sun hat dressed with pink ribbons and ostrich feathers.

'Good morning, Barbara. How are you today?'

'Entirely better for seeing you two, my dears.'

Maddy threw her travel bag onto the coat rack and sat next to the window.

'Do you mind if I join you?' Tony asked.

Her heart leapt, but she managed to keep her voice steady. 'Please do.'

Eventually, with the luggage stowed and everyone safely strapped in the bus pulled away. Stan drove slowly down the long hotel drive, giving them a last chance to experience the extensive grounds. Maddy spotted a flock of magpie. *One for sorrow, two for joy, three for a girl and four for a boy.* A boy, a son? Two more magpies joined them. *Five for silver, six for gold.* She'd settle for that. And then another arrived. *Seven for a secret never to be told.* Her secret weighed heavy. Disturbed by the passing bus, the magpies cackled loudly and flew off into the undergrowth.

Maddy's excitement and anticipation quickly dissolved, when she glanced at Tony and realised, he'd fallen asleep. They hadn't even reached the end of the hotel drive.

Half an hour later, she jumped as Bailey shouted. 'Kangaroos, to the right!'

Tony sat bolt upright.

Maddy pointed. 'Oh look, there they are. Our first kangaroos.'

Five dark grey kangaroos sheltered in the shade of a small copse of graceful trees, similar to weeping willows but covered in small white flowers.

'I wonder what kind of trees they are?'

'Peppermint.' Tony rubbed his temple. 'I'm sorry I've not been very good company this morning. I didn't sleep too well.'

'Did your story bring back painful memories?'

'I miss Archie and Emily, of course, I do. But it's been over two years now, and life has to move on.'

'Easy said.'

Tony looked into her eyes and smiled. Maddy's stomach took another somersault. It was as though he probed deep into her psyche.

'So, what or who are you trying to move on from?' he asked.

Heat rose in Maddy's cheeks.

'I'm sorry. Ignore me, I shouldn't pry.'

'No, I'm sorry.' She looked around to make sure no one could overhear. 'I went out with Peter for six years. My first – in fact, only – serious boyfriend. A detective inspector in the fraud squad. I worked with him for a couple of years until I got promoted to sergeant and transferred to work in domestic violence – advising women to get out of abusive relationships. Ironic.'

'How so?'

'Our relationship by then had itself become abusive, and yet I continued seeing him. I convinced myself I could change him, that he loved me. I believed him when he cried and said it would never happen again. But of course, it did.'

'So, what happened?'

'A broken wrist.'

'Ouch.'

'We argued, and he pushed me down the stairs. I was lucky to get away with a broken wrist. The stupid thing is, I would still have taken him back, but he met someone else and dumped me. I've been on my own for over a year now.' She felt a weight lift from her shoulders. 'You're the first person I've told. I felt so stupid.'

'It wasn't you who was stupid.' Tony patted her hand gently. The hairs on her arm bristled.

Tony's head lolled against her and nestled on her shoulder. He was either very comfortable in her company, or she was very boring – she wasn't sure which.

Bailey finished handing out the boarding tickets, retreated to a quiet corner of the lounge and sank onto one of the uncomfortable plastic seats. She glanced at her watch. Surely Suzy would be around at this time of the day? She dialled the office number.

'Oh hello, Jayne, I hoped to talk to Suzy.'

'Bailey, is that you? Hold on, Jim wanted a word.'

'Bailey.' Jim's voice was sharp and unfriendly.

'Jim? I hoped to speak to Suzy. Is she in today?'

'Who gave you permission to provide free cocktails to everyone, and where's this ridiculous story idea come from?'

'I'm using my daily allowance for the drinks. It isn't costing the company any extra. And the guests seem to like story time.'

'Story time. You're supposed to be managing a tour, not a kindergarten. Look Bailey, I can't put it any plainer than this... get off this phone and for fuck's sake get on with your bloody job. Otherwise you won't have one. Do I make myself clear?'

'But Suzy–'

'Forget Suzy. Suzy's not here. Get on with your job. Do you understand me?'

'What do you mean, Suzy's not there? Is her daughter ill or something?'

'If you must know, she's on gardening leave – suspension. And she's been told that any contact with you will result in her instant dismissal. So, for her sake, and yours, forget it.'

'But–'

The line went dead.

Bailey's head spun. Suzy suspended? Why? An overwhelming sense of guilt flooded over her. Suzy, a single mum with a three-year-old daughter, would be in a mess if she lost her job?

'I've brought you a strong, black, coffee, Bailey. You look like you could do with one.'

Bailey looked up. Miller stood before her holding a cup of coffee.

She took it gratefully and smiled. 'Thanks, Miller. That's so thoughtful of you.'

'We need to keep our leader in good form. Listen up, Bailey, you're doing a great job. But you mustn't forget to take care of yourself as well as us.' He winked at her and then wandered off in the direction of the others.

What a topsy-turvy world. Miller, of all people, had demonstrated concern for her wellbeing, while her boss, who should have been offering motivational encouragement, told her to pull her finger out and get on with her f – ing job.

She took a sip of coffee. The caffeine fired through her and she jolted upright. How did Jim know the details about the cocktails and stories? Someone had fed back information. Had he planted a secret shopper on her tour? A spy reporting back on her every move? Who could it be? Is this the reason Suzy had been suspended? Had she been about to reveal the secret shopper's identity?

PART TWO

10. E-mail

To Suzy Bird
From Kate Bailey
Subject: Where's my wing bird?

I've been trying to get you at the office, but Jim tells me you're on "gardening leave."

Your cell phone goes direct to answer-phone and I don't know if you even have a land line. I've texted, and checked your social media – nothing. Then I remembered I had your home e-mail.

Try not to worry about being suspended. It must have been a shock, but go and see the union rep. I can't remember her name, but she's supposed to be very good. Knowing how hot-headed Jim can be, he's probably broken every protocol in the book.

He let it slip that he has inside information on my tour that could only have come from one of the guests. I guess I must have some sort of secret shopper. I don't know if you found out anything? As I see it, the new owner is going to be tied up with strategic issues, so I expect the secret shopper is likely to be employed as a spy. If I knew who, it might just give me the edge, and the best chance of keeping my job.

Let me know what you think.

11. Arrival – Alice Springs

Bellini Cocktail

- *120ml Prosecco*
- *20ml fresh peach juice.*
  Pour peach juice over ice, top up with Prosecco, stir and garnish with a slice of peach.

Bailey glanced around the small but comfortable lounge that the hotel had made available for her guests. No doubt Jim would have something to say about the extra cost. He'd probably dock the money out of her wages but, to be honest, she didn't care. She'd do anything to improve her chances of keeping her job – well, almost, she had her pride.

Furnished with small sofas and armchairs covered in rich teal upholstery and dove grey scatter cushions, the room created a snug and relaxed impression; far more conducive for cocktails and storytelling than the formality of the hotel's main lounge. Surely this attention to detail would impress the secret shopper – or the spy in her camp as she'd come to think of them.

'Good evening, Ladies and Gentlemen, and welcome to Alice Springs. Have you all got your Bellini?'

A chorus of agreement circled the room.

'Tomorrow's trip is your opportunity to explore the amazing

scenery and vastness of the outback. The coach leaves from the front door at nine. Don't forget your hat and bottled water.'

'We wouldn't dare,' Miller grinned.

Bailey glanced at him. 'And sun tan cream,' she added.

She turned her attention to Barbara and gave her a thumbs-up. Barbara nodded. Thank goodness Barbara had agreed to tell her story tonight. At least she'd get a tick in the box for remembering to address gender balance. Of course, she had tried to get Angie involved, but memories of that night simply inflamed her insomnia.

'Tonight's storyteller is our resident agony aunt, Barbara Bath. Thank you, Barbara, whenever you're ready.'

Barbara sat in the chair, placed carefully by Bailey to face the audience, and adjusted her pink pillbox hat and veil. Her diamond rings caught the soft glow from the wall lights and flashed blue, yellow and then bright pink as they picked up the colour of her silk skirt and jacket. She smiled to reveal pink lipstick on her front teeth.

'I married my first husband when I was eighteen, and very naive. He drank far too much and often came home drunk. He would then proceed to take his frustrations out on me. He left after eighteen months. In one of his rare sober moments he said that he'd kill me if he stayed.

'My second husband earned good money, but cultivated expensive tastes. Before I knew it, we were up to our necks in debt, with several overstretched credit cards. They were a fairly recent phenomenon at that time, but one to which he quickly became accustomed. I did what I thought was for the best. I waited until he took his evening shower, then raided his wallet and cut them all up. I negotiated a repayment plan, took on an extra part-time job and we eventually got our debt down. Unfortunately, he took it all very badly and became depressed. I tried everything I could to help him, but... despite my best efforts... he eventually took his own life.'

Barbara paused and patted her pockets.

'Oh, Barbara, you poor, darling.' Angie reached over, stroked Barbara's arm and offered her a delicate lace handkerchief from her shoulder bag. Barbara took it and dabbed at her nose.

'Thank you, Angie dear. I appreciate this. I'll return it tomorrow – freshly laundered of course.' She stuffed the hankie into her pocket, sniffed and brushed down her skirt. 'I felt so guilty, but eventually it turned out for the best. I met Jack, my last husband. A love match if ever–'

'Come on, Barbara, cut to the story,' the Brigadier demanded.

Bailey's heart thudded so loudly she felt sure the others would hear. How could this charming man be so rude? And to Barbara of all people?

Sumner sat in the armchair beside the Brigadier and shifted his position to confront him. 'Where's that sense of charity you're always bragging about, Friar?'

'Brigadier to you, and I'll show you about meddling when we get to my story. It's all about a corrupt photographer.'

'That's OK. Mine's about a fraudulent fundraiser.'

Bailey watched the colour drain from the Brigadier's cheeks. 'Gentlemen, please.' She held up her hand to silence the bickering. Either the Brigadier was behaving out of character or she had made, yet another, gross error of judgement. She couldn't believe the way the two of them were acting – like small children. 'Barbara, please continue.'

Barbara smiled. 'I'm sorry gentlemen. I'm only telling

you my experience of marriage so you can understand how I gained the necessary skills to become an agony aunt. I became so successful that I was recruited by... shall we say, a famous daily tabloid.'

'My tale tonight is about one of my clients. A young man called Steve, and his quest to find true love. I remember Steve's e-mail as though it arrived yesterday. He wrote with such yearning and incredible eloquence. He described how he'd fallen desperately in love with the most wonderful woman. His feelings for her scorched the ether as he pinged his meteoric declarations of adoration. The list of her attributes went on, and on, but I think you get the general idea?'

Her question was met by a flurry of nods and smiles of encouragement.

'He'd met her when he auditioned with the amateur dramatics group and was chosen to play the part of Lancelot in the summer show. Steve begged me to advise him, to tell him what he needed to do to win the affection of this beatific paragon he'd met at rehearsals. He swore he'd do anything, absolutely anything, to achieve his ambition and win her love. How could I refuse such a profound appeal? After all, Pryor, as your bracelet says: *love conquers all.*'

Pryor glanced at her bracelet. Nigel smiled fondly at her and gently stroked her hand.

'I told him I wanted to help, but warned him that he must instantly curb his enthusiasm in her presence. We didn't want her to perceive him as an out of control puppy. I insisted he keep me constantly updated on progress, so we could tweak his approach and that, if the advice worked, I wanted an invitation to the wedding. Any excuse for a new outfit. He agreed, and we embarked on the seven-week plan for him to become the epitome of the perfect husband. It works like this:'

Barbara Bath's Tale

When a woman is looking for a life partner, she, either knowingly or unknowingly, searches for seven qualities that will complement and encourage her own achievements, make her feel safe and happy and provide a good father for their children.

'Good grief, Barbara,' Fyrne said. 'We women can achieve success and happiness without men. We can even enjoy motherhood these days.'

'I'm aware of that, my dear, but I'm sure you would agree that for many young women, not all I grant you, but for many, the perfect man is high on their agenda.'

I agree,' Bailey said. 'And for some of us that are not so young. Thank you, Barbara. Please continue.'

'Thank you, my dear.'

You men are all capable of displaying these qualities, but do you demonstrate them consistently, in a way that will make the object of your desire convinced that you are the ideal husband for her?

I started Steve on the H.U.S.B.A.N.D programme, one letter a week, starting with 'H' for honesty.

A woman demands honesty from her man. She would not want him to lie about major issues, things that matter. In other words, she would not want to be patted on the head, told not to worry or be patronised. However, she may not want total honesty all of the time. The brutal truth may sometimes be a step too far. If she asks: "Do you like my outfit?" and you actually loathe it, you may be best to use the: "I preferred the one you were wearing yesterday" approach, rather than an outright: "no." It's a matter of getting the balance right.

A woman also needs to know her man has sufficient trust in her to share what is going on in his life, what his thoughts are on important issues, things that have happened to him in the past and his dreams for the future. She needs to be able to explore his life and decide if it is something she can climb into and share. But remember the puppy dog. He should not reveal too much, too soon, about his feelings for her.

Rehearsals were progressing well, until Guinevere, otherwise known as Gina, chastised Steve in front of the entire cast and crew. She demanded to know why he had pulled away early from their final stage scene that ended with a passionate embrace and a long smouldering kiss. Steve, remembering this was his week to practice honesty but with diplomacy, stumbled through his apology.

'I got... uhm... distracted.'

'Distracted by what?' she demanded, placing him in an impossible position.

'I'm afraid I have this thing about the smell of garlic. I'm sorry, it makes my stomach churn.'

'You're kidding me? You mean that garlic bread I had for lunch? Most men would give anything to share an ardent clinch with me, garlic breath or not.'

'I'm sorry. I don't mean to offend you. It's just that garlic... well unfortunately it has that effect on me.'

She turned her back on him and walked towards the changing room, her long skirt swishing. Steve sighed as he watched her leave.

'Bad luck, Steve.' Alex, the stage manager, patted him on the shoulder. 'Good excuse though. I thought for a minute she was going to make you admit you were enjoying yourself too much.'

Steve sat in one corner of the pub, ostracised, while Gina and her entourage stood around the bar laughing. He couldn't hear the full conversation, but heard Gina mention the words "garlic" and "vampire," to which someone else added, "too much at stake," causing even more laughter.

Alex left the others at the bar and joined him.

'You're taking a risk,' Steve smiled.

'I can take it.'

'How are the ticket sales going?'

'Two days completely sold out, and there's still seven weeks of rehearsals 'til the first show.'

'All down to your hard work. Stage manager, ticket sales, wardrobe... is there no end to your talents? Don't you ever think of swapping all the admin and auditioning instead?'

'Me? You've got to be joking. I'd be hopeless.'

'I'm not sure I'm any good. I've always wanted to act. Only as a hobby, you understand; I love being a primary school teacher. But this is the first major part I've had since I was six years old and played the Innkeeper in my school nativity play.'

'You're a natural. I can't believe how quickly you learnt your lines. And your stage presence is exceptional. I can't think of anyone better for the part.'

Steve glanced back at the bar. Another burst of laughter erupted.

'I suppose I will have to perfect my honesty with diplomacy skills if I'm ever going to get Gina to agree with you.'

Alex laughed. 'Don't worry. She'll have forgotten all about it by next week.'

The second week we tackled the letter 'U' for understanding. A woman wants to be understood by her partner at all times, even if she doesn't understand herself. She doesn't want to explain why she's feeling grumpy or snappy, why she doesn't want to go to that particular event, why she can't be bothered to cook dinner. She wants him to know, and empathise with her, and respond to her needs accordingly. Because if she knows he understands her, then she can be comfortable in her own skin, knowing that her man truly loves her, whatever.

This time, Steve's attempts appeared to fare better. After rehearsals, he sat in the pub with Alex discussing the complexities of stage management, its major contribution to the success of a production and the lack of recognition the role attracted. Gina arrived and joined them. She apologised profusely for her behaviour the week before, said she'd been 'feeling a bit hormonal.' He assured her she didn't need to explain; he completely understood and offered to buy her a drink.

When he got back, Alex had disappeared. He handed Gina her drink. 'Where did Alex go?'

'Oh, you know, two's company, three's a crowd. I wanted you to myself to tell you my news.' She sipped her drink and smiled. 'I've had an offer – a part in the Nottingham pantomime.'

'Wow, congratulations! You must be pleased.'

'It's only a small part to start with, but before the season closes I plan to have a major role.'

'I'm sure you will. You'll bowl them over.' Steve raised his glass and chinked it against Gina's. 'I'm so pleased for you, but promise you'll come back.'

'After the panto' season? I doubt it. My absolute dream is to act full time. This could be my lucky break, a fresh start.'

Steve frowned and stared at his beer. 'I… err… we'll miss you. Maybe, between now and then, we'll persuade you to stay?'

'Perhaps, but don't hold your breath.' She finished her drink. *'Let's have another to celebrate. A double gin and slimline tonic for me.'* Gina pushed her empty glass towards him. *'With ice and slice.'*

Twice more Gina asked for a top-up, both times with doubles. She downed the last drink, glanced at her watch and struggled to her feet.

'Gosh, it's hot in here, I feel quite faint,' she said as she swayed and clutched onto Steve's arm for support.

'Hang on. I'll give you a lift home, Gina.'

'I've got a lift. My mate Ade's has a brand-new BMW. He's picking me up at ten to show me how she goes.'

'A lot better than my antiquated Fiesta I imagine.'

'Be a dear and walk me out to the car park, would you?'

Steve escorted her out to Ade's car and helped her into the passenger seat. She waved to him as they roared away, wheels spinning and gravel flying.

The third week we concentrated on 'S' for strength, both mental and physical. A woman may not be looking for Mr Universe, but she wants a man who is strong for her. Strength laced with compassion and kindness to make her feel safe and secure.

Steve arrived at the hall to find Alex struggling to erect a heavy backcloth. He offered to help.

'Everything OK last week?' Steve asked

'Sure, why do you ask?'

'You disappeared. I hope Gina didn't make you feel awkward.'

Alex mumbled something about having an errand to attend to and Steve dropped the subject.

Gina displayed her very demanding side that day. She wanted Steve to move this prop here and there and then back again. He wrestled with one particularly heavy cupboard and revealed a terrified baby mouse cowering beneath.

Gina screamed. 'Kill it. Please. Keep it away from me.' She jumped onto a stool and pulled her long skirt up to her knees.

'Don't worry. He's more frightened of you than you are of him. He's only a baby.' Steve recovered an empty glass from the table, placed it over the mouse, and slipped his script papers underneath. The youngster stared out at them, whiskers twitching, entrapped within its glass prison.

'Take it away. Get rid of it,' Gina screeched.

'It's OK, I've got it safe. Has anyone got a shoe box, or something similar?'

Alex produced a box and held it carefully while Steve transferred the mouse and closed the lid firmly.

'I'll take it to the park and release it after we finish rehearsals,' he said.

'All this trouble over a stupid mouse,' Gina mumbled as she climbed from the stool and brushed down her skirt.

'B' was our fourth week's objective, blind devotion; because a woman needs to know that she is adored, no matter what. To know that her man will always be there to care for her, that she will never be alone, whatever state she's in. We know we may not be perfect, but we want him to think we are.

They were in the pub after rehearsals. Alex nudged Steve's elbow, and pointed to a brown and white dog who sat at his owner's feet, watching every move he made. 'Look at that Springer Spaniel, isn't he a beauty?'

Occasionally the dog would rub his nose under his owner's hand, wagging his tail whenever the man rewarded him with a pat on the head, or a stroke of his long silky ears.

'My aunt had one just like him,' Steve said. 'Called Flynn. They were inseparable. They went everywhere together. If dogs weren't allowed, she refused to go. Flynn died of a broken heart a week after my aunt.'

'Gosh,' Gina said. 'Your aunt must have been quite young?'

'She struggled with lung cancer for several years. She was a heavy smoker so I suppose we should have expected it. She didn't want to die in the hospital – she wanted to be with Flynn – so my uncle nursed her at home. Always there for her ministering to her every need, an absolute saint.'

'Crazy.' Gina said. 'That's why we have hospices.

'But surely, that would be everybody's dream,' suggested Steve. 'To die in peace, at home, looked after by the one you love.'

'Nightmare, more like. For the carer that is.'

'But Gina, wouldn't you want to do whatever you could to make the life of someone you love happy and comfortable?' Alex asked.

'Leave it to the professionals, I say. That's why we pay them.'

The following week it was the time of letter 'A' for assertive.

It could be controversial this one, sorry if it causes you any offence, Fyrne, but try and accept it as part of the story.'

Fyrne held up her hands in a gesture of surrender. 'Go for it, Barbara. Just don't expect me to agree.'

'Thank you.'

Most women want to feel in control, not only of their own life but also, of their partner's. At the same time, they want to feel safe and secure in the knowledge that when it comes to important issues, her man will obviously take her views into account, but is not afraid to take control and make the final decision.

They were all in the pub following rehearsals. The discussion had drifted to the wedding of a former member of the theatre group. Several of them had been at the wedding the previous Saturday.

'I can't believe she promised to obey,' Gina said.

'I think she's right,' Steve said.

Gina gasped. 'You male chau–'

'Now before you all get excited about this, let me explain. To obey is not the same as blindly following an order, or expecting someone to comply with your words of wisdom. It's about opening your ears heart and soul to listen, and then making a loving response. It's because people don't always recognise the true meaning that we have all this controversy over the marriage vows.'

'I can't believe you said that. You won't ever catch me promising to obey any man.' Gina turned on her heels and flounced off in the direction of the ladies.

'Oh dear, I appear to have put my foot in it again,' Steve sighed.

'Never mind, she'll get over it.' Alex picked up Steve's empty glass. 'My round. Same again?'

The following week was the letter 'N' for nice. A woman wants a man who is nice to her, nice to her parents, nice to everyone. Nothing wins over a woman's feelings as quickly as being told by everyone how lucky she is to be with such a nice young man. Steve's clearly what you would call a nice young man, but he wasn't one to talk about his good deeds normally. I persuaded him that he needed to make a few of them more apparent than his usual reticence would allow.

'Sorry I'm late for rehearsals, everyone,' Steve said. 'Hope you

got the message. I had to take my neighbour to the hospital for his appointment, and then on the way back he wanted to call in at the supermarket for some groceries. I've brought you some doughnuts by way of an apology.'

'Well, now your here, at last, we'd better run through that last scene again,' Gina said.

Steve handed the bag of doughnuts over to Alex.

'Maybe these will sweeten her up,' Alex whispered.

'I can but hope,' Steve whispered back before heading for the stage.

Later, at the pub Steve sat chatting to Gina, Derek and Alex. Derek had just become a father for the first time. He and his wife could only afford one car and his wife needed it to ferry the baby back and forth to the childminders. Derek faced a bike ride of over five miles each way.

'I could give you a lift,' offered Steve.

'But it's out of your way.'

'Not really. I could cut through on the back road. It would only add an extra mile or two to my journey.'

'How much would you charge?' Derek asked.

'Nothing. I go that way anyway, and I know you can't afford to pay me, not with the little one.'

'Are you sure?'

'Sure, I'm sure.'

'Thanks, Steve. That will be such a help. You're right… money is tight at the moment.'

Derek rushed off to tell his wife the good news.

Alex leaned over. 'Steve, has anyone told you? You're such a nice guy. Don't you think so, Gina?'

'Soft more like,' Gina sniffed. 'You'll simply get walked all over.

People will take advantage.'

'I like to help people if I can,' Steve said.

'You'll learn.' Gina picked up her coat and handbag. 'Bye, guys. Got to go. Hot date.'

The final week was 'D' for being good Daddy material.

Steve had been invited to the local primary school to talk to the young pupils.

'They want me to go on Friday afternoon and tell them the story of King Arthur and the Knights of the Round Table, and what it's like to be an actor playing the part of Lancelot. It will be great fun. Who wants to join me? Gina, how about coming along? You don't work on Fridays, do you? You could dress up as Lady Guinevere?'

'Are you crazy? I've got far more important things to do with my Friday afternoon. My nails, hair and waxing appointments for a start.'

Steve watched her walk away.

'Don't worry, Steve,' Alex said. 'She's very snappy at the moment. I think she hoped to hear about the pantomime by now. You know she had her eyes set on an upgrade to a more important role?'

'I know, I just hoped...'

'I'll come if you like. I know it won't be the same and I'd look a right plonker dressed as Guinevere, but I can always hand out leaflets for the show. We still have a few seats to sell. I think it's great. The support you're giving these youngsters is inspirational.'

Steve's visit was a resounding success, as Alex made a point of telling Gina at the next rehearsal.

'He's a natural with children. He'll make a fantastic Dad. They loved him,' Alex said.

'Yuk, kids,' Gina said.

Everyone turned to look at her.

'Why are you all looking at me like that? Kids ruin your life. I've seen it with my sister's two boys. They're dreadful little monsters.'

'But Gina,' gasped Alex. 'Surely you'd want children of your own one day?'

'You must be joking. Why would I want to wreck my figure and ambitions by having children?'

'I could name several actors that seem to be doing OK, despite the fact they have children,' Alex said.

'Not this one. Motherhood is not on my agenda. Anyway, I have to go now; I've got an audition tomorrow for a part in a pantomime.'

'But I thought you already had a part, the production in Nottingham?' Steve asked.

'I have, but this is a better part,' Gina said. 'In fact, I may as well tell you all now. After our last show next week, I'll be leaving this dump of a town. I'm moving to follow my dreams, wherever they take me. Hollywood here I come.' She picked up her coat. 'Bye.'

'Better part, my foot,' Alex said. 'I heard she has the part of the Ugly Sister in a small production somewhere in Doncaster.'

'Good for her, I suppose, if it's what she wants.'

'Cheer up, Steve.' Alex patted his shoulder. 'What are your plans for the rest of the evening?'

'I've won a meal for two with champagne at the Red Lion in their monthly draw. Don't suppose you fancy keeping me company?'

'Gina's loss is my gain. Lead on.'

Steve rang me the next morning.

'How did it go last night?' I asked.

'Brilliant. The dinner, in fact the whole evening, was ace.

Your plan worked just as you predicted. Alex thought I was besotted with Gina. She had absolutely no idea it was *her* I was crazy about.

Six months later he sent me an invitation to the wedding.

Bailey stood to lead the applause. 'Thank you, Barbara. Now we know who to come to with our affairs of the heart.' Thank goodness, a simple, happy tale with hardly any contentious issues. She waited until everyone finished clapping and then announced, with relief: 'And now, Ladies and Gentlemen, dinner is served.'

12. Day Six – Tour of Alice Spring

The ghostly, silver-grey gum tree provided little shelter from the scorching sun. March sipped from her water bottle and glanced across the courtyard towards the dry hollow of the legendary Alice Spring. Her husband leaned against the perimeter fence, deep in conversation with Frank. Typical! At this rate there'd be no time left to visit the Telegraph Station.

James's voice boomed across the courtyard. 'It's appalling. They can't even serve a decent bottle of wine. I paid the earth for that bottle of Australian Syrah last night and it tasted like cat piss. I told them to take it back and replace it with something more expensive. At no extra cost, of course.'

Her heart sank. This holiday was supposed to bring them back together – an impossible dream. It wasn't just James's behaviour, or his arrogance and disregard for the opinion of others; it was *her* feelings for him that had changed. She no longer felt a surge of happiness when he walked into the room. More a sense of dread.

Hard to believe it was only a year ago.

'What do you mean, you're not staying for dinner?' she'd said. 'I've cooked your favourite – lamb shanks.' Her heart had pounded, her voice trembled. She'd struggled to hold back the tears. 'I've spent hours preparing this meal.'

'I didn't ask you to cook. I told you I'd be late.'

'That's why it's lamb. The cooking time is flexible.'

He flumped into the kitchen chair facing her, leaned his

elbows on the antique oak table and rubbed his fingers through his hair.

'Can't you delay your meeting, so we can eat first?' she begged.

'I'm not seeing a client. I came home to pack a suitcase.'

'Unbelievable.' She leaned back in her chair and folded her arms. 'You must have known about this trip earlier.'

'I'm sorry.'

'Sorry? Sorry isn't good enough, James.' She swallowed and breathed deeply.

'Oh, for heaven's sake, March. Put the lamb in the bloody freezer.'

'It isn't just the meal, it's your thoughtlessness. Why couldn't you have warned me?'

'Because I didn't know until today.' His face drained of colour. 'March, I need you to understand–'

'Oh, my God, James. I'm so sorry. Is it your mother? Is she ill?'

James's mother lived three hundred miles away. Although James only visited her two or three times a year, he spoke to her by telephone every week. Her sudden illness – or worse – was the only possible explanation for the pained expression on his face.

She leaned towards James and covered his hands with hers. 'I'll come with you.'

James pushed her hands away. 'It's not my mother... it's Tina.'

'That young leggy blonde from your office? What's she got to do with it?'

'I've fallen in love with her... that is, *we've* fallen in love. We're moving in together.'

She pulled back. 'You've got to be joking.'

He didn't look like he was. He looked totally stunned. His hands were clenched and she noticed for the first time that they were splattered with brown age spots.

'I know it's a cliché, but for goodness sake, you're old enough to be her father.'

James flinched. 'She adores me.'

'Does she? Does she really? How long will it take before she gets tired of all your annoying little habits? We've been married for twenty-seven years. We have a wonderful son, two adorable granddaughters. What do we tell everyone? That you're having some sort of midlife crisis and things will be back to normal any time soon?'

He slammed his fists on the table.

'We love each other.' He leapt to his feet, sending his chair clattering across the kitchen. 'I'm going to pack. If you need to talk to me, ring me on my mobile. Don't ring the office. I don't want any scenes.'

He didn't want any scenes? What about what *she* wanted?

March couldn't move. Her legs had turned to jelly. Tears streamed down her cheeks and dripped onto the table. She listened as he crashed around upstairs, stomped down the stairs and slammed the front door behind him.

Was this it? The end of everything they'd built together?

She'd sat at home for two weeks, avoided everyone, refused to answer phone calls, and lived off food from the freezer. Not that she felt much like eating – and lamb was definitely off the menu. She couldn't even bring herself to tell their son, who lived in London, oblivious to her suffering.

Ian and Angie, their best friends, arrived on her doorstep,

full of concern about the countless unreturned answer-phone messages. Ian agreed to take James out for a drink and brokered a meeting. A tearful occasion, at which James agreed to: 'give her another chance.'

She still wasn't quite sure how his infidelity turned out to be her fault, or how she always found herself apologising. Perhaps, as he said, she was boring, didn't take enough care of her appearance, never had anything interesting to say, but she didn't need reminding of her failings every day. She had loved him until then but, these days she found his theatrical flamboyance distasteful and his sarcasm and criticism of everything she did or said unbearable. Her love had withered and died – like the grass beneath her feet.

She jumped as a flock of pink and grey cockatoos rose from the ground before her. They were beautiful, with grey backs, white crests and the most delicate dusty pink breasts. They fluttered, flapped, and screeched as they flew into the gum tree and perched above her head.

'Penny for your thoughts?'

'Sorry, Fyrne, I didn't see you there. I'm enraptured by these birds.'

'Beautiful, aren't they? I asked Bailey about them. She said they were known as Galha birds, until the name became associated with someone stupid, or doing something stupid. Now they simply refer to them as pink and greys.'

'Shame. I like the word, galha.' March glanced over her shoulder. James was still deep in conversation. 'I suppose we're all a bit galha at times.'

Fyrne smiled. 'I'm about to visit the Telegraph Station. Come and keep me company.'

They walked into the cool building and stood before a display of photographs.

'I can't believe this.' March could hear the tremble in her own voice as she struggled to comprehend the horror of what she read. 'Why would they confiscate Aboriginal children to raise them here?'

'I can't imagine how that must feel, but the sense of loss must have been dreadful for these poor women.'

'James and I were lucky enough to have our son, John. You know how rough and tumble young boys can be? Always covered in bruises. I lived in terror that we'd be reported by some do-gooder at the school and that he'd be snatched away by social workers. Silly, isn't it?'

'Not really. I expect every parent feels the same.'

They continued to read the harrowing stories of children snatched from the loving arms of their mothers. Engrossed, they failed to notice Bailey approach.

'Shocking. isn't it?'

'Oh, hi there, Bailey,' March said. 'I wasn't expecting this. I thought it used to be a telegraph station.'

'Originally, but then it became a home for what they called half castes – illegitimate children born to Aboriginal mothers and white fathers.

'But why?' Fyrne asked.

'They didn't trust the Aboriginal women to care for their children in what they described as being "an acceptable way".'

'I suppose it's more *acceptable* to seize babies from their mothers and condemn them to a life in care?' Fyrne scoffed.

'It's no defence, I know, but they believed it would save them from becoming savages – as they were thought of at that time.

At one stage there were almost a hundred children living here. Now, I'm sorry to drag you away, ladies, but I need to get you back to the bus.'

The risk assessment Jim had demanded half an hour earlier, had threatened to be an impossible task in the timeframe he'd allowed – another pathetic attempt to ramp-up the pressure. He obviously hadn't taken account of her ability to cut, paste and tailor a document that provided everything he'd stipulated. Relieved, she pressed *send*, closed her laptop, grabbed her bag and rushed from her room.

She arrived slightly out of breath in the small lounge that the hotel had made available again for them tonight. She spotted Barbara bravely attempting to engage the Nunnes in conversation.

'Oh, my dears did you see that delightful little Aborigine boy in the School of the Air Maths lesson today? Wasn't he simply delicious?'

'Mm, it seems like an expensive set up for two hundred children,' Mr Nunne said.

'But the school covers hundreds of square miles.' Barbara frowned. 'How would the children experience a proper schooling without it?'

'Parents should think about their circumstances before they bring children into the world.'

Barbara, for a moment, resembled a goldfish.

Bailey cut in. 'Come now, Mr Nunne, how would our Northern Territories – mines, cattle ranches and parks – be managed without these young families?'

'It's irresponsible, in my opinion.'

'Well, I certainly enjoyed seeing what a marvellous job the

school does,' Barbara said, quickly recovering her composure. 'The grades they achieve are outstanding.'

'That's as maybe, but at what cost to the general public? Come, my dear, lets claim our seats.'

Bailey watched the Nunnes push their way through the other guests in their rush to grab the best seats.

'Ignore him, Bailey. He's such a grouch.'

'As long as you enjoyed it, Barbara.'

'Oh, my dear, I did indeed. And that flying doctor service. Isn't it incredible?'

'They do an amazing job, and cover huge distances.'

'I never realised how vast it was out here, until we flew over mile after endless mile of barren red soil. Hardly any roads and very few signs of life.'

'Exactly. Now, if you'll excuse me, I need to get the show on track.' She smiled, and hoped she appeared calm. She felt anything but. She'd gone out on a limb to have this excursion added to the itinerary and she needed it to be a triumph. 'Ladies and Gentlemen, could I have your attention, please? Our evening adventure, the Kangaroo Sanctuary Sunset Tour, will leave in about half an hour.'

She glanced around and smiled; relieved to see they had taken her advice. They were all dressed sensibly with long sleeves, trousers and flat shoes.

'Our visit is timed to coincide with the sun going down and when the kangaroo's start to wake. No need to change for dinner, it will be an informal private function in the Alice Suite, with a free glass of wine in lieu of our usual cocktail. Brigadier Friar has agreed to tell his story now, while you enjoy some iced water. Remember, it's important to keep up your fluids, even when the sun's going down.'

Brigadier Friar walked to the front of the group and stood beside the sofa occupied by Barbara and Angie.

'Barbara, may I compliment you on your story last night. I now know why I have failed to find a wife and what I must do to improve my chances in the future.'

'Why, Brigadier, I'm sure you would make an excellent husband. In fact, don't forget, I have a vacancy at the moment.' She patted the spare space on the sofa beside her.

The Brigadier's eyes widened. He smiled nervously. 'Dear lady, you're very kind.' He breathed deeply and regained his poise. 'My story is about a lecherous photographer. No offence intended, Sumner.'

'None taken. But, be assured, I *will* return the compliment.'

'Fred made a living from glamour photography, corrupting the lives of young women, encouraging them to believe they had a future in modelling. Grooming young girls into posing for more and more risqué shots, until eventually they were involved in photographic sessions that were only just shy of pornography.' The Brigadier smiled at Sumner. 'You know the sort of thing.'

'I'm sure I don't. I prefer wildlife.'

'Oh, I'm sure there's plenty of wild life involved. Fred made a good living from his sordid activities. Unfortunately for him, he was both greedy and careless:'

Brigadier Andrew Friar's Tale

Fred sat at the bar of his local pub – his back to the wall so that no one could sneak up on him. A tall man in a grey trench coat approached the bar.

'Evening Mr White, have you got my cash?'

'Have you got my photo's?'

'Money first, you know the rules.'

Mr White (although after eight months of research Fred knew that his customer was, in fact, Mr Drake, head of the local high school, and ripe for blackmail) slapped a small padded envelope onto the bar.

'Eighty quid, plus a new roll of film. It's all there. No need to count it.'

'Price goes up next month. A hundred from now on.'

'You've got to be joking?'

'The cost of developing has gone up. Then there's the considerable risk I take. If you don't like it, you can always go elsewhere.'

'And where would I go?'

'Exactly. So quit moaning. By the way, arrange to come in half an hour earlier next month. Time for our review.'

'What?'

'Just part of the service I offer to my older and more valuable customers.'

Fred picked up the padded envelope and put it in his shoulder bag – four hundred and eighty quid. Not bad for one night. He looked forward to his next meeting with Mr White. He always enjoyed their look of total shock when he revealed his research findings and made his first demand. The look of sheer terror in their eyes, the smell of fear, as they realised they were trapped. They all paid up. Except for the Judge.

Mr James, (real name Judge Jerry Winthrop) had been meeting him for almost six months. Every couple of weeks he would turn up on a Wednesday evening at seven o'clock and put his padded envelope on the bar, collect his envelope of photographs and disappear without a backward glance. Always in a rush to get back to his wife; Geraldine, who thought he'd nipped to the local off-license to collect his weekly indulgence; a bottle of Bushmills.

Fred had followed the Judge one evening, watched him leave the off-license and then entered the store. The shopkeeper was re-stocking a shelf.

'A run on Bushmills?' Fred asked.

'Judge Winthrop just had the last one. He comes every Wednesday, regular as clockwork. Always Bushmills.'

'It must be good if it comes recommended by a Judge. I'll take one.'

After that, Fred easily found out as much as he needed about his client, who had more reason than most to cover up his illicit hobby. Yes, Judge Winthrop would be keeping Fred in Bushmills for a long time to come.

Unfortunately for Fred, things didn't go as planned. Judge Winthrop had been found dead at his home the day after Fred had informed him of their future financial arrangement. He chose suicide over disgrace. The one that got away.

Fred had been furious, but he wasn't the sort of guy to be thwarted by such a setback. He had left the grieving widow alone to bury her dead husband, but planned to visit her on Friday to share his findings. No way would she want her dead husband's name dragged through the dirt; she'd pay up. Fred smiled as he anticipated the meeting.

'Excuse me, is this seat taken?'

Fred looked up from his musings. A young, smart, professional looking man stood beside him pointing at an empty bar stool.

'No, help yourself.'

'Great, thanks. Let me get you a drink?'

'Half a draft lager would be good, thanks.'

Fred noticed that all the other bar stools were occupied by a gaggle of young women. One wore a silver crown, a pink T-shirt emblazoned with I'm getting married on Saturday and a short white skirt that revealed white suspenders holding up white stockings. She had white balloons tied to her wrists and a pink silk sash encircled her slim waist.

Fred's benefactor handed him the lager and held his glass up to toast the group of women who giggled and held up their bright pink cocktails to toast him back.

'Thanks for the drink,' Fred said.

'My name's Bradley. A friend of mine recommended you.'

'A friend?'

'Sure, he goes by the name of Sexton. I planned to meet him earlier, to be introduced, but I got held up.'

'How do you know Sexton?'

'We share the same hobby. We sometimes swap photographs. He tells me you do a great job of developing film. I wondered if you could do some for me.'

'Fifty quid deposit today and fifty next Tuesday. Same time, same place.'

'Fifty?'

'Is that a problem?'

'Sexton said forty up front and forty on collection.'

'The price just went up. Take it or leave it.'

'No, no, fifty's fine. Here you go.' *Bradly handed him fifty pounds in crisp ten-pound notes and a roll of film.* *'I'll see you next Tuesday.'* *Bradly drained his glass and left.*

Fred stowed the cash and film in his shoulder bag. Tonight, got better and better. Now, where's that bride-to-be?

Fred had been enjoying a good week. Bradly would be an interesting client; the photographs were extremely explicit and the boys very young. He wondered what Bradly did for a living.

Fred paused outside the Judge's home. The front porch light shone brightly. She'd be expecting him. He'd phoned the day before and told the widow Winthrop that he had something belonging to her husband that he wanted to return. He'd refused to give any details on the phone, simply assuring her that she'd definitely want to take procession of the items.

He rang the doorbell. The door opened immediately; she must have been waiting anxiously in the hall. A good sign.

'Mrs Winthrop?'

'Fred, I presume?'

She sneered as she said his name, and looked at him disdainfully. He didn't care. She would soon change her tune. He looked forward to the shock, the tears, the pleading and the payment.

'May I come in?'

'If you must.'

She opened the door just wide enough for him to enter, closing it behind him. Then she walked down the hall and into the lounge, where she perched on the sofa leaving him standing.

'Your husband left these pictures with me to be developed. As you can see, he is present on several of them, so I think you'll agree

there's no denying they're his.'

She looked at the photos, holding them at arm's length by one corner. Then she took them in both hands, ripped them in half and threw them on the floor.

'And what do you expect me to do, Fred?'

'I have the negatives, and I want payment for their safe return. I reckon they are worth about twenty thousand pounds. If you're not prepared to pay that I'm sure one of the newspapers will be only too happy to recompense me.'

She laughed, high pitched, almost hysterical. 'Do you think I don't know about my husband's sordid life? He left me a suicide note confessing everything. What he had done and how you were using these dreadful pictures to blackmail him. I've been married to a monster for all these years and I never knew. Now I'm left alone to face his shame. Get out.'

'I don't think you understand—'

'Oh, I understand all right. You facilitated and encouraged my husband's disgusting behaviour and now you expect me to give you money.'

She stood up and walked towards the door. 'I think we're finished here, Fred or whatever your name is. Out.'

'Unless you agree to pay, copies of those photos will go to the press.'

'You can't collect money without revealing your involvement, and I'm sure the police will be happy to find out about that. You can't hurt me anymore than you already have. Thank God the judge and I never had children.'

'But—'

'I'll revert to my maiden name and move away, so what do I care? You can go to the devil. You'll get nothing from me.'

'But—'

'Get out!' she screamed, pointing at the front door.

Fred stormed out of her house. He slammed the door behind him and swore under his breath. He'd get even with her. Even if he had to sacrifice any reward from the papers to preserve his identity, copies of those pictures would be in the Sunday papers next week.

Geraldine retraced her steps and walked towards the kitchen door.

'You can come out now Inspector Bradly. Did you get everything you needed?'

'Everything, thanks to you. Come and sit down, let me pour you a drink. This must have been very upsetting.'

He moved over to the silver salver on the drinks cabinet and poured her a large gin and a splash of soda water.

'Ice?'

'No... thanks. Will this be enough to convict him?'

'It will. We already had him on tape accepting money from me to develop pornographic photographs. Now, thanks to your tip off, we have him on film for attempted blackmail. You're one very brave lady, Mrs Winthrop.'

'Geraldine, please. I'm determined he'll pay. Jerry was a very wicked and evil man, I know that now, but I wasn't going to let this Fred get away with his part in all of this. That's why I contacted the police when I got his call.'

'And thank goodness you did,' Brady assured her. 'As I said, you were very brave. I've been working undercover on this case for months. With your help, we now have enough evidence for a search warrant.'

The police raided Fred's house, obtained all the information they needed to commit him to trial and as a result of the information in his files they were also able to arrest several active paedophiles in the local area. The town will be a whole lot safer for its youngsters from now on, thanks to Mrs Winthrop.

Pryor burst into tears. 'I'm so sorry... it's just... oh, Nigel.'

Nigel placed his arm around his wife's shoulder and pulled her close. He searched in his pocket and handed her his hankerchief. 'Come, come, my dear. Don't go distressing yourself. I know it's difficult, but it's only a story.'

Bailey looked on, horrified. Not again! How could the oh-so-charming Brigadier cause this upset? What would the secret shopper make of this?

Barbara rushed over to Pryor and patted her free shoulder. 'Paedophilia, such a dreadful subject. It touches the lives of so many people, creeping over them like an insideous cloud, tainting their very souls.' Barbara glared at the Brigadier.

'I know what you mean,' Paul said. 'It casts a shadow on the victim's lives. It never leaves them. Even when the abuse is over, the nightmares continue. I have several clients–'

'I don't think we should talk of such things, Cynthia said. 'We have to remember patient confidentiality.'

'I wouldn't name–'

Cynthia held up her hand, like a traffic cop on duty. 'I'm sorry, Paul, I didn't mean to be rude, but it's too upsetting,'

'But if no one speaks up, it will never be stopped,' Miller said. 'Look at how many people knew about Jimmy Savile – nothing happened.'

'Dear ladies, I'm so sorry if my story has caused offence. I merely... oh dear. Sumner, this is all your fault.'

'Not me. You were so intent on having a go at me and my profession, you landed yourself in this one.'

The Brigadier sank into an armchair and put his head in his hands. He looked genuinely mortified.

Bailey wanted to throw her arms around him and give him a hug. 'Ladies and Gentlemen, I'm sure the Brigadier had no intention of causing any upset. Now, moving on, as they say, to something I know you're all going to enjoy. If you would like to make your way outside, our bus is ready to take us to the kangaroo sanctuary.'

Bailey counted her guests as they scrambled onto the coach. She blamed herself; she'd been so proud of her story idea but, so far, it had caused more tears than laughter. Should she abandon it? Dare she risk any more upsets? She needed to think this through. Yet another sleepless night.

13. Kangaroo Sanctuary

Chris 'Brolga' Barnes strode towards them dressed in khaki shirt and shorts, with black leather walking boots. He was exactly as Bailey remembered him: extremely tall; at least six foot seven; very tanned; good looking, with a warm smile that could melt anyone's heart – with the possible exception of the Nunnes. A baby kangaroo followed in his shadow.

'G'day everyone. Welcome to the Kangaroo Sanctuary. Please come inside and help yourselves to some cold bottled water.'

The simply constructed building had dark terracotta walls, concrete floor, corrugated roof, and large Perspex windows. Chris reached over and plucked a padded cotton bag from a peg on the wall. The Joey watched his every move. Holding the pouch low, Chris waited patiently while the young animal somersaulted, head first, into it. Moments later, the baby kangaroo poked his head up and looked around.

Chris told them how the sanctuary began. He'd discovered a female kangaroo killed by a vehicle after she'd strayed onto an unfenced road. Her young Joey, safely cocooned in his mother's pouch, had survived the impact. As his reputation grew, so did his orphanage. He began with two acres but then rented a further ninety of adjoining land from the Government and expanded his reserve to accommodate his growing passion.

Bailey had first heard about Chris when she'd been in Alice Springs the previous summer. She knew instantly that a tour of the sanctuary would be an ideal addition to the itinerary, and negotiated terms. She also knew that the stumbling block would be Jim. He would have dismissed her suggestion; because it was her idea, not his. Instead she submitted her proposal straight to Smithy, the MD, who enthusiastically agreed. Jim erupted with fury, and her already fraught relationship with him reached a new low. She didn't care. Her instincts told her this trip would be one of the highlights of the tour.

'OK, Ladies and Gentlemen, we are going to move outside and watch some of the younger 'roos come for their supper.' Chris smiled at Maddy. 'Would you be able to carry this one for me, while I lead the tour?'

'Really?' Maddy gasped. 'I'd love to.'

Chris gently handed the pouch to her.

She gazed down at the youngster. 'He's so cute.' The kangaroo turned his head and licked her wrist making her laugh. 'It tickles, his tongue is prickly.'

'Turn this way, Maddy,' Sumner said. 'I must get a photo.'

'Follow me, Ladies and Gentlemen, and stay close. It gets dark very quickly now, and although you will come to no harm from the kangaroos, you could do yourself some damage if you fall down a pot-hole, or trip over a termite's nest.'

Chris picked up two buckets of food, led them into a fenced sandy paddock area, and began to rattle them. Within moments a group of small kangaroos arrived.

'As you can see, these young 'roos are older than the baby carried by Maddy. Some are rescued orphans raised on the sanctuary, others were born here.'

He threw a few handfuls of food over the fence. The youngsters pounced on the pellets, which gave Chris the opportunity to open the gate, and usher the guests through.

'We'll go and visit Roger first. He's kept in an enclosure. Don't worry, it's a large one and he has female company, but he can be quite dangerous. Even though I bottle fed him as a baby, he'd still like to give me a good beating if he could. Kangaroos are quite capable of ripping your guts open if they feel inclined, so, as you can imagine, I handle him with all the respect he deserves.'

'Would you like to hang onto my arm?' Bailey asked Barbara.

'That's sweet of you, my dear, but I'll be fine.' She pointed to Maddy and Tony who strolled beside Chris, Maddy still cradled the youngster. 'Aren't they simply the most wonderful couple? I bet you they'll be swopping that kangaroo for a baby within the year.'

Bailey laughed. 'Barbara, you really are the most impossible romantic.'

Chris entered the enclosure and slowly approached Roger. He reared up on his back legs, balanced with his tail and positioned his arms into a classic boxing pose. They were almost the same height, but Bailey could imagine Chris would come off worse in the event of a match. Chris spoke softly to Roger, taking care to maintain a safe distance between them.

Bailey breathed a sigh of relief as Chris left the enclosure. He obviously knew how to handle Roger, but she didn't want any incidents to spoil the magic.

By now it was dark. Stars were scattered across the night sky. A few bats swept past, and an owl hooted.

'What sort of owl is that?' Cher asked.

'It's a male Boobook owl. We were fortunate to have a nesting pair and a couple of chicks this year. They made their nest in that old gum tree.'

By the moonlight it was possible to see several kangaroos, sometimes alone, sometimes in small groups. Chris knew each one by name. He paused frequently, called them to him, and while he fed them handfuls of food from his bucket, he explained their individual history. He pointed to a tree. 'Does anyone know the name of this tree?'

'Is it an Acacia?' Celia asked.

'The Aborigines call it the Witchetty bush, but it is a type of Acacia known as Black Wattle. They call it Witchetty after the grubs that live in the roots. The grubs are a very important part of their diet, being rich in protein and fat. They either eat them raw, or roast them in their camp-fires.'

'Yuk, I can't imagine anything worse,' March said.

'They tell me that they taste like almonds, but I must admit I've never plucked up the courage to test the theory.'

Bailey and her guests followed Chris in silence, soaking up the atmosphere.

'Barbara, oh my goodness, Barbara, darling. Are you all right?' Angie's voice pieced the stillness.

Last time Bailey had looked in their direction, Barbara and Angie had been walking side by side giggling like two schoolgirls as Barbara pointed to Chris and whispered something in Angie's ear. Now, just moments later, she lay sprawled on her back in the dusty track, her legs and arms waving franticly. She resembled a ladybird that had inadvertently landed upside down.

Bailey rushed to her side. 'Let me help you up.'

'Let me.' Chris pulled Barbara into a sitting position, placed his arm around her waist and lifted her to her feet. 'Are you OK? Can you stand?'

'So sorry to cause such a fuss, my dears. I simply tripped over my own shadow. How silly of me. Please don't worry.'

The Brigadier suddenly materialised beside them. 'I've picked up your handbag, Barbara. You dropped it when you fell. I'll carry it back to the bus for you.'

'Thank you, my dear. How kind of you.'

'The path circuits the sanctuary, so we're not far from the shed now,' Chris explained. 'Will you be OK to walk, or shall I fetch the trailer?'

'I'll be fine. No harm done, apart from my pride. I'm simply a clumsy old woman.'

Chris and Bailey slowly supported Barbara along the path, until they arrived back at the shed, where they guided her to a chair.

Bailey knelt beside her. 'Does anywhere hurt?'

'My wrist is a bit sore,' she held up her left arm.

'It looks like a sprain. Your fingers are beginning to swell. I think you'd better take off your rings before it gets any worse.'

Barbara sucked her fingers and slowly twisted three diamond rings and one wedding band from her fingers. 'Could you put them in my handbag, Brigadier?'

'Of course.' The Brigadier took the rings, opened her bag and unzipped a small pocket. 'I'll put them in this section here,' he said, before he closed the bag and handed it back to her.

'Let's get you on the bus, Barbara.'

'Where's my baby?' Chris asked over the heads of the remaining guests who were making their way onto the bus.

'Here he is,' Maddy said. 'Thanks for a wonderful evening. Your sanctuary is, as Bailey would say, amazing.'

'Glad you enjoyed it.'

Bailey returned from the coach. 'So sorry, Chris. Let's hope our next tours are a bit less eventful.'

'Is she going to be OK?'

'I'll get the doctor to give her a check over when we get back, but I think it's just a slight sprain. She says she can't even blame the termites. She simply stumbled.'

Sumner paused at the lounge entrance, and listened to the pianist's rendition of *She* – very good, much better than your average.

Sumner glanced across and spotted Tony and Maddy on a secluded sofa, well away from eavesdroppers. Two's company, three's a crowd he mused, just as Tony looked up and beckoned him over. Sumner spoke to the piano player, took out his wallet, dropped a $10 note into his basket, and walked over to join them.

'I thought you two lovebirds might prefer to be alone?' he teased.

'You're as bad as Barbara,' Tony laughed. He shuffled closer to Maddy, allowing space for Sumner to sit.

Sumner sat beside them and leaned back on the cushions. Most of the tour guests bored him, but these two were not only good company, but obviously made for each other.

There was a round of applause for the pianist, who nodded towards Sumner and began playing the Van Morrison classic: *Have I told You Lately?*

'I *love* this song,' Maddy said.

Tony patted her hand. 'Any good photos of those kangaroos, Sumner? Mine have all come out a bit dark.'

'I believe I've got a contender for the front cover.'

'That baby kangaroo was awesome,' Maddy said. 'I wanted to take him home.'

'I got some great shots of you carrying him. Really cute.'

'He *was* very cute.'

'I meant you.' Sumner winked at Tony.

Tony bent his head closer. 'Can I have a word?'

'Hey, Tony, only joking. No offence, Maddy, but you're a bit older than I normally go for.'

Maddy laughed. 'Thank goodness for that.'

'No listen, it's not about Maddy, it's about the Brigadier. Did you notice how he reacted to that reference about a fraudulent fundraiser?'

'Well now you come to mention it, he did look a bit shocked,' Sumner slowly rubbed his chin. 'Should we take something from that do you think?'

'Maddy and I became suspicious about him a couple of nights ago. I chatted to him about his army service. He... well, we didn't want to read too much into it, but we both thought him rather evasive.'

'How so?'

'I asked if he'd seen much action. He said he had, in the Falklands. I mentioned my uncle, he was a major out there, and he suddenly remembered he needed to be at a meeting with Bailey. He dashed off and seems to have avoided me ever since.'

'We were wondering if you had any pictures of him?' Maddy asked.

'I think I've got a rather good one of him standing by the lighthouse at Cape Leeuwin.'

'Can you send it to me?' Tony asked. 'I've a friend who still works in the service. I could ask him to do a bit of sleuthing.'

Sumner hesitated. The word *ethics* sprang to mind. 'Why?'

'I've got this niggle in my head, and Maddy agrees. I can't help thinking his reaction may indicate his involvement in some sort of scam with *Help the Heroes*. I know that's a big leap to make, but it's a charity close to my heart. They've helped several friends of mine. This may sound a bit silly, but I'd like to do a bit more digging.'

'Happy to help. It'd be lovely to find something to burst his bubble. Pompous snob. He and James make a good pair. Give me your e-mail address. I'll send the photo after dinner. I'll also send you both a couple of Maddy and the baby 'roo. Oh look, I think they're ready for us. I'm starved after all that walking.'

14. Day Seven – Uluru

Rob Roy

- *40ml Scotch*
- *20ml Sweet Martini*
- *Two dashes of orange bitters*
- *Splash of sugar syrup according to taste*
  Shake with ice cubes before straining into a martini glass and serving with a twist of orange zest.

Another day, another town and another chance to impress the secret shopper. She still had no idea who. For the umpteenth time that day, Bailey checked her messages – nothing from Suzy.

'Ladies and Gentlemen, I hope you enjoyed our coach trip from Alice Springs to the Uluru Resort today. I'm so glad you managed to see one of our road trains. Aren't they amazing?'

James moaned, 'I wouldn't want to get stuck behind one of them.'

Bailey stifled the urge to point out that not everything needed to be viewed through that egocentric lens of his. Instead, she smiled graciously.

'Grab yourselves a cocktail everyone, and then, when you're settled, we'll listen to tonight's tale from our celebrity photographer, Sumner. Afterwards, our coach will transport us to our venue, where we'll enjoy a spectacular view of Uluru as the sun sets, and a romantic evening meal under the stars.'

She paused. 'OK, Sumner…' Bailey beamed encouragement at him, 'over to you.'

'Thank you, Bailey. And thank you, Brigadier, for last night's imaginative story about a corrupt photographer. My story, you won't be surprised to hear, is about an evil fundraiser who raised vast amounts of funds for a charity, but in fact kept most of the money for himself.'

Sumner grinned at the Brigadier, who glared back. She could almost sense the heightening of testosterone as they stared unblinking, like two prize boxers at a pre-match photo shoot.

She settled back nervously in her chair. She'd checked out Sumner's story with him earlier. She'd been reassured by his description of a fraud story with a happy ending.

'My story,' began Sumner, 'is a true one about good friends of mine – Thomas, and his wife, Tanya:'

Giles Sumner's Tale

Thomas and Tanya, a deeply devoted couple and, at the time my story begins, desperate for a child. They'd suffered from infertility for ten years. Finally, in their late thirties, they made the decision to try IVF.

The process was traumatic; countless counselling sessions, weeks of painful injections for Tanya and excruciating embarrassment as the eggs were harvested and fertilised.

They sat holding hands, waiting to be called back for the procedure to transfer any viable embryos. Would it be one? Could it even be two? Or – a miracle – more, with an option to freeze some?

The phone rang.

Not one viable embryo had survived.

And so, their first round of IVF, free on the NHS, resulted in failure. They then found themselves trapped in a post code lottery. A few miles further south and they would have been entitled to a second free treatment. Twenty miles north and they would have received two more chances.

But not in their town.

They dug deep into their limited savings to fund the next round. Imagine their joy when this time they discovered they were expecting a baby.

A happy ending, you might think. But, unfortunately, their son was born with leukaemia and spent six months in and out of a hospice. Thomas and Tanya were able to stay with him whenever he was admitted, and being able to spend every minute with him gave them some comfort. Even so, their lives were devastated by his death and Tanya fell apart.

Bailey thought she might well follow Tanya's example. She glanced nervously at her guests. No tears. Yet.

About three months after they had buried their son, a man called Adam approached Thomas and–

Bailey watched with horror as the Brigadier sprang to his feet. 'What are you playing at, Sumner?'

'Playing, Brigadier? I can assure you I'm not playing at anything.'

'You deliberately used my name.'

'I'm so sorry Brigadier, pure coincidence I assure you. I'll change it to Andrew if it makes you feel better?'

'Gentlemen, I beg you. Calm down.' Bailey rose to her own feet. 'Brigadier, could I ask you to sit down? I'm sure Sumner didn't intend to cause offence.'

The Brigadier threw himself back into his chair. Good grief! Could they not have just one story that didn't traumatise the other guests?

'Sumner, please, do continue with your tale.'

'Now, where was I?' Sumner rubbed his chin. 'Oh, yes, we'd just met Andrew, as we are now calling him.'

The man, Andrew James, made an appointment to meet with Thomas at Thomas's office.

'Please forgive me for contacting you in this way at what must be a very difficult time, but I believe your story could be what the hospice needs to help raise funds for a much needed expansion.'

He showed Thomas an authorisation letter from the charity and explained that he managed a project to raise £120,000 for an extension. Andrew showed him the plans, which would provide three new family rooms. Thomas agreed to discuss things with his wife and let Andrew know their decision.

Thomas used his key to let himself into the cold building he'd once thought of as home.

'Tanya, darling, I'm home.'

'I'm in the kitchen.'

He found her, sat at the kitchen table, her hands clasped around a beaker of cold coffee. He often returned home to find her like this. Still in her pyjamas, her hair un-brushed and with no obvious signs of any activity since he'd left home that morning. His job in accountancy was very demanding and guaranteed to keep his mind occupied for at least twelve hours a day. But Tanya didn't go out to work, not since she'd given up her job as a receptionist to become a full-time mum. She had too much time on her hands, and too much to brood about.

He switched on the kettle, sat beside her and reached for her hand.

She snatched it back, pushed both arms under the table and into her lap.

'Don't touch me,' she whispered.

'I'm sorry, darling. I know you're raw with grief, but I'm so worried about you.' He picked up her coffee mug, emptied the dregs down the sink and then made them both a fresh drink.

'I met a really nice guy today. He does voluntary work for the hospice. He wondered if we'd be interested in doing some fund-raising with him.'

Thomas sat beside Tanya and pushed the coffee in front of her. 'Here you go, just as you like it.'

Tanya met his gaze. *'I'm sorry.'* Her eyes filled with tears. *'I don't deserve you.'*

'Nonsense, you've been through a lot. We both have. It's just that I find it easier to cope. I lose myself in work. Perhaps some fundraising would help take your mind off things?'

'I'll never forget our beautiful boy.'

'Neither of us ever will. But maybe helping the hospice might ease the pain a little? Why don't we invite Andrew around one evening? See what he has to say?'

Thomas watched his wife as she poured over the plans. It was the first time he'd seen her take an interest in anything for months.

'But what would I have to do? I've no experience of marketing.'

'I'd take care of all that,' Andrew said. *'I'd write up your story, advertise any fundraising events you undertake, supply photographs for the local paper. It will be an opportunity for you to throw your energies into a good cause.'*

They arranged to meet a week later to go through the details.

Tanya and Thomas stood on the doorstep to see Andrew off. Thomas allowed his arm to slip around Tanya's waist. For the first time in months, she didn't push him away.

'I'm sorry.'

'Tanya, darling, I promised to be here by your side, for better or for worse. This has been the worst of times, but there will be better ones.'

She kissed his cheek.

Thomas and Tanya spent the next few months running garden fetes, car boot sales, auctions, music festivals and raffles. Their nursery was full of the prizes they collected from local businesses and other *donors. They spent their evenings packaging the various gifts into baskets, then touring the pubs and clubs selling raffle tickets to anyone sympathetic to their cause.*

They were exhausted, but happy that their hard work would help the hospice.

Six months after they first met Andrew, Thomas looked up from his paperwork as a smiling Tanya walked into his home office. This was the first time he had seen her look happy since the day their son had been diagnosed.

'I've added up all the receipts from Andrew,' she said, 'and we've raised £119,500. We're only £500 short of the target.'

'No, we're not. I forgot to tell you, they had a whip round at the gym last night and raised £400.'

Tanya whooped. 'Let's round it up to the £500? Then we can go out for that meal we promised ourselves. A bottle of champagne and a taxi home. I think we've earned it.'

Four weeks later, Tanya walked into Thomas's den, her eyes sparkling. 'I have some news for you.'

'And I have some for you,' Thomas said staring at the letter before him. 'But you go first.'

'Well you're not going to believe this, but... well, I don't know how, but I'm pregnant.'

'What?'

'We're expecting.'

Thomas stood and threw his arms around Tanya.'

'Are you sure?'

'I've just done a test. It's positive.'

She wiped her eyes and smiled up at him. 'So, what's your news?'

'Oh nothing, just a mistake, I think. We've had a letter from the

hospice, thanking us for the £30,000 contribution to the extension when it should say £120,000. I'll check it out tomorrow. It can wait for now. Let's get you sat down with a cup of tea while I ring for an appointment with the doctor.'

A few days later Thomas decided to contact the hospice to check if they'd made a mistake with the letter. The charity manager thanked Thomas for their donation of £30,000. He asked if they would attend the opening ceremony, but warned it would be some time yet. Apparently, they were still somewhat shy of the total needed. Thomas called Andrew and asked him to visit them that evening.

'Hi Thomas, hello, Tanya, sweetheart, you're looking well.'

'Come in, Andrew. Thanks for calling by. We wanted to discuss the fund-raising with you.'

'Missing it are you? We could always do some more if you are up to it, they always need as much as they can get.'

'So how come they have only received £30,000 when we raised £120,000?' Thomas demanded waving a copy of his letter in front of Andrew.

'£30,000 each. Didn't I explain it properly? I work as an agent for four hospices, in four different towns. Any funds I receive, including your £120,000, gets divided across the four.' He reached into his briefcase and took out three letters. 'Here, this gives you the full story.'

Thomas took the letters and read them:

Dear Mr James,

I am writing to thank you and your team for the very generous contribution of £30,000.

Thomas checked the next one:

Dear Andrew,

Thank you so much for yet another generous contribution of £30,000.

And the last:
Dear Andy,
Once more I write to say thank you, this time for the generous contribution of £30,000.

'I knew it must be a mistake,' Tanya said. 'We didn't realise you were collecting for a group of hospices.'

'Yes, I'm sorry if we sounded suspicious. We just assumed it all went to the hospice we knew.'

'Well, it amounts to the same thing in the end, every time I reach a reasonable amount, I send it in so they can all carry on with their building programmes. The next cheque may come from one of the others, but your hospice will get 25% of that cheque in the same way that they have received 25% of yours. It's simply a way of keeping funds rolling in on a regular basis.'

'Yes, I can see that,' Thomas said. 'Could we possibly keep a copy of the three letters?'

'Of course,' Andrew handed them over. Thomas quickly made copies and handed them back.

'Let me know whenever you feel like more fundraising,' Andrew said as he waved them goodbye and walked towards his new BMW saloon.

'There,' Tanya picked up her knitting. 'I knew it would be OK.'

Thomas looked at the name cc'd at the bottom of one of the letters provided by Andrew. Mr and Mrs Longhurst – not an especially common name, maybe worth an internet search. He typed in the name, town, and added death of a child. A newspaper report came up with a story about the couple. They were raising funds for the local hospice, following the death of their eight-month-old daughter, who'd died from leukaemia.

Thomas pondered his dilemma for several days before plucking up the courage to telephone the Longhursts. He waited until Tanya went to visit her mother. He didn't want her upset, not in her condition.

'Hello, is that Mr Longhurst?'

'Speaking.'

'Mr Longhurst, you don't know me, but my name is Thomas, and I believe we have something in common.'

The two men quickly realised that they did indeed have quite a lot in common, particularly with regards to monies raised. Mr Longhurst had been told exactly the same as Thomas, when he'd queried the amount collected. It was clear to them both, that Andrew was taking large quantities of the funds raised for himself. They both agreed to hand everything they had over to the police. The fraud squad were able to prove that Thomas's suspicions were correct.

Bailey watched the Brigadier in fascination as his face flushed red before deepening to purple blotches. Goodness, he's bursting a blood vessel, having a heart attack, or about to start a fight.

The Brigadier stood and took a step closer to Sumner. 'Absolute tosh. You obviously know nothing about the stringency of systems within charities.'

'I assure you, Brigadier, it's a true story.'

The Brigadier placed his empty glass down on the nearest table. 'Excuse me everyone, I'm not feeling well – a sudden headache.' He turned on his heels and walked out of the room.

Bailey's stomach churned. Whatever would the secret shopper make of this? Come to that, what did any of them think? What on earth had just happened?

'Oh dear, I'm sorry to have caused an upset,' Sumner said. 'Do you suppose he'll be all right?'

Bailey bit her lip. 'I'll go and check on him in a minute. You promised me a happy ending, Sumner. Remember?'

'Ah yes, a happy ending indeed. They arrested Andrew for fraud. Some of the funds were recovered, although unfortunately nowhere near all of it. Thomas and Tanya had a beautiful daughter, followed by a son the following year. To my knowledge, they have never undertaken fund-raising again. I suppose their hands are full with family business these days.'

Everyone clapped, Miller whistled.

'The bus will be here to collect us very shortly, so if you could finish your drinks and make your way to the front entrance?' Bailey picked up her shoulder bag. 'Please excuse me while I go and check on the Brigadier.'

Sumner settled on the sofa beside Tony and picked up his drink. 'That didn't go too bad then.'

'Touched a raw nerve all right,' Tony said.

'It seems so. Did the photograph help?'

'I sent it, but Uncle didn't recognise him. He did remember a Sergeant Adam Friar, discharged in 1994 for fraud.'

'Do you think that's him?'

'Not sure, but that's why I asked you to use the name Adam

for your fraudster. It certainly got a reaction.'

'Where do we go from here?' Sumner asked.

'I've another friend – Steve – who works for *Help the Heroes*. I've asked him to check the Brigadier out, see how much fund-raising he's actually doing.'

'Nice one. Let's keep our fingers crossed. I'd love for you to get something on him. Bring him down a peg.'

Tony stood up and helped Maddy to her feet. 'Come on, let's go and find that bus.'

'Oh, good, are they here? Hope it's not far, I'm starving,' Sumner said.

'You're always starving,' Maddy laughed as she linked her arm through Tony's.

15. Uluru Under the Stars

Jujh sipped from his water bottle and gazed over the flat, red scrubland. He loved this evening temperature; it reminded him of summer evenings back in India. However, the clarity of the air was nothing like home, where scenic views were often semi-obscured by yellow fuggy fog. A slight breeze stirred the leaves of the nearby Eucalyptus tree that clung to life despite the harsh conditions. He breathed in the distinctive smell, hard to describe, somewhere between mint and pine with just a hint of honey.

He could hear James talking loudly as usual, making derogatory comments about the *inferior* quality of the Australian sparkling wine.

The didgeridoo player began playing a new tune, or at least Jujh supposed it was new. To be honest, they all sounded much the same. He could hear, and feel, the resonance of the instrument as it droned away in the background. Occasionally the monotonous soporific sound was interspersed with a wail or squeal, like the cry of a wounded animal.

This setting had obviously been selected to provide a stunning vantage point. Five kilometres to the left, Uluru, or Ayers Rock as he knew it, shimmered in the dying rays of the sunlight. The flat top and steep sides of the escarpment were a familiar sight. He'd never visited before, but he had seen the image on countless photos and postcards. In contrast, Kata Tjuta, a few kilometres to his right, was completely unknown to him until this evening. It had a decidedly more interesting shape, with all its lumps, bumps, and protrusions silhouetted against the evening sky. According to Bailey, the Aboriginal community also thought Kata Tjuta a more spiritual place than Uluru.

'Hello.'

He looked down to where the tiny voice had come from. Two big brown eyes looked up at him. A small Aboriginal girl with a mop of curly black hair grinned at him, revealing the whitest teeth he had ever seen.

'Hello,' Jujh smiled at her. 'What are you doing here?'

The young girl grinned again.

'Where's your mummy?' Jujh asked.

'She died.'

'Your father?'

The small girl shook her head. She reached up and grasped his hand.

Jujh's heart wrenched. She must be about the same age as his daughter. A wave of guilt engulfed him. His beloved wife had died giving birth to Chaunta. It had been impossible for him to care for the tiny baby who constantly reminded him of his loss. He wondered if she was happy living with her Grandmother, or if she felt totally abandoned.

His thoughts returned to the present and the young girl hanging onto his hand as though her life depended on it. So vulnerable. He looked around for Bailey and spotted her on the far side of the sandy dune, talking to Miller.

'Bailey!' he called over to her.

She looked across, frowned and rushed towards him. Miller followed closely behind.

'Dorothy,' Bailey said. 'I've told you before… it's not safe here.'

'I came with Uncle Nardoo.' Dorothy pointed to where the didgeridoo player sat serenading the group.

'But he's busy. I've told you and your uncle. You shouldn't be here.'

'She's not causing any harm.' Jujh patted Dorothy's hand. 'I always find children instinctively know who they can trust.'

'But what if she's attacked by a Dingo, or goes missing while her uncle's distracted?'

'I'm happy to keep my eye on her until he finishes.'

'That's kind of you, but I need to get you all into dinner while it's light. The path is uneven and I don't want any more accidents.'

'I'll catch up later, don't worry. We'll be fine, won't we Dorothy?'

The child nodded enthusiastically.

'But I couldn't impose.' Bailey looked flustered. 'Besides, I'd be putting you in a difficult position, leaving you on your own with a young child.'

'I'm not a paedophile, Bailey, I assure you.'

'Oh, I know, I wasn't suggesting that you were.'

'No one would even think of such a thing in India. Child over-protection seems to be an invention of the Western World.'

'A bit like the Western World's rules on health and safety,' Miller laughed. 'I know whose rules I prefer. I've seen your scaffolding and electricity cables. Nightmare.'

'I'm not being over protective,' Bailey said. 'It's not that, it's just… well… you know how it is. We have to consider every eventuality, and risk-assess everything.'

'Don't worry, Bailey, I'll stay with them,' Miller volunteered. 'You'll be OK with us Dorothy, won't you?' Miller knelt down to be level with the child, who clapped her hands and nodded.

'Well, if you're both sure?'

Dorothy jumped up and down and grinned.

'OK, but as soon as Dorothy and her uncle are ready to leave, follow the path over the dunes. You will see the dining area when you get to the top.'

'Save us some grub,' Miller said. 'And I don't mean those Witchetty grubs Brolga told us about. They may be a prized delicacy, but I'm not into bush tucker food.'

'Are you sure I couldn't tempt you?'

'You can tempt me anytime, Bailey, but not with Witchetty grubs.'

'We will be there as soon as possible.' Jujh patted his stomach. 'I am ravenous. As you English say, I could devour a horse.'

'No horse, I'm afraid, but we can manage kangaroo and crocodile.' Bailey laughed. 'See you later, and don't go giving Dorothy any money. It will only encourage her to do it again.'

Bailey nudged Jujh's arm, smiled and pointed towards Miller drawing a hopscotch grid in the sand for Dorothy. 'Look at that, he's a natural.'

The sun had disappeared completely. Jujh used the torch on his cell phone to negotiate the pathway.

Bailey rushed to his side. 'What have you done with Miller?' she asked.

'He sends his apologies, and his earnest assurances that he will see you on the sunrise tour tomorrow morning. He's been invited to Mutitjulu for dinner and an overnight stay.'

'Miller has? My goodness, that's a first.'

'Dorothy's uncle offered to teach us to play the didgeridoo. I declined, but Miller's effort impressed everyone. Pleased with his extraordinary progress they invited him back to develop his skills.'

'I just hope he behaves himself. He has such a tendency to say the wrong thing at times.' Bailey sighed. 'I hope we don't end up with an international incident. And I can't believe he chose tonight, of all nights, to go walkabout. Tomorrow's such a tight schedule.'

'He made a promise, Bailey, and I believe Miller is a man of his word.' Jujh could see she was still worried, but he could say no more to re-assure her.

'Yoo-hoo, Mr Singh! I've been saving this seat for you.' Barbara patted the chair beside her.

'Please excuse me, Bailey. And try not to worry. Miller is an extraordinary man. Everything will be perfectly fine.'

Barbara smiled as Jujh sat beside her. 'I hoped to speak with you, Mr Singh.'

'It's *Jujh,* ma'am. Please call me Jujh.'

'I do so want to find out more about this wonderful hotel you and your father own. I intend to holiday in India next year and your hotel sounds just like the sort of place I may be looking for. Now where exactly is it?'

'I will get you a brochure when we return to our hotel.'

'That will be kind of you, my dear.'

Barbara was distracted momentarily by the wine waiter giving Jujh a chance to look around. The group sat at four tables covered with white linen tablecloths and canopied with large cream umbrellas. The only lighting came from lamps placed in the centre of each table. The glass shades were splattered with flies, grasshoppers, moths and other winged insects, lured to their deaths by the bright lights. The waiters hovered discreetly, delivering bread rolls and offering a choice of wine to each guest.

Tony leaned towards Jujh from his seat beside Barbara. 'Good timing, Jujh. It's our turn to go up and help ourselves from the buffet.' Tony stood. 'Come on, Maddy. Let's see what's on offer.'

Jujh surveyed the choices. He always avoided beef, but he fancied trying the kangaroo steaks. The crocodile Caesar salad didn't look particularly tempting, but the grilled chicken appeared simply cooked. He helped himself, added salad, a few new potatoes and a small dish of apple crumble and custard. As he walked back to the table, his foot scuffed against a small rock of red iron ore, about the size of an apple. He picked it up and placed it carefully on his tray.

'What's that you have Jujh?' Sumner asked.

'It's a stone, the perfect size for a paperweight. I shall take it home as a reminder of my visit.'

'This red colouring is stunning,' Sumner said. 'I've taken some incredible landscape shots for the calendar.'

'It's like Mars,' Tony said. 'I keep expecting to walk around a corner and bump into a NASA robot.'

Jujh tasted the kangaroo steak – surprisingly tender and a pleasant flavour.

'Good, isn't it?' James sat opposite. 'Of course, my wife won't even try it, some nonsense about them being too cute to eat.'

'I won't eat Skippy,' March said.

James snorted. 'More fool you. It's delicious. A bit

like venison.'

'I won't eat Bambi either.'

He waved his loaded fork under March's nose. 'Try it.'

'No, James, I've told you. I'm happy with the chicken.'

'I'm with you, March, dear.' Pryor pointed at her salad. 'I like to know what I'm eating. I'm mostly vegetarian, although I will take fish once in a while.'

The lights dimmed and an Aboriginal man appeared wearing jeans and a T-shirt. He picked up the microphone. 'Welcome to our cultural evening of storytelling, shared with you tonight through the medium of traditional dance.'

Two more performers arrived. They wore black shorts, and carried spears. Their black skin glistened in the lamp light and contrasted with the painted white streaks highlighting their rib cage, slashes down their legs and arms, with their palms painted completely white.

'They look like pantomime skeletons,' James said.

'Shush, James, you'll upset them,' March snapped.

Jujh noticed Paul at the next table. He whispered into Frank's ear, pushed back his chair and strode off into the darkness as the performance began.

Maddy's stifled sob drew Bailey's attention. Something was clearly wrong in paradise. After finishing their meal, the couple had retreated to the edge of the glade, taking their drinks with them. They were perched on an old tree trunk, stripped of bark and polished to provide informal seating. She watched as Maddy stood and put her arms around Tony's neck. He pushed her away, rose to his feet, marched back to the dinner table and threw himself into his seat next to

Barbara. Maddy stared after him, and then turned and fled across the dune in the direction of the toilet block. Should she go after her? She really didn't want to abandon her guests. She hovered, undecided.

Barbara rushed over. 'Leave it to me, Bailey.'

'If you're sure? Take one of these torches and, please, no more falling over.'

The performance ended and a few extra lights came on to illuminate a pathway.

'Ladies and Gentlemen, I hope you have enjoyed your evening under the stars. Unfortunately, the performance has now come to an end, so if you would like to make your way down this path, your coach is waiting at the bottom.'

Bailey counted. 'I'm three missing. Four if we include Miller. I know Barbara and Maddy went to the loo.'

Tony glanced at his watch. 'Some time ago,' he frowned. 'I thought they'd be back by now.'

'Who else is missing?' Bailey asked.

'Paul went to the astronomy glade.' Frank said. He's always very disparaging about what he calls these "phoney cultural evenings." He said he wanted to go and look for the Southern Cross.' Frank looked at his watch. 'He promised to be back before now. I'll fetch him.'

'No, you stay here. I'll find them.'

'I'll come with you,' Tony offered. 'My mobile phone has a torch.'

Bailey and Tony strode over the sand dunes, their torches cutting shafts of light through the inky black.

'It's so dark,' Tony said.

'They keep the light pollution to a minimum to give us the full impact of the stars, so we–' something caught Bailey's eye. She shone her torch onto a bundle. A body, dressed in black jeans and long-sleeved shirt. A long blonde ponytail shimmered in the light.

'Maddy!' shouted Tony. He raced towards the prostate figure, threw himself to the ground and turned the body over.

'It's not her.' Tony's gasped with relief. 'It's Paul.'

Bailey's heart raced as she sank to the floor and felt for a pulse in Paul's neck. It might not be Maddy, but it was still one of her guests. 'He's OK. Looks like he's knocked himself out.' Bailey glanced up as another powerful torch beam lit the scene. Maddy, closely followed by Barbara.

'What's happened?' Maddy asked.

'Maddy.' Tony stood, threw his arms around her and kissed her forehead. 'I thought it was you.'

'Paul, can you hear me?' Bailey squeezed his shoulder.

Paul groaned, lifted his hand to his forehead and slowly opened his eyes.

'Who turned my lights out?' he croaked.

'Did you slip?' Bailey asked.

'Someone bashed me.'

'Surely not,' Bailey said.

'I was my way back, next thing I knew – bang.'

'Can you sit up?' Bailey asked.

Paul grabbed Bailey's hand and hauled himself into a sitting position. 'I'm OK, just a bit wobbly.' He ran his hand over his head. 'This bump's as big as an egg.'

Bailey examined Paul's head. 'No blood, but you'll have a headache. I'll get the hotel doctor to give you a check-up when we get you back. He'll have to sign you off as fit to fly tomorrow morning.'

'I'll be fine.'

'Here you go, mate. Let's get you up.'

Tony and Bailey each took one of Paul's hands. They pulled him to his feet. He swayed a little, but remained standing.

Barbara and Maddy held the torches to light the way, and Bailey and Tony supported Paul as they all walked slowly towards the coach. Frank rushed towards them.

'Paul, whatever happened? Bailey?'

'Paul had a bit of an accident,' Bailey said.

'Accident, my foot. Someone clobbered me.' Paul rubbed his head and groaned.

'Thanks, Tony, I'll take over from here.' Frank put his arm around Paul's waist and helped him towards the bus.

Bailey followed. 'I need to phone the incident through to the police. I don't suppose they can do much, but they may want a statement from you, Paul.'

'No point. My wallet and passport are in the safe at the hotel. Nothing stolen.'

'Even so, we need an incident number, just in case.' Bailey thought it best not to mention the chances of bleeding on the brain, complications, or death. She walked to the back of the bus counting the guests. 'All present and correct, Driver. We can go now.'

She glanced down at Jujh polishing his rock with his handkerchief. 'What do you have there?'

'Beautiful, isn't it? I will keep it on my office desk as a reminder of my trip.'

'It's rumoured to be bad luck to take rocks away from Uluru.

Perhaps you should leave it behind? Best not tempt fate.'

'I don't believe in luck. Life is what you make it.'

'Others have thought the same, but many experienced such bad luck that they were compelled to return their stones. There's even a special postcode for people to use.'

'My dear Lady, I am thanking you for your concern, but I would rather keep it.'

Bailey decided not to argue. Besides, she had more important things to worry about. As the bus pulled away, she turned to face her guests.

'Don't forget, I need you in reception at five tomorrow morning.'

James groaned.

'It's up to you, of course. Leave a message at reception if you decide to have a lie in but, I promise you, sunrise over Uluru is well worth the early start.'

Bailey slumped down in her seat and began to make a mental check list for when they got back. First, she needed to sort a doctor to check Paul over, and then she needed to contact the police and report the attack. It must be an attempted robbery. Who else would want to injure Paul?

Maddy watched Tony as he ordered their drinks. The other guests had gone to their rooms and the lounge was empty, apart from themselves and the barman. It was still very early days, but she so wanted this relationship to work. She'd even allowed herself to believe he felt the same. Now she'd come close to losing him. Of course, she'd taken a risk by sharing her guilty secret. She'd guessed he might be shocked, or even upset, but she hadn't expected him to react quite like he did.

Tony placed two glasses of sparkling white wine on the table. He smiled tenderly and sat beside her on the sofa, his thigh pressed against hers. Her skin tingled. She knew she had to say something to get things back on track. She could feel the blush creep up her neck and across her cheeks as she struggled to find the right words.

'I'm so sorry,' she gushed. 'I should have told you earlier.'

'No. I'm sorry. I behaved appallingly.'

The line of tiny bubbles rose slowly to the top of her glass. 'I feel so guilty. But Peter told me his marriage was over, and I naively believed him.' She plucked up courage and looked into his eyes. 'I didn't want any secrets between us. Do you hate me?'

'I could never hate you.'

'You pushed me away.'

He fiddled with the stem of his glass and frowned. 'It was a shock. For me marriage is for life. I can't believe he treated you like that.'

'Have I ruined everything?'

'I'm angry at him, but I could never be angry with you… well, not for long anyway.'

He rubbed his thumb gently over her knuckles and gazed into her eyes. Her pulse raced. She felt a surge of desire. It was going to be OK. Please let it be OK.

'I'll never forgive myself for letting you rush off into the dark like that. That could have been you lying there.' He leaned over and kissed her, a long, slow kiss that made her stomach flip.' He pulled away. 'Actually, while we're sharing guilty secrets, I also have a confession.'

Her heart sank. 'You're not going to tell me you're married, are you? I don't think I could stand it.'

'No, not married. But I have a son. He's called Oscar.'

Not a wife, thank goodness for that. A son. She could cope with a son.

'He's twenty, and he lives in Melbourne.'

'I thought this was your first visit?'

'It is. I met his mother at university. We had a bit of a drunken fling, failed to take sufficient precautions and she fell pregnant. I offered to do the honourable thing, but I think we both knew it wouldn't work out. She moved back to her home, here in Australia, shortly before his birth.'

'So, you've never seen him?'

'The occasional photograph.' He shuffled his feet and frowned. 'I did wonder if I should look him up when we get to Melbourne, but I'm not sure how I'd be received.'

Maddy drained her glass. Tony watched her, waiting for her reaction.

'Look, why don't you contact him tomorrow and invite him to our hotel in Melbourne? Ask him to join you for a drink?'

'You wouldn't mind?'

'Course not.'

Tony swept her into his arms and kissed her passionately. So, this was what swooning felt like.

'Do you need to go back to your room for anything?' He kissed her again, 'I think you should spend the night in my room tonight.'

'Why, because there's some maniac's going around hitting people over the head?'

'Because it's time for us to move our relationship on a step, don't you think?'

Thank goodness she wasn't standing; her legs had turned to jelly.

Bailey rang the hand bell. 'Wake up, wake up!' she screamed, as she raced along the hotel corridor, pausing briefly to hammer on each bedroom door. 'Get up, we'll miss the plane.' The walls of the corridor faded away, and the floor tilted. An explosion? An earthquake? She opened her eyes and blinked. She lay flat on her back in bed, her cell phone ringing. She grabbed it from the bedside table.

'Frank? Is Paul worse?'

'It's Jujh, I need your help. Urgently.'

'Where are you?'

'In reception. Can you come? Now?'

'On my way.'

'Please hurry.'

She pulled on her clothes and ran to reception, her heart racing.

Jujh paced up and down. He saw her and rushed towards her.

'Oh my dear Lady, you were so right. Please take it back.' He thrust the small red rock into her hands.

'Whatever's the matter?'

'My daughter. She is dangerously ill. I've just received a phone call. My family tracked me down from our tour schedule. I have to return to India immediately. They say her only hope is a bone marrow transplant and I am her best chance for a match.'

'I didn't know you had a daughter.'

'It's a long story.'

'Save it for now. You go and pack, then meet me back here

as soon as you can. I'll contact the airport and sort out the best flight to get you home.'

'The rock, you will take it back? I wished I'd never—'

'Consider it done.' She patted his arm. 'It'll be OK, I'm sure. Now go.'

16. Day Eight – Sunrise at Uluru

The group took Bailey's advice and meandered their way up to the viewing platform. Alone at last, she slumped onto the wooden bench.

Her head felt light. Not surprising. By the time she'd thanked the doctor last night and left Paul in Frank's capable hands, it was way past her normal bedtime. Then she'd contacted the police, who'd taken her statement, given her an incident number and told her they would keep her informed of progress. She got the distinct impression that the report would be filed under *drunken tourist trips and falls*.

She'd tossed and turned, going over and over the events. Who on earth would want to hurt Paul? Not the staff; they relied on the tourist trade. Not his partner, Frank, who'd been devastated – unless he was a very good actor. None of the other guests would have any reason to hurt him. It made no sense. And what on earth would the secret shopper make of it all? She'd only just dropped off to sleep when Jujh rang needing help.

She'd travelled with him to the airport and ensured he was safely checked onto his flight. He'd said he'd e-mail and let her know what happened. She hoped he did. This was what she loved about her job. Jujh could be the secret shopper, a troublesome guest or the nicest guy on the planet. It didn't matter, he required help and she had given it gladly and professionally. By the time she returned to the hotel, sleep was no longer an option and she'd settled for a quick shower and a strong coffee.

Now, at Uluru, she listened to the birds as they awoke. First a solitary call, then an answer, followed by a cacophony of noisy twitters from a bush filled with budgerigars. She forgot her weariness as the familiar black outline of Uluru gained definition against the inky blue sky.

She would never tire of watching the first light of day as it crept across the red desert plain; the colours so intense. Of course, she knew the theory: water vapour and red dust particles in the atmosphere filtering out the blue solar rays, allowing more red light through to enhance the colours. But the science could never fully explain the magic of watching Uluru as it turned to burnished gold.

Bailey took Jujh's rock from her pocket and rolled it into the shrubbery. 'Let's hope that's the end of your bad luck,' she whispered. She heard footsteps approaching and looked up. 'Miller. Glad you're here. I thought you might miss our flight.'

'Naidoo dropped me off. He said I'd find you here.' He sat beside her and looked towards the sandstone escarpment. 'Spectacular, isn't it?'

'I've visited many times, but I still find it breath-taking.'

The sun rose behind them and Uluru changed to the more familiar red of the picture postcards.

'The way the rock strata folds like that always reminds me of a large cake covered in red marzipan,' she smiled.

'Look, a Martian,' laughed Miller. He pointed to the right-hand side of the rock. 'Do you see it? There's a large domed head, two eyes and a mouth.'

'I suppose... if you have a vivid imagination.' Bailey turned towards him. 'How did your evening in Mutitjulu go? I worried about you.'

'And here was me thinking you didn't care.' He looked across the sandy ground. A slight frown creased his brow. 'What an eye opener. We sat outside under the stars and grilled kangaroo tails over a campfire. They were delicious. But the village was something else. Streets littered with plastic bags, old tyres, food packaging, flies everywhere. The stench was unbelievable.'

'Not just Mutitjulu. Most townships are the same.'

'Why doesn't the Government do something about it?'

'What can they do? Move in with big skips and clean up? Implement health education programmes? They've tried everything, with little success. The problem goes much deeper.'

'How come?'

'It's cultural. Before the settlers came, the Aborigines were nomadic hunter-gatherers.' She picked up an empty crisp packet someone had discarded and stuffed it in her pocket. 'Their food didn't come in plastic wrapping. It was bio-degradable. They'd drop their left-over food on the ground and when the smell and flies got too bad, they'd simply move on.'

'Something needs to happen. Dorothy took me to see her father. He lay sprawled on a filthy bed in the back room. I thought he was ill at first, until I realised, he was drunk. Naidoo reckons that of the three hundred people living in the village, half of them suffer from alcoholism, and the level of obesity and diabetes is staggering. I wish I could do something to help.'

Bailey glanced at him. He wasn't smiling now.

'Perhaps you can. I have friends in Sydney who work on various youth projects. I could give you their contact details if you're serious?'

'I don't think I've ever been more serious. I also want to help Dorothy. I may set up one of those educational trust funds, like Jujh did?' He looked towards the other guests gathered on the viewing platform. 'Where is he by the way?

'I'm afraid you won't be seeing Jujh. He had to fly back to India last night. His daughter's seriously ill.'

'Daughter? My word, he never let on he had any family. He's full of surprises.'

He's not the only one, she thought.

Miller placed a hand on her shoulder. 'Are you OK, Kate?'

'What happened to you calling me Bailey?'

'I like the name Kate. It was my mother's name. You look tired.'

Bailey felt the pressure of his hand and looked up to meet his gaze. 'I didn't get any sleep. I had Jujh's flight to organise.'

'You should try and get some rest.'

Her eyes prickled with tears. She couldn't cope with this unexpected empathy. How many more e-mails from Head Office would be waiting for her when she got back to her laptop. The demand for reports and risk assessments increased daily, mostly from Jim, and mainly because he wanted to cover his own back.

'Chance would be a fine thing!' she snapped.

Miller removed his hand from her shoulder. 'I'll go. Leave you in peace.'

Bailey watched him saunter up to join her other guests. She'd offended him. The last thing she wanted. He'd tried to be kind, but he was wrong. She wasn't tired; more like exhausted. She'd been so busy, frantically trying to be all things for every guest and at the same time discover the identity of the secret shopper and for what? Why should she distrust all of them for the sake of one? She'd be better off taking them at face value. Her ridiculous endeavours had resulted in her distrusting everyone. They didn't deserve this. Even if she had found out, what could she possibly hope to achieve or do differently? Besides, since she became a Tour Manager, she'd never had a complaint. Only compliments.

Sod all this identifying the secret shopper crap. In future, she would simply get on with doing her job. First things first; time to get them all on the flight to Melbourne.

PART THREE

17. Day Eight – Afternoon in Melbourne

The Brigadier surveyed the empty lounge in search of a comfortable seat. He needed some support for his back, which was giving him gyp after that morning's flight. He chose one of the high-backed wing chairs that faced the window with a superb view across the river. God, he needed a stiff drink. Where's that bloody waitress? He heard the tip tap of her heels as she came closer.

'Can I get you something, Sir?'

Bugger, she'd stopped to serve someone on the sofa behind him. He was about to complain – he'd been here first – but then the guest placed his order.

'A bottle of sparkling wine and three glasses, please?'

Sumner! Three glasses? He must be expecting that meddlesome couple.

He wondered if he should try and make a quick exit before they arrived. He could do without a confrontation with that pipsqueak, Captain Knight. On the other hand, the chair shielded him from view. He decided to stay put.

He should never have lied to Tony about seeing active service in the Falklands, but how could he have known Tony's bloody uncle had been in command out there. Nor should he have over-reacted when Sumner used the name Adam in his fraud story. He assumed they were baiting him after they'd somehow discovered he'd exaggerated his rank. He may only have been a Sergeant, but countless others inflated their rank on retirement. Why shouldn't he?

He jumped as Sumner called out.

'Tony, Maddy, over here!'

He shrank back further into his chair. They wouldn't even be here if his plan had worked. It was a spur of the minute thing, when he saw Maddy walking back through the sand dunes last night. He'd hoped that a crack on the head would make her unfit for this morning's flight. With her and Tony out of the way, the trio would be apart for a day or two, giving him some time to think. Obviously, his plans had come to nothing when he'd mistakenly knocked out that pansy, Paul, instead. What sort of man wore a pony-tail? A stint in the army would soon sort him out.

'What's with this drinking at lunch time? Tony and I are off shopping.'

'You've got all afternoon, and I wanted to hear your news.'

Tony laughed. 'Honestly Sumner, I do believe the Brigadier has gotten under your skin.'

He'd been right. The bastards *were* out to get him.

Sumner snorted. 'I never liked him from the start – he's so pompous. If he's lied about his rank, well, that's just sad. But if he's stolen money from a charity, he deserves to be exposed.'

He clenched his fists. Stolen! He'd spent every bloody weekend working for that charity – raised thousands for them.

'You remember I told you about my friend, Steve, who works for *Help the Heroes*? Well, I think he's come up trumps.'

'OK then, deal me in,' Sumner said.

'The Brigadier *has* made some contributions to *Help the*

Heroes, but Steve cross-referenced those against the archives of the Brigadier's local newspaper. They carry reports on thousands of pounds being raised. The discrepancy is enormous – at least fifty thousand pounds over this past year alone. I had my suspicions, but I'm stunned by the scale. Steve's handed everything over to the fraud squad. They'll check the Brigadier's bank accounts, and if they agree there's a case to answer, they'll be waiting for him when he gets home.'

'I'll drink to that. One more for the road?' Sumner asked.

How dare they celebrate his downfall with such glee? What difference did it make to any of them? What if he did top slice funds? He needed to top up his pittance of a pension somehow. Anyway, all charities took their admin fees and he only took half. The charity still benefitted. He unclenched his hands and rubbed the red indented marks where his nails had dug into his pale, bloodless palm. He shook his hands and loosened his collar. He really needed that drink now. Why didn't they get a bloody move on and finish their drinks?

'Bottoms up,' Sumner said.

He leaned forward and glared at their backs as the trio left the lounge.

Time for Plan B.

18. Afternoon in Melbourne

Cynthia looked forward to an afternoon free to explore Melbourne, but at the same time, she worried. What if she got lost? Or mugged? After all, it happened to Paul. What if...? oh, for goodness sake, Cynthia, pull yourself together.

She picked up a map and a hotel address card from the reception desk, and placed them in her purse. Now, if she did get lost, she could get a taxi back to the hotel.

She walked purposefully towards the bridge that spanned the Yarra River and paused to watch the cruise boat as it sailed beneath her, leaving a trail of white foam in its wake. A woman stood on the bow and gripped her partner's arm. She pointed towards the Casino complex and they both laughed. He placed his arm over her shoulder and gave her a hug. The simple gesture filled Cynthia with a deep longing. If only she had someone to share her life with.

It hadn't bothered her while she worked. Returning to an empty home after a long day at work was almost a relief. Since she'd retired, the emptiness wrapped around her like a cold mist. A chilling reminder that there was no one with whom she could discuss the weather, the news, or the latest book she was reading.

She consulted her map, and made her way towards the arcades. Wandering through the bustling narrow streets, she gazed in through shop windows and paused to admire a display of opal jewellery. She turned away and caught sight of the Brigadier disappearing into a shop. Perhaps she could persuade him to join her for a coffee. She hurried up the street and glanced inside the jewellers. The shop was empty, apart from a young girl behind the counter. Had her desperation for company played tricks on her mind?

Cynthia continued through the arcade admiring the windows adorned with Ugg boots, Aboriginal artefacts and knickknacks. This was exactly the sort of place to come for presents. In the past, she would have found something interesting for her secretary, but now there was no one; no one at all.

Her spirit lifted as she saw Sumner walking towards her. Perhaps she could persuade him to join her for a drink?

'Hi there, Ms Clerk. Are you enjoying Melbourne?'

'It's thirsty work. Could I tempt you to join me for coffee?'

'I'd love to, but I'm on my way to meet someone.'

'Someone?'

'The Brigadier.'

'That's funny. I thought I saw him go into a shop, down that way,' she pointed.

'Sorry, must dash.'

Sumner hurried off in the direction she'd indicated. Her heart sank. He didn't have to be so abrupt.

She checked her map and turned towards Federation Square wondering what had brought on this unexpected sense of melancholy. She'd never needed company in the past. Her mother had died a month after Cynthia's nineteenth birthday, her father a year later. She had a few friends in her twenties and thirties, even an occasional boyfriend, but her job kept her so busy they'd drifted away.

This holiday she'd hoped, perhaps, to make new friends.

She hadn't expected to suddenly feel lonely for the first time in her life.

She looked up from her musings. At the entrance to the railway station was a red and white striped barrow filled with buckets of fresh flowers. She picked up a posy containing three stems of orchids – cream with a pale pink throat and a heavenly scent.

'Hello, Ms Clerk. Let me get those for you.' The Dean stood at her side, holding out a $20 note to the vendor.

'Oh no, you mustn't. It will be such a waste.' She could feel the heat rise in her cheeks. 'We fly to Cairns in a couple of days. They won't let me take them through security.'

'I insist,' he smiled. 'Leave them in your room for the cleaner. At least enjoy them until then.'

'That's so kind of you, thank you. And please, call me Cynthia.'

'And I'm David,' he said as he handed the flowers to her. 'I always used to buy flowers for my dear wife. Orchids were her favourite. May I walk with you?'

They ambled towards the hotel.

'I'm looking forward to our evening meal,' David said. 'I hear the tram car is like the Orient Express.'

'I'll have told my story by then. I'm *so* nervous. Terrified I'll mess it up.'

'Nonsense, you'll be fine. Why don't we sit together on the tram and celebrate?'

She smiled. 'That would be lovely, thank you.'

Bailey's cell phone rang. She didn't recognise the number, but took the call.

'Bailey, is that you?

'Sumner?'

'Listen, Bailey. Something is definitely going on with the Brigadier.'

'Is he ill?'

'No. He's going around all the shops that buy second hand jewellery.'

'He's probably shopping.'

'Has anyone reported anything stolen?'

'Sumner! How could you think such a thing?'

'Mostly because Tony's discovered he's not a Brigadier, he was dishonourably discharged from the army for fraud, and he may be involved in a scam to steel thousands of pounds from *Help the Heroes*.'

Bailey sank onto her bed and tried to make sense of what Sumner was saying. 'Surely not. He's a charming man. I realise there's no love lost between you, but–'

'What about Barbara? She's not worn her rings since the fall. Are they still safe?'

'I'll go and check, but I'm sure you're mistaken.'

Bailey went in search of Barbara. She found her in the lounge, reading a magazine and sipping a cup of tea.

'Bailey, how nice to see you. Would you like some tea?'

'Barbara, I know this may sound a bit odd, but have you checked your rings since you took them off?'

'Rings?' Barbara looked confused. 'I haven't moved them since the accident.'

'Could you check?'

'Of course, my dear. If it makes you feel better.'

Barbara reached for her handbag, unclipped it and unzipped the side pocket. 'This is where the Brigadier put them.' She pushed her hand in and rummaged. Frowned. Rummaged some more. 'Oh, my dear, someone must have stolen them. How did you know?'

'Don't worry Barbara. We may know what's happened. I promise I'll do my best to get them back. I have to leave you for a while. Will you be OK?'

'I'm so sorry to cause all this trouble.'

'Don't worry about it. This is not your fault.'

Bailey dashed back to her room and dialled 000. Her heart raced as she explained the situation to the duty policeman. He promised to get someone over to the hotel immediately, and asked for Sumner's contact number.

How could she have been so blind? Surely the Brigadier must have realised Barbara would discover the theft. There must be some horrible misunderstanding.

She raced back to the lounge, where she was surprised to find Maddy and Tony with Barbara.

'It's OK, Bailey,' Maddy said as she stroked Barbara's hand. 'Sumner told us the latest. We came back to help.'

'I can't believe it,' Barbara said. 'How did he think he'd get away with it?'

'I think he's desperate,' Maddy said.

'He must have known the police would be involved once I reported the theft.'

'Maybe he planned to post them to the UK, and bluff it out,' Maddy said. 'He probably hoped a member of staff would be suspected. After all, without the rings there'd be no proof he'd stolen them.'

'But I don't understand,' Barbara said. 'Why change his

mind. Why sell them now?'

'He must have discovered that the police have him under investigation,' Maddy suggested. 'Perhaps he's been tipped off by someone in the UK.'

Tony ran his hand over his cropped hair and shook his head. 'If he sells the rings for cash, he could abandon this trip, get back to the UK and try to put his affairs in order.'

'Easy to find out,' Maddy said. 'If that's his plan, he'll have his bags packed, ready to scarper as soon as he sells them.'

'I'm still convinced there must be some awful mistake,' Bailey said. 'But I'll get the manager to check his room. I'd go myself, but the police are on their way. Are you all OK to stay for a while and give your statements?'

'Anything to help, Bailey,' Tony said. 'I feel somewhat responsible.'

Bailey rushed over to the reception desk and returned several minutes later, a young man by her side.

'This is Detective Inspector Finnegan. He's here to ask us a few questions. Apparently, the Brigadier, if indeed he is one, has been arrested and taken to police headquarters for questioning. The arresting officers have confirmed that he was in procession of several diamond rings. They'll be sending them over for you to identify, Barbara.'

'I'll be relieved to have them back.'

D. I. Finnegan smiled at Barbara. 'I'm afraid that may be a few months, Madam. They'll be needed for evidence, but we'll keep them safe.'

Bailey sank into a chair. 'I really can't believe this. By the way, Maddy, you were right. The manager has checked the Brigadier's room. His bags are all packed and have UK flight tags ready to go.'

'Can I get you that cup of tea now, Bailey?' Barbara asked. 'You look very pale.'

'Thanks, but I've ordered a tray of sandwiches and some fresh tea. I think we'll be in need of sustenance after all this excitement.'

Excitement she could well do without. Jim would enjoy twisting this around to ensure she got the blame. No doubt he would take another swipe at her for organising the kangaroo sanctuary tour. After all, this whole sorry story had begun there. And how would she explain that yet another guest had left the tour?

19. Evening in Melbourne

Mai Tai:

- *20ml Bacardi*
- *20ml Jamaican Rum*
- *10ml Orange Curacao*
- *20ml fresh lime juice*
- *7ml Orgeat syrup*
- *7ml sugar syrup*

Fill a tumbler glass with crushed ice. Shake all of the ingredients together and strain into glass. Garnish with a slice of fresh pineapple and a cherry.

Miller watched Bailey as she walked towards him carrying a tray of drinks.

'Cocktail?'

'Thanks, Kate.' He reached up and took two.

'Thirsty tonight?'

'In need of company. Will you join me?'

'Not just now, but you could do me a favour and invite Cynthia Clerk. I think she gets a bit lonely and she may also be nervous – it's her story tonight.'

'God, I love a bossy woman.'

Bailey bent her head closer to his ear, and spoke in a soft voice. 'I'm not being bossy. I'm appealing to your chivalrous side. I know it's in there, somewhere.'

He grinned and watched her walk away. Glancing around the lounge he spotted Cynthia Clerk. Bailey was right; she did look nervous. He realised, with a twinge of guilt that he'd hardly spoken to her before, other than to say hello.

Cynthia's attention was drawn towards Miller. He beckoned her over to join him. A slight blush warmed Cynthia's cheek. No one, apart from David earlier today – and Bailey of course – had sought out her company since the holiday began. She hurried over and sank into the armchair next to him.

'Mrs Clerk, do try this delightful Mai Tai.'

'*Miss*,' she picked up the drink. 'I've never been lucky enough to marry.'

'Or foolish enough, eh?' Miller winked.

'Please, call me Cynthia.'

'What a nice name. Tell me, Cynthia, what have you been up to today?'

'What my dear mother would have called pottering. And you?'

'Oh, I went off to explore the ice bar.'

'Me too,' Barbara said as she bustled into the armchair opposite. 'My dear, wasn't it absolutely wonderful? I loved the way the bar, the seats, and even the glasses were carved from ice – utterly marvellous.'

Cynthia's mood sank. Barbara's brightly coloured clothing and her exuberance always made Cynthia feel insubstantial. She looked down at her own grey wool skirt and matching fitted jacket, white blouse and sensible black shoes. The only colourful touch was one of David's orchids pinned to her collar.

By contrast, Barbara wore a lime green suit, with a matching hat and high heeled shoes in a colour Cynthia had once been shocked to hear described as *nude*. Cynthia already felt excluded from their conversation. She knew it wasn't intentional, but how could she make any comment when she hadn't even seen this bar. How could you sit on seats made of ice? She didn't want to show her stupidity by asking. Perhaps she would visit tomorrow and find out.

Bailey stood and waited for the chatter to die down. Cynthia's stomach cramped. She may have been confident in her career life, but she was essentially shy with strangers. And her story included sex. What had she been thinking? A sixty-five-year-old virgin telling a story that included sex, a subject she knew little about. She sat back in her chair, sipped her cocktail and tried to compose herself.

Bailey clanged a glass with her pen. 'Ladies and Gentlemen, before we begin tonight, I'm afraid I have some rather sad news. The Brigadier, as you may have noticed, is not with us this evening. Unfortunately, he's been forced to leave the tour.'

'Is he ill?' asked James.

'On the advice of our legal department I'm not allowed to say any more. But no, he's not ill.'

'I knew he was a villain,' Mrs Nunne turned to her husband. 'I told you, didn't I? He had shifty eyes.'

Bailey ignored her. 'Tonight's story is from Cynthia. Afterwards we will leave the hotel and join the tram car for our tour of Melbourne and evening meal. Cynthia, over to you.'

Cynthia's legs trembled as she stood and turned to face the

group. 'I hope you will enjoy my story. It's not a true one, and I'm hopeless at making things up. So, I'm afraid it's one I borrowed from a magazine:'

Cynthia Clerk's Tale

Griselda's taxi drew up at the gateway of the quaint little church set beside a small lake. The pale golden stonework of its classical square tower reflected on the shimmering surface of the water. Fragrant pink roses clambered chaotically over the porch. A peel of bells rang. She wanted to run down the path, breathe in the heady scent of those roses, walk through the doorway, and feast her eyes on her groom; Simon.

'Good luck, darlin',' said the driver as she climbed out of the cab and adjusted her dress. The cream lace clung to her figure and emphasised her small waist, before falling gently over her hips and cascading into a short train. She felt…delicious. She picked up her bouquet of white lilies and yellow roses, noticed that they sadly had very little perfume, stepped through the rustic lych-gate, and into the churchyard.

The bells fell silent. The only sound was the persistent call of a wood-pigeon.

Her matron of honour, Ella, rushed towards her; a look of absolute horror on her face. 'Oh, Griselda, darling, I'm so sorry. Simon says he can't marry you today. He's got a big presentation to make at work.'

The alarm on her mobile phone wrenched her awake. She opened her eyes, her heart pounding. Thank goodness. Only a nightmare.

Simon lay facing her. She studied his straight nose, long eyelashes and the dark stubble on his chin with that oh-so-cute dimple and experienced a surge of happiness. It was their anniversary, twelve months since they'd met at a local quiz night. She still couldn't believe her luck.

She wondered where she'd left her clothes and then blushed as she remembered how they'd returned from the pub and ripped off their clothes in the hall, like reckless teenagers before collecting a bottle of champagne from the fridge on route to the bedroom.

She swung her legs out of bed

'Don't go,' he begged.

'She may need me.'

'Surely, just one night won't hurt.' She leaned over and kissed him softly on the lips. 'You go back to sleep. Good luck for tomorrow's presentation.'

She made her way back to the hall and retrieved her clothes. She hated this getting up late at night to go home. She'd never yet spent a whole night with Simon, even though he frequently pleaded with her to stay. How much longer could she expect him to wait?

She crept in and closed the door carefully. Marmaduke met her as she took off her coat and hung it up.

'Hello, sweetie pie. How are things?' she whispered. Marmaduke purred and rubbed against her legs. She reached down and stroked him. 'Let's go and check on Mother, shall we?'

She climbed the stairs, careful to avoid the top one, which always creaked, and pushed open the door. The bedside night light glowed softly; she could easily make out her mother's shape beneath the duvet. She paused, waiting to hear her mother's gentle breathing, but there was no sound. Alarmed, she rushed to the bedside and watched. Nothing.

'Mother, are you all right? Wake up.'

Griselda shook her mother's shoulder and then felt for a pulse. Her skin was cold to the touch. Griselda grabbed the extension phone from the bedside table and punched five; the speed dial for the Doctors surgery. Her hand shook as her call was re-directed to the Out of Hours Service.

A sleepy voice answered. 'Hello, Dr Andrews speaking.'

'It's my mother... I think she may be... she may have died.'

The doctor asked for her mother's name and their address and said he'd be with her within fifteen minutes.

Griselda gripped her mother's cold hand. 'I should have sat with you, read you a story, instead of leaving you here alone. Please, don't be dead. Give me another chance.' She dissolved into tears.

The doorbell rang. She flew down the stairs.

'Doctor Andrews. Thank goodness you're here. I checked on Mother, and she's... she's not responding.'

'How about you make us both a cup of tea while I go and see her?'

Griselda pointed to her mother's bedroom door and watched the doctor as he climbed the stairs. She wanted to shout out to him to miss the squeaky top step, but stopped herself just in time.

She staggered into the kitchen and switched on the electric kettle. By the time the doctor joined her she had mashed the tea, as her mother would say, and placed the knitted tea cosy over the pot.

'I'm so sorry, my dear.' He sank into the chair opposite her. 'She wouldn't have known a thing. She simply died in her sleep. Painless. I only hope I go in the same way when my time comes.'

Griselda stared into her teacup. 'But that's the point isn't it? It wasn't her time. She's only sixty-six.'

'Your mother wasn't a well woman, not since the pneumonia weakened her heart. That must be getting on for eighteen years ago.'

'I should never have left her tonight.'

'You have nothing to reproach yourself for.'

Griselda stifled a sob. 'What happens now?'

'I'll ring the coroner and have your mother collected.' He patted

her hand. 'Is there anyone I can ring? You shouldn't be on your own.'

She instantly thought of Simon, but then remembered the presentation. She shook her head. 'I'll be fine.'

'Come and see me in the next day or two.'

The doctor finished his tea and left her to her thoughts. What would life be like now? What about Simon? Would he propose? How could she even think such a thing? Another huge wave of guilt rose up from her toes, flooded her chest and left her breathless.

A loud knock on the front door broke the silence. Her heart raced as she un-bolted the door. A tall man of around fifty years of age with large brown eyes and a hooked nose stood on the doorstep. A younger chap stood behind him, with a trolley.

'Miss Jones, I presume?'

She nodded.

'We're sorry for your loss.'

Griselda held the door open, wide enough for the two men to manouvre their trolley into the hallway. She pointed out her mother's bedroom and remained by the front door. She couldn't look as they manoeuvred the body bag down the stairs. She turned her face to the wall as they lifted it onto the trolley, and closed the door behind them as they wheeled her mother out to their van.

The next morning, she woke with a start as the events of the previous night came flooding back. She lay on the sofa, fully clothed with the blanket over her feet and legs. Marmaduke had taken advantage of this unusual sleeping arrangement, and curled up beside her.

'Tell me it's all a bad dream, Marmaduke.'

But of course it wasn't and he didn't.

She rang the primary school where she worked part-time as a playground supervisor and explained she wouldn't be in for a few days. The head teacher was very understanding and told her to take all the time she needed.

She wondered if she should ring Simon, but she didn't want to disturb his preparations for the presentation. Instead, she decided to clean the house from top to bottom, not that it needed it, but it gave her something to keep her occupied.

Griselda pounced on the phone as it rang.

'Hi, guess what? We won the account.'

Her voice became strangled in her throat. She'd vowed this wouldn't happen.

'What's the matter?'

'It's Mother,' she managed, before she burst into tears.

'I'm on my way.'

He arrived within minutes. She fell into his arms. He held her gently, waited for her sobs to subside, placed his arm around her shoulder and led her back into the lounge. Sitting beside her on the sofa he held her hand.

'Tell me when you're ready.'

She stumbled through the sorry saga of how she'd discovered her mother, the doctor's visit and the awful indignity of her mother leaving her home for the last time.

'Why didn't you call me?'

'You needed to be at your best for today.'

'You're always putting others first. I should have been here for you.'

'Oh, Simon, I feel so guilty,' she sobbed.

He rubbed her neck and shoulders. 'Come on. You can't blame yourself. You've always done everything you could for her.'

'But I owed it to her.'

'We all think we owe our parents, but there's a limit.'

'No, you don't understand. I know I should have told you before now, but I had a baby. It nearly killed my mother, she never got over it.' She shook her head slowly. 'I was fifteen, and very foolish.'

'Aren't we all at that age?'

'Mother became ill – a bad cold that turned into pneumonia. At least it gave us an excuse to move to my grandmother's home in Norfolk, away from prying eyes.'

'So, what happened?'

'I wasn't even allowed to see my baby girl. She was placed for adoption. A month later we returned home, but mother never recovered her health. The pneumonia weakened her heart. She's been an invalid ever since.'

'Do you think about her – your daughter?'

'Every day. She was adopted at the time by a family in Hampshire. I wonder if she's still there, how she is and what she's like. She'll be eighteen in June.'

'Come on,' Simon got to his feet. 'We've got lots to do. Let's make a start.'

Simon stood by her side at the funeral, helped her to clear her mother's belongings and assisted with the mountain of paperwork. Griselda resigned from her job at the school. Her mother had left her enough money to live on for some time, as well as a mortgage free house. Besides, she wanted the space and freedom to be with Simon whenever she could. She hoped that he would pop the question now, but the weeks flew by with no proposal.

Using her key to let herself in, she walked into the hall and could hear Simon talking on the telephone. She opened the office door gently, not wishing to disturb him, but simply to wave and let him know she'd arrived.

He jumped and turned to face her. His face flushed as he spoke hurriedly into his mobile.

'Got to go, I'll ring again to confirm, bye.' He slipped his phone into the back pocket of his jeans. 'Griselda, darling, you're early.'

'It's six o'clock.'

'Is it?' He glanced at his watch. 'Sorry. Busy afternoon, I lost track of time.'

He followed her into the kitchen and poured them both a glass of wine while she emptied the shopping into the fridge and organised the ingredients for their pasta dinner.

'Who was that on the phone?' she tried to keep the suspicion from her voice.

'A potential client.' He flopped down on one of the bar stools and watched her as she peeled and chopped an onion. 'He wants me to go and see him. I thought I'd take up Dave's offer of his holiday cottage for a couple of days. It's pretty close to where this guy lives.'

'Good idea. I'll get Lucy to feed Marmaduke and come with you.'

'No need,' he said hastily.

A bit too hastily she thought.

'You'll be bored. I'll be totally immersed in this bid and there's nothing going on down there. No shops, no nothing. It'll only be for the one night.'

'OK. I'll ring you in the evening, see how it's going.'

'No reception, according to Dave, so I'll be incommunicado, but I'll ring you from a call box if I get the chance.'

Don't nag, she told herself. 'No worries, it'll give me the chance to finish decorating Mother's room. I want to rent it out. I could do with the income.'

Tears stung Griselda's eyes as Simon dropped her back home the next morning and kissed her goodbye. He waved as he drove down the road and disappeared from view.

Marmaduke rubbed against her legs, purring loudly.

'Let's go and get some breakfast, shall we?'

She had a thumping head. The smell of fresh paint didn't help, nor her lack of sleep. She'd lain awake for most of the night wondering if she was about to lose Simon. She made some toast and took a bite, but the lump in her throat threatened to choke her and she ended up throwing the rest in the bin. She picked up the cat, burying her face in his soft fur.

'Oh, Marmaduke, it's no good, I have to know.'

She packed a small sports bag with a change of clothes and set off for Simon's house, let herself in with her keys and de-activated the alarm. Moving into the kitchen she saw the postcard from Dave pinned to the message board. Her hands trembled as she took it down. The picture showed the village green, duck pond, church and a row of pale pink thatched cottages. She turned it over to see the name of the village – Meonsworth. Of course. Now she remembered.

It took her two hours to drive to the village and park on the road beside the green. The village pond was home to a flock of white ducks. Two young mums and their toddlers fed them. They all laughed as one of the birds pecked another's tail, creating a frenzy of splashes and quacks. Daffodils and crocuses grew in clumps under the weeping willow trees that fringed one end of the pond. From where she had parked, she could see along the row of pink thatched cottages and the unusual thatched church.

She had no idea which cottage Simon was staying in, although she could see his car parked on the far side of the pond. She glanced at her mobile, 1:00 p.m. And three bars of signal. Simon had clearly lied. Why would he do that unless—?

The front door of the centre cottage opened and a young woman stepped onto the street, closely followed by Simon. Griselda gasped as the young woman linked her arm through Simon's and they sauntered towards the pub. Her chest ached as she saw Simon laugh at something the girl said. Griselda watched through her tears as they climbed the steps and entered the pub.

Marmaduke purred as she walked through the front door, shrugged off her coat, kicked off her shoes and threw herself onto the sofa. How could he treat her like this? Just when they were free to be together, he'd lost interest. Why would he chase after a girl young enough to be his daughter?

Marmaduke jumped up beside her and nuzzled his head under her chin. She stroked him and his purring grew stronger as he pummelled her belly, turned around several times, flumped down and licked her fingers.

'At least someone loves me.'

That night and the next day were a nightmare; every piece of music, TV programme, each book she picked up to read — they all reminded her of Simon. She dreaded his return. He'd told her he planned to be back at about six, but had his visit changed everything?

He rang at half-past six. 'I wondered if you could come around. I have something I want to talk to you about.'

'Can't you come here?'

'I'd rather you came here, if that's all right.'

'OK.' She paused. 'I'll be about an hour.'

She dashed off to take a shower, dry her hair, and carefully apply her make-up. She wasn't going to make this easy for him.

Simon opened the door before she could use her key, threw his arms around her and kissed her passionately.

'Come into the lounge. I've opened some wine.'

This demonstration of affection was the last thing she'd been expecting.

He handed her a glass of wine.

'Here's to us.'

'Is there an, us? I thought you were about to tell me it was over.'

'You're joking!'

'I don't understand? I thought you'd met someone else.'

'Well, in a way, but not how you mean. Remember when you caught me being a bit secretive on the phone. I was talking to the private detective I'd employed. He's tracked down someone I hope you'll want to meet.'

'Who?'

'Your daughter. Soon to be our daughter, I hope.'

'My daughter!' Griselda sank into the armchair. 'But how...?'

'We knew she went to live in Hampshire and that she turned eighteen in June. Apparently, the electoral records show the birthday of anyone coming of age in the current year. It's to demonstrate their eligibility to vote from that date. He discovered that she lived with her adoptive parents in Meonsworth, which is why I went down there to meet her. She's always wanted to trace you.'

'This is such a shock.'

'Nice shock?' Simon watched her with a pensive expression. 'I hoped you'd be pleased. She's waiting to hear from you. Do you want to meet her?'

Griselda burst into tears and threw herself into his arms. 'Yes please.'

'I also want to ask you…' He dropped onto his knee, reached into his trouser pocket and held up a small box. 'Will you marry me?' He opened the box to reveal a diamond solitaire ring.

Her mouth fell open in surprise.

'Can I have an answer? My knees aren't as young as they used to be.'

And for the second time that day, she said yes.

There was a ripple of applause.

'Well done Cynthia. Clever twist,' Bailey said.

'A triumph, my dear,' Barbara said.

Cynthia could feel the heat rise in her cheeks. A triumph? Barbara, of all people, thought it a triumph? She floated back to the sofa and sat beside David.

'I told you not to worry,' he said. 'Excellent. Quite moving.'

'Oh, thank you so much.'

'It reminded me of that song,' March said.

'Song?'

'You know the one: *She knows her mind all right your Aunty Grizelda*. As a teenager I adored the Monkees.'

'And I thought you were a classy lady.' Miller tutted at March. 'A manufactured boy band with no talent.'

'That describes most of the bands on talent shows today. Nothing changes,' James said. 'Oh look, Bailey's getting her knickers in a twist about us getting a move on.'

Cynthia gathered her things together, reluctant to leave the scene of her moment in the spotlight. David offered her his arm and she allowed herself to be led out into the night.

20. Day Nine – Puffing Billy

It had rained earlier. Cynthia loved that after-the-rain smell, that sweet, fresh aroma that promises new life. She also adored its name. *Petrichor.* A Greek word, which roughly translates as: *fluid from the veins of Gods flowing onto stone.* How romantic. Although perhaps not quite so romantic once you discovered it's created by the chemical reaction of bacteria in the soil.

Now, last night, *that* was truly romantic. The tram journey through the town had been magical. The coach interior dazzled with its mirrors, polished wood and candelabras. The food – especially the fillet steak – was divine and David had been the perfect host. Oh, what an evening. She'd gone to sleep dreaming of sharing her autumn years with him, living in a small bungalow by the sea, enjoying cosy chats on the veranda as they gazed out to sea, before spending a relaxed evening beside a log fire.

Her childish dreams had been dashed that morning. She'd looked out for him, hoping he'd sit beside her on the bus, but he never showed. According to Bailey, he had an appointment in town with an old university friend and wouldn't be joining the tour.

The steam train whistled and chugged slowly out of the station. The wooden bench seating was hard and uncomfortable, but the view through the gum trees was spectacular. Ragged tendrils of bark hung down like half stripped wallpaper and glistened from the recent downpour. Underneath the canopy of trees, the forest floor was covered with ferns and moss.

She stood to take a photograph from the side window. From her position in the fifth carriage, the engine, *Puffing Billy*, was clearly visible as it turned a right-handed bend and passed over a precarious-looking wooden bridge. In the first two coaches, youngsters sat on the window sills with their legs hanging over the sides, kicking, laughing, and enjoying the exhilaration of the drop below them. Oh, what fun! She suddenly felt her age. Her wrists ached from the cold and damp. Her knee still hurt from her climb into the train carriage. She hadn't thought about getting old before she retired. She was too busy. But now, the thought of the years passing by, the aches and pains, the loneliness – was this all she had left to look forward to?

She looked through the connecting door and into the next coach. Barbara sat chatting to Angie. How could Angie look so fresh? Last night Miller and Bailey had practically carried her back to the hotel. Barbara, as ever, looked smart in her cream trouser suit. The pink scarf around her neck exactly matched the pink ribbon on her sun hat. She always looked so confident, and you could just tell that everyone instantly liked and admired her. Why couldn't Cynthia be more like her?

When the train drew to a halt, she clambered down onto the platform and watched as Barbara reached the carriage doorway.

One of the volunteer porters rushed to her side. 'Would you like a hand, my dear?'

Barbara smiled, reached to take his hand and stepped elegantly onto the platform.

'Thank you so much. Come on, Angie dear. Let's see if we

can find ourselves a decent cup of tea. Bailey says we have half an hour before the bus gets here.'

Cynthia realised this was her time to grasp the initiative. She stepped forward. 'Good morning, Ladies. I don't know if you had anywhere in mind, but I was recommended *Ye Oldie Tea Shop* across the road.' She pointed towards a thatched bungalow with leaded glass windows. 'It looks like the setting for an Agatha Christie novel, don't you think?'

'Oh, yes. It looks fascinating, my dear,' Barbara smiled at her.

Cynthia hesitated, wondering if they would ask her to join them. Then something inside her clicked. She forced her shoulders straight and smiled with a confidence she didn't feel.

'Would you like to join me?' she asked, half-dreading their response.

'Oh, my dear, that would be lovely. Wouldn't it, Angie?'

'Divine.'

They'd said yes. It had been so easy. Why hadn't she tried that before? She led the way towards the platform gate, her head held high.

21. Second Evening in Melbourne

Dry Martini:

- *40ml Gin*
- *20ml Vermouth*

    Shake ingredients together and strain into martini glass. Serve with a small twist of lemon and an olive on a cocktail stick.

March entered the lounge. Bailey must have been watching out for her, because she came rushing over to her side.

'Ah, there you are, March. Everything all right for your story tonight?' Bailey asked.

'Fine. Although… it could be controversial.'

Bailey smiled. 'Aren't they all?'

March Hunt's Tale

Damien Rajit lay in his bed. If only his wife was with him, he might forget his tiredness. He looked around. Paint peeled from the window frame. The metal grid, installed to prevent intruders, was speckled with rust. The walls sprouted with green and black mould and the carpet, once cream, was patched with sticky filth. The stain at the side of the bed resembled a map; if he concentrated carefully, he could make believe it was an image of Malaysia and not the result of the previous inhabitant's pool of vomit.

Living above the restaurant helped him to save money, but he could never get the smell of cooking out of his hair. No matter how often he showered in the tepid, trickle of water, laughingly referred to by his employer as a power shower, he could still smell the spices and grease.

January, had told him he'd only charge a low rent and that he'd pay four times more anywhere else. However, he'd failed to mention that Damien would be required to open up at 7:00 a.m. each morning and take deliveries from suppliers trying to beat the loading restrictions. He'd also omitted to mention that, after the last orders had been taken and January had emptied the till, Damien would be expected to serve the final customers, polish and set the tables ready for the next day, mop the restaurant floor, clean the kitchen and lock up. He rarely got five hours sleep before deliveries were due again the next morning.

He took out his wife's photograph – he always carried in his wallet. It may be curling at the edges and the colours were fading, but the memory of their wedding day would never fade. She smiled at him from the doorway of her parent's hovel, a one-roomed shack built on stilts, fashioned from woven reeds and thatched with straw. It had been taken a year ago on the morning after their wedding. Her parents had stayed with her uncle to give the couple some privacy. His heart raced as he remembered that evening.

He'd travelled from Kuala Lumpur to England the next day to take up his post as chef in January's restaurant. At the time, he was convinced that their separation would only last a few weeks while they applied for her visa. But then the rules changed. Either he needed to be earning three times his current wages or he needed an impossible amount in savings before a visa would be granted. They were trapped.

He had enough money saved for her air ticket. Or he could use the money to return home, but where would that leave them? They'd have no work, and nowhere to live. They needed to find a way to be together here in the UK. He placed the photograph carefully in his wallet, took two of his sleeping tablets and drifted off to sleep dreaming of his wife.

January stood in front of his restaurant; his heart swelled with pride as he admired the new sign. He especially liked the gold writing against the burgundy background –January's Authentic Malaysian Cuisine. Proprietor: January Bin Ah Fatt. Classy.

He didn't care if his customers laughed at him behind his back – Fatt by name and fat by nature - he'd done well since arriving penniless in Manchester forty years before. OK, so he may be a bit overweight, but he loved the food of his home country, and so did they. That's what made the restaurant such a success. Occasionally he would get the odd grumble from a customer, complaints about the quality of the food, but usually they were fishing for a discount.

They also made jokes about him being single, even questioned his manhood, but who cared. Even in his younger days, women had never appeared that interested in him and why should he spend money on dating a woman when he could pay by the hour for a tart to service his needs. Not that he bothered much these days, his libido had diminished as his girth expanded. Give him food any day.

He walked inside and looked around. The marble-tiled floor shone. The wooden bar and tables were polished to perfection and smelt strongly of beeswax. He never used tablecloths. No point. Cotton needed laundering and paper ones were expensive; they simply eroded his profit margin. Each table was laid with cutlery, burgundy paper napkins and a small vase of plastic flowers. He sighed with approval, checked the answer-phone and made a note in the diary.

Damian stood in the kitchen preparing onions, tears streamed down his cheeks, but it wasn't the onions, well not entirely. Today his wife celebrated her thirtieth birthday and he couldn't share it with her.

January walked into the kitchen. 'Hi, Damien. Those onions must be fierce.'

Damien brushed the tears away with the back of his hand.

'Looks like we could be busy tonight,' January continued. 'I've just taken a reservation for a table of eight, we already had four tables booked and then there's the passing trade. Perhaps we should give Pete a ring and see if he's free, we could do with an extra pair of hands.'

Damien nodded. 'Yes boss'.

'It's on days like this that I need a wife – a bit of help in the restaurant, someone to keep my house clean and do my laundry.'

'You could hire help,' Damien suggested.

'Why pay for help when it could come free. I'm surprised I haven't thought of it before. I'll be sixty next month. I'm not bothered about the sex anymore, but I could save a fortune on cleaners and laundry bills.'

Damien suddenly realised that this could be his opportunity. 'Wife is very good idea, but you need Malaysian wife. Good housewife, obedient, and very beautiful.'

'Mm, perhaps your right. I'll get onto the internet and check out these mail order brides I've heard about.'

'I could help. I have big family back home. Perhaps one of my cousins would be happy to live in UK?'

'Thanks, I appreciate that. Better the family you know, eh?'

The next afternoon, Damien watched in disgust as January entered the kitchen and yanked his trousers up over his obese belly. Was he really doing the right thing? Too late for doubts.

'Boss, I consulted my family and my cousin is looking for a husband.'

'Have you a photograph?'

'I thought you wanted help – does it matter how she look?'

'Good looks go down well with the customers. They'll tip more.'

'Tips?'

January frowned. 'They go towards the overheads. Photograph?'

Damien fished in his wallet and pulled out a picture.

'She is very beautiful.' January rubbed his chin thoughtfully. 'Will she be put off by my advanced years?'

'She is looking favourably at a more mature husband.'

'Shall I write to her, invite her over, or what?'

'She would be happy to visit if you are prepared to offer

accommodation in a hotel and pay for the air fare. Should I make the arrangements?'

'Where will she stay?'

'The hotel overlooking the park is a reasonable price. Shall I make enquiries?'

Two weeks later, Damien stood in the arrival hall at Manchester Airport. He waved as he spotted May pushing her suitcase through the swing doors. He ran towards her and threw his arms around her.

'May, my precious, my darling wife. I can't believe you're here.'

'Damien, I've missed you so much, but I'm worried about your plan.'

'I'll explain it all later, but not here. Let's get to your hotel.'

'Is January going to be there?'

'Not until this evening. I told him you were arriving on a later flight. We have several hours alone together.'

Damien and May spent the next few hours recapturing the joys of their wedding night. Eventually, satiated, their thoughts returned to Damien's daring idea to bring May to England.

'But what do I do if he…' May blushed. 'You know… if he wants—'

'To have sex? Don't worry. He's not interested in that side of things. He just wants an unpaid servant. It's a small price to pay if it means we can spend time together.'

'Come on. We'd better be ready.' He kissed her gently. 'Well, perhaps another half hour won't hurt.'

January arrived in the reception of May's hotel and spotted Damien chatting to a beautiful young woman. They sat in the corner drinking tea.

Damien stood to greet him.

'January, I am proud to introduce you to my cousin, May Musa. She is very shy and speaks very little English, but she wants you to know how grateful she is that you consider her for your wife.'

January smiled at the young woman. She was even more stunning than her photograph.

'I'm afraid, after forty years of speaking only English, my Malay is very poor, but I'm sure Damien won't mind acting as interpreter. Would you like to visit my home? I want to be sure that you'd be happy taking it on.'

'I like, thank you,' she smiled.

'After that I'll show you the restaurant. I've asked Pete and his daughter to come in this afternoon to help you, Damien. I've also asked Pete's daughter to stay on to waitress tonight so that I can spend the time with May.'

January thought the evening a tremendous success. Damien had prepared a special meal – Chili Pan Mee. May appeared to like the house and the restaurant, and seemed to understand that she would work in both. Of course, her stunning good looks were a bonus. He experienced an unexpected stirring of his nether regions, which had not happened in a long time.

It was agreed that the following morning Damien would collect May from the hotel and take her to January's house for a late breakfast and discussions about the possible wedding. January offered to walk May back to her hotel, but Damien insisted that, as her chaperone, he would make sure she got back safely.

Damien clung to May's arm as he walked her slowly towards January's house. They had spent the night at the hotel together and were reluctant to end their time alone. The night had convinced them both that they would do anything to prevent May having to return to Malaysia.

January met them at the front door before they had a chance to ring his doorbell. 'Come in, do come in. Please, go through to the lounge, I'll bring tea.'

Damien reached over and patted May's hand. 'You're sure?'

She nodded.

January returned carrying a tray loaded with three mugs, a sugar bowl, pastries, butter and jam. 'Sorry, I don't appear to have any cups. Please help yourselves.'

Damien cleared his throat. 'My cousin is very impressed with you, your home and your restaurant. She wants me to tell you that she would be very proud to become your wife.'

January picked up a croissant and smothered it, first with butter and then jam. 'How soon can this take place?'

'If you are happy, May will stay at her hotel until the wedding. You can see her, but I will need to act as chaperone. You must have an agent to complete all the formalities in Malaysia. I can recommend someone – he is a cousin of mine and familiar with all the necessary paperwork. It will take about ten days to organise everything. We are sorry to ask, but neither of us have any savings and May will need some funds for her wedding dress and some warm clothes suitable for England.'

'I'll get you a couple of hundred. What about the ceremony?'

'The hotel is licensed to organise the ceremony, and the wedding reception could be held in their restaurant.'

'We'll celebrate in my restaurant. I'm not wasting money.'

January stood nervously beside Pete, his part-time member of staff and best man. He didn't have anyone else he could class as a best friend; in fact, he didn't have any friends.

The music began to play and January turned to watch his bride walking towards him, clutching Damien's arm. She looked radiant in a cream lace dress. January could not believe his good fortune, thanks to Damien. He would reward him with a pay rise. Or even better, a one-off bonus – a small one.

Formalities over, the small group walked to the restaurant and enjoyed a lavish meal; lamb biryani, a chicken dish called ayam masak merah, vegetable dhal and curried prawns, followed by a selection of sweet dishes, all washed down with champagne.

January enjoyed the champagne, but was eager to get May back home. The now familiar stirrings were back whenever he looked at her.

'Damien, I'm leaving you in charge here. It's time to get my bride home and claim my conjugal rights.'

Damien's eyes widened. But... but I thought you had no interest in sex.'

'I didn't. But, thanks to you, I appear to have banished my impotence.'

'I must speak with May before you leave.' Damien rushed over to where she sat. 'May, January has had a change of heart. He's planning a traditional wedding night.'

'But, Damien, you promised–'

'Shush, we don't have much time. Go along with it. Tell him you want to share some more champagne, and then slip three of these sleeping tablets into his drink. He'll be knocked out and he won't remember a thing. Then come back to the restaurant and we'll plan what to do next.

May emerged from the bathroom looking nervous, but radiant in a cream nightdress of silk, edged with lace. January patted the bed to encourage her to take her place beside him.

'You are so beautiful, and I am such a lucky man.'

He reached over to pull her close but she evaded him and poured him a glass of champagne.

'Cheers, my husband.'

January awoke the next morning to a throbbing headache. He remembered nothing since finishing the glass of champagne. Surely, he hadn't passed out and failed in his matrimonial duties? He looked up as May walked into the bedroom carrying a tray with coffee and toast.

'Husband, I bring breakfast to recover strength after night of love.'

He breathed a sigh of relief; everything was as it should be, except for the fact that he could remember none of it.

'I will be recovered by tonight, my angel.'

'My husband, in my country we believe a woman should rest after wedding night, to cultivate seed and make baby. Do not worry, I will stay in my room, very comfortable.'

January felt a pang of disappointment. He had hoped to enjoy an evening that he could remember, but he didn't want start an argument so early in his marriage. He sighed. He'd simply have to wait.

Three weeks later May came looking for him in his study.

'Good news, my husband, we are with child.'

'That is good news. Will you be moving back into my bedroom now?'

'Oh no – too dangerous. We must wait.'

'Where are you going?'

'I take walk in park. Good for baby.'

January watched her leave. So far married life had cost him a lot of money, in return for a night he couldn't remember and a wife that continued to reject his sexual advances.

He worked on his account books until ten, and then decided to deliver them to his book-keeper who lived two streets away. Afterwards he planned to cut through the park, find May and invite her to walk back to the restaurant with him for a coffee.

He looked around the park. The scent of roses wafted over him, but he was the only one enjoying them this morning. In the play area a young mother pushed her young son on the swing while her younger child slept peacefully in the push chair. The bowling green was devoid of players, or anyone. Where could she be?

He decided to call in at his restaurant. May would surely be there, chatting to her cousin about the baby news.

He found the front door locked. Surprised, he rang the doorbell and waited on the doorstep for a couple of minutes before Damien arrived looking somewhat flustered.

'Sorry boss, I lock door for safety while I'm out back with deliveries.'

'Good man, you can never be too careful. Have you seen May?'

'She came to tell me about the baby.'

'It's good news, don't you think?'

'You must be a very proud man.'

Was he proud? He'd never really counted on becoming a father at his age. He was certainly frustrated. After years of not thinking about sex, he now did nothing but think about it. How long could this, no sex for the baby's sake last?

Two days later January walked into the kitchen. He stopped in his tracks, transfixed.

'What is the meaning of this?' he demanded.

Damien and May sprang apart.

'Sorry Boss, my cousin is upset. The baby makes her feel sick all the time. I consoled her.'

'I've heard of kissing cousins, but really? May, go home and wait for me.'

'But—'

'Get out!'

January watched her go and then turned back to Damien.

'This is how you reward me, after everything I've done for you? Pack your bags. I want you out.'

'Look, January, I'd better tell you. We were desperate to be together. You said you were only interested in a housewife. No sex. May isn't your wife, she's mine. We didn't plan a baby, but it isn't yours. The baby's mine.'

'You're telling me I spent all that money on a sham wedding?'

'I understand you're angry. I'm sorry. We didn't know what else to do. I'll come to collect May in an hour. We'll leave together.'

January snarled. Spittle ran down his copious chins. He lurched towards Damien and delivered a fierce uppercut. Damien fell back heavily against the kitchen door and slid to the floor. He didn't move.

January ran from the building, pounded down the pavement and, panting heavily, reached his home. He raced upstairs and barged into May's bedroom. She turned towards him, her face white and streaked with tears.

'You lousy tart. Come here.'

January snatched her arm, pulled her to her feet and pushed her backwards onto the bed.

She screamed. 'The baby, please, don't hurt the baby.'

He slapped her hard across the mouth. 'Quit that noise. Take me for a fool, trying to pass off another man's bastard as mine.'

He yanked at his belt, unzipped his flies and threw himself on top of her.

May couldn't breathe. She struggled to push January away, expecting any minute that his hands would rip at her clothing, but he didn't move.

'January, get off. January?'

He didn't answer. She heard someone running up the stairs.

'May, darling, where are you?'

Damien raced into the room and yanked at January's shoulders. January rolled off the bed and onto the floor – lifeless.

'Did he–'

'No, he must have passed out.'

Damien pressed his fingers into the side of January's neck. 'There's no pulse. I think he's had a heart attack.'

Twelve months later, Peter cut through the park on his way to the restaurant. He saw Damien, with May pushing the pram. He smiled. Damien couldn't have done more for May and that baby boy. He wouldn't be surprised if they didn't get married sometime soon. He understood they were only distant cousins.

The restaurant had gone from strength to strength under their shared management. The new staff, including Peter's daughter, worked reasonable hours, received decent pay and were paid a share of any tips. It made for a happy team. The customers enjoyed the improved quality of the menu, wrote good reviews and tipped well.

He felt sorry for January, dying so young, but he should have looked after himself better. An obese, sixty-year-old man with a beautiful young wife – a heart attack was always on the cards.

March smiled as the guests applauded. She looked around for James. He'd been sat behind her earlier, but now he stood at the bar chatting to the waitress – again.

Fyrne smiled and patted the spare seat next to hers. 'Have a drink.' She reached for the bottle of sparkling wine in an ice bucket. 'I thought you might need one, so I ordered us a bottle.'

March took the glass and glanced over to the bar. 'He didn't even stay long enough to hear the end of my story. Honestly, I could... oh, what's the point?'

'Don't let him get to you, or you'll need his services. He told me when we were first introduced that he's a doctor.'

'He's not a physician. He has a Doctorate in Business and Marketing.'

'Impressive.'

'Not really. Promise me you'll never say a word?'

Fyrne nodded and leaned closer.

'He bought it from some internet college in America. He filled in a questionnaire, sent them $4,000 and the certificate came in the post. Not that he ever stops bragging about it.'

'I suppose it's good for business?'

'Good for his ego more like. Oh look, I think they're calling us in for dinner.

22. Day Ten – Melbourne

Oh no. What did Mrs Nunne want this time? Bailey tried to assume a neutral face as Mrs Nunne arrived, quivering, beside the hospitality desk.

'Bailey, I need a room.'

'Is something wrong with your room?'

'My husband. I can't stand to be in the same room with him a moment longer.'

Bailey stopped herself from laughing. Mrs Nunne's scowl indicated that she meant every word; this wasn't some sort of horrible joke.

'Let's go and sit down in the corner. Would you like a cup of tea?'

Mrs Nunne stalked off in the direction Bailey indicated and slumped into the chair, her back to the room. Bailey scribbled a note for her guests – Back in fifteen minutes. She left it on the desk and hurried over to join Mrs Nunne.

'I don't want tea, or sympathy. I just want a room. A single room for the rest of the tour.'

'Well, I'll do my best, Mrs Nunne, but it may not be as simple as that.'

'What about the Brigadier's room? He won't need it now.' A single tear broke free and drizzled down Mrs Nunne's puffy cheek. She brushed it away with the back of her hand.

'What's brought all this on? I thought you two were close?' Bailey stopped herself from adding, *united by your spitefulness and misery.*

'He told me I'm a spiteful and miserable old woman.'

'That doesn't sound like him.'

'How would you know?'

'Mrs Nunne, I'm sure it must have been one of those... heat of the moment things.'

Mrs Nunne sniffed.

'Let me go and see what I can do. In the meantime, please, use my room.' Bailey scrambled for her keys. 'It's room 201. Make yourself at home. I may be a while, but I'll be with you as soon as I can.'

Mrs Nunne snatched the keys and bustled off in the direction of the lifts.

Bailey's temple throbbed as she rang Jim's direct line.

'Jim? Bailey here. I need authorisation for an extra single room. The Nunnes have had a falling out.'

'Their problem. They can sort it.'

'But, Jim, we're two rooms light on our original schedule. Surely, we can use one of those? We must have made some savings.'

'Savings! What about all the legal costs we need to sort out your mess?'

Bailey could hear the blood pumping in her ears, God, she actually hated this man.

'*My* mess?'

'You're the one that twisted the Managing Director round your little finger with that bloody kangaroo tour. Personal injury to a guest, theft, legal affairs, do I need to go on?'

'Forget it. I'll sort it myself.'

'You'd better. You won't find the new Managing Director as

easy to manipulate. He'll keep a close eye on everything you do, so you'd best make the most of what will undoubtedly be your last tour.'

The phone went dead.

She was clearly on her own with this one. She returned to the hospitality desk, sorted a few queries from her guests and then hurried over to the manager's office. He looked up as she walked in, put his sandwich down and brushed a few crumbs from his pot belly.

'Hello, Bailey. Hope things have settled down after yesterday's excitement?'

'I've got an issue with two guests. They've fallen out and want separate rooms.'

He clicked on his computer and scrutinised the screen. 'I have got a few rooms free, but none of the superior rooms your tour is booked into.'

'What about if I give her my room?'

He glanced back at the screen. 'I've got a small single you could have. I'll give you a staff discount, but it will still cost you $150 a night.'

'Hold it for now. I'll get back to you.'

Bailey studied her guest list and hurried up to the second floor. The door opened immediately.

'Oh Bailey, I thought you were…'

'She's in my room, Mr Nunne. I've come to see if there's anything I can do?'

'Can you make her come back? I know you must think she's a pain at times?'

'No, no, Mr Nunne, not at all.' Bailey inwardly cringed at her lie.

'You see, I love her. But she just made me so angry, going on and on about the Brigadier and how right she'd been about him. I told her to drop it, it had nothing to do with us, but she said she thought Barbara knew what had happened because she'd seen her talking to a policeman. She threatened to go and ask her about it.' Mr Nunne studied his fingernails. 'That's when I lost it. I said some unkind things I'm afraid.'

'We all do at times. I'm sure she still loves you.'

Mr Nunne snorted. He looked up, his eyes swimming with unshed tears. 'Last spring, I went into the garden to peg out some clothes. The path was slick, and I slipped over. I lay flat on my back in the flowerbed. She came running out from the house. I thought she was worried about me, but do you know what she said?'

Bailey shook her head.

'She said: "Get up, you're crushing my tulips".'

Bailey reached over and stroked his hand.

'I want her to come back. She's talking about going to live with our daughter when we get home. I can't live without her. Please help me.'

'I'll go and talk to her. I can't promise anything, but why don't you order her some sparkling wine and a bunch of flowers?'

Bailey left the room as Mr Nunne dutifully called room service.

She tapped on her own door.

'Come in.'

She walked in and flinched. Mrs Nunne lay on her bed watching the TV. She ate grapes from a fruit bowl that she balanced on her rounded stomach. Bailey might have told her to make herself comfortable, but really, this was taking it too far.

'Mrs Nunne. The Brigadier's room is no longer available I'm afraid. Are you sure you want a separate room?'

'Absolutely, Charles was horrid to me. I shall move in with my daughter when we get back to the UK. I don't suppose that husband of hers will be very happy, but they owe it to me.'

'Your son-in-law wouldn't be too keen? How would that make you feel?'

Mrs Nunne paused, and then placed the last few grapes back in the bowl. 'It could be a bit uncomfortable, now I come to think of it. He can be very sarcastic.'

'I suppose you could make the guest room comfortable, then you could stay out of his way if needs be.'

'Hmm, now you mention it, their spare room is very small. And the bed is dreadfully uncomfortable.'

'Perhaps more time in the garden? I know you enjoy your garden.'

'And that's another thing. They have no garden to speak of. And you're right, I do love my flowers.'

'Mrs Nunne, I've spoken to your husband, and—'

'You've no right to do that. How dare you?'

'Here's the thing. Your husband loves you very much. He's desperately unhappy about your decision to leave him. He told me he can't live without you.'

Mrs Nunne burst into tears. She put the fruit bowl onto the bed beside her, grabbed some paper hankies from the bedside table and buried her head in her hands. Bailey moved to her side and patted her shoulder.

'So why did he say those awful things about me?'

'We all say things in the heat of the moment. I can assure you, he's very sorry.'

'I'll just use your bathroom to freshen up and then I'd better go and see what the silly bugger's up to. Hopefully, he'll have learnt his lesson by now.'

Bailey could hear her running the taps, opening the bathroom cabinet, ferreting around her toiletries, invading her personal space. God, the woman didn't have a sensitive bone in her body. Bailey switched off the TV, straightened the bed, placed the virtually empty fruit bowl back on the bedside table, and turned on her lap-top. Mrs Nunne emerged a few minutes later, hair combed, makeup freshly applied and doused in Bailey's perfume.

'Good luck, Mrs Nunne. I hope it all goes well. See you this evening.'

She closed the door behind her. Another catastrophe averted. Now she could add marriage counselling to her list of achievements.

23. Last Evening in Melbourne

Daiquiri Cocktail

- *40ml Bacardi*
- *10ml fresh lime juice*
- *8ml sugar syrup*

   Shake ingredients together and strain into martini glass. Serve with a wedge of lime.

Frank wasn't expecting to be nervous about telling his story, but that annoying heartburn was back. He picked up his cocktail and swallowed a couple of antacid tablets, followed by a swig of Daiquiri. Mm, that tasted good, not too sweet. Perhaps lime would become his new coke. He looked up as Paul walked into the room.

'Paul, I wondered where you were.'

'We don't need to be tied at the hip, do we?'

'I worried you might miss my story.'

'The times I've heard you practise, I could tell it myself.'

'Sorry. By the way, don't forget we have to pack tonight.'

'Quit nagging.'

'OK, I was only saying. Oh look, here come Tony and Maddy. Hello there, I see you had company today.'

Tony smiled. 'My son, Oscar. We've never met. His mother

moved back to Australia before his birth.'

'Goodness. You must have some catching up to do.'

'Only brushed the surface, but he's promised to visit the UK when he finishes university next June. I'll try to persuade him to do his Masters in the UK. That way we could really get to know each other.'

'I'll keep my fingers crossed. It's hard when you lose touch with your children.'

'Thanks, and good luck with your story tonight.'

Maddy picked up her cocktail and clinked her glass against Tony's. 'Cheers.'

'That went well, don't you think?' he asked, an anxious frown creased his brow.

'Very.' She smiled. 'I knew you were nervous.'

'I kept thinking he'd change his mind.'

'You must be proud Oscar's doing so well?'

'I hope he does come to visit us next summer.'

Maddy had been about to sip her cocktail, but paused. 'Us?'

He blinked, as though unaware he'd said it. 'Yes, that's what I'd like to happen.' He lifted her hand and kissed her fingertips. 'You do know I've fallen for you, don't you?'

There, at last, he'd said it.

'I feel the same.' She'd known for several days, but she wasn't going to say it first.

Tony leaned towards her and kissed her gently. His lips tasted of lime juice. She wanted to suggest they skip dinner and go back to her room – or his – but she didn't want to appear too eager.

He frowned. 'You know we'll need to make a few decisions. For example, *where* will we live?'

'Well, I have my home, and I do have a job to go back to in a few months, but I'm not sure how you'd feel about returning to Birmingham?'

'There's another option. I told you Dad died last year.'

Maddy reached for his hand. 'That must have been so hard for you, especially so soon after losing Archie and Emily.'

'He always wanted me to take over the family business… it's a farm and some woodland, about 20,000 acres.'

Maddy gasped. 'That's enormous.'

'I've dabbled a bit, but basically, it's been looked after by an estate manager. He's retiring this year so Mum's asked me to decide if I want to take over the ancestral home or if it should be sold.'

'Where is it?'

'Back of beyond and infested with midges, but it has a certain charm.'

'Scotland?'

'Not far from Inverness. You don't need to say anything now. We'll visit when we get back.'

'Remind me to pack my jungle strength beastie repellent.' Maddy leaned over and kissed him on the cheek. 'That was a nice gesture, giving Oscar your father's signet ring.'

'Dad gave it to me just before he died. I wanted Oscar to know he's important to me, even if I've been absent from his life so far.'

She settled back on the sofa, enveloped by a warm tingle. Tony talked as though they had a future. That was all that mattered. To be honest she didn't care where they lived, so long as they were together.

Frank took his place at the front of the group, and mopped

his forehead with his handkerchief. Maddy hadn't thought it was that warm tonight. Nervous perhaps?

'My story is not true.' Frank pushed his damp hankie into his pocket. 'But it is based on true geographical events that happen in two of my favourite vacation spots. The first is a small Caribbean island and the other is a magical place in Tragoess, a small village in Austria.'

Frank Lynne's Tale

Aurelius watched the young woman as she stood, motionless, staring out to sea. The wind caught her long blonde hair. Tendrils fell across her face. She reached up and tucked the errant strands behind her ear, revealing a classic nose and perfect cheekbones. He moved closer, until she sensed his presence and turned to face him. Her beauty took his breath away.

'You must be our new neighbour, the magician?' She smiled.

'Illusionist.' He wanted to charm her with his wit and make her laugh, but for once he was lost for words.

'I've seen you on the TV. How did you make that elephant disappear? Incredible.'

'Thanks.' He was usually so quick on chat up lines, but now his behaviour resembled an adolescent schoolboy – struck dumb.

'I'm Dorien.' She held out her hand. He could smell her delicate perfume.

'Aurelius.' Her touch sent a shiver down his spine.

He raised her hand to his lips and brushed her fingers with a light kiss. She gently, but firmly, removed her hand.

'You're my husband's favourite illusionist.'

She'd emphasised her marital status, darn it. On the other hand, he'd never allowed a partner to cramp his style before.

'In fact, you're the only one he'll watch. Gyles will be interested to find you're staying on the island.'

'He's here?' Darn and double darn! He'd hoped she was one of the proverbial lonely housewives that were always his happy hunting ground on the island.

'Tomorrow night, he's arriving on his new yacht. I offered to pick

him up from the marina, but he's determined to sail into the bay. So stubborn.' She shook her head. *'I should have sailed with him, but I hate boats. Silly really, I'm a good swimmer, but somehow they make me so nervous.'* She twisted her wedding band and returned her gaze to the sea. *'Just look at all those rocks. He's bound to be shipwrecked,'* she sighed. *'If he survives, it'll be a miracle.'*

'Perhaps I could help? You saw the elephant vanish? A few rocks are easy in comparison.'

'Really? She turned to face him; one eyebrow raised quizzically. *'If you make them disappear you can name your reward.'*

'You're on.'

'Gyles aims to arrive at high tide tomorrow, but look, the flow has stopped. This is the highest the water will get and that approach is impossible. No wonder there's a lighthouse.'

She pointed to the right-hand side of the cliff top, where a tall white building flashed its warning every thirty seconds.

'I promise to keep him safe. But remember…' Aurelius winked at her. *'I will claim my reward.'*

She returned her gaze to the ugly rocks protruding from the shallows like broken, blackened teeth.

'I'll see you tomorrow,' he said as he waved goodbye.

She appeared engrossed and failed to reply.

The next evening, her heart racing, Dorien arrived on the beach. The first thing she noticed was that Aurelius was already there. The second thing was that the rocks had disappeared.

'Goodness! How did you do that?' Dorien gasped as she reached his side. *'Where did they go?'*

'Tricks of the trade.' Aurelius tapped his nose. *'Look, I do believe that's your husband.'*

He pointed towards a yacht as it edged its way cautiously towards them. Dorien waved, and a tall figure in a white T-shirt and blue shorts waved back. Within minutes the yacht reached the beach, and the sail and anchor were lowered. Dorien rushed into the waves as her husband climbed down and raced through the shallow water towards her. He picked her up, kissed her, and carried her back to the beach.

'Oh, Gyles, I've been so worried. You should have seen the rocks here yesterday.'

Gyles kissed her forehead, placed her carefully on the sand and then turned towards Aurelius. 'I don't believe we've met, although you do look familiar.' *He reached out his hand.*'

Aurelius grasped his hand and shook it. 'I'm your new neighbour, Aurelius.'

'The magician?'

'Illusionist.'

'We have Aurelius to thank for your safe arrival. He made the rocks disappear.'

'And I thought the high spring tide did it,' *laughed Gyles.*

'What!'

'It's well recorded. If you wait for the high spring tides, align your mast with the lighthouse this bay becomes navigable. Excuse me, I must check the anchor.'

'You tricked me,' *Dorien glared at Aurelius.*

'An illusion. One of my best. Now, when can I claim my reward?'

Gyles returned to where they stood. 'Ready, darling? The boat will be fine – the twin keels will sit on the sandy floor when the tide goes out.' *He patted Aurelius on the shoulder,* 'Why don't you join us for dinner tomorrow evening? Do you play Poker?'

'Shall I bring wine?'

'Just loads of dosh. I'm feeling lucky. Come about seven.'

Dorien loaded the dishwasher while Gyles hand-washed the glasses.

'What's wrong?' Gyles asked. 'You've barely spoken a word since the card game.'

Dorien threw the soap tablet into the dispenser and slammed the door. The machine instantly began to whirl and swish.

'Aurelius, that's what's wrong. His final hand was rubbish. He forced you to surrender a huge pot of winnings.'

'That's the name of the game. I'll get my revenge next time.'

'But Gyles, he tricked you. You shouldn't let him get away with it.'

'I always honour a promise. It's something my father taught me.'

'Even if it's a scam?'

Gyles shrugged his shoulders.

'So, if I promised to repay someone for solving a problem and then found out it had been solved through deception, you'd still expect me to honour it?'

'If the problem is solved. A promise is a promise.' He hung the tea towel over the oven door. 'Let's go to bed, I seem to remember that you're on a promise tonight.'

She laughed as he chased her up the stairs.

Aurelius arrived on the beach three days later in time to see Dorien waving goodbye to Gyles as he sailed his yacht out to sea. Tears streamed down her cheeks.

'He's gone then?'

'He had to leave before he lost the spring tides, I won't see him again until he gets back from his business trip to France. I miss him terribly when he's away.'

'You love him very much.'

'He means everything to me.'

Aurelius picked up a small stone and skimmed it across the flat surface of the water. It bounced several times, leaving a row of expanding circles.

'Well, while he's away, I'm sure I don't need to remind you of your promise.'

'But you tricked me.'

'Even so.'

'What do you want?'

'You.'

'What?'

She turned to face him, her eyes widening.

'I want you. I can't remember ever wanting any woman so much.'

She realised he wasn't joking. 'But I'm married. Happily married.'

'A promise is a promise.'

Her heart sank. 'That's what Gyles says.'

She glared at him her eyes brimming with tears.' She kicked the sand, turned away from him and focussed on the yacht. It sailed close to the horizon and would disappear any moment. Disappear, as if by magic.

She experienced a noticeable quickening of her heart.

'OK, if you must. I'll meet you tomorrow. Do you know the park at the foot of the valley behind our house?'

'I visited it last autumn.'

'Did you see the bench under the apple tree?'

'A magical setting.'

'I'll meet you on the bench at six tomorrow evening. But if you're not there, the slate is clean. Agreed?'

'Agreed. But don't get your hopes up. Nothing will keep me away, although I did hope for a more comfortable location.'

She turned her back on Aurelius and walked away.

Aurelius glanced at his watch – ten to six. He quickened his pace. The mist swirled around him; the air damp and heavy – a bit like his mood. He'd hoped she'd see tonight as a bit of fun, but he'd seen the way she looked at Gyles. Never had he felt so torn over a potential liaison. It looked as though he would have to release her from her promise – shame.

He'd explored this area last autumn, when he first moved to the island. He'd discovered a small park with a gentle stream, spanned by a rickety wooden bridge. A pebble path led down to a wooden bench situated beneath an apple tree. He'd sat for some time, soaking up the peace and tranquillity.

The mist grew thicker, obscuring his view. As he descended, he could make out a few features, but the scenery looked completely different to his last visit. At last, he stumbled across the footpath that would take him to the footbridge and down to the bench where she'd be waiting. But no, he must be wrong. Through the mist, stretching from one side of the valley to the other, instead of the park he expected to see, there was a lake. Surely, he was in the right place. He looked around for features he recognised. This was definitely the beginning of the footpath, but it disappeared under the water.

As he stood trying to work things out, the water rippled. A dark shape broke the surface. Was it a fish? If so, it was a big fish for such a small lake. Gradually the shape moved towards him, and with a start he realised it was a diver wearing a wetsuit and snorkel.

'Where were you,' she asked, as she pushed back the hood of her

wet suit revealing her long blonde hair. A soft smile played across Dorien's lips.

'What's this?' he said as he waved his hand towards the lake.

'Meltwater. It happens every spring. The park floods, but because it happens so slowly, the water remains undisturbed. It creates this small lake with crystal clear water, giving the appearance of an aquarium. It's like flying as you swim over the bench, past the tree, and over the bridge. I discovered it last year.'

'You tricked me,' Aurelius smiled.

'Now at least we're even.'

Bailey smiled at Frank and began the applause.

Fyrne stood and clapped her hands together loudly. 'Well done, Frank.'

Bailey got to her feet. 'Yes, well done, Frank, an interesting tale. I must check out this Tragoess in Austria, it sounds amazing. I must also remember never to play cards with an illusionist.'

Everyone laughed. Well, almost everyone – not the Nunnes.

'OK everyone, I think we have a few minutes before dinner, so if I can remind you, our coach to the airport leaves from the front car park tomorrow morning at nine. Please don't be late. I can assure you, Cairns is a treat you will not want to miss.'

Bailey thought about Frank's story. The use of trickery and deception was an interesting change from earlier stories, but somehow it had left her feeling uncomfortable. Normally the illusion of the rocks being made to dissapear by magic would have enthralled her. She was still captivated by David Copperfield's illusion when he'd walked through the Great Wall of China. Dorien had been so easily deceived – although obviously she'd come up with a brilliant soution.

It was so easy. Hadn't she been deceived by Tyler? He'd sold her the dream, persuaded her to get married, leave Scotland and move to Australia. She was seventeen, madly in love and excited about starting a new, idylic life on the opposite side of the world. Without much thought, she'd abandoned her parents and friends. She'd fallen pregnant almost immediately, but quickly found her dreams turning to nightmares. Night after night, Tyler would spend long evenings in the pub. He left altogether shortly after Duncan's birth.

Of course, she could have gone home to Scotland and patch things up with her parents. She'd thought about it, but she couldn't face crawling back and admitting to such a crass error of judgement. And then it was too late. They'd both died in a car crash when Duncan was six months old. So she'd stayed in Australia. Her and Duncan against the world.

Her judgement hadn't even improved with age. She'd thought the Brigadier charming, a real Gentleman. Look where that had got her.

'Are you joining us for dinner tonight, Kate?'

Bailey looked up. Miller stood before her, his brow creased with a frown.

'You OK? You look a bit down.'

'Miles away, sorry.'

'Come on, we can't start without our host. The others have all gone through for dinner.'

She stood, allowed him to take her arm and escort her into the dining room.

24. Day Eleven – Cairns

Sex on the Beach

- *40ml Vodka*
- *20ml Peach Schnapps*
- *14ml Crème de Cassis*
- *50ml orange juice*
- *50ml cranberry juice*

   Shake ingredients together with ice cubes and pour into a chilled highball glass. Garnish with an orange slice and cherry.

Bailey spotted James and waved to attract his attention. 'OK for tonight?' she asked.

'Moi?'

She frowned. Surely, he wouldn't let her down?

'Your turn for a story.'

He winked. 'Don't worry, Bailey. I'm only teasing.'

She breathed a sigh of relief. She gave everyone a few more minutes to get their drinks and settle down, and then made her way to the front. 'I hope you all enjoyed our journey up to Cairns today.' There were murmurs of appreciation.

'Well tonight we have another treat for you. Our story teller,

Dr James Hunt. Thank you, James.'

James stood and turned to face the others.

'Hey, James,' said Sumner. 'I didn't know you were a doctor.'

He stood, rolled up his trouser leg and revealed a Mickey Mouse sock and hairy leg.

'Could you check out my gammy knee?'

Bailey smiled. Several guests chuckled. James and Sumner laughed.

James straightened his shoulders and puffed out his chest. 'As Dr of Business and Marketing I'd say your chances of earning any money from legs like that are zilch. I suggest you stay on your side of the camera.'

Bailey's smile widened as the guests laughed. This was a good start to the evening.

'And now for my story. It's based on a true story and raises some difficult issues:'

Dr James Hunt's Tale

Virgil is sitting in a small treatment room. You know the sort, we've all seen them. The walls are magnolia. There are no windows and no pictures to break up the stark walls. A small white porcelain sink in the corner and four chairs, covered in pale blue leatherette, are the only relief from the cream monotone. The room smells strongly of antiseptic and bacterial hand gel.

Virgil's wife, Mary, sits across from him, head bowed, refusing to meet his gaze. He has never seen her fall apart like this. Tears stream down her cheeks and drip from her chin. She makes no effort to wipe them away. He wants to reach out and put his arms around her, kiss the top of her head and tell her it'll be OK, but the anxiety is paralysing him. He can't move.

He clutches the hand of his daughter, Virginia. She sits motionless beside him, pale to the point of transparency, her lack of colour broken only by the dark blue smudges under her eyes.

None of them speak. No one knows what to say.

The door opens. Virgil leaps to his feet as a young man steps briskly into the room, wearing a white coat and clutching a pink folder.

'Please take a seat.' The doctor smiles and indicates the seat that Virgil has just vacated.

Virgil collapses back onto the chair and reaches again for his daughter's hand. He wonders why they couldn't send someone older to give them the results, someone who would understand, rather than this young whippersnapper who was clearly only just out of short trousers.

'I'm Doctor Claudius, Senior Consultant Haematologist. I'm

sorry, but it's not good news.' The doctor riffles through the folder. 'Our tests show that Virginia is suffering from acute myeloid leukaemia, an illness that is invariably fatal if not aggressively treated.'

Virgil can't breathe, it's as though somebody has kicked him in the stomach.

Mary gasps, throws her arms around Virginia and pulls her close. 'There must be something you can do to save her. She's such a good girl. Our only child. Please.' Mary's unchecked tears continue to flow. She stifles a sob.

'There is some better news. We have recently obtained very promising results by administering a new chemotherapy treatment, together with a series of blood transfusions. Virginia would have a forty; perhaps even fifty percent chance of a full recovery. I suggest we start the treatment immediately.'

'No.' Virgil is back on his feet. He places his hand on Virginia's shoulder and squeezes it gently.

'I don't understand? It's practically painless, and it can be totally successful.'

'We're Jehovah's Witnesses. The Bible and our faith prohibit us from taking blood.'

'I'm offering your daughter the possibility of life. This treatment will give us the chance to save her.'

'Please, Virgil, I beg you.'

'Mother, please don't cry.'

'For God's sake, man! Don't you realise, without a transfusion Virginia will die?'

'It's God's law. The Bible is very clear. "But flesh or meat with blood ye shall not eat." Genesis, Chapter 9, Verse 4. "No soul of you shall eat blood; whosoever eateth it shall be cut off." Leviticus, Chapter 17, Verses 12 to 14.'

'But that's about eating blood. I can understand that. Refrigeration didn't exist in Biblical times. Abstaining from eating undercooked meat was simply common sense. But this is the 21st Century.'

"That ye abstain from blood." Acts, Chapter 15, Verses 19 to 21. "Gentiles keep themselves from things offered to idols and from blood." Acts, Chapter 21, Verse 25.'

'Mr White, we save countless lives with blood transfusions. No one would have dreamt such a thing would be possible at the time the scriptures were written.' The doctor kneels beside Virginia and takes her hand. 'What do you think, Virginia?'

Her voice is soft but steady. She holds her body erect with her shoulders back and speaks directly to the doctor. 'If I violate God's law, I may live, but I will be shunned. It will damage my relationship with God. I will never experience an eternal life.'

'Well spoken, my darling child. I've never been prouder.'

'No, Virginia,' Mary says. 'You can't do this. I won't let you. Please, baby. For my sake as well as yours, please, say you'll try the treatment. I can't live without you.'

'Mary, stop this emotional blackmail. I won't allow it. Virginia has made her decision, and so have I.'

Doctor Claudius stands. 'I'll leave you to discuss things. Stay as long as you need, but let my nurse know when you're ready to leave. I'll come back to receive your final decision, but remember, without this treatment you are condemning Virginia to certain death. She could have her whole life before her. Please don't reject this chance she has.' He leaves the room.

'Please, Virgil, don't let her die. Give them a chance to save her,' Mary begs as she falls to her knees before him. She clutches his legs. 'I accepted your faith when we met. I loved you. I would

have accepted anything. I agreed to bring our child up in the truth, but I never thought it would mean losing her. Please, Virgil, the elders could be wrong.'

'Mary, I'm sorry, but I will not violate our religious beliefs and authorise this treatment. It goes against God's word.'

'What does that matter if Virginia lives?'

Silence descends. Virgil's thoughts run through the day Virginia was born. Such a tiny scrap of a thing, with the biggest blue eyes and a cute button nose; his heart had melted at first sight. He looks at her now. She returns his gaze, her eyes full of trust, for him and her beliefs. He looks at Mary, who glares back at him, her eyes full of hatred. Life will never be the same again.

Virgil leaves the room and approaches the nursing station.

'Could you please tell Dr Claudius we are ready to leave?'

'Of course, Sir. I'll fetch him immediately.'

She scurries off, while Virgil returns to the sterile and silent room.

Doctor Claudius steps into the room and looks at each of them in turn. 'You have reached a decision?'

Virgil nods. 'There will be no transfusions.'

'Then I am forced to inform you that I have applied to the courts for permission to treat your daughter. I have submitted my evidence and agreed to serve as a witness.'

'You can't do this!' Virginia screams. 'Daddy, tell them they can't do this. I won't let them.'

'I'm sorry, my dear, I really am, but you're twelve years old. You're still a minor. If your parents won't give their consent then I have no alternative but to have you taken into care and administer the treatment you need. A member of my staff is currently racing across town to the Judge's chambers to obtain a time and date for the hearing, hopefully tomorrow.'

Virgil slowly shakes his head. 'I will fight you on this,'

'That is your right. But I can assure you that Section 1(a) of the Children Act places the child's welfare as paramount. We have never lost an application.'

Judge Apius sits on his throne-like chair, dressed in his red and ermine gown and an uncomfortable-looking white wig, slightly askew. His black spectacles have slipped down his nose, which Virgil thinks give him a rather snooty appearance as he looks down at them. On one side of the court, Virgil, Mary, and their daughter Virginia sit with their barrister, Eliot Parry. On the other side, representing the hospital is John Allen QC, with Dr Claudius at his side.

Judge Apius opens the proceedings. 'I understand that time is of the essence in this case. I intend to hear what you all have to say this morning, and I will make my decision later this afternoon. Mr Allen, would you like to open for the applicant?'

'Thank you, my Lord. I would like to call Dr Claudius.'

Dr Claudius climbs into the witness box, picks up the Bible and takes the oath. He explains the illness that Virginia is suffering from and how her blood count has fallen to dangerous levels, making it impossible for them to use the chemotherapy drugs that could potentially save her life. He goes on to explain that the only treatment at this stage is a series of blood transfusions, followed by chemotherapy. Without the treatment, Virginia will become increasingly breathless, her organs will begin to shut down and she will suffer internal haemorrhaging – a painful death.

Mary moans quietly and rocks in her chair. Virgil glances at Virginia, who remains outwardly calm, holding his hand and staring at the judge.

Eliot Parry refuses the opportunity to question Dr Claudius. Virgil's feels sick as he takes the stand.

The usher asks Virgil to take the Bible in his hand. He refuses on the grounds that it isn't the New World Translation. There is a short delay, while the usher is sent to the adjacent court to hunt down a copy.

Virgil takes the oath and, in response to Eliot's gentle questioning, explains how he had been brought up in the truth by his parents, how his wife had entered the faith after they met and fell in love, and how Virginia has always been brought up as a faithful follower. He explains the passages in the Bible that forbid the taking of blood in any form, and how the elders maintain that blood is sacred and should not be taken in, which therefore excludes eating, drinking or transfusions. He confirms that Virginia is twelve years old, but insists that she is fully in agreement with the decision to refuse treatment.

Virginia nods emphatically at this point, so that the Judge is left in no doubt.

'And is your wife in agreement?' Judge Apius turns his attention to Mary. She nods.

A wave of relief washes over Virgil. He'd been convinced Mary would object and weaken their case. He smiles fondly at his wife before turning back to Judge Apius to reply.

'She is my Lord, although she finds the situation impossible. It's tearing her apart.'

Mr Allen declines his opportunity to ask questions, and Virgil is allowed to return to his seat.

'I will retire to my chambers now, and the court will resume at four this afternoon when I will give my ruling.' Judge Apius departs.

Virgil looks around the courtroom. There is no jury, but a couple of reporters are in the gallery, together with a dozen teenagers, probably law students. He holds onto Virginia's hand, casting a glance at her now and then to gauge how she is coping. She appears to be doing better than her mother, who has refused to enter the courtroom and has remained outside in the vaulted marble waiting hall.

Dr Claudius is chatting to John Allen. They looked confident. Dr Claudius leans closer and whispers in John's ear. Both men laugh.

Virgil can feel the rage churn his stomach. How dare they demonstrate such inappropriate behaviour?

'All rise.'

Everyone stands to attention as Judge Apius enters the room and takes his seat. He waits for them all to settle down before clearing his throat to speak.

'This has not been an easy decision. I have taken into account numerous precedent rulings, too numerous to go through in detail given the need for a quick decision, but they will all be included in my written judgement. I have decided that, although I respect the conscience of Mr and Mrs White, and indeed their daughter Virginia, this cannot override my duty to uphold the law. I have therefore signed the necessary paperwork, and authorise the hospital to undertake the required treatment.'

Virgil knew this would be the outcome, but it didn't stop his anger. How could this pompous judge make such decisions? This would be ruination for Virginia.

Judge Apius removes his glasses and turns towards Virgil and Virginia.

'Mr White, Virginia, I know this is not the outcome you hoped for, but I require you to respect my decision and report to the hospital at 9:00 a.m. tomorrow. Doctor Claudius, please do whatever

you can to prevent this young girl from dying needlessly.'

Virgil glares at Dr Claudius. At first, it looked as though Dr Claudius would approach him but, evidently thinking twice about it, he turns back to finish his conversation with John Allen. Virgil steers Virginia out of the courtroom and over in the direction of her mother, who remains seated with her head in her hands.

'The Judge found for the hospital. We have to attend at nine tomorrow morning for Virginia's treatment. I suppose you'll be happy now.'

'Happy? How can you say such a thing? I can't imagine being happy ever again. But at least this way I may still have a daughter this time next year.'

She stands and embraces her daughter.

'I'm sorry if you think me selfish, darling,' Mary's voice brakes. 'But this decision is such a relief. It's over now, out of our hands.'

Virginia tugged on her father's sleeve. 'We could run away and hide.'

Virgil glanced across to Mary. 'We could defy them. Virginia could die peacefully and be assured eternal life, and so would we.'

'No Virgil, they would arrest you for contempt of court. If Virginia were to die, you would be charged with manslaughter. It's over. The court has ruled. If you won't bring her tomorrow morning, then I will.'

The next morning Virgil was ready at eight o'clock. He had spent most of the night in prayer and reading his Bible. His decision made, he placed a sealed envelope on his computer as he left his office and descended the stairs to join his wife and daughter.

Mary checked her watch. 'It's early, are you sure we want to leave now?'

'I want to drive the scenic route, along the cliff road. We had such happy times there, taking our picnic to the car park, looking out over the sea and eating ice-cream. Do you remember how we used to watch the sailing boats?'

Virgil drove past the docks, around the point and into the car park, packed with memories, but this morning mercifully empty of vehicles. He drove to the far side of the car park, from where they could view the rocks fifty feet below. Waves crashed, seagulls screeched, and the engine ticked over. A single magpie landed on the flimsy wooden fence in front of them. His black feathers glinted blue and green in the early morning sunlight.

Virgil revved the engine and put the car into gear. I know God will never forgive me, but I hope you understand that I'm doing this because I love you both so much.'

'Virgil, what do you mean? What are you doing?'

'Goodbye, my dears.'

He pressed the accelerator to the floor and drove over the cliff edge. The car hit the rocks with a sickening crunch, bounced, and landed on its roof, wheels spinning. A tiny flame licked the front bumper, and then, boom! The car was engulfed in flames and stinking black smoke. No one could survive such a fall.

No one did.

Two hours later, the court officials entered Virgil's house and found the letter:

To the Coroner

Dear Sir, I have been blessed with the most wonderful wife and daughter. They have made me the happiest and proudest man alive. Nobody could ever hope for such a family. I love them both more than life itself. I have therefore decided that I cannot stand back and watch my daughter deprived of her eternal life. Nor can I watch my wife being torn apart by her beliefs, or the loss of our daughter. I know that by taking this course of action I condemn myself to Hell. It is a sacrifice I am prepared to pay.'

Sumner recovered first. 'He took his own life. Isn't that a sin?'

James turned to face him. 'Indeed it is, as is murder, which let's face it is what he did.

'But he loved them both more than life itself.' Fyrne said. 'That's the point isn't it? He sacrificed himself to ensure they would enjoy eternal life.

'I've found that most parents would sacrifice anything to save their children from disaster,' Frank said, 'but that has to be the most extreme. What do you think, David? You must have experienced this in your line of work?'

David leaned forward and ran his finger around the edge of his clerical collar. He cleared his throat. 'I believe that the Jehovah Witness's position is what I would call one of an erroneous conscience. They believe something that is, in my opinion, mistaken. As your story suggested, James, science has progressed to a level where many lives are now saved, in ways never envisioned at the time of Our Lord Jesus Christ. I believe that, if a minor is in jeopardy and intervention offers the possibility of life, then it is right to override the will of the parents.'

'But surely not.' James ignored March as she grabbed his arm 'They hold profound convictions. We should respect that. It's a person's right to refuse treatment. To go against their decision would be an infringement of their human rights.'

'James, you don't believe that. I've heard the way you carry on when they come to the door,' March said.

'I'm just playing the devil's advocate, dear. Putting the other side.'

'You're just being bloody minded,' March snapped. 'As usual.' She glanced around the silent room. 'Please excuse me, everyone, I need to fetch my shawl. The temperature appears to have turned somewhat cool.'

Fyrne felt a powerful need to follow March and comfort her. She wanted sympathise with her about that odious husband and the disparaging way he treated her. She looked across at Bailey, who appeared to be watching her closely. Bailey made an almost imperceptible shake of her head before rising to her feet.

'Thank you, James. As promised, an interesting tale which tackled some difficult issues. I'm sure the debate will continue, but for now, folks, would you please follow me through to the dining room, where our evening meal is about to be served?'

25. Day Twelve – Cairns Balloon Flight

March looked around the basket: there was her husband, James; Maddy and Tony clutching hands; Frank and his partner, Paul; Harold and Cher Reeves; Sumner, with his camera poised, and Miller. James had laughed at her when she'd admitted to being nervous, but at least she'd come. The others had said they found the thought of a balloon flight quite terrifying; no engine, little control on direction and always that tiny, but ever-present fear that the balloon could burst into flames. The burner roared.

'This heat is scorching my head,' James moaned. 'Why didn't you remind me to bring my hat?'

'Here, take my scarf.'

James took it, examined it and screwed up his nose. 'It's not my colour.'

'Oh, for goodness sake.' She snatched the scarf back and tied it around her neck.

The burner blasted again, and the basket rose from the ground slowly.

March forgot her irritation as she gazed around. 'Isn't this amazing?'

James leaned over and whispered, 'You're beginning to sound like Bailey. If you can't say anything more original, shut up.'

Her eyes stung with tears. She should be used to his put

downs by now, but they were still painful, especially as somebody could overhear. She looked around, but everyone appeared occupied with the views. She turned her back on James.

Below her, she could see two other tour groups clambering into their baskets. Their balloons, one red and one yellow, remained tethered, while the burners continued to blast hot air. March glanced at her watch: five o'clock. The early morning mist hung over the valley. She looked towards the hills where the sun was making an appearance. It tinged the sky grey, mauve, pink and red in horizontal bands that merged in the mist. The other two balloons were now airborne and silhouetted against the hills.

'Kangaroos!' Maddy shouted.

March looked down and smiled as a large herd of kangaroos, disturbed by the shadow of the balloon, raced out of the woods and scattered in different directions.

'Look at them go,' Maddy hugged Tony and grinned. 'They must be clearing over two metres with each hop.'

One large male stood in a central clearing; his fists raised in a boxing pose as he prepared to take on the unknown threat to his herd.

March watched the tapestry of fields float beneath them. A white farmhouse passed by, large bushes laid out in a grid and an orchard of fruit trees. The sensation of floating, disturbed only by the occasional roar of the burner, was unreal. Thank goodness she hadn't let her nerves get the better of her. Perhaps she should start to live a little more dangerously. She'd been a mouse for far too long.

'Look, there's our collection team, racing after our shadow.'

Miller pointed to a truck and trailer. 'I hope we don't cross any more rivers, or we could lose them.'

'No worries. We're going to head for that field over there.' The pilot pointed to a large grass field, mercifully devoid of telegraph poles and electricity pylons.

The balloon descended quite quickly. March gripped the basket as the ground came closer.

Fyrne reached over and whispered in her ear. 'Don't worry; we'll be down in a minute.'

March smiled at the words of comfort. She gasped as the basket hit the ground and bounced, but then on its second attempt, settled gently onto the grass. Three men from the recovery team raced over and tethered the balloon. James jumped from the basket and walked away. One of the recovery crew offered March his hand while she clambered out.

Fyrne climbed out next and stood beside her. 'Gosh, how exciting.'

'I appear to have lost James.'

'He's over there, talking to one of the crew.' Fyrne pointed to the rescue vehicle, where James stood chatting to a young woman. 'I think our task is to transfer the balloon onto the trailer.'

March joined the others as the pilot demonstrated how they should smooth the air out of the balloon ready for it to be rolled and packed into its cover case.

'Come here, March!' James bellowed from the trailer.

'It's OK. I don't mind helping.'

'We didn't pay all this money to work as skivvies.'

March looked up as Fyrne caught her eye and winked.

'I'd rather not, thank you. I'm enjoying myself.' March

looked back at Fyrne and grinned.
'Good for you,' Fyrne whispered.

26. Second Evening in Cairns

Long Island Tea:

- *10ml Vodka*
- *10ml Gin*
- *10ml Bacardi*
- *10ml Tequila*
- *5ml Triple Sec*
- *5ml fresh lemon juice*
- *50ml cola*

   Shake alcohol and lemon juice together with ice cubes and then pour into chilled highball glass. Top up with coke, stir and add two slices of lemon.

'It's your turn tonight, Paul,' Bailey said. 'Can we expect some light entertainment, even perhaps a funny tale?'

There's no doubt James's story last night had been thought provoking, but Bailey lived in hope of something a bit more cheerful for once.

'I'll do my best,' Paul promised. 'Let me finish this iced tea, and then I'll begin.'

'I see you always choose the non-alcoholic drinks,' Miller said.

Paul placed his empty glass on the coffee table beside him.

'I don't drink alcohol.'

Frank patted Paul on the shoulder. 'He doesn't swear either. You could say he's the picture of perfect purity.'

Mrs Nunne snorted. 'That's a new word for it.'

Paul ignored her and sat back in his seat. He positioned his elbows on the chair arms, placed his fingertips together as if in prayer and lightly rested his chin on them.

'My tale is a moral tale. It could well be true. I hope it is. I like the idea of disrespect and greed being rewarded with revenge:'

Paul Pardoner's Tale

Harrison Spencer Jackson stood in his front garden deadheading roses. Their fragrance wafted over him making him sneeze. He employed a gardener to attend to his large garden and expansive lawns, but he always enjoyed culling the faded blooms.

Three youths stumbled along the pavement and drew level with the large granite pillars at the end of his driveway. Harrison could feel his blood pressure rising. Since they'd moved in next door, they'd trashed his garden with their beer cans and pizza boxes, kept him awake at night with their loud music and abused him whenever he was unfortunate enough to cross their path. This kind of behaviour didn't belong in a neighbourhood where houses were worth the best part of £2,000,000.

Ade, the slob who'd inherited the house, stuck up his finger. The sort of vile gesture Harrison had come to expect.

'You should be ashamed of yourself!' he shouted. 'What would your dear grandmother say if she could see you now?'

'She'd tell me to enjoy it while I can!' Ade shouted back.

'Drunk every day. Drugged half the time. You don't deserve to live in such a beautiful home. She'd turn in her grave.'

'We're living the dream, old man.' Ade laughed. 'You can't take it with you.'

'I'll have a bloody good try. I won't make the mistake your grandmother did. I'll not indulge my family's lazy lifestyle. You youngsters are all the same – leave school, go on the dole and waste your lives on drink and drugs.' He sank down onto a conveniently positioned concrete mushroom and rubbed his chest. 'Complete trash the lot of you.'

'And you're old, ugly and miserable, you stupid—'

'Leave him be,' the one called Sam said. He grabbed his friend's arm. 'It's not worth it. We'll miss the start of the Grand Prix if we don't get a move on.'

Sam dragged Ade along the pavement, and while he paused to unlatch the gate, Ade took the opportunity to turn around, and this time, stuck up two fingers.

Harrison waved his secateurs at them. 'You've made my life a misery, but I'll get even with you. You see if I don't.'

The church bells rang mournfully. Ade, Paul, and Sam hardly noticed as they sat in the Flanders Arms drinking their second pint of Tribute Ale. They were engrossed in the racing pages of the Morning Post.

'I fancy Seneca. The odds are good,' Sam said.

Paul laughed. 'That's because she's got three legs.'

'She's worth an each way bet,' Ade concluded.

Today was a normal day for the three of them: a couple of pints, a visit to the bookies and a trip to the local supermarket for a box of beer. They would round off the evening by ordering a takeaway, smoking a couple of spliffs and watching sport. Any sport would do.

'What's that noise, it's been going on for ages?' Ade asked as the bells slowly infiltrated his consciousness.

'The bells… the bells.' Paul hunched over his glass and gave a realistic impersonation of Quasimodo. 'It's the funeral for the old geezer from next door.'

'Good riddance,' Ade spat on the floor.

'I wonder what he did with his money.' Sam said. 'He must be worth a bob or two. He's written loads of books.'

Paul picked up his glass and gulped down the last of his beer.

'He did an interview with the Morning Post last month. He said he'd never leave his money to charities because they'd spend it on admin. Tight git.'

'And he told us it wouldn't go to his family.' Ade folded the newspaper.

'Perhaps he did find a way to take it with him.' Paul put his empty glass on the table.

'What do you mean,' Sam asked.

'Well, think about it…' Ade leaned forward and lowered his voce. 'If he didn't leave it to family, or charity, where the hell is it?'

'Is he being buried? If he is, we could dig him up and find the loot.' Sam pushed the newspaper aside leaned forward. 'He could have converted it all into gold and have it put in his coffin. That way, it'll be buried with him.'

'I don't think so.' Paul tugged at his ear lobe. 'I seem to remember it's a church service followed by a cremation. Gold would be difficult. It would be obvious when they raked the ashes out.' He picked at a zit on his chin making it bleed.

'Perhaps its diamonds?' Sam suggested.

'Whatever it is will finish up in the casket, won't it?' Ade asked.

'Right,' Sam nodded.

'So where will that go? My gran's ashes were sprinkled in the garden of remembrance, but that wouldn't work if he's intent on keeping his riches to himself. What about in his house?'

Paul leaned over and scratched his ankle. 'I read that his house has been gifted to the National Trust, in lieu of income tax debts and death duties. They plan to open it up as museum showcasing his work, with a gift shop and café.'

'What about his log cabin?' Sam suggested 'He apparently wrote his books in there.'

'You could be right,' Paul said. 'He wanted it maintained and open to the public. Apparently, future revenue from his books will go into preserving it as a shrine.'

'Pompous old codger,' Ade sneered. 'But you're right, Sam. I bet that's where the casket will be.'

The man arrived mid-morning two days later. Sam, hearing their ex-neighbour's gate squeak, looked out in time to see the man as he limped up the path carrying a cardboard box.

'Quick guys, this could be his solicitor.'

They watched as the tall, thin man in a dark suit, pin striped waistcoat and bowler hat stood on the front doorstep struggling to balance the box on one hip. He reached into his pocket for a set of keys, opened the door and entered the house.

'What do you think he's doing?' Ade asked.

'Delivering something,' Sam said. 'Looks heavy.'

'Gold ingots?' Paul suggested.

'He won't leave anything in the house,' Sam said. 'Don't forget, he's given the house to the National Trust. My bet is it'll be where he wrote his books.'

They raced upstairs and looked out over their rear garden, littered with fag ends and beer cans. They could see over the fence into the author's immaculate garden and then down to the log cabin and the lake beyond.

The man limped down the path, paused on the veranda and fumbled in his pocket to find his keys. He unlocked the door and entered the building. After ten minutes he emerged folding up the empty box which he put under his arm. They continued to watch him as he returned to the back door of the house and entered. Moments later, he emerged from the front door, locked it, and walked back to his car. He drove off without a backward glance.

'Stupid bugger. That cabin hasn't even got a burglar alarm.' Ade clapped his hands. 'This is going to be easy-peasy.'

They waited until after midnight and then, dressed in dark clothes, made their way into their backyard, over the old man's fence and down the path.

No one saw them. No CCTV cameras covered the grounds. No alarm protected the cabin. The door was secured with a Yale lock. Ade jiggled a thin strip of plastic in the lock and opened the door. They walked inside and closed the door behind them.

Ade swept the torch beam around the interior of polished oak, lined with bookshelves, and an open fire surrounded by a sandstone fireplace. Glass patio doors led out onto a small balcony overlooking the lake. The author's desk was placed in front, his chair positioned to achieve a spectacular view over the water. The full moon shimmered in the water, creating a silvery path to the shoreline.

Anyone else would have paused and soaked up the stunning beauty, the tranquillity and peace framed through the doors, but not these three. They had one thing in mind, to find the casket and claim its treasure.

'What are we looking for?' Paul asked.

'Gran's casket looked a bit like an urn.'

'Like this?'

Ade shone the torch onto a black urn which stood on the mantelshelf. It was about twelve inches tall and embellished with a necklace of cream plaster pearls swathed around its neck.

Paul picked it up. He had to use both hands to lift it. 'Gosh it's heavy, this must be it.'

'Empty it out, so we can see what's mixed in with his ashes. I'm still betting on diamonds,' Sam said.

Ade pushed the author's blotter to the floor, while Sam removed the casket's lid and tipped the ash across the desk's highly polished surface. Ade shone the torch onto the dust.

'Can't see any diamonds, can you?' asked Ade. 'And these ashes are the whitest ashes I have ever seen.' He pushed his fingers through the pile and sniffed the powder. 'My God. These aren't ashes. This is cocaine.'

Sam dipped his finger in the powder and rubbed his gum. 'Good stuff too. There must be a good Kilo here. What's that worth?'

'Not as much as diamonds,' Ade said. 'But better than a kick in the teeth. Bazz'll give us a good price. Let's bag it up. Then we can leave the urn, wipe our fingerprints off everything and no one will be any the wiser.'

Leaving the cabin, they returned to Ade's house, carrying the cocaine in a carrier bag. Paul grabbed three beers from the fridge.

'I think we should keep a small amount back for recreational purposes,' suggested Ade. 'It'll make a change from spliffs.'

'I agree,' Sam said. 'Let's try a line now and find out how good it is. Otherwise Bazz will try and knock us down, saying its third grade.'

They spread three good lines on the coffee table, rolled up a five-pound note and snorted one each. They lounged back on the sofa and waited for the blissful feeling to set in.

Mr Rose Junior, of Rose and Rose family solicitors unlocked the door of the terraced house that served as his office and bent down to pick up the envelopes from the hall floor. He groaned, rubbed his knee and limped towards the small kitchen. He filled the kettle, clicked it on and turned his attention to his mail.

The first letter contained a bill for the creation of a solid gold urn-shaped casket, laced with a necklace of brilliant-cut one carat diamonds. A plaster coating had then been applied and painted black, with the diamonds picked out in cream. The cost, together with his fees, almost emptied his client's account. He understood why his client had wanted the diamonds disguised in that way. Security. Only three people knew the value of that plaster urn: the maker, who didn't know the client or its location; the deceased owner; and himself. Good job he was honest. Many people in this position would have been tempted to help themselves.

The second letter came from the Inland Revenue, confirming that his client's income tax debt and death duties were covered by the gift to the National Trust. Only the long-term management of the Trust remained. Mr Rose had confidence that the income from future book sales would cover the maintenance of the shed and his ongoing executive fees. Job Done.

He still puzzled over the reason why his client had given him a bag of chalk, with strict instructions to place it in the urn, especially when he had requested his ashes to be sprinkled on the lake, but then his contract required him to carry out his client's instructions to the letter. He had done exactly as asked.

He opened the final piece of post, the local paper and read the front page:

"Three bodies found at No.7, Watling Street."

Next door to his client, Mr Harrison Spencer Jackson. How unfortunate can you get? He continued reading:

"Police, alerted by neighbours complaining of a terrible smell, broke down the front door of the house in Watling

Street and discovered the three bodies. The autopsy showed that they had all died of an overdose of cocaine that had been laced with digitalis – a deadly combination, according to the coroner. A verdict of accidental death has been recorded."

Bailey started the applause. 'Thank you, Paul. An interesting tale.'

'And a reminder that we can't take our wealth with us when we die,' said Harold.

'Would you like to go through for dinner everyone?'

As the guests meandered their way towards the dining room, Bailey approached Harold and Cher. 'Are you all right Harold, you look as though you're worried about something.'

'I'm fine, Bailey. I just have an important decision to make before I return home. My father died last month.'

'I'm so sorry.' Bailey patted his shoulder.

'Oh, he had a great life. He was ninety-six. But I'm his executor and I have to decide what to do with the farm he inherited from my uncle, JD – the one in my story. I want to be sure I do the right thing by the families who depended on it for their livelihoods, but at the same time I want to do the right thing by Cher.'

Cher stroked his hand. 'You know whatever you decide will be fine by me.'

'Where would I be without you?' he kissed Cher's hand.

What a special relationship these two had Bailey thought. One she envied.

27. Day Thirteen – Cairns to the Beach Resort

Two missing, thought Bailey as she counted heads for the second time. *And* we're ten minutes late leaving.

Bailey shouted down the coach. 'Anyone seen Angie this morning?'

'Barbara's gone to Angie's room to check,' March said. 'Would you like me to go and find them?'

'Thanks, but I'll go.'

Bailey hurried towards Reception and sighed with relief as she spotted Barbara.

'Bailey, my dear. I'm afraid you will have to leave without us. Angie is somewhat… indisposed, should we say.'

'You mean she's worse than normal?' How on earth could she fix this one? Her other guests were all on the bus, waiting patiently. Or, in the case of the Nunnes, not quite so patiently.

'I'm so sorry. I should have kept a closer eye on her with those Long Island Iced Teas. They were lethal. You go, we'll follow up by taxi later.'

'But, Barbara, it's a two-hour drive. It'll cost a fortune.'

'Never mind that. Give me the details and leave it to me. You get back to the bus.'

Bailey sat in her comfortable bamboo chair beside the open patio doors and looked down through the dense jungle landscape. The pleasant smell of wood smoke wafted up from below. Someone had a bonfire burning.

At least the journey up to the Beach Resort had gone well and everyone appeared happy with their log cabin accommodation. She'd recommended the luxury picnic lunch to her guests, and taken her own advice. Several of the younger ones had agreed to take their feasts down to the beach, but she looked forward to an afternoon alone and had politely declined their invitation. The hamper would be delivered in about half an hour but, for now, she'd opened a bottle of cold Sauvignon Blanc, poured herself a generous glass and settled down to catch up on some admin.

She sipped from her glass and opened her laptop, still in two minds: should she tell Jim about Barbara and Angie travelling up by taxi? He would demand a new risk assessment, and take great pleasure in laying the blame for their alternative travel arrangements at her door. On the other hand, if she didn't inform him and something happened... Bailey's hand trembled as the screen opened to reveal a new e-mail from Jim.

The title jumped out at her: *REDUNDANCY.*

She looked up at the air conditioning fan as it circled lazily above her – whhup, whhup, whhup. She shivered, took a deep breath and double clicked.

Dear Katherine Bailey,

As you will be aware, Australia Unleashed is under new ownership and a restructuring is currently being undertaken. We are, at present, looking at the need to make financial savings, which will inevitably include a reduction in the number of staff employed.

As a result, I am sorry to inform you that your post of Tour Manager is at risk. No final decision has yet been made. We will be consulting with you over the next 30 days – details to follow. A final decision will be made by the 1st December.

I regret informing you of the situation by e-mail and appreciate that you will find this news distressing. If you would like to discuss the redundancy issue, or the process, please contact The Head of Human Resources, Kelly Price, on extension 310.

Yours sincerely
  Jim Tennant, Head of Administration.

She read it through a second time. Yours sincerely? Jim didn't know what the word meant. Pressing that send button must have made his day. Why couldn't he ring? She'd get back to Sydney in two days; couldn't this have waited?

She thought back to all the other spats they'd had: the unfounded accusations he'd made about her expenses claim (he hadn't even apologised when proved wrong); his refusal to split the final group of last year (even when the numbers reached forty-eight); their huge row over the kangaroo tour. OK, she'd gone behind Jim's back to get it approved, but did she really deserve to be treated like this. Did she?

The real reason, she felt sure, he'd never managed to make her cry. He appeared to take great pleasure in reducing the women in the office to tears, and hated her especially because she'd always stood up to his bullying.

She didn't care. Well, she did, but she'd never give him the satisfaction of knowing just how much. If the new regime worked liked this, then sod it. She'd take her redundancy and move back to Scotland, close to Duncan. She'd get a job escorting tours in Scotland and become a grandmother-in-waiting.

PART FOUR

28. First Evening at the Beach Resort

Bloody Mary:

- *40ml Vodka*
- *120ml good quality tomato juice*
- *5ml fresh lemon juice*
- *Two dashes of Worcester sauce*
- *Two dashes of Tabasco sauce*
- *Pinch of salt*
- *Pinch of ground pepper*

  Shake all of the ingredients with ice cubes, strain into a tumbler glass and serve with a stick of celery and a slice of lemon.

Bailey looked around the Beach Resort's lounge. She was especially pleased to see Barbara and Angie who had contacted her mid-afternoon to say they'd arrived safely and without incident. Thank goodness she hadn't told Jim. Now he'd never know.

'Good evening, Ladies and Gentlemen. According to my list, it's Fyrne's turn to provide us with a tale tonight. Is that OK with you, Fyrne?'

Fyrne expected this, but her heart rate still increased. She knew others thought she was full of confidence but, on occasions like this, her tummy churned. She'd practised her story several times this afternoon, but her legs trembled as she walked to the front and turned to face her audience. March smiled and gave her a supportive thumbs-up.

'Thanks everyone.' Fyrne smiled at March. 'My story is about a woman that yearned to find true love:'

Fyrne Schipmanno's Tale

Lowena wriggled her toes in the cool sand. A long line of spray blew from the wave tops and sprinkled her face with a fine mist. She breathed deeply, enjoying the salty taste and the distinctive smell of the sea. Could she really leave all this behind?

A young mother and her toddler walked by. Lowena watched as the mother leaned over and whispered in her son's ear. Her words made him giggle with delight. Lowena's familiar and painful yearning for a child flooded back. She blinked away the tears, and returned her gaze to the horizon. These foolish hopes and dreams were pointless. Not only had she been single for over a year, but despite her best efforts to mix, mingle and socialise, she hadn't even come close to finding a new relationship.

She rolled her jeans up to her knees and walked ankle deep in the cold water, smiling as the receding waves tugged the sand from beneath her toes and threatened to unbalance her. She used to walk here with Sam every Saturday morning. She looked across to where a young couple sat on the terrace of the beach café. He read her something from his newspaper. They both laughed. Eighteen months ago, that could have been her and Sam, planning their lives, marriage and children. And all that time her biological clock had been tick, tick, ticking away.

Her mother hadn't helped. 'Happy thirtieth birthday, darling,' she'd said, and then in the next breath, 'When are you and Sam going to settle down and give me some grandchildren?' She'd tried to explain. Sam expected a promotion soon. His marketing firm might need him to re-locate. Her job was flexible – as a primary school supply teacher she could easily move. But with all the uncertainty, as Sam had insisted, it was better to wait.

In March he'd been invited to attend a training course in London, a pre-cursor for his promotion. He'd been gone for two weeks when a knock came at the door. Lowena put her coffee mug in the sink and raced through the lounge to answer it.

'Hi Pete! Come in. Sam's not here, he won't be back for another week.'

'I know.' Pete had walked into the lounge and threw himself down on the sofa. 'Lowena... I'm not sure how to say this, but—'

'What is it? Is it Sam? Has he had an accident?'

'Have you checked your texts this morning?'

She grabbed her phone from the coffee table and checked her in-box. There was a message from Sam. Her fingers shook as she opened it.

'Sorry babe. Offered job in London and accepted. Won't b back. Realise now not ready 2 settle down. Pete will be over 2 collect my stuff.'

She felt the blood drain from her face. Her legs trembled as she collapsed on the sofa next to Pete. Dumped? By text?

She turned to face him. 'Is this a joke? Please, tell me it's a joke.'

Pete shook his head slowly.

'How can he do this to me? Three years, for God's sake—'

'Come on, Lowena. You must have realised things weren't right?'

'It couldn't be better. He was about to get his promotion and I've spent the past fortnight planning the nursery.'

'Lowena, it would never happen. Not with Sam.'

She'd sat in dumb silence while Pete gathered Sam's things. He'd given her a quick hug; told her she'd soon find someone else and left her to her misery. She'd tried ringing Sam, texting, messaging, but he'd obviously blocked her number.

Two seagulls swooped over Lowena's head, squawking loudly as they chased a big black crow.

Despite the painful memories, she still enjoyed these early morning walks on the beach, but this was her last before the taxi arrived to take her to Newquay Airport. She'd promised her sister that she'd visit her in Australia for a few months. Alison and her husband, Baz, had just become parents for the first time and found life with a newborn baby quite demanding. Lowena wasn't sure if she looked forward to playing the maiden aunt, or dreaded it. How would it feel to hold a child that wasn't her own?

'Good morning. What a beautiful day.' A tall, military looking gentleman in a tweed jacket, white shirt and cavalry twill trousers, strode towards her. His highly polished brown brogues crunched on the shingle.

'Morning,' Lowena smiled.

'Have you seen out there?' He pointed with his walking stick to a spot beyond the breaking waves. 'I think there's a seal.'

'Really? We don't often see them in the bay.'

'Perhaps it's a young one that's lost its way.'

Lowena peered out to the floating object. 'Mm, you're right. There's definitely something there, but I'm not sure it's a seal. Wrong colour.' She blinked. 'Oh, my God, It's a person! Call an ambulance!'

She threw her jacket and shoulder bag onto the dry sand and raced into the water, gasping at the coldness as it reached her waist. She dived through the next wave and swam out strongly. She could see clearly now. A man floated on his back. His dark green T-shirt and blue jeans blended with the blue and green of the waves, the pale flesh of his face and hands contrasted starkly.

'I'm here, I've got you.' She grabbed him under his arms and

supported his head as she swam back towards the shore.

Relief surged through Lowena as she heard the old man shout, 'Emergency services are on their way!'

The old man, close now, splashed his way through the surf towards them and together they pulled and tugged the lifeless man the last few metres to the shore.

'Is he alive?' the old man asked.

Lowena sank to her knees. 'I can't find his pulse.'

Her own pulse hammered in her ears. He was a young man. Early thirties, she decided. She felt a sudden surge of anger towards him.

'I've put too much effort into this for you to go and die on me!' she raged.

She tipped his head back, held his nose and breathed into his mouth. His chest rose and fell. She pumped his chest and tried again. He spluttered, turned his head towards her and vomited sea water all over her jeans. His long dark lashes fluttered open, revealing eyes the colour of the sea; dark blue flecked with green.

'Welcome back,' Lowena smiled at him.

'Thanks…' He gasped, turned his head towards her and wretched.

She pulled him onto his side and into the recovery position. 'That's better. Don't want you choking, do we?' She patted his shoulder.

'Amazing! You've saved his life,' the old man said.

Lowena was pleased to see he'd taken off his beautiful, and no doubt very expensive, brogue shoes before wading into the surf to help.

'We did.' She smiled at the old man. 'Although it's still early days. He's very cold.'

'Here, my jacket.' The old man draped his tweed jacket over the younger one, who remained prostrate, but now breathed evenly.

A wailing siren heralded the arrival of an ambulance. Only then did Lowena notice that a small crowd had gathered around them. The crowd parted as two men ran across the sand carrying a stretcher and thermal blankets. One checked the victim's vital signs while the other wrapped him up. Satisfied, they rolled their patient onto the stretcher.

'Was he breathing when you pulled him out of the water?' the first paramedic asked.

'Dead as a Dodo,' the old man said. 'Still would be if it wasn't for her.' He reached down and picked up his redundant jacket.

Lowena and the old man followed the paramedics back to the ambulance.

'Come on.' The second paramedic gestured for Lowena to climb into the ambulance.

She glanced at her watch. 'Gosh, I hadn't realised how late it is. I have to go.'

'But we need to check you over.'

'Sorry, I really must dash, my taxi's due in half an hour.'

The old man shouted after her. 'Well done, you saved his life.'

This was Lowena's first shopping trip into Truro since her return from Australia. She'd expected to feel a sense of excitement, but instead the hairs on the back of her neck prickled. Sensing someone behind her, she spun around. No one there.

An old couple strolled past, clutching each other's arms. The woman grinned at Lowena. 'He thinks I'm hanging on so I don't slip on these granite slabs, but actually, it's just so I can get my hands on him.'

The old man winked at Lowena and chuckled. 'Any excuse.'

They'd obviously found love, a love that had lasted. Why

couldn't she?

During her four months stay in Australia, Alison and Baz had organised one barbeque after another and invited every single male they knew, all of them charming, fit and eager to meet an English babe. Not one had appealed. In despair her sister had accused her of being too picky and warned her to drop this "Goldilocks" approach before it was too late.

Now she was back she'd decided to take Alison's advice and join a dating agency. Easy enough until it came to completing her personal statement.

I've been single for over a year — could be interpreted as, I'm now desperate for sex.

I'm now ready to move on — may give the impression of, being psychologically damaged.

I'm a fun-loving kind of girl — might suggest, shallow with no brain, and a sex maniac.

She'd finally settled for: Back on old turf and looking for that someone special. Maybe, someone had recognised her agency photo and she was being stalked? Stop it!

She re-focussed her attention to her immediate situation. Across the street, outside the public toilet block, a man stood with his back to her — blonde curly hair, blue jeans and a leather jacket. He spoke into his mobile phone, presumably waiting for someone.

She crossed the road, dived into the doorway of a jewellery shop and pretended to examine a tray of second hand rings. If anyone was following her, they would have to walk past. This is absolutely ridiculous, she told herself. There's no one there.

A man walked by. She recognised his leather jacket. He walked slowly, and alone.

Lowena stepped out from her hiding place.

'Why are you following me? Who are you?

He spun around and smiled. 'I knew it was you.'

'Never mind who I am, I asked—'

'I never forget a face.'

So, he had seen her online, and now he stood there, bold as brass, thinking he somehow had the right to accost her.

'You're my guardian angel. You saved me.'

Oh God, an out and out crazy.

'I would have drowned that day if you hadn't rescued me.'

Lowena blinked and looked at the stranger again. It was him. The man she'd pulled from the sea. 'I'm so sorry, I didn't recognise you. I thought… well, I'm sorry.'

'Please. I'm the one who should apologise – scaring you like that. Only I tried and tried to find you. Even put a piece in the West Briton, asking for you to come forward.'

'I left for Australia that same day to visit my sister and her family. I only got back this week. I did ring the hospital when I got to London that day. They said you were "doing well," but wouldn't give me any details. Data protection. But you're all right?'

'I was only in overnight, for observation. I went home the next day.'

'I'm so glad.'

'Look, can I buy you coffee?' His eyes pleaded with her. 'Please, I always hoped I'd find you and get the chance to say thanks. There's a good Costa around the corner, top floor of the book shop.'

She nodded and fell into step beside him.

While they rode the escalator to the coffee shop, he introduced himself – Clive. He complimented her name – very pretty, very Cornish. They ordered two cappuccinos and Clive carried their tray to a corner table.

'What have you been up to since? Rescued anyone else?'

'I hope that was a one off. I'm not sure my nerves will take another scare like that. I thought you were dead.'

'From what the hospital said, I was. Your skill brought me back.'

'Anyone would do the same.'

'I'm not so sure.'

'How did you finish up in the water?' She could feel herself blush as she suddenly realised it could have been a suicide attempt. *'Don't tell me if it's too painful.'*

'My own stupid fault. I went out in my kayak, too arrogant to wear a safety jacket and too pig-headed to check the weather forecast.' He smiled at her. *'A big wave flipped me over and the rest is history. Anyway, tell me about yourself. Are you married, local, working, do you have kids, hobbies?'*

Lowena laughed, *'Single. Falmouth born and bred. I work as a primary supply teacher. I have no kids, love music and walking on the beach.* She sprinkled a sachet of sugar over the foam of her coffee and stirred it in slowly. She took a sip, taking care to avoid getting coffee froth on her nose or top lip. *'So, what have you been up to since your accident?'*

'You changed my life.'

Lowena looked at him. She thought he was joking but his face looked deadly serious.

You forced me to accept that I was a total pratt.'

'I did?'

He nodded. *'You made me realise how precious life is. So, I donated a kidney to my brother.'*

'Wow, that's brave.'

'Not really, I'd spent weeks trying to make the decision. I have to admit, the thought of donating scared me. I was pathologically

terrified of the surgery. While I recovered in hospital, on the day you saved me, I realised how selfish I was. You didn't even know me, yet you put your own life at risk without any hesitation.'

'It wasn't much of a risk. I'm a strong swimmer.'

'Nevertheless, I was ashamed. I immediately took the tests and discovered I was a perfect match.'

Lowena looked at Clive's hands. They were well proportioned with manicured nails. Hands designed to caress. His eyelashes were to die for, long and dark, in contrast with his blonde curly hair that flopped casually over his forehead. His eyes were that wonderful dark blue flecked with green, which reminded her of the sea and the day she'd pulled him free from his watery grave.

'Let's have another,' he said, as he collected up her empty cup and placed it next to his on the tray. 'Same again?'

'Thanks.'

She watched as he returned to the counter. She should be drooling over this handsome hunk, and yet... what was wrong with her?

'Here we go,' he sat down and pushed one cup towards her.

Lowena stirred her coffee, taking pleasure in messing up the carefully created palm tree that floated on top.

'I wondered,' he paused. 'How would you feel about coming around to my place for dinner tomorrow night? We're having a barbeque. The whole family would be there and I know they would love the chance to meet you. We've also got a live band booked. Do you like blues music?'

'I love it. That sounds like my idea of heaven.'

'Here, I'll write down the address and phone number.' He fumbled in his pocket and produced a pen and piece of paper. 'Come about seven. Don't bother bringing any food or drink. You're our guest of honour.'

She smiled at him as she took the paper and placed it carefully in her bag. Gosh, meeting the family on only the second date, or would that count as the first? He must be interested.

But what about her? This was Australia all over again. Yes, she wanted to settle down and have kids, but, as she'd told Alison, she needed to be sure it was with Mr Right.

'Wear that sexy little black number,' Esald, her flat mate said.

'I'm aiming for sophisticated.' Lowena wriggled into the dress she'd selected, a simple dark blue silky dress, full length with thin shoulder straps.

'Mm, very nice, but you need to knock his socks off. He could be your best chance yet. Don't forget, tick tock, tick tock.'

'Thanks, Esald. I'm well aware of that.'

'What's wrong with you?'

Lowena grabbed her hair brush and swept her hair up, securing it in place with a handful of grips.

'I'm not sure about him.'

'But you said he was drop dead gorgeous.'

'He is, but he didn't make my pulse race, or the hairs on my arms stand to attention, or my stomach churn with butterflies. After all, there's more to attraction than good looks.'

'It's a good starting point.'

'OK, I'll keep an open mind.' She applied her lipstick and checked her reflection in the mirror. 'Thanks for offering me a lift.'

'No problem, anything to help the cause. I'll pick you up at midnight, unless you ring to say otherwise.'

Lowena slipped her feet into a pair of black ballet pumps, put her comb, lipstick and mobile phone in her clutch bag and picked *up her pale blue pashmina shawl.*

'OK, I'm ready. Let's go.'

She could hear the blues band playing Howlin' Wolf's "How Many More Years". How appropriate, as Esald would say. The appetising smell of barbequed meat filled the air. She walked down the path at the side of the large Victorian house and emerged into a backyard that looked like something out of Homes and Gardens: perfectly manicured lawn with flawless stripes, Cornish Palm trees, clumps of Agapanthus. Lowena looked across to the patio where the blues trio were breaking into Muddy Waters's "Everything's Gonna Be All right."

'Hello there. You must be Lowena.'

A young blonde woman raced towards her, a glass of something bubbly in her hand. Her dress, long and flowing, could not disguise the fact that she must be at least seven months pregnant. Lowena felt a sharp stab of jealousy.

'I'm so pleased you could come. I'm Fliss. Here, I hope you like Champagne.' She offered the glass to Lowena. 'Great, now I can give you a big hug.'

Lowena found herself enveloped in a warm embrace. Usually uncomfortable about sharing her personal space, she felt surprisingly drawn to this woman. She looked over Fliss's shoulder and saw Clive approaching. He wore an apron and had a bottle of beer in one hand and turning prongs in the other.

'Hello there! How's my guardian angel?'

Once again Lowena found herself wrapped in a huge bear hug. The embrace was pleasant, but disappointing – no quickening of her pulse or fluttering stomach. Esald would definitely be disappointed.

'I'm so pleased you're here,' Clive said. 'I see my wife is looking after you.'

Wife? He was married? Course he was. She swallowed some of her drink and waited for the disappointment to kick in, but instead she felt relief.

Clive put his arm around Fliss and patted her swollen belly. 'How's our baby girl?'

'Dancing to the music and making me hungry.'

'Do you still want chocolate sauce on that hot dog?'

'I'll settle for tomato,' she laughed.

Clive smiled at her and returned his attention to Lowena. 'Fliss has been so looking forward to meeting you. You'll really get on. I just know it. I must dash back to the barbeque. I've left Dad in charge and he's a dab hand at burning everything.'

Fliss put her arm through Lowena's and guided her across the patio to the gaggle of guests gathered around a table laden with salads, bread rolls and a large stainless-steel bowl containing ice, bottles of beer and champagne.

'Listen up everyone… this is our guest of honour…Lowena. Without her we would not be here tonight celebrating. Lowena, this is my mum and dad, Clive's mother – his dad's on barbeque duties – and these are our neighbours, Laura, Reg, Joy and Phil.'

Lowena felt a bit like the package in pass the parcel as she received one hug after another. Clive's mum wept as she hugged Lowena and kissed her on both cheeks. This was one tactile family.

Clive returned with a tray of sausages.

'Here we go folks. Starters. I'll cook the chicken next. But first, Lowena, let's go and meet the rest of the family.'

The excited squeals of happy children could be heard before they turned the corner and approached the tennis court. Two young boys *were playing football with a man.*

'These are my two boys... Toby, he's six, and Jacob, he's seven. And this is their favourite uncle, Charlie. Actually, he's their only uncle.'

Lowena looked across and gasped. With the two boys clutching his hands, Charlie walked towards her – a perfect replica of Clive.

'Let me introduce you to my younger brother, Charlie. We're twins, but he's ten minutes younger than me. I know you two are going to get on. You have a lot in common. He also loves blues music, barbeques and walking on the beach.'

Her eyes met Charlie's. She felt a shock of sexual attraction. She had never fancied a man so instantly or intensely in her life before. Her stomach erupted with a cloud of butterflies. The fine hairs on her arms prickled and her hand trembled as she shook his hand.

His handshake was firm, but gentle. His hands were practically identical to Clive's, but she noticed his shoulders were slightly different. After all, Clive's did slope a bit.

'I can't thank you enough for what you did that day.' Charlie gave her a chaste peck on her cheek.

Lowena's skin tingled. 'My pleasure.'

'Before the transplant I could only dream about settling down and having a family. Your generosity, and Clive's, has now made that a real possibility. Now all I have to do is find the right woman.' His eyes twinkled as he smiled at her.

She noticed the band had begun to play again: Etta James's

> *"At last my love has come along*
> *My lonely days are over and life is like a song."*

March leapt to her feet and applauded loudly. The others joined in.

'That was amazing,' said Bailey.

'Absolutely,' March grinned at Fyrne.

Fyrne realised her nerves had gone. March looked happy and that was all that mattered.

'Dinner, Ladies and Gentlemen?' Bailey gestured towards the restaurant where the waiters were hovering at the door to great them.

29. Day Fourteen – The Barrier Reef

Bailey stood waiting patiently for her guests to assemble below deck in the boat's saloon. She'd asked them to gather at 10:15 a.m., giving them plenty of time to explore and find their sea legs while they cruised out towards the reef.

It was hot. The open windows provided a pleasant breeze and plenty of ozone rich fresh air. She was pleased that she'd decided to break company protocol and wear her comfortable dark blue shorts instead of her usual uniform trousers. She'd made sure her white shirt and silk scarf were as pristine as ever. No one would even know that she'd broken the rules.

The long white trestle tables running either side of the central aisle reminded her of filleted fish bones. Several members of the group already sat around the tables and sipped from their water bottles. Others had collected drinks from the bar and shuffled onto the bench seats, a process made difficult by the fact that they were bolted to the floor, allowing very little wriggle room.

Bailey waited for them all to settle down. 'Ladies and Gentlemen, I will never forget my first visit to the Great Barrier Reef. I knew it was the largest coral reef in the world, I'd seen pictures, but I was unprepared for the scale of it. It is mon-u-men-tal, iconic, and today I'm so very proud to introduce you to this extraordinary ecosystem. We will swim in it, dive into it, snorkel, sail and helicopter over it and witness, in the process, every possible shade of blue.

'The Great Barrier Reef is a World Heritage Site and the planet's largest protected marine area. One of the seven wonders of the natural world, it stretches for 1,430 miles along the Queensland coast – from Bundaberg to the Torres Strait. It consists of almost 3,000 individual reefs containing 400 different types of coral. It's home to over 1,500 species of fish, along with whales, dugongs, turtles, dolphins and more than 4,000 types of mollusc. In addition, it is an important bird habitat.'

'And sharks, Bailey!' James bellowed. 'Don't forget the sharks.'

'Reef sharks. Nothing to worry about.' Bailey reached down into the sports bag at her feet and held up what looked like a long fishing net.

'One word of warning, if you go into the water you should wear one of these. It's a stinger suit, designed to protect you from our very nasty jellyfish. It's not very elegant, I know, but a sting would put you in the hospital for a couple of days, and I'm sure that's something we all want to avoid. It also offers some protection from the sun, which can be very fierce.'

'Do you recommend a wetsuit?' asked Sumner. 'I'm always game for a bit of dressing up in rubber.'

James laughed.

Bailey decided to ignore their schoolboy humour. 'A wetsuit isn't necessary for swimming or snorkeling. The water temperature on the surface is a lovely 30° Celsius, or 86° in old money.

'OK, well I hope that's enough to whet your appetite. We should arrive at the reef in about half an hour, and moor up alongside the activity platform. If you have any questions, come and see me.'

Bailey moved to the bar, where the waitress had a coffee waiting. She perched on a stool next to Miller and smiled as he turned towards her. She noticed him glance at her legs.

'Mm, nice legs Kate. You should give them an airing more often.'

'Mr Miller, you really should behave yourself.' Bailey could feel herself blush, although she had to admit she had enjoyed the compliment.

March struggled into her stinger suit.

Fyrne looked her up and down. 'Wow. I thought Bailey said they weren't very elegant. How come you manage to look like Cat Woman?'

'Only because I'm too proud to admit that small is a bit snug.'

'You look great.'

March blushed; she wasn't used to compliments of this nature, especially from another woman.

Fyrne looked across to the boat. 'Where's James? Is he coming to see you off?'

'I told him I'd accepted your invitation to scuba dive. He's gone to prop up the bar and sulk.'

'Sulk? He could have come with us. I didn't think he was interested.'

'He's not. But he doesn't like the idea of me enjoying myself without him.'

'Oh, for goodness sake!' Fyrne reached over to March and touched her arm. 'He doesn't deserve you.'

March could feel her skin tingle under Fyrne's touch. If Fyrne was a bloke, she would think he was flirting with her. Perhaps this is how it is with a good friend? She realised that she hadn't had a girl friend since her school days. She'd met James during university fresher week and they'd built up a small circle of friends together. Although, to be honest, they were mostly his friends and their partners.

Fyrne took March's hand and led her towards the edge of the platform. They sat and dangled their feet in the water. March giggled as a couple of fish swam up and nibbled her toes.

'Come on, March. Forget James. Let's explore.'

March slipped her fins onto her feet, shrugged on her tank and dipped her face mask into the water. She could taste the salt as she positioned the mouthpiece and adjusted the straps to fit comfortably. Holding hands, they eased themselves gently into the water, swam to the edge of the demarcated swimming area and paused. Fyrne pointed down to indicate they should start their dive. March nodded before sinking down into another world.

After only a few yards, Fyrne tapped March on the shoulder and pointed to a giant purple clam nestled on the sandy seabed. The shell, more than two feet across and covered with downy seaweed gaped wide open. Bright green globules edged with turquoise lined the inside rims. Deeper inside the shell, a purple and black heaving mantle pulsated, and a fringed ring of waving hair-like tentacles siphoned the water for food. March paused to take a photograph. She hoped she could capture the colours and recreate them in a silk scarf. It would make an interesting addition to her range.

March knew she would struggle to find the words to describe the beauty and wonder of gliding over this brightly coloured coral. The colours were stunning: brilliant yellow; orange; pastel pink and violet; mint green and an intense blue. They resembled a rich tapestry draped over the lumpy seabed with a colour palette borrowed directly from Disney. And to think, if Fyrne hadn't insisted, she would have missed all this.

A three-foot long, smiling Maori Wrasse swam right up to them, big lips pouting in front of their faces as it came up close for a peek. The wrasse followed them and its body twisted and snaked between their legs as they swam into deeper water.

March noticed that the colours here were no longer as bright. Was this the bleaching she'd heard so much about? And was it really all down to global warming? March shivered as they sailed over a dead patch of blackened coral.

Fyrne pointed up and together they swam to the surface.

March trod water and lifted her mask to speak. 'That's so sad.' A cold sense of dread crept down her spine.

'The bleaching can apparently be reversed, given time and the right conditions,' Fyrne said. 'But not once the coral is dead.'

'It was so lovely up to that point.'

'Come on. Time to move on.'

They replaced their masks and sank back below the surface. March shook off her uneasy feeling as a large cuttlefish came into view. Easily eighteen inches long, maybe nearer two foot. His skin flickered and rapidly changed colour, as he hovered and pointed his tentacles towards them. Glassy eyes watched with an unfathomable expression as he tracked their movements and used the constant motion of his flamenco frill to maintain his distance.

March feasted her eyes on the vast expanse of corals. The architecture was spectacular, with cliffs, canyons and cathedral like arches.

Every now and then they paused to take photographs of staghorn heads filled with shoals of damsel fish, and shelf corals with baby Nimmoes hiding in their shade. Anemone arms fluttered and waved as they swam over them. Shrimp danced before them. Algae and sponges coated the rocks. Every crevice housed some creature or another.

A sea cucumber floated by, closely followed by a shoal of blue and silver fish with yellow lips and fins. A turtle swam up close, so close March could have reached out and touched it, but remembering their briefing before entering the water, she resisted the temptation. Unperturbed by their presence, it glided alongside them.

All too soon, it seemed, Fyrne tapped her watch and pointed to the boat. Their time was up.

March's heart sank.

Fyrne climbed out of the water and pulled off her tank and flippers. 'How was that for you?'

March grinned. 'Awesome. I loved it.'

Fyrne reached down to help March. 'Up you come.'

'Must I? I don't want this to end.'

'And you were prepared to miss out? Remember, you need to grab life's chances.'

'I know. It was just that—'

'Ah, there you are.' James arrived beside them. 'I wondered how much longer you were going to keep me waiting. Come on! I want to try the helicopter flight and get back before they stop serving lunch.'

'Have I got time to change?'

'You'd better. You look ridiculous in that outfit. I'll wait in the bar.'

March avoided Fyrne's eyes as she scurried off to the changing room, wondering how her confidence could somersault so drastically, depending on who she was with.

30. Second Evening at the Beach Resort

Mojito:

- *40ml Bacardi*
- *20ml fresh lime juice*
- *10ml sugar syrup*
- *Ten fresh mint leaves*
- *Soda water*

    Place ice cubes and mint leaves in layers into a highball glass. Pour over the Bacardi, lime juice, and sugar syrup and stir gently. Add crushed ice and a splash of soda water and serve with a sprig of mint.

Bailey always enjoyed the Beach Resort's recital room. She glanced around as she stood chatting with Pryor and Nigel. Beside them, a Steinway grand piano, polished to perfection, supported two silver candelabra, each dressed with five emerald green candles. A waiter strolled over, lit the candles with a plastic disposable lighter, and then wandered off in the direction of the bar.

Bamboo canes lined the walls of the room. Large windows revealed views of the surrounding trees. Pots, containing huge ferns were clustered against the walls, creating the impression that the room was an extension of the patio area and gardens.

Bailey counted her guests - nineteen, all present and correct.

'Ladies and Gentlemen, could I have your attention please?' She paused while everyone stopped talking and looked towards her. 'I hope you all enjoyed the Barrier Reef?'

'Oh, my dear, absolutely incredible.' Barbara clapped her hands together. 'I never thought I would fly in a helicopter. I'm so glad we did.'

Angie nodded in agreement. 'I was reluctant at first, but Barbara convinced me. Exhilarating, don't you know? I'll remember those views for the rest of my life.'

Bailey smiled. This was what made her job worthwhile.

'This evening is a different format to usual. I know we usually gather in the bar, but as you will see, our *first tale* is in fact a piano recital. You may have wondered – I know I have – at the meaning of Pryor's bracelet. Tonight, she has agreed to reveal the secret through a song, accompanied on this amazing piano by Nigel. Nigel, Pryor, whenever you're ready.'

Pryor walked over to stand beside the piano. Her husband followed and settled himself on the piano stool. He pressed a key to produce a perfect C sharp, and sat with his back straight, hands poised, waiting.

'Ladies and Gentlemen, I am going to sing you a song called *Love Conquers All*, the words that many of you have noticed engraved on my bracelet. In 1985 my husband and I lost our only child, Jeremy.'

Bailey's stomach lurched. Not another dead child? She'd hoped this would be a joyful event. Last year, she'd organised a piano recital for her guests and she could still remember the perfect pitch of this piano.

'When he turned seven, we allowed him to walk home from school on the understanding that he always shared the journey with his best friend, Matthew, who lived next door.'

Pryor paused, turned, and smiled nervously at her husband. He smiled back and nodded encouragement.

'Jeremy loved to sing. On this particular evening, they were both scheduled to stay behind at school for choir practise. Unfortunately, Matthew had a sore throat and came home straight from school, unbeknown to us at the time. When Jeremy didn't arrive, we checked with Matthew and, realising Jeremy was alone – and late, we organised a search party. We informed the police and spent agonising hours, days, weeks and months searching and hoping for his return, but to no avail.'

Bailey's eyes prickled with tears. Why did the nicest people have to suffer so much?

Pryor reached for her glass of water and took a large sip before continuing.

'This song was released shortly after Jeremy went missing. It became our song of hope for Jeremy.'

Pryor reached out and touched her husband's hand. 'Ladies and Gentlemen, tonight we would like to share that song with you.

Nigel played the haunting introduction, and Pryor's perfect mezzo-soprano voice filled the room:

Pryor and Nigel Monk's Song

It seemed that our lives almost ended
On that day that you failed to come home
The pain and the grief, overwhelming
The fear never left us alone
But LOVE conquers all.

If it takes us forever, we'll find you
And we pray you may still be alive
We trust in the Lord that you're still safe and sound
And by His grace you somehow survive
Because LOVE conquers all.

But for now, all we have are the memories
Your singing and angelic looks
Your fluffy blue rabbit and Paddington bear
The pictures, the toys and the books
Our LOVE conquers all.

Imagine the peace when we're with you again
Our brilliant and beautiful boy
Maybe in this life, or maybe the next
Together, forever, such joy
When LOVE conquers all.

Oh yes, LOVE conquers all.

Nigel finished playing with a final flourish and the room erupted into applause.

'My word,' Miller said. 'What a voice.'

'Moving, so very moving.' Cynthia wiped a tear from her cheek.

'What lyrics,' Frank sighed. 'They bring back so many memories.' He reached over, placed his hand on Paul's shoulder and gave it a squeeze.

'Thank you, everyone.' Pryor waited for the applause to finish. 'Jeremy would be thirty-seven now, but although it's thirty years since he disappeared, we haven't given up hope. We have his photograph *digitally aged* every five years, and create posters, which we distribute wherever we go. All over the UK, France, Spain, even here in Australia. After all, if he's still alive now, he could be anywhere.'

She reached into her handbag, pulled out a piece of paper, smoothed it flat and held it up for them to see.

'This is what he would look like now. We also have his DNA on file, taken from some of his hair that I kept in a locket. So, if he is ever found, we will be sure that it's him.'

Barbara dabbed at her smudged mascara with her handkerchief. March sat with huge tears rolling down her cheeks. Angie coughed, mumbled something about "bathroom" and disappeared.

Bailey moved to the front and cleared her throat. 'Thank you for that wonderful performance.' Her voice caught and she coughed. 'You are both so brave. I can't think of anything worse than losing a child.'

She'd spent the last few weeks moping over the thought of losing Duncan, when in fact she should have been happy at the prospect of gaining a daughter-in-law, the possibility of grandchildren and the promise of holidays back in her native Scotland.

'Ladies and Gentlemen, we are now going to hear our second performance of the night. If you would like to go through to the bar?' Her eyes were drawn to the far side of the room. 'Please excuse me. I think Barbara is trying to attract my attention.'

She rushed across to where Barbara stood, looking agitated. 'What's the matter?'

'Angie has locked herself into the loo and she's sobbing. I think I should be with her. Could you make our excuses for a while? I'll let you know what's what.'

'That's so kind of you.'

'Leave it to me. I'll get to the bottom of it.'

Bailey walked back into the reception room. The guests had all gone through to the bar. The waiter, who Bailey remembered was called Clive, collected the empty glasses. Bailey saw him pick up the poster of Jeremy, fold it, and put it in his pocket. How thoughtful. He obviously intended to return it to Pryor and Nigel. She made a mental note to pass on her compliments, about Clive's level of service, to the hotel manager.

Barbara tapped on the cubicle door. She could hear Angie sobbing quietly.

'Angie, come out of there. Let's go for a drink and talk about this.'

'Go away, leave me alone.'

Barbara heard Angie blow her nose and choke down a sob. Something had obviously caused Angie to breakdown like this, but what? Yes, it was a sad tale, especially when such an adorable couple have lived with this tragedy for so many years, but surely there must be more to it.

Barbara leaned closed to the cubicle door, and lowered her voice. 'Angie, dear, I'm not leaving you like this.'

'I don't want to talk.'

'OK, then let's go back to your room – or mine – and have a drink.' She experienced a twinge of guilt at the thought of encouraging Angie's habit.

The lock clicked and Angie emerged. Her turban had slipped and strands of silver-grey hair protruded from beneath it. Black smudges streaked down her cheeks where the tears had caused her mascara to run. Angie clutched a wodge of toilet paper in a tight ball and continued to dab at her swollen eyes and red runny nose.

'Oh, my dear, let's do a bit of emergency repair work.' Barbara pulled out her lace edged handkerchief, soaked it under the cold tap and wiped Angie's cheeks. 'There, that's better. You don't quite look like a Panda now.'

Angie looked in the mirror, straightened her turban and blew her nose.

'Ready to go?' Barbara asked.

Angie nodded.

'Your place or mine?'

Angie sniffed, threw the tissue in the bin, and rinsed her hands under the cold tap. 'Mine. I've got a fresh bottle of gin. I need a drink.'

'I'll just nip back and tell Bailey we're going back to your room. Wait here for me.'

Bailey followed her guests into the bar. 'Ladies and Gentlemen, it is now time for the final part of our evening's entertainment. Cher, over to you.'

Cher walked to the front of the group. 'Tonight, I'm going to tell you a story based on the book by Miguel de Cervantes.'

James groaned. 'But we all know that one. Tell us something new.'

'A good story is always worth re-visiting. Besides…' Cher looked at James and smiled. 'I'm telling it as a poem:'

Cher Reeves's Poem

Don Quixote, a nobleman by birth,
Was determined to improve his worth.
He studied many books on Knights
And vowed that he would roam the earth
With Sancho as his humble serf,
In search of gallant fights.

'Come, Sancho, let us forge ahead
And prove that chivalry's not dead.
Let's seek our foe and fight our duel.'
He rode his horse, a steed well bred,
Who pawed the ground and flounced his head
While Sancho followed on his mule.

Quixote with his lance in hand,
Said: 'Come, Sancho, let's leave this land.
We'll search and find much better things.
An island home will come to hand
With cocoa palms and golden sand,
A paradise! We'll reign as kings.

'But first we'll travel far and wide
Loyal companions, side by side;
Destroy the wicked, defend the weak.
Turn the tables, turn the tide,
Restore justice where'er we ride,
We'll gain the respect and honour we seek.

'Sancho, look, a monstrous arm
A giant who intends us harm.
See how he swings his limbs around?
Courage my friend we must stay calm,
As we attack, we'll sing a psalm.
God will defend us I'll be bound.'

'But Don Quixote, those limbs are sails!
They circulate in wind and gales.
They grind the corn and make the flour.
They are not giants; your eyes have veils;
You've read too many noble tales.
These are not a test of valour.

They're harmless windmills, don't you see?
They'll never ambush you and me.'
Windmills-'

Cher broke off from the poem and looked over Bailey's shoulder towards the door. Bailey turned and followed her gaze. Barbara was waiting in the doorway. As she realised Bailey had spotted her, she began waving franticly, giving an impressive imitation of Don Quixote's windmill.

Bailey rushed over. 'Is something wrong, Barbara?'

'I didn't want to interrupt Bailey. I just wanted you to know – I'm taking Angie back to her room. She's had a bit of a meltdown, but I'll stay with her until she settles. I don't think she should be on her own.'

'OK, thanks. Don't forget the early start tomorrow. Breakfast is at 5:00 and the coach leaves for the airport at 5:45.' She walked back into the lounge. 'I do apologise, Cher. Please, continue.'

James called out. 'Do you have to?'

'No, no, I was almost finished.'

'Please, Cher,' Bailey begged.

'No, it's fine. Honestly, Bailey, after all, it's not exactly Chaucer.'

'That's fairly rude of you, James, but it's probably as well,' Fyrne said. 'I'm all for green energy, but windmills fill me with dread. They've applied for planning permission to erect a forest of the damn things in the field behind my home. Since then I've developed an aversion.'

'An aversion to windmills?' gasped James. 'Surely not? They are beauteous creations. They march across our skylines.' He cupped his hand around his mouth to create a megaphone and spoke even louder than usual. 'They declare FREEDOM!' His voice ricocheted around the bar.

Clive, the barman, turned around and stared in his direction.

March grabbed his arm. 'Shush, James, not so loud.'

Fyrne jumped to her feet. 'Freedom from what exactly? Wildlife destroyed by their merciless blades? Beautiful landscapes destroyed by 200-foot metal eyesores? Or–'

'Freedom, my dear lady. Freedom for us Brits from imported Russian gas. Freedom for Australia from imported Chinese coal. Freedom from power stations with huge chimneys that burn fossil fuel, pollute the atmosphere and contaminate our earth. Freedom from the risk of catastrophe, caused by nuclear accidents, or from terrorist attacks.'

Fyrne stepped closer to him.

Bailey wondered if she needed to intervene. Surely Fyrne must realise that James was only arguing for windmills in an attempt to wind her up. Ironically, for once he was talking some sense, but only because it gave him a chance to take centre stage in that annoying flamboyant way of his.

Fyrne continued. 'We don't have to rely on windmills to achieve all that. Windmills destroy the peace and quiet with their noise and vibration. How is that freedom?'

'It's freedom from global warming. Do you realise that wonderful coral we saw today will die if the temperature continues to rise as it has? Australia is already highly at risk from climate change and is also one of the biggest contributors per capita of greenhouse gasses. The only solution is more wind farms.'

'What about waterfalls, solar panels, wave hubs, heat source pumps, reducing our consumption through better insulation, electric cars that generate their own power, etcetera, etcetera. We don't need bloody windmills.' Fyrne turned her back on James, returned to her chair and threw herself back down.

Sumner patted Cher's shoulder. 'Well, well, well. Who would have thought that the dashing Don Quixote could cause such a stir? This is entertainment at its best.' He leaned forward. 'You have to admit James, they are ugly.'

'Ugly? How can you say such a thing? They have such grace. Have you seen an orchard of turbines at sunset? They are truly magnificent.'

'Well, beauty, as they say, is in the eye of the beholder,' Sumner continued. 'But they can be noisy blighters, I'm told.'

'As their white blades slice through the air they create a gentle murmur, like the tender beat of angel wings,' James said softly.

Sumner snorted. 'Personally, I don't recall ever hearing the sound of angel wings.'

'That Sumner,' James lowered his voice, 'is because they are so quiet.' He smiled and winked at Bailey.

Bailey ignored him. 'Ladies and Gentlemen, I'm so sorry to have cut short your evening's entertainment, but perhaps it's no bad thing after all, as I see the retaurant are ready for us now. I did ask for dinner to be slightly earlier tonight. You will remember that we have a very early start tomorrow. The advantage is that we will be in Sydney for lunch and you will have the rest of the day to explore.'

Fyrne walked over and sat beside March. She leaned towards her and whispered. 'How on earth do you put up with him?'

'God knows.'

'Then why do you?'

'Habit, I suppose. It's not much fun these days, that's for sure.'

'Today's dive was fun.'

'I'm so pleased you talked me into it.'

'You can't come all this way and miss out.'

'I don't suppose I'll ever hear the end of it.' March glanced at James. He stood at the restaurant door chatting to a young waitress. She sighed and turned back to Fyrne. 'I loved it, thank you.

Barbara sat in the arm chair in Angie's room, while Angie fixed them both a large gin and tonic.

'Do you want to tell me what that's wrong?'

'That hauntingly sad song, and Pryor's story.' Angie reached for a tissue from the box beside her. She perched on the bed and took a large gulp of her drink.

'I don't want to pry, Angie, but you're obviously in considerable distress. Won't you let me help?'

'I'm just a stupid old woman who drinks far more than I should. Ignore me.'

'Angie, my dear, I can't. You're obviously in so much pain. How long have you been drinking – in your words – far too much?'

'Five years.'

'So, what happened five years ago?'

Barbara could see that Angie's eyes brimmed with tears. She reached across and placed her hand over Angie's.

'Did you lose someone?'

'I lost everything. My daughter, Vicky. My reason for living.' Angie's tears ran freely once more. 'So beautiful, kind and intelligent.'

Barbara stood, topped up Angie's empty glass and handed it to her. 'What happened?'

'A hit and run. She was at a bus stop when this idiot lost control of his car and smashed into her. She didn't stand a chance. He didn't even have the decency to stop and help her.'

'Oh, you poor dear.' No wonder Angie drank. 'You say *he*. Does that mean he was traced?'

'They caught him a mile from where she lay dying. He'd crashed into a parked car.'

Barbara moved over to sit on the bed beside Angie. She put her arms around her to give her a hug, and in doing so, knocked Angie's turban off.

'Sorry, my dear, I… oh, what beautiful hair. Silver. I'd kill for such a pretty shade. Why on earth do you keep it covered up all the time?'

303

'My hair fell out when Vicky died. The shock, don't you know? It grew back, eventually, but by then it had turned this colour. It's so fine. I hate it.'

'You should have a really good cut. Keep it a bit longer on top and short at the side, like Dame Judi Dench. It would be stunning. I tell you what… I've been recommended a stylist in Sydney. I knew I'd be ready for a tidy up by then, so I made an appointment. Let me book you in as well. My treat.'

'That's so kind, Barbara. I'll get us both another drink.'

'OK, one more and then that will be my limit if I'm to make breakfast at 5:00 a.m. Now, why don't you tell me a bit more about Vicky? If you feel up to it?'

31. Day Fifteen – Sydney

March looked up from her visitor's guide book of Sydney, as James closed the wardrobe door. He shrugged on his sports jacket. She'd planned an expedition along George Street to get something for their two granddaughters. Perhaps a pair of Ugg boots, or one of those cute, cuddly koalas she'd seen at the airport. Or should she get them both an opal necklace for when they got a bit older.

'Are we going now?'

'You stay and read your book, I'm off out.'

She noticed James smelt of aftershave, unusual for him during the day.

'Where are you going? You're not rushing off to find that blonde waitress you were chatting up over lunch, are you?'

'Which waitress?'

'Don't which waitress me. You must think I'm blind.'

'I thought I'd nip down to the marina. Sumner came to Sydney last year to sort out the contract for that calendar he's working on. He went out on one of those ocean yachts. It only cost him a couple of hundred quid.'

'But we were going shopping?'

'Take that new friend of yours. You seem to prefer her company to mine these days.'

'I went on the dive with her because you refused to go.'

'Well then, you did what you wanted. Now it's my turn.'

So, this was her punishment for enjoying herself so much.

Yesterday, with Fyrne, was the first time in ages that she'd laughed for joy? She tried to remember the last time she and James had shared a laugh together, but failed, it was so long ago.

He picked up his man bag, hitched it over his shoulder and strolled out of the room. He didn't even say goodbye.

March walked over to the window and looked across to the Sydney Opera House. She had paid extra for the upgrade to enjoy this view. James had insisted it came out of her bank account, rather than the joint account that usually covered their holidays and household bills.

'You suggested upgrading, you pay!' he'd snapped. He had strange ideas about money. Just lately she'd caught him looking at expensive houses. She knew he planned to spend her inheritance as soon as her elderly demented mother passed away. She could hardly believe how harsh he'd been when they'd discussed the last nursing home bill.

'If she doesn't hurry up and die soon there'll be nothing left. We should move her to somewhere cheaper.'

'But she likes it there. She thinks it's her home. She told me on my last visit that the other residents were friends who have come to visit her and that the nurses were all loyal servants.'

'She lives in cloud cuckoo land. She'd never know the difference.'

'She's my mother, and I won't move her.'

She'd felt like stamping her foot, but resisted behaving like a petulant child. He didn't. He'd sulked for two days.

The phone rang. Perhaps he'd had a change of heart. She picked up the handset.

'Hi March, it's me, Fyrne.'

March's heart lifted.

'I bumped into James in the lobby. He told me he's out for the afternoon. Fancy some retail therapy?'

'I'll meet you in ten minutes.'

'I'm in the lounge.'

March stroked the black silk camisole and French knickers trimmed with delicate cream lace. 'They're so beautiful. I'd feel like a million dollars wearing them, they're so sexy.'

'Buy them,' urged Fyrne. 'They'd look great on you.'

'But they're so expensive and utterly frivolous. Who would ever know I wore silk underwear costing the best part of a hundred pounds?'

'You would, and that's all that matters. They'll give you confidence. Make you feel good about yourself.'

'My confidence has taken a bit of a battering lately.'

'I'm not surprised with that husband of yours. He talks to you like you're a... well I'm not quite sure, but it's not what you deserve.'

'He's always been the same. He's always quick to remind me that he got a better degree than I did, he got a better job, has always earned more money than I have, and–'

'And you kept the house in good order, all the cooking and cleaning. Brought up your son and still went on to create your own designer textile business. Think about yourself for a change.'

'Your right. I'll buy them. I can wear them under my evening dress tonight. I wonder what James will say when he sees them.'

Fyrne frowned. 'Well if you're late coming down for the evening, I'll know why.' She turned away and walked over to examine a display of silk scarves while the sales attendant wrapped March's purchases in tissue paper and popped them into a carrier bag.

March stepped out of the shower, towelled herself down, dried her hair and dabbed a small amount of perfume onto her wrists and behind her ears. She stepped into the silk knickers, slid them up over her thighs and then pulled the camisole over her head. The silk felt cool against her flushed skin. Fyrne was right; they did make her feel confident.

She stepped into the bedroom, where James lounged on the bed, drinking a beer and watching the TV.

'I went shopping today.'

'I know, you told me. Cuddly koalas and Ugg boots for the girls.' He didn't look up from the programme. 'Can't think why. They'll be grown out of them in six months. I hope you used your own account.'

'I treated myself to some sexy underwear too. What do you think?'

He dragged his gaze away from the TV show, where a fisherman struggled to land an enormous fish.

'Sexy? Call that sexy? You look like a tart.'

March grabbed her evening dress from the wardrobe and retreated to the bathroom. She locked the door. James treated her like dirt and expected her to take it. Well, she'd had enough. She'd show him. She applied her make-up carefully, stepped into her dress and checked the mirror. Not bad for a fifty-six-year-old.

'I'm going down for a drink. See you in the bar. Don't be late. It's story time in half an hour.'

James grunted and continued to watch the TV. She walked

out, allowing the door to bang behind her. By the time she reached the bar, her confidence had evaporated and her eyes brimmed with tears. She was relieved to see Fyrne at the bar drinking a glass of sparkling wine.

'May I join you?' March asked.

'I'll get you a glass of wine. How did it go?'

'Don't ask.'

'You look stunning. How could he not be impressed?'

'He said I looked like a tart.'

'What? I can't believe that man.'

Fyrne ordered them both a glass of sparkling wine each from the barman. 'Come on, we'll go and sit over there in the corner.'

March watched while the waiter took two small coasters from his tray and placed them on their table. He then transferred two frosted glasses filled to just below the brim with bubbly white wine, followed by a bowl of peanuts.

'Thanks.' Fyrne smiled at the waiter, handed a glass to March and took the other, raising it in a salute. 'Cheers!'

'I don't feel very cheerful. I do believe today was probably the last day of my marriage. I can't take anymore.' March's eyes filled with tears as she sipped the chilled wine. 'I thought my world had ended when he walked out last year. I thought everything would be all right when he came back, but it isn't. I don't feel the same way about him anymore.'

'Oh, March, I'm so sorry.'

'I used to find him amusing. Now I think he's arrogant, pompous and rude. He makes me cringe with these flamboyant performances of his. I wouldn't care as much if I thought he actually believed what he said, but most of the time it's just for effect.'

'What will you do?'

'I'll probably have to close the shop. Most of my sales are through the web page these days, and it'll save money to move everything online. I suppose I'll have to rent somewhere to live while things are sorted out. I could even move out of Cornwall, somewhere nearer to the grandchildren and Mother's nursing home. At least if I go now, he can't get his hands on her money. I intend to start divorce proceedings as soon as we get home.'

'Good for you.' Fyrne took March's hand and squeezed it. 'You know I'll help in any way I can.'

'You're a good friend. Thanks.'

'I could offer you a room in Reading. I have a large rambling pile of a house. Although it may soon have a field of windmills close by.'

'Thanks. I'll think about it.'

'Please do.' Fyrne patted March's arm. 'Courage and confidence, that's what you need. This is your chance to find happiness. Oh, look! I think the group is gathering over there for story time. Do you feel up to it?'

'Let's go.'

32. First Evening in Sydney

Singapore Sling

- *30ml Gin*
- *10ml Cherry Brandy*
- *5ml Benedictine*
- *10ml fresh lemon juice*
- *Two dashes of Angostura bitters*
- *Soda water*

   Fill a chilled highball glass with ice, pour in the ingredients, stir and top up with soda water. Serve with a slice of lemon.

Maddy smiled as she and Tony joined Miller and Sumner at the cocktail bar. She raised her glass in a toast. 'Cheers!' She took a sip. 'Mm, these cocktails taste even better knowing they're free.'

Sumner laughed. 'You do know they simply add an extra fifty quid on everyone's bill to pay for them, don't you? They're not exactly free.'

'Maybe not, but I prefer to think they are.'

Bailey walked over to join them. 'Good evening, everyone. Maddy, I checked with the Nunnes today. As I suspected, they have declined the opportunity to tell a story.

'Chickens,' Sumner scoffed.

'I hope it isn't inconvenient for you to bring your story forward?'

'Not at all. As I said last night, I'm happy to step in.'

'Thank goodness. I hope you're all enjoying your Singapore Slings?'

'It's a fun way to start the evening,' Maddy said.

'I'm glad. The cocktails are a new introduction this year.'

'Great idea.' Miller picked up his cocktail. 'I wonder how the company absorbed the cost. I'd noticed the holiday price remained the same as last year.'

'Oh, I'm sure it's not very expensive,' Bailey said.

Maddy noticed that Bailey looked slightly flustered as she rushed over to the corner of the lounge where the other guests were gathering. She weaved her way between the collection of burgundy sofas, mushroom and burgundy striped armchairs and dark chestnut coffee tables that had been clustered together earlier to create a cosy and discrete area for the group.

'Ladies and Gentlemen, could you'd please take your seats?' Bailey waited for them to settle down. 'You will be pleased to know that Maddy has agreed to tell us her tale tonight. Please give a hand to our courageous police officer.'

A ripple of applause greeted the introduction.

'Good evening everyone,' Maddy said. 'As you know, I work for the police, but obviously, I could not reveal the details of a true investigation, so my tale tonight is completely fictitious.'

'Come on, Maddy,' laughed James. 'You don't expect us to believe that, do you?'

Maddy smiled and continued. 'There are two teams involved in bringing a criminal to justice, the police, who investigate the crime, and the prosecutor who must persuade the jury that the defendant is guilty. Sometimes we may know someone is guilty but are unable to assemble sufficient evidence to prove it. Sometimes, we need a little luck. My story is about one such case:'

Maddy Manciple's Tale

Brendon and Phil had been friends since school. Brendon went to university to study Business Studies, Phil to college to study beer mats and pies. Brendon went to the Gym twice a week to keep trim, Phil to the pub every day and didn't bother. Brendon had his hair styled once a fortnight by Kelvin, Phil's mother gave him a trim whenever his fringe grew too long.

I think you get the picture. They made an unlikely pair, but they were the best of friends.

Brendon sat in the pub, explaining to Phil how he'd popped the question to Pheobe, a young woman he'd met at university.

'Of course, she said yes and obviously you'll be my best man. Honestly, Phil, she's the most beautiful woman in the world.'

'But then, you may be a little biased.'

Brendon laughed. 'You'll love her when you meet her. She is petite and blonde, with huge almond-shaped blue eyes. She also comes with the added advantage of a wealthy family.'

'I hope you're marrying her for the right reasons.' Phil finished his drink. 'See you tomorrow,' he stood and picked up his coat.

'Leaving so early?'

'Stomach's a bit sour tonight, sorry.'

The wedding took place a month after Brendon and Phoebe finished university. It was a lavish affair, paid for entirely by Phoebe's parents. Brendon's parents were both dead, and although Brendon offered to make a contribution, somehow, he was never around whenever there was a bill to settle. Or if he was, he had forgotten his chequebook and promised to pop one in the post. One way or another, the anticipated cheques never arrived.

After the honeymoon in Hawaii, paid for by Phoebe's grandparents, Brendon met with Phil over a pint to discuss various options for their future employment. Phil had recently inherited some money from a distant aunt, which he'd agreed to contribute as start-up funding. Brendon had inherited his parents' rather nice home, where he and Phoebe now lived, but his extravagant lifestyle at university had ravaged his financial situation, or so he claimed. Phil accepted that the cash-strapped Brendon was unable to match his funds, and at least his inheritance gave them enough to get started.

They decided to set up a small corporate hospitality business. You know the thing: organising someone a box at the races, football or rugby to entertain their potential clients; or arranging the hire of marquees to accommodate weddings, parties or festivals. Phil was good at organising venues, the catering, logistics and hard physical work, and Brendon excelled at marketing, socialising and the financial side of things. Together, they made a good team, and over the next three years their business boomed.

Brendon looked up as Phil entered the office, panting as usual. His jacket lay draped over one shoulder. Damp patches spread from under his arms and across his chest. The buttons on his shirt strained. His stomach hung over the top of his belt. His body shape resembled a pear sat on top of an apple. He slumped into his chair and sighed deeply.

'Christ, what drove us to choose an office on the top floor. Never again. Those stairs get steeper every day.'

'No, Phil, it's you getting fatter every day. When do you start that diet?'

'Don't go on at me. I'm already getting it in the neck from my GP.'

'Someone needs to tell you the truth. You're a heart attack waiting to happen.'

Phil sighed. 'Fancy a pint after we finish?'

'Wouldn't say no. As long as you're paying, I'm broke. I'll give Phoebe a quick call and tell her to hold dinner.'

Phil's perched on a small stool that threatened to collapse under the strain. 'How is Phoebe?'

'She's great. The perfect little woman. She keeps a nice house, rustles up a cordon bleu meal at short notice, like when I need to entertain a client. She understands about the hours I work – and play if you catch my drift – and she's very accommodating in the bedroom. Although to be honest, that side of things has trailed off a bit of late. She's a bit moody at the moment. You know how women can be when their hormones kick in.'

'You don't appreciate her enough. She's a gorgeous, kind, intelligent woman.'

'Phoebe? Sure you're talking about my wife? Gorgeous, no question. Kind – I suppose so. But intelligent? No way. Last week she told me we needed to check our catering suppliers. Apparently, there's been a case of Ebola. I ask you. She meant E-coli of course.'

'Easy mistake to make.'

'Well I grant you, they can both cause an upset tummy, but Ebola is rather more deadly.' Brendon laughed.

'I'm warning you, you'll lose her unless you wake up and start to appreciate her more.'

Phil's words stirred a vague feeling of unease in Brendon. Phoebe had been acting a little out of character of late. More evenings out with her friend, Lucy, a little less of the "dinner is on the table" and more of the "help yourself to cold cuts from the fridge."

Brendon made excuses and left Phil to finish his pint. He decided that after two pints he should leave his car in the office car park. He walked down the high street towards home and bumped into Phoebe's friend, Lucy.

'Oh hi, Brendon. How's Phoebe, I meant to ring her to fix up an evening out, but I've been so busy this past month I haven't had the chance.'

His stomach lurched. If she hadn't been meeting Lucy, who the hell had she been seeing for the past three weeks?

'She's fine.' Brendon forced a smile. 'I'll tell her I saw you. Get her to give you a ring.'

Brendon called as he unlocked the front door and walked into the hall. 'Phoebe, I'm home. Where are you?'

'I'm up here, in the bath. There's a bottle of white wine open in the fridge.'

He walked into the kitchen. Her handbag lay on the table with her cell phone beside it. By now, he was angry and his brain was in overdrive. He reached over and checked her contacts list; Brendon, Home, Lucy, Phil – hang on a minute…why would she have Phil on speed dial? He pressed the button to connect.

Phil answered immediately. 'Phoebe, darling, are you OK? He's just left me. How can you bear the way he talks about you? Tell him you're leaving him. Just do it, then we can be together. Phoebe? Phoebe?'

Brendon disconnected. His head was bursting with fury. How could she be unfaithful to him, especially with that lump of lard? What had Phil got to offer? He still lived at home with his mother for God's sake.

His hand shaking, he poured a glass of wine and headed for the bathroom. She lay submerged in a steaming bath of bubbles, only her neck and head visible. She smiled as he handed her the wine.

'Thank you. Enjoy your drink? How's Phil?'

'Fine!' he snapped. 'I forgot to ask you... how did the drink with Lucy go last week?'

'Good. We had a good time. Lots of girlie chat. What's up? You're frowning.'

'I bumped into Lucy on the high street. She told me to say she's been meaning to get in touch for the past few weeks. She wants you to ring her.'

'Oh.'

'Oh? Is that all you have to say?'

'What do you want me to say?'

'How about telling me why you betrayed me? And with that fat oaf, Phil? He's grotesque for Christ's sake.'

She sipped her wine. 'He enjoys my company. Loves me for who I am. It's so refreshing – so... exhilarating... to be adored.'

Anger swept through him. Overwhelmed with rage he grabbed her ankles and pulled hard. Taken by surprise, she dropped the glass, which sank beneath the bubbles. She tried desperately to get a grip on the bath, but he continued to hold her feet, forcing her head under the water. Her struggles grew weaker. Then stopped altogether. He held her under until there was no doubt.

She was dead.

Panic swung in. Now what? He thought quickly. No one had seen him return; his car was still in the parking lot below the office.

He could get back there and try to establish some sort of alibi. But would the police believe it was an accident? Someone else needed to discover her body and become the suspect. He grabbed his cell phone and dialled the home number. It went to answerphone.

'Darling, it's me. I'm really sorry but I've bumped into a few mates, and we're going for a curry. I won't be home till late. I'll make it up to you when I get back. Love and kisses.'

That should establish his absence, ongoing love, and lack of suspicion. He rolled up his sleeve and reached for the wine glass, wiped it with the towel and let it fall back into the bath. He had no idea if fingerprints could survive hot soapy water, but he wasn't about to take chances.

Now for the alibi. He raced downstairs, into the kitchen and carefully picked up her phone with his handkerchief. He used his pen to tap in the message – B is out for the night, come now. I'm in the bath, door on latch. Can't wait to see you XXX. He scrolled through her address book to Phil's number, and pressed send.

Leaving the front door on the latch, he left by the back door, through the gate in the fence and headed down the jetty; a short cut to the office. The lights were still on in the second-floor advertising office.

'Hi guys, you lot working late I see.'

'Rush job, but we're just finishing off. Is Phil with you?'

'He left earlier, some mysterious date. Do you fancy a curry? I'm starving, and the wife has threatened me with cold cuts – again.'

'Sure, I'm up for it,' Brian said. Gail and Steve also agreed and they set off to the nearest curry house.

Brendon got back to the house two hours later. Two police officers were standing on the doorstep. One spoke into his radio.

'Good evening, Officers. What's all this about? I have had a few drinks, but I left the car at the office.'

'I'm afraid we have some bad news, Sir. Shall we go and sit in the police car?'

'Of course, let me just tell my wife I'm back.'

'I'm sorry, Sir. She's not here. Let's sit down in the car.'

One policeman opened the door and protected Brendon's head as he sat on the back seat. The second policeman scrambled in beside him.

'What's all this about, officer?'

'There's been an accident. I'm very sorry to tell you, but your wife has drowned in the bath. She died a couple of hours ago.'

Brendon gasped. 'This can't be real. It can't be true. It's our third wedding anniversary next week. What do you mean, she died?'

'I'm sorry for your loss. A family friend discovered your wife's body. He's down at the police station helping us with our enquiries.'

'Family friend?'

'Phillip Hardcastle. I believe he had a text from your wife and came around. He discovered her body in the bath.'

'Phil? Why would my wife contact Phil?'

'I'm sorry Sir, but it seems they were involved in an affair.'

'No... no officer, you have it all wrong. My wife would never be unfaithful. And even if she did, it wouldn't be with someone who weighs twenty-five stone. Phil? You must be mistaken.'

'He's admitted it, and their phone records would appear to indicate that they were indeed involved. Now, Sir, can we take you to stay with a relative, a friend, or at a hotel for the next couple of days.'

'I'll be OK here.'

'Sorry, Sir, this is a crime scene. We'll hand it back to you as *soon as we can.'*

Brendon shook his head. 'I can't believe it. Any of it.'

Nor did we. Oh, he put on a good act and he'd covered his tracks well. But the anguish and loss demonstrated by Phil Hardcastle was so genuine. There was no doubt in our minds that Brendon killed his wife in a fit of rage. Unfortunately, we had very little evidence, certainly not enough for us to make an arrest. We allowed him to continue with the belief that Phil Hardcastle was our prime suspect and watched him closely in the hope that he would make a mistake.

The inquest was inconclusive. It could have been an accident, but the coroner was concerned about the marks on Phoebe's ankles. It could have been murder or even suicide. The court recorded an open verdict.

The day before the funeral, Brendon decided to go to the office and sort through the paperwork, cancel a few bookings and get things straight. He had e-mailed Phil earlier in the week and told him they could no longer work together. He'd suggested that they sell the business as a going concern and split the proceeds 50/50, completely ignoring Phil's rights to have the initial start-up funding refunded. Brendon argued that this was easier than a protracted court case over who gets what. Brendon held a very healthy life insurance on Phoebe. He was confident it would pay up eventually, once they failed to prove her death was a suicide. The sale of the house, business and the insurance policy would give him plenty of funds to start over again.

We can only surmise what happened next. Brendon never admitted the sequence of events, but we believe it went like this:

It was stuffy in the office. Brendon opened the patio window that gave access to the tiny Juliet balcony, with a view onto the car park four floors below. It was almost dark. He could just make out his car. Phoebe would have moaned at him about taking the car for such a short distance, but the forecast suggested rain before the night ended.

He thought about Phil. He knew he'd been released on bail, pending further enquiries, and that he was still under suspicion. The police had told him that they believed Phoebe had tried to break things off with him and, in a fit of rage, he'd killed her, but they had no evidence.

Brendon looked up as Phil entered the office, panting as usual.

'You're the last person I expected to see, Phil.'

'It was you, you bastard. I don't know how you did it, but I know it was you.'

'But why? I had no idea you were involved with my wife until the police told me.'

'You found out somehow. I'll prove it if it's the last thing I do.'

Brendon stood and moved from behind his desk. Philip lunged towards him. Brendon sidestepped, and Phil, wrong-footed, hurtled forward and stumbled through the open patio window, over the balcony railings, and fell with a heavy thud into the car park below.

Brendon leaned over the balcony railing. It was totally dark and the only light came from the street lamps on the main road. He could just make out the crumpled heap of Phil's white shirt. There was no movement, not that he expected any. No way could anyone survive landing head first onto a tarmac surface from the fourth floor. No one was about; no one had seen the incident. His was the only car in the car park, Phil must have walked. It would look like a leap of suicide, an admission of guilt. Brendon breathed a sigh of relief. He was safe.

He left the office, leaving the door unlocked and the lights on. Everyone would assume that Phil was the last person to leave the building. He dashed to his car, refusing to look in the direction of Phil's body. If he paused to look, he would risk being sick, or he might be seen from the footpath. He needed to get home as quickly as possible. He drove to the edge of the car park without his headlights, not wanting to alert anyone to his presence.

Damn, what was that clunk? He must have hit a stray boulder on the car park, better get the tyres checked in the morning. He switched on his lights as he pulled onto the main road and turned on the CD. He began to hum as he drove the short distance home.

He was humming the next morning when he opened the door and recognised the two police officers, the ones who had delivered the news of his wife's death.

'Hello there. Do come in. Would you like a cup of tea?'

'No Sir, I'm afraid this is not a social call. Is that your car on the drive?'

Brendon looked over the policeman's shoulder to where his silver Ford Focus was parked.

'Yes, that's mine. Is there a problem? It's not my road tax, is it? I didn't think that was due until next month.'

'If you would come with us, Sir? There are some questions we need to ask you down at the station.'

Brendon sat on an uncomfortable plastic chair in a small interview room. The same two policemen sat opposite him.

'Would you mind telling me how you came by the damage on the front wheel hub, on the passenger side?'

'Oh that? Yes, I caught it on a boulder yesterday, as I was leaving the car park at work.'

'Can you account for the fact that there are traces of blood on the paintwork?'

Brendon felt the colour drain from his face. The police officers watched him.

'Perhaps I hit a cat? Perhaps it wasn't a boulder?'

'Come now, Sir. You don't expect us to believe that? We know you pushed your partner out of the patio window of the office and left him for dead. It must have been a shock when you realised, he'd recovered sufficiently to crawl across the car park towards the road. You deliberately aimed your car and drove him down, didn't you?'

'Don't be ridiculous. I haven't even seen Phil since the day of my wife's death.'

'Then how do you account for this?'

The policeman pulled out a small tape recorder. It was about the size of a mobile phone, with a clip to keep it in place in a shirt pocket. Brendon's own voice broke the silence.

'You're the last person I expected to see, Phil.'

'It was you, you bastard. I don't know how you did it, but I know it was you.'

'But why? I had no idea you were involved with my wife until the police told me.'

'You found out somehow. I'll prove it if it's the last thing I do.'

There was the sound of a scuffle, a scream from Phil, followed by a heavy thud as Phil hit the ground.

'Well, OK, perhaps I did see him that evening, but I didn't

push him. He ran at me and I moved out of his way. It was an accident.'

'In that case, why didn't you ring the police and an ambulance? The doctor has confirmed he was still alive after the fall. You could have saved him.'

'I... I didn't think he could survive such a fall, and... well, to be honest officer, I didn't want to be involved. After all, he killed my wife.'

'Did he really, Sir? That's not how it sounds from the tape, is it? We think it was you who killed your wife, after finding out about the affair.'

'That's not true. You can't prove I killed Pheobe, or Phil, for the matter. They were both accidents.'

'Wait a minute, Sir. There's more.' He switched the machine back on.

There was the sound of heavy breathing, a few gasps and a sound like a sack of potatoes being dragged across the floor.
'Brendon. Help me, please help... noooo-'
Then a sickening clunk as Brendon's car hit Phil's head.

'Brendon James, we are arresting you for the murder of Phil Hardcastle. You are not obliged to say anything, but anything you do say may be taken down, and may be used in evidence. Do you understand?'

We would probably never have proven that Brendon killed Pheobe, or that he pushed Phil off the balcony, but the tape and the doctor's evidence proved that Phil was still alive after the fall. The fact that Brendon failed to call for assistance, and then drove Brendon down with his car, led to his conviction for manslaughter.

'Wonderful, my dear.' Barbara clapped loudly. 'Isn't she wonderful? Don't you think so, Tony?'

'I do indeed.' Tony smiled broadly and clapped along with the others.

Maddy blushed. She wasn't used to such approval, but she could certainly get to like it. She linked arms with Tony as the group followed Bailey into the restaurant for dinner.

33. Day Sixteen – Melbourne Cup Day and Sydney Opera House

Bailey stood at the hospitality desk chatting to James and Sumner. She looked up as Barbara floated into the room wearing her pink trouser suit and matching hat, accompanied by Angie, in an orange kaftan and matching turban.

'Good morning, Barbara and Angie. Are you joining us for the Opera House Tour?'

'No thank you, my dear. Angie and I are off to the hairdressers.'

'Darling, I'm to undergo a metamorphosis and become turban-less, don't you know.'

'I look forward to seeing the results. By the way, Dean David has agreed to tell his story tonight, ladies, so don't be late. Six-thirty in the lounge.'

Bailey picked up her list and proceeded to check off names as guests continued to arrive and gather around the desk. 'Good morning, Frank. Are you reporting in for the Opera House Tour?'

'I'm so sorry, Bailey. I may catch up with you later, but I must try and find a pharmacist. My indigestion has got worse. I think I need something a bit stronger.'

'You'll find a large Walgreens on George St, about a quarter of a mile down on the right-hand side – just past the town hall. Check what's best with the pharmacist. They often know far more than the doctors. Miller, how about you? Opera House Tour?

'Not for me, thanks. I have an important meeting.'

'What can be more important than a tour of Sydney's most iconic building?' Sumner asked.

'Well, actually, I'm off to see a solicitor.'

'But you're on holiday.' Sumner slapped Miller on the back. 'Come on, let's do the tour, sink a few drinks, and then we can decide which horses to back in this afternoon's race.'

'I'd love to, but I need to find out how to establish one of these educational trusts for Dorothy and some of the other kids in Mutitjulu.'

Bailey blinked and stared at him. He was obviously serious. 'You are a surprise, sometimes, Miller.'

'You've seen nothing yet.' He winked, waved, and walked away.

She did a quick head count: fifteen. 'OK, Ladies and Gentlemen, if you could follow me, we'll walk the short distance to the Opera House, where you will be met by your guide for the morning. After the tour you will be free to explore the city, or remain on the quay, which, because it's the Melbourne Cup day, will be buzzing with excitement and parties. If you fancy a flutter on the race, you'll find temporary bookie stalls set up on the quay, opposite the ferries.'

Bailey usually loved Melbourne Cup days. Everyone dressed up in their best clothes, and the women wore extravagant hats. Champagne was consumed in vast quantities. Parties began before lunchtime and continued until the small hours of the next day. Today she didn't feel the excitement. She was too anxious about the upcoming meeting with Jim. She'd left several messages and e-mails, telling him she wanted to discuss the possible redundancy notification, but he'd ignored her calls, and then overnight sent an e-mail:

From: Jim Tennant
To: Katherine Bailey
Subject: Disciplinary Proceedings

Please report to my office at midday. I want to discuss:
Your blatant disregard for Australia Unleashed policy, specifically in relation to company uniform.
Your misuse of the daily allowance, which I understand you have used to purchase alcohol, in the form of cocktails.
Failure to notify Head Office, specifically in relation to arranging alternative travel arrangements for two guests.
These are considered to be serious breaches of your employment contract and may result in disciplinary action being taken against you.

Something she did not look forward to. But for now, it she needed to get her guests delivered to their guide for this morning's tour.

Fyrne and March sat in the armchairs either side of the bay window in Fyrne's room. The room service waiter had just left, having delivered two flute glasses, an ice bucket and a bottle of sparkling wine.

'So, where's James gone?'

'He said he was going back to the marina. I don't really believe him. He's wearing aftershave again, which is always a bit of a giveaway. And he told me not to bother waiting up for him tonight.'

'Does it worry you?'

'It makes me more determined to divorce him.'

Fyrne poured March a glass of wine. 'Here's to you, and your new life.'

'It still feels pretty scary, but I'm determined to make the break before I'm too old. I don't think I'd have had the strength to even think about leaving him if I hadn't met you. You're a good friend.'

Fyrne frowned and picked off a piece of fluff from her black shirt. 'Could you...' she looked at March. 'Do you think we could ever be more?'

March's cheeks grew hot. She hadn't been wrong then. 'In what way?'

'Do you remember Miller's story?'

'Did it upset you?'

'It was his dismissive attitude of Hazel and Nicola that I found so offensive. And your husband's suggestion that lesbian relationships are in some way second class. I guess you know I'm gay.'

'I think I knew that.'

'I am not fortunate enough to share my life with anyone at the moment, and I'm too old now to go cruising around bars searching for a soul mate, but believe me, the desire to find someone special is always there.' She looked at March and smiled. 'I envied Hazel and Nicola their relationship. It reminded me of Chaucer: "Grass time is gone, for me its winter hay." Fyrne put her glass on the coffee table. 'How do you feel about making some hay while the sun shines?'

March could feel her heart pounding. Was she being seduced by a woman? She couldn't do this, could she? Something about

Maddy's story last night sprang to mind. Phoebe had fallen for the unlikely lover, Phil, because he adored her. Seeing the way Fyrne looked at her now, she could understand how special that felt. She'd never been adored by anyone before. Could her unlikely lover be a woman?

March hesitated. 'Oh, Fyrne, I'm a middle aged, heterosexual, married woman. I've never even had an affair. James is the only man I've ever known – sexually that is. I can't even begin to imagine what it's like to have a sexual relationship with a woman.'

'Why don't you let me show you?'

34. Second Evening in Sydney

Cuba Libre

- *40ml Bacardi Rum*
- *15ml fresh lime juice*
- *80ml cola*

Fill a highball glass with ice, pour over Bacardi and lime juice, stir and top up with cola.

Bailey stood at the entrance of the hotel lounge reflecting on how awful her day had been. It had started well enough. She'd handed her guests over to their Opera House tour guide and then walked to Head Office for her twelve o'clock meeting with Jim, only to be told that he was with the new Managing Director and would not be available for the rest of the day.

She'd returned to the hotel and checked her text messages and e-mail throughout the afternoon, but had received nothing. She tried to concentrate on catching up on some paperwork, but her mind had wandered constantly. It was so unsettling to have Jim's accusations hanging over her. How *was* Jim getting all his information – who is the secret shopper?

Frank and Paul smiled at her as they walked past and entered the lounge, closely followed by the Nunnes, who were not smiling at anyone. As they walked towards the bar, Frank placed his arm over Pauls' shoulder and gave him a squeeze.

'Look at that,' Mrs Nunne nudged her husband in the ribs. 'Shocking behaviour. It's bad enough him being gay with a partner young enough to be his son, but to be demonstrative in public... well, it's a disgrace.'

Bailey cringed. She hoped neither Paul nor Frank had heard Mrs Nunne's evil comments. A friendly voice whispered in her ear.

'Never mind, Bailey, my dear.'

Bailey turned, and smiled at Barbara.

'That one will never change,' Barbara said, sadly.

'Unlike, Angie.' Bailey glanced over to where Angie sat on one of the lounge sofa's chatting to Nigel and Pryor. 'What an amazing transformation you've made there, Barbara. Well done you.'

'Doesn't she look stunning with her new hair style?'

'I hardly recognised her.' Bailey patted Barbara on the shoulder, and together they walked over to where the group were congregating.

Sumner sat in an armchair reading the sports pages of the evening newspaper.

'Anything interesting?' Bailey asked.

'I'm just reading about the race earlier. I'll scan through it for you.' He opened the page and folded the paper, making it easier to handle. 'The favourite, Red Admiral... the race in his stride... 800 metre mark... something dreadfully wrong... labours over the line... dead horse walking... reaches stall... collapses... stable hands, like firefighters... buckets of cold water... no good... the flame is out... owners heart blown apart, like a dandelion seed head in a cyclone.' Sumner looked up from the paper. 'So sad.'

'Serves him right,' Paul threw himself down in the armchair next to Sumner. 'Forcing horses to race like that. It's obscene.'

'I think they enjoy it.' Sumner folded the newspaper and tossed it onto the coffee table. 'I'm always amazed at how the horses that unseat their riders continue to race.'

Nigel stood to give Barbara a seat next to Pryor. He perched on the sofa arm and cleared his throat. 'In my younger days, and before it was banned, I used to enjoy hunting. The horses definitely enjoyed that experience.'

'More than can be said for the poor foxes,' Paul snorted.

Bailey sighed. More controversial subjects. More conflict. Why couldn't they all get on? She'd never had such a prickly group before. She was grateful James wasn't around to throw in his opinion. She wondered where he was.

'Ladies and Gentlemen, tonight we have our final story, told for us by our very own, Dean David.'

David stood and smiled at his audience. 'Dearly beloved, we are gathered here today.'

There was a ripple of laughter.

'But no, folks. Seriously. Today I will tell you a true story, set within the beautiful undulating countryside of Leicestershire. The setting is close to the site of the famous Battle of Bosworth, which took place on the 22nd August, 1485. You may remember: Henry Tudor was victorious; King Richard III was slain and the War of the Roses came to an end. Richard's death has recently been in the news because his remains were discovered under a car park in Leicester.'

Miller laughed. 'I'm glad I didn't have to pay his parking ticket.'

David smiled as he waited for the chuckles to subside.

My tragic story begins two-hundred and fifty years later, and involves a man, who, I'm sorry to say, ignored the perils of the seven deadly sins... pride... avarice... lust... envy... gluttony... wrath... and sloth. And so, my story begins:'

Dean David Parsons' Tale

The 4th Baronet Sir Wolstan Dixie was born in the year 1700 at Bosworth Hall. His parents arranged for their young son to be educated at home, and employed a series of governesses. None lasted long. Wolstan hated to be cooped indoors. He would play tricks on his teachers, run away from his lessons and disappear into the extensive grounds of the estate. Eventually, his father, in despair, sent him to boarding school, where he misbehaved so badly that when he ran away for the third time, the school refused to take him back.

As a young man he became renowned for his quick temper and a tendency to settle any disputes with his fists. One classic example of his many long-running feuds, involved a footpath that crossed his land. He took great objection to a neighbour using it, and physically attacked the man, beating him senseless.

He was a large man, prone to gluttony. His favourite food was the very rich lamprey, an eel-like fish that thrived in the clear water of the streams that ran through his estate.

Despite his lack of formal education, his quick temper and his size, he was a successful man. At twenty-seven, he became one of the youngest Sheriffs of Leicestershire. When presented to King George I, the monarch remembered his history and said, 'Bosworth! Big battle at Bosworth I believe?' Whereupon Dixie replied, 'Yes, Sir, I thrashed him.'

He was a proud man, especially of his beautiful and most precious daughter, Anne. They were particularly close because he'd raised her alone, after his wife died in childbirth.

He was also, unfortunately, a selfish and greedy man, never satisfied with his own substantial wealth. He envied his neighbour, a self-made man who owned a huge estate and an extensive herd of Longhorn cattle. Although Dixie considered the family to be lower class and inferior, he negotiated for Anne to marry the eldest son, in return for a dowry - half the herd and several hundred acres, increasing his wealth considerably. Even though he loved his daughter with a passion, he never asked her opinion on the union and failed to notice her lack of joy when the engagement was announced.

Tragedy struck shortly after the betrothal, in the year 1758. Dixie heard a rumour that Anne had been entertaining a young man in her room at night. He was appalled; not only was this man without title but he also came from an impoverished family. How dare this man ravage his daughter, putting her reputation and forthcoming marriage at risk? Furious, he became determined to seek his revenge.

He discovered that Anne would leave the back door to the stairs unlocked so that, under cover of darkness, the young man could sneak up to her room for their illicit meetings. This could not continue. Imagine if her intended found out and broke off the engagement. His plans for a comfortable early retirement, paid for by her dowry, would come to nothing.

The evening after he made this discovery, he planted an animal trap. The jaws of the contraption were stretched open to reveal huge jagged teeth, capable of snapping a man in half. The spring on the trap was incredibly strong, so Dixie enlisted the support of his coachman to carefully prime and install it under the sandy floor at the base of the staircase. This would be a fitting vengeance on this scoundrel, who dared to upset his careful plans.

He hid in the stable block nearby to watch the eagerly anticipated events unfold. He intended to then drag the body and trap into the nearby woods, and claim the young man had suffered an unfortunate accident while poaching.

Unfortunately, things didn't go as Dixie planned. The coachman horrified by his boss's plans, warned the young man to stay away. Anne, wondering where her visitor had got to, and fearing she may have forgotten to unlock the back door, descended the stairs and stepped into the trap.

Her cries of agony alerted Dixie. His heart pounding, he raced to Anne's side. Nothing could have prepared him for the shock of seeing her so badly maimed and screaming in agony. He freed her from the trap, swept her into his arms and carried her up to the bedroom. Her injuries were so severe it was obvious she was dying and he could do nothing, nothing at all to save her. Overwhelmed with remorse he begged her to forgive him. He explained how he had been trying to prevent her from making a dreadful mistake and how he hadn't wanted Anne's reputation to be ruined when her fiancé discovered her love affair.

Despite her injuries, she laughed, and told him there was no love affair. Anne and the young man, Francis, were meeting every night to undertake bible study together. He wanted to join the priesthood, and she had no intention of going through with the arranged marriage, but instead wanted to become a nun. They both sought to dedicate their lives to God.

As her life blood drained from her, streamed across the floor and seeped into the very fabric of the building, she forgave her father, on the condition that he promised to spend the rest of his life penance. She begged him to live a life of humility, love and kindness. She beseeched him to dedicate the estate to the care of the sick, and commit his life to charitable work, as she had planned to do.

He pledged to do all of these things.

'He did. That building became a hospital for the poor. Countless lives were saved. Two hundred years later, under the NHS, the building became the Bosworth Park Infirmary. After the hospital closed, the Hall was restored to its former glory as a Country House Hotel.

'Even today, Anne's ghost is said to haunt the building, and no matter how many times they paint the ceiling beneath her bedchamber, her life blood re-appears as a dark stain, and a reminder of the perils we face if we succumb to all, or even any, of the seven deadly sins - pride, avarice, lust, envy, gluttony, wrath, and sloth.'

Bailey stood to lead the applause. 'Thank you, David.'

'Before I take my seat,' the Dean said. 'I want to say thank you for your company and friendship over the past three weeks.'

He glanced at Cynthia, who, Bailey noticed, blushed.

'I didn't think it possible to enjoy life after the death of my dear wife, Mildred. Indeed, I only agreed to come on this holiday because this trip was a retirement present from my Cathedral congregation.

'While I've been here, I have given my future a lot of thought. Since the days of being a theology student I was drawn to the Roman Catholic faith, but then I met my wife at university and selfishly decided I wanted the best of both worlds: a life serving God and a married life shared with Mildred. I therefore chose to become an Anglican.

'I know I made the right decision at the time. We were blessed with a very happy marriage. Our only regret being that we were never able to have children. Now that I find myself alone, I feel free to reconsider my faith. After considerable prayer I have decided to convert to the Roman Catholic Church. Your friendship and support has helped me through this process, and I am truly grateful, thank you.' He raised his glass in a toast.

Oh dear. Bailey glanced at Cynthia who looked crestfallen. This would appear to be the end of any romance. Poor Cynthia.

Bailey heard a gasp. She turned around in time to see a glass fall from Frank's hand, hit the edge of the coffee table and shatter, splattering the remnants of his drink over the cream carpet. Frank clutched his arm. His eyes widened. His face paled. Beads of sweat appeared on his forehead.

'Dad, what's up?' Paul leapt to his feet, sending his chair crashing to the floor behind him. He grabbed Frank's shoulder. 'Dad, Dad, what's the matter? Talk to me.'

'This pesky... indigestion.' Frank struggled to breathe. He clasped his hands to his chest, tried to stand, but his legs crumpled and he collapsed to the floor.

Paul threw himself down at Frank's side. 'Help!' Paul shouted. 'Get a doctor.'

Bailey felt sick with panic. My God, he's having a heart attack. 'Call an ambulance!' she shouted to the waiter. She raced over to where Frank lay and fell to her knees opposite Paul. Come on, Bailey, she told herself, you know what to do. You've trained for this.

Alerted by the commotion the group gathered round.

'Stand back, give him some air.' Bailey looked up as someone knocked against her foot. 'Mrs Nunne, get out of my way.'

Bailey loosened Frank's tie, undid the top button of his shirt and felt the side of his neck. Sod it, no pulse. She'd never had a guest die on her before. Please, God don't let this be the first. She placed her hands in position on his chest and started to pump.

'Paul, pinch his nose hard. When I say go, breathe into his mouth.' She pumped eight times. 'Go.' She looked up at Paul. Tears streamed down his cheeks. 'Paul, for Christ's sake, now.'

Paul held Frank's nose and blew into his mouth. Frank's chest rose.

'Good. Well done, Paul. Now wait.' She remembered her trainer who taught them the technique, and pumped again in time with the Bee Gee's tune. 'One, two, three, four, staying alive, staying alive. Your turn, Paul.'

Paul took a deep breath and blew into Frank's mouth once more. He stroked Frank's forehead, as Bailey resumed her pumping. 'Come on, Dad. Please.'

'Bailey, let me help,' offered Tony.

'I'm OK. I can do it.'

'Let's take it in turns? It's less exhausting.'

'If you're sure?'

Tony dropped to his knees beside Paul.

'OK, Tony, the next round is yours.'

Bailey sat back on her heels as Tony began pumping. She checked Frank's neck. 'Keep going, both of you, we have a faint pulse here.' Her head swam with relief. She could feel the surge of adrenalin kick in, banishing her tiredness. She heard the siren, shortly followed by the clatter of trolley wheels. Two paramedics arrived.

'Good job, you three. We'll take over now,' said the first. He knelt beside Bailey and felt for Frank's pulse.

The next few minutes were a blur. Bailey suddenly realised

that Frank had been lifted onto the trolley, his face covered with an oxygen mask. Thank goodness, he was still alive.

'I'll come with you, Paul. Tony, will you keep an eye on everyone? I'll be back as soon as I can.'

'Don't worry about us. You look after Paul. We'll go in for dinner and be in the lounge when you get back.

'It may be late.'

'Go.'

Bailey walked across reception. She could see her group in their usual corner of the hotel lounge. As she approached, she heard the shrill voice of Mrs Nunne. 'I don't understand it. Did Paul say Dad?'

'Subterfuge,' her husband replied.

'I don't think so,' Barbara said. 'It sounded genuine enough to me.'

'You don't call anyone Dad, except your dad,' Fyrne said.

Mr Nunne huffed. 'If you believe that...'

Barbara stood as Bailey walked in. 'Oh, my dear. What news?'

'Dead on arrival. Nothing they could do.' Bailey slumped onto the nearest chair and put her head in her hands. 'In case you're interested, Mrs Nunne, Paul is devastated about losing his dad. Completely broken.'

Mr Nunne took his wife's arm. 'Come, my dear. We'll leave now. No use upsetting yourself.'

'I'm so sorry, Bailey.' Barbara walked over and placed her hand on Bailey's arm, giving it a squeeze. 'You were brilliant, my dear.'

'So, Paul was his son?' asked Fyrne.

'Apparently so.' Bailey sniffed, and Miller handed her a

cotton handkerchief.

'Thanks. I never guessed because of the different family name, but Paul explained that he took his mother's maiden name when his parents divorced.' She paused to wipe her eyes and blow her nose. 'They were reunited shortly before his mother died last year. This holiday was Frank's treat, so they could get to know each other better.'

'Oh, the dear boy. Where is he?' Barbara asked.

'He wanted to be alone. He's gone straight to his room. I'll take him back to the hospital tomorrow morning to sort all the paperwork. It means I won't make my nine o'clock hospitality desk slot tomorrow morning. I hope you'll forgive me.'

'Of course, Bailey, don't even think about it.' Miller turned to the others. 'We'll manage, won't we? Now, can I get you a drink?'

'Brandy and soda please, on the rocks.'

'That's my girl.'

35. Day Seventeen – Sydney

Cynthia looked through the large picture window. She'd been excited by this view when they first arrived, but this morning the view failed to lift her spirits. It was impossible to tell where the drab grey sky ended, and the dreary steel coloured sea began. To her left, the metal arches of the Sydney Bridge towered above her. A ghostly cruise ship glided towards the International Dock. The boat was longer than the iconic Opera House and almost as tall as the structure's distinctive roof. The early morning mist swirled around the large white boat so that it appeared to fuse and merge with Australia's famous building.

She had grown fond of Frank during the tour; always polite, never moaned, always attentive to his companion. How wrong had they had all been about Paul, about them both? A clear demonstration of how prejudice can manifest itself. Everyone, even Bailey, had assumed that Paul was Frank's young homosexual lover – until last night. Not that it would have mattered to her if they were a gay couple. She hadn't thought about it until she overheard the Nunnes moaning. She had worked alongside many gay men and women in her time, and as a sixty-five-year-old single woman, many may have questioned her own sexuality. What did it matter? But it mattered that Frank was dead.

A loud click made her jump. The kettle had boiled. She welcomed the routine of making her first cup of morning coffee. She stirred in one heaped teaspoon of sugar – for the shock. Usually, she took it without milk or sugar, but today she needed the energy. She breathed in the bitter yet inviting aroma. It cleared her head. She took a sip and then carried the drink back to the window.

It was so unfair, Frank dying like that. And he was too young to die – younger than she was. What if it had been her? Would anyone miss her? Would anyone go to her funeral? She couldn't die yet; she hadn't made a will, and with no relatives, or friends, she needed to make sure her estate would be divided between her favourite charities. She reached for her diary and added *Solicitor* to her list of things she needed to do on her return to England.

She thought about David's thank you speech, made just before Frank had collapsed. David's conversion to the Catholic faith had obviously drawn the final curtain on her foolish dreams of an autumn romance between them. However, he had looked at her when he gave thanks for the friendship and support, he'd received. He'd made her feel that she was an important part in him making his difficult choices, and she realised that his 'rejection' of her, as she had seen it, was nothing of the sort. He had offered and taken friendship from their acquaintance and she had been granted pleasure from that.

A dark green and pale-yellow ferry sailed into view. Two small boats, like drone bees, followed. The mist had cleared a little and she could now make out the promenade, lined with deep purple Jacaranda trees in full flower – a respite from the tedious grey. That's what she needed: some colour in her life. Colour and friendship. She opened her diary again and added: *sort out wardrobe, check out local clubs and possible charity work.*

Cynthia made her way down to breakfast and approached the table where Barbara sat buttering a slice of toast.

'Good morning, Barbara. May I join you?

'Please do.'

Cynthia gave the waitress her order for tea, toast, and a soft-boiled egg. 'How did you sleep after that dreadful evening?'

'Oh, my dear, wasn't it frightful?'

'So sad.' Cynthia looked across at March and Fyrne, who were having breakfast together. 'How nice they've become friends. Especially when March has to put up with that dreadful husband of hers.'

Barbara nodded in agreement, and then noticed Angie enter the dining room. She lifted her hand and waved.

As Angie reached their table, Cynthia said. 'That hair cut really does suit you. I can't believe the transformation.'

'Oh, thank you, Cynthia dear. I have Barbara to thank for it. She treated me, don't you know? She's also helped me to give up the alcohol, after five years of excess, and you know what? I feel amazing, as Bailey would say. Poor dear, I suppose she will be at the hospital for hours.' Angie smiled as the waitress arrived with Cynthia's order. 'Tea for me, please. I usually take my coffee, black, oops, sorry, Cynthia, coffee without milk, but I think I will enjoy tea this morning. I could even manage a slice of toast. It was so late when we eventually got off to bed last night.'

'Gosh, wasn't it awful?' Barbara shook her head. 'Such a nice man.'

'And his poor boy. I wonder how he is this morning,' Cynthia mused.

Mr and Mrs Nunne entered the room. They totally ignored

everyone else, and walked over to a corner table.

Barbara glared at them. 'They'll get their comeuppance. You should have heard her last night. She made outrageous comments about how Frank behaved disgracefully, giving Paul a hug.'

Angie reached for a slice of toast from the rack and spread a thin layer of butter across it. 'This holiday has made me realise that life is too short. There are so many things I could be doing and I intend to start now, don't you know?'

'That's my plan, also,' Cynthia said. 'I don't know where you both live, but I wondered... is there any chance you could both come and stay with me for a few days, sometime soon? I live in Derbyshire. I have some lovely walks on my doorstep, which I've never had time to explore, and there's a spa hotel nearby. We could book in for a few treatments, perhaps some swimming and cream teas?'

'Why, Cynthia, that's a wonderful idea. Thanks, I'd love that.' Barbara clapped her hands together. 'I've decided, while we've been away, that I'll take up some voluntary work for the Samaritans, but I will only do one week in four, so I'll have plenty of free time. Do you think the spa hotel attracts any rich widowers?'

Cynthia laughed. 'I've always been too busy working to enjoy the facilities before now. It'll be great fun. How about you, Angie? Please say you'll come.'

'Why not? We can swap photographs, reminisce and enjoy a few meals out. It will be like a second holiday.'

Cynthia smiled. Now she had two colourful personalities she could count upon for friendship, not just for the holiday, but for the future.

Tony reached across the breakfast table and took Maddy's hand in his.

'Maddy, I wondered… well, Frank dying like that last night, it made me think.' Tony squeezed her hands and gazed into her eyes. 'Will you marry me?'

'Yes.'

'You don't have to give me your answer now. Not immediately, of course. I mean we could stay together when we get back to the UK and then if things go the way I think they will – say in six months… what did you say?'

'I said yes.'

Tony jumped to his feet, pulled her into his arms and kissed her.

'Oh Maddy, I was so afraid you'd say no. Come on, let's go and find an Australian engagement ring. How do pink diamonds sound?'

'I think Barbara will approve.' Maddy looked over to where Barbara, Angie, and Cynthia were watching them and smiling broadly.

Bailey called at the reception desk and collected her messages. She wondered if she had time for a quick snooze before her guests gathered for the final evening meal. She was exhausted. The arrangements needed for Paul to fly back to the UK with Frank's body were complex. Jim had refused to help, suggesting it should be up to Paul and his insurance company. She couldn't leave Paul to deal with it all on his own. He was an emotional wreck.

She glanced at the top message:

Dear Ms Bailey,
URGENT.

Could you please meet with me in room 388, as soon as you return from the hospital?

Yours sincerely,
  Clive Wilson.

Wilson? That didn't ring a bell. She'd take a quick shower and then swing by the room. Not that she had any intentions of entering the room of an unknown man.

Clive opened the door. She recognised him at once. The last time she'd seen him he'd been clearing tables at the Beach Resort when he'd picked up the Monk's poster of their missing son.

'Bailey, come in.'

'It's OK, can't stop, I'm in a bit of a rush. What can I do for you?'

Clive pushed his door wide open. Bailey's eyes were drawn to a second man, who stood by the bed. Her nerves jangled. One virtually unknown man was bad enough, but two? She took a step back, but then paused as she realised that the second man was also familiar. Late thirties, with dark blond hair that flopped over his eyes, his nose reminded her of someone, and something about his eyes.

She gasped. 'Are you? Is it…?' Her gaze swung between the figure near the bed and Clive. Both men nodded. 'Oh, my God.'

'Take a seat,' Clive offered. 'I thought I recognised the poster as Jeremy. We've known each other for years, from scuba diving, but I didn't want to say anything until I'd spoken with him.'

She collapsed into the armchair and continued to stare at the Monk's long-lost son, Jeremy. On closer inspection, he wasn't exactly like the poster, but there was a strong resemblance.

'Do Nigel and Pryor know?'

'No,' Jeremy said in a broad Australian accent. 'I waited for my DNA to be checked in England. We contacted the number on the poster and had my profile faxed over. Unfortunately, they confirmed the match yesterday afternoon.'

'Unfortunately?'

'Obviously, the fact that it's now confirmed that I'm a missing person has opened up Pandora's Box. I was clearly kidnapped as a young boy. I don't remember anything, apart from being told that my parents had been killed in a car accident and that I was going to live with a new Mum and Dad. Now that I've put my DNA in the frame, the police will have to investigate if it was my parents who snatched me, or someone on behalf of the agency.'

'What do they say about it?'

'They both died several years ago. Apparently, the agency no longer exists, so I'm not sure how this will ever get sorted.' Jeremy perched on the end of the bed and rubbed his hand through his hair.

'So how long have you been living in Australia?'

'We moved out here shortly after my parents adopted me. They told me all their savings had gone on the agency fees for my adoption, so we emigrated. That's why I can't believe they were the guilty party.'

'So, when are you intending to break the news to Nigel and Pryor?'

'I'm not even sure if I should.'

'Believe me, Jeremy, Nigel and Pryor are an adorable couple and they have spent their lives searching for you. Surely you won't deny them of knowing that you're still alive? Especially after you've come this far. After all, the investigation into your kidnapping will continue whatever you do.'

Jeremy stood and walked to the window.

Bailey held her breath for what seemed like ages, but was probably only seconds.

Jeremy shrugged his shoulders and turned back to face her. 'Of course, you're right.' He smiled. 'I wonder if you could help. It will no doubt be a bit of a shock, and I don't want to give them a heart attack.'

Bailey flinched. She was still coming to terms with Frank's.

'Perhaps I should speak to them first and prepare them. Walking into the bar and saying: "Hello, Mum," could be a little overwhelming.' Bailey smiled at him. 'Give me about half an hour.'

36. The Final Evening

Moscow Mule Cocktail

- *40ml Vodka*
- *20ml fresh lime juice*
- *80ml Ginger Beer*

   Fill a chilled tumbler with ice cubes. Pour the ingredients over the ice, stir and serve with a slice of lemon.

Miller watched Bailey rise to her feet and raise her glass. 'Ladies and Gentlemen, I want to propose a few toasts on this our final evening together. For the first time on an Australia Unleashed tour, we have an engagement. Congratulations to Tony and his beautiful fiancé, Maddy.'

March raised her glass. 'To the happy couple.' She turned towards Fyrne, who stood beside her, sipping her drink.

Miller saw Bailey glance at the two women and smile. He wondered what she'd picked up on that had completely passed him by. She was such a sharp cookie, and that smile was obviously some recognition of something. He looked around and spotted James on the sofa, as far away as possible from the two women. He was frowning as he glared at Fyrne. Aha, now it made sense. Serves him right. He should have treated her better.

'Also, I'm sure you will all be happy to toast Nigel and Pryor, and celebrate the very welcome return of their son, Jeremy. As the words of their song said: *love conquers all.*'

Nigel and Pryor sat proudly with their son between them. Pryor's eyes brimmed with tears as she chinked her glass, first with Nigel and then with Jeremy.

'I would also like to raise a toast to absent friends, Frank and his son Paul.'

'Absent friends,' the group echoed.

Bailey's voice caught in her throat. She coughed. 'I also want to propose a vote of thanks to you all. This has definitely been the most remarkable tour of my career to date. Thank you.

'Cheers.' They all responded in unison.

Miller nudged Sumner's elbow. 'What about you, Sumner?'

'What about me?'

'Well, everyone appears to be making life changing decisions; walking away from unhappy relationships, re-establishing or forming new ones.'

'I'm happy as I am. I'll find a new woman when we get back. Preferably she'll be in her early twenties, so that I'll get a few years of her keeping my bed warm before she starts clucking.'

Miller laughed. 'You do know that one of these days you'll move someone in with you who fails to cluck. Then what will you do?'

'Never thought about it. By then I'll be approaching my sixties. Perhaps a non-clucking thirty-year-old could be the answer to my comfortable old age? Who knows?'

Bailey had sunk back into her armchair. 'What about you Harold? Have you solved your dilemma?

'I have, thanks to Miller. We had a long chat about how I didn't want to spend long periods of time in the US. I hate to be away from Cher,' he smiled at his wife. 'But at the same time, I wanted my father's estate and the ginning mill to continue supporting his loyal employees. I didn't want to sell it, we don't really need the money and as Paul reminded us with his story, we can't take it with us. Miller suggested setting it up as a co-operative, which solves everything. My attorney is looking into the details for me for when we get back.

'I'm impressed, Miller,' Bailey said.

'Praise at last,' Miller grinned.

Angie leaned forward. 'Are you going to tell us a story tonight, Bailey, darling?'

'Not a story, but I do have a letter to read to you. Actually, it's the epilogue of a story we heard earlier on our trip.' She pulled a few sheets of paper from her bag and unfolded them. 'I've had a long e-mail from another absent friend, Jujh. I'll read it out to you:'

Dear Bailey and my travel friends,

I hope you have enjoyed your magnificent tour. I am writing to update you on the news of my daughter, who is recovering well.

First, allow me to explain how it was that my daughter and I became separated.

My wife and I fell in love when we were at the University of Delhi. She was very beautiful, but I am Sikh and she was Hindu, and unfortunately my parents forbade our marriage. After considerable protestations, they finally agreed, on the condition that our astrology charts demonstrated that we were a good match. In India, we believe very much in the astrology charts to predict a good union, with a minimum score of eighteen out of a possible thirty-six points needed to indicate compatibility. Regrettably, when I went to collect the chart from the astrologer, it only amounted to a score of eight points. I persuaded him to recast the chart, reminding him of several factors he must have accidentally failed to appreciate until we reached the magic score of eighteen.

My bride arrived at the ceremony by elephant. She was stunningly beautiful, wearing a red and gold sari and draped in her dowry of gold jewellery. Her hands were exquisitely painted with henna. The service took place over two days and ended with a spectacular firework display.

One year later, our child was born. I hoped for a boy. I know what you will be saying, but it's a cultural thing, please forgive me. I happily accepted a girl. I could not, however, accept that my wife would die in childbirth. In respect of my dear wife's wishes, I named our daughter, Chaunta, which means: one who outshines the stars. It seemed appropriate, but I couldn't help but wonder if my wife's death was retribution for trying to outwit the stars by tampering with the astrology chart.

My mother-in-law agreed to care for the child at her home in the far northern territories of India, until I recovered from my grief. After a couple of months, I wrote to make the arrangements for my daughter to join me. But my mother-in-law wrote back to say, she couldn't cope with losing her granddaughter, after already suffering the loss of her daughter. She suggested it would be best for all concerned if the child remained with her. I agreed. By now my cricket career was at its height, which required me to spend long periods of time away from home and it seemed better for Chaunta that she remains with her Grandmother. Looking back, I realise that I was still angry, consumed with grief, and confused about my feelings for Chaunta.

Somehow, I never managed to find the time to visit. I thought it would distress the child, and I knew it would distress me, especially if she resembled her mother.

When we arrived in Uluru, you may remember, we met the young girl, Dorothy, who took my hand and smiled into my eyes. She was about the same age as my Chaunta, and my heart melted. As I held her hand, I realised what a fool I had been. What I had missed. This could have been my own daughter stood by my side, smiling at me in that trusting way.

On arrival back at the hotel I received a telegram to say Chaunta was dangerously ill in hospital, and the only thing that may save her was a bone marrow transplant, preferably from a close relative. I flew back immediately, convinced throughout that terrible journey that this was God's punishment. I will thank God every day that I got there in time. Miraculously, my bone marrow matched, and now my darling daughter, is well on the road to recovery.

My mother-in-law has agreed to come and live with us and will continue to contribute to the care of Chaunta. I will never let my daughter leave my side again.

I would like very much to thank Bailey for all the arrangements she made to get me home quickly and to thank you all for your friendship. I look forward to seeing you one day in our splendid hotel, (address below) where you will be assured of top-class accommodation, wonderful food and a healthy room discount.

From your very good friend, Jhujhaar Singh.

Miller watched Bailey fold the printout and push it into the front pocket of her bag. He thought he glimpsed a tear in her eye. She really was a beautiful, kind and generous person, and obviously touched by Jujh's story.

'For those of you who would like to contact Jujh, he has asked me to circulate his e-mail address, and details of his hotel web page. They will be included in your final newsletter, which will be delivered to your room tonight. Don't forget I need you and your suitcases in reception at nine sharp tomorrow morning, with your bar bills paid.'

'God, I love a bossy woman,' Miller said loud enough for Bailey to hear.

Bailey blushed, but continued with her well-practiced instructions.

'If you could follow me, we will walk down, past the Rocks area to an amazing waterfront restaurant, the venue for our final evening meal. Any questions?'

'Is it far?' asked Mrs Nunne.

'Five minutes, Mrs Nunne, but I could get you a taxi if you prefer?'

'Oh no, don't bother. We wouldn't want to be a burden.'

'If you're sure. Would you all like to follow me? We'll be leaving the hotel through this entrance and crossing over the piazza. Off we go.'

The group began to shuffle through the revolving door, following Bailey. Miller placed himself in front of the Nunnes, blocking their exit.

'That's a first,' he snorted when he had their attention.

'Why, Mr Miller, whatever do you mean?'

'Let's face it, Mrs Nunne, you two have done everything possible to make Bailey's life a misery on this trip.'

Mr Nunne moved forward and stood between his wife and Miller. His face flushed; he wagged his finger under Miller's nose. 'Now look here, Miller, I won't have you talking to my wife like that. We paid a fortune for this holiday and we expect the best service possible.'

'In my opinion, you've had the very best. Far better than you deserve. Bailey must have the patience of a saint. You even told me yourself how supportive she'd been to you.'

Mrs Nunne glared at her husband. 'You told him about our personal business.'

'I'm sorry, my dear. But you told Bailey, and I was so upset at the thought of losing you. I–'

'I hope you remember to show her your gratitude with a healthy tip tomorrow morning,' Miller said.

The hotel door swung behind Miller as he joined Bailey and the group outside, leaving the Nunnes gasping like goldfish.

37. Day Eighteen

Bailey's last task was to deliver the group to the correct gate at the airport. Then she'd be free to return home. The thought filled her with dread. She'd been counting down the days until Duncan finished University, looking forward to him being around again. His decision to remain in Glasgow would mean returning to solitude, and his empty room. Loneliness was the one downfall of this job. The week turnaround between trips didn't give her much time for friends or socialising. By the time she had caught up on the mail, the laundry and the dusting, it was time to go again. Now all she had to look forward to was a weekly Skype call.

Counting each guest as they handed their suitcases to the porter for loading onto the bus, she was reminded of Agatha Christie. Twenty-one guests quickly became twenty when Jujh left for India, then nineteen with the arrest of the Brigadier. Paul was flying back with Frank's body separately, which took it down to seventeen. Re-arranged flight tickets had been sorted for Nigel and Pryor Monk, who were staying on for a holiday with their son, which left fifteen. She checked again, fourteen. One missing – Miller.

He leaned casually on the reception desk, waving at the others. His cheeky smile lifted her spirits, she realised that she would miss his cheerful banter.

'No suitcase, Miller?'

'No, I'm not going back. Cancelled my flight and checked

in here for another couple of weeks until I can find something more permanent.'

'Too much to see in Sydney?'

'Too much to do. I've set up that educational trust fund for Dorothy, but now I'm working with those contacts you supplied. I'm sponsoring an apprenticeship scheme for Aboriginal youngsters. The idea is to get half a dozen talented young lads who are keen on music, teach them the trade, put them in touch with some good writers and produce a number one CD with vocals backed by didgeridoos and drums.'

Bailey laughed. 'You're creating an Aboriginal boy band?'

'Pretty much.'

'After all you said about manufactured boy bands?'

'What do you think?'

'Amazing, but what about the girls?'

'That's the next project.'

Bailey slowly shook her head and chuckled. 'You amaze me, Miller. I'm usually a good judge of character, but you have taken me by surprise.'

'I surprised myself. This trip has made me realise, it's time I put something back.'

'But how long are you staying? Haven't you got work to go back to?'

'I'm a stockbroker. In a global economy, I can work from anywhere.'

'Goodbye, Miller. I'll miss you.' She experienced a twinge of sadness, and realised that she really meant it.

'Perhaps not. I'm hoping we'll be seeing a lot more of each other.' He reached for her hand, raised it to his lips, and kissed her knuckles.

Bailey blushed and snatched her hand away. 'Don't be such a tease.'

'Kate, I'm serious.' his eyes sparkled, and his smile was warm.

'You're the archetypical perpetual bachelor. You admitted that you hate the idea of commitment. That's not the kind of relationship that interests me. Thanks all the same.'

'Me neither – at least not since I fell under your spell on that first day in Perth. You promised me magic, but I didn't count on you turning my life upside down – quite literally. I didn't intent to make my home here down under. Will you have dinner with me tonight? How about eight o'clock at the Scaffold's restaurant, near the Harbour Bridge? Do you know it?'

Bailey's stomach flipped. She realised that the prospect of a date with Miller was an exciting one that she would look forward to.

'Why not? I'll see you there at eight.'

Aeroplane engines roared above her as Bailey turned away from the checking in desk. She sighed with relief. The last of her guests were now safely delivered through to the departure lounge. This tour had been challenging but, being honest, enjoyable. She'd even surprised herself. On the one hand, she'd enjoyed her best tour ever and now looked forward to a date with an attractive man. On the other hand, it looked as though she was either going to be sacked or made redundant. Where was the justice in that? She still hadn't heard from Jim, but no doubt there'd be a letter waiting for her at home.

Her phone buzzed, indicating a text from Duncan.

Dear Mum, try and get as much time off as you can over Christmas as Sarah and I will be visiting, along with her parents. We have been discussing the future and have decided that we may all move to Australia on a permanent basis. Tell you more when I Skype you at the weekend. Love you, D xxx

Two weeks before, this would have been the best news ever. The fact that she was about to be sacked, slightly took the edge off things. The tour industry in Australia was quite competitive, and with a dismissal on her record she wasn't going to find a new position very easily. Perhaps she should resign? Maybe she'd talk it through with Miller tonight. She felt a warm glow at the thought of having someone with whom she could discuss her hopes and aspirations.

She walked out of the airport building. The blistering heat bounced off the tarmac, which shimmered like the surface of a deep, black, watering hole. She sneezed as the smell of aviation oil tickled her nose.

Her phone buzzed, indicating another text. This time, from Franklin James, PA to the former Managing Director and secretary to Jim.

Dear Kate, could you please come into Head Office immediately, as the new Managing Director wants an urgent discussion with you.

Her heart sank.

Bailey scurried into the reception area of Head Office. The first person she saw was Suzy.

'Suzy, what are you doing here?'

'I've been reinstated by the new MD. I'll tell you all about it later – but hurry, he's waiting for you.'

Suzy pushed Bailey towards the double doors of the MD's office. 'Go on, in you go. We'll speak later.'

Bailey could feel her palms sweating as she tapped on the door and turned the big brass knob. She pushed the door open.

A figure stood with his back to her, looking out of the picture window. His hair, burnished by the sunlight, resembled a halo. He turned to face her.

She gasped.

'Hello, Kate. Did you get everyone to the airport? Why do I ask? Of course, you did.'

'Miller. You mean... oh no. Surely you're not the secret shopper?'

'Guilty as charged.'

'How can you be so cruel? You made me believe you were interested in me. You asked me out on a date. How could I be so naive?'

'It was all true. I am interested in you, personally. I've never met anyone like you and I really hope we have a future together. But I wanted to keep our personal and professional life separate, or at least as far as it's possible. I'm not playing a game here. I meant every word earlier. But now it's time to talk about our professional relationship.'

'You're here to report me to the new Managing Director?'

'I am the new Managing Director, and the owner.'

Bailey gasped again, reached out for the chair positioned in front of the large mahogany desk and lowered herself into it.

'I'm sorry, Kate. I wanted to find out as much as I could about Australia Unleashed, which is why I took the tour.' He sat down behind his desk.

'But why was I under investigation?'

'They told me you were the best. That's why I came on the tour to see for myself. They were right, you are the best. But the way you risked everything, even the job that I know means so much to you, to help that objectionable Nunne woman and her husband – that has to be a lesson to us all.'

'Mrs Nunne. But how did you find out about that?'

'Jim told me you'd asked for an extra room, which he thought you'd mentioned was for the Nunnes. I was at reception when Mr Nunne, slightly out of character, rang down for flowers and sparkling wine. I bought him a drink that evening and we chatted. He told me what you'd done.'

'I thought Jim would sack me and I'd be out of a job.'

'He tried, but it's him that's out of a job. He knew I was the secret shopper, but had no idea about me being the new owner. I sent him information about the tour as a bit of a test – to gauge his reaction. I told him yesterday, I don't tolerate bullies; threats and intimidation have no place in my team. That's why I need you in a new job as my Director of Customer Services, training and managing others to replicate your commitment. You're a true advocate for good service, the very best. I want every member of our staff to care the way you do.'

'But I'd miss the tours.'

'Yes of course, but you can still do some. Such as induction training for new Tour Managers. I also intend to expand. I hope the two of us will get the chance to check out potential new tours – to New Zealand, Tasmania, etc. But mostly, I want you working alongside me here in Sydney, much more than your current schedule allows. My admiration of you, and my need to have you here, are for professional *and* personal reasons.'

Bailey rested her head in her hands. 'I'm so confused.'

'When I bought the company, I planned a hands-off approach. I intended to appoint a Managing Director rather than undertake the role myself. You made me realise how important it is to really care about my staff, as people, rather than to worry about how much money they could make for me. And now you've even got me dabbling in philanthropy. You did this to me. You made me look at everything from a different perspective. Please believe me, I need you. You've stolen my heart.'

'But I work for you. I can't be involved with you. Not romantically. It will make life impossible.'

'Not if we're determined to make it work. Please say you'll try. Will you still have dinner with me tonight? We can celebrate your new job.'

Bailey remembered back to the first day of the tour. The waitress had suggested she needed romance in her life, and she'd been quick to forcefully denounce the idea. She'd been exasperated throughout the tour by Miller's cheeky and often annoying behaviour. And yet when the time had come to say goodbye, she'd realised that she would miss him. Could it work? Should she give it a chance?

'Kate?'

'Well, I'll have to do a risk assessment.' She grinned. 'But I can't see why not.'

THE END

Acknowledgements

I offer my heartfelt thanks to my husband, Harold, our daughter, Rachael, her husband, Dan and our two adorable grandsons, Hector and Arthur. Without their love and encouragement, this book would never have been completed.

I am also indebted to Kath Morgan and Elaine Singer, my fellow beta-readers. I am eternally grateful for their friendship, constructive advice and suggestions.

My thanks go to Barbara Henderson, my tutor at Random House, who helped me to shape my manuscript, and also to Ed Handyside at Cornerstones, whose editing and insightful comments helped me to polish the final draft.

I would also like to thank James Essinger, principal of The Conrad Press, for his support and humour, the title, and for putting the finishing touches to my book.

Also, to Charlotte Mouncey, for turning my vague design thoughts into a brilliant cover.

Unusually, for fiction, Chris 'Brolga' Barnes, is a real person and the Kangaroo Sanctuary at Alice Springs is an actual place. The work they do there is wonderful, and a tour should be an essential part of any visit to the area. I am indebted to Brolga for allowing me to use his sanctuary as the setting for part of my novel.

Thank you, one and all. X.